Smoke & Mirrors

The *Coup*, the *Con*, and the Neo-*Cons*

by **Stephen Paine**

"Some boast of being friends of government; I am a friend to righteous government, to a government founded upon the principles of reason and justice; ... but I glory in publicly avowing my eternal enmity to tyranny...."

"This people will never be enslaved with their eyes open."

John Hancock, at the annual oration in commemoration of the Boston Massacre; 5 March 1774

Smoke & MiRRORS - the concise story

by Stephen Paine

Special provocative edition - share with the world!

ISBN: 978-0-6151-4671-3

Dedicated to Thomas Paine, Benjamin Franklin and the brave founders of a new experiment in government.

http://www.culturefix.org/common_sense_revisited_treason/evidence

"Patriotism is supporting your country all the time

and your government when it deserves it."

Mark Twain

Smoke & MIRRORS

The *Coup*, the *Con*, and the Neo-*Cons*

by Stephen Paine

"In the following pages I offer nothing more than simple facts, plain arguments, and common sense; and have no other preliminaries to settle with the reader, than that he will divest himself of prejudice and prepossession, and suffer his reason and his feelings to determine for [himself]...."

Thomas Paine, **Common Sense**, 1776

O

The question is not what you look at

but what you see.

Henry David Thoreau

Optical illusion
(hint: the wheels are not turning, your mind is)

"Only the educated are free."

- Epictetus

"Our lives begin to end the day we become silent about things that matter."

- Martin Luther King, Jr.

~ ~ ~

"Patriotism means to stand by the country. It does not mean to stand by the president or any other public official save exactly to the degree in which he himself stands by the country. It is patriotic to support him insofar as he efficiently serves the country. It is unpatriotic not to oppose him to the exact extent that by inefficiency or otherwise he fails in his duty to stand by the country."

– Teddy Roosevelt

Smoke & MiRRORS

The *Coup*, the *Con*, and the Neo-*Cons*

Table of Contents

Smoke & Mirrors I
Mesmerism and Hypnotism
The Varieties of Hypnosis
Hypnosis and Society
Sacred Cows
Creating Criminals
Cultural Paradox

Smoke & Mirrors II
Blinded by the Right
The Neo-Con Extremists

The Case
The Coup
& Iraq as Mirror of the Coup

Florida
Freedom!
Everywhere but here.
The Bottom Line

How did this happen?
Brainwashed, bamboozled
The media *slants* the message.
Stifling Truth for Patriotism
Shame on the Press

Propaganda = Lies
A Precarious State of the Union
Slanting the News
Just like a Hollywood movie!
The African Bush?
Top Gun Bush
Euphemisms of our times
Rumors: George Soros

The Bush Regime
Republicans are not all alike
A Republican Police State?
Changing of the guard

9/11
> Something stinks at the bomb site.
>> 9/11 - the Big Picture
>> Blowback

Crimes
>> So many, let me count the ways ...
>> The pervasiveness of the mind-set
>> Almost investigating those corporate scandals
>> ... needing a diversion ...

Iraq
>> The Story
>> The *Inside* Story
>> The War Itself
>> Iraq as Mirror of the Coup
>> Who says it's not the oil?
>> Pigs at the Trough
>>> Pigs requesting Pork
>>> Still following the money ...
>> Behind Our Backs
>> Helping Israel

hearing voices

How to Create Terrorists: a recipe
>> Abu Ghraib
>> Gitmo ... and worse

Tight security? Or the public on a leash?

Economy: Con, Cash-in & Cripple
>> Fiscally Irresponsible

Compassionate Conservatism?
>> Guns for sport?
>> Women and their Choices
>> Health Care
>> The Environment

Where is this Leading?
>> Un-American Activities
>> *Another Homeland Security scandal...* A Texas Brew
>> Big Brother and the Holding Tank
>> Technology & the Takeover
>> Post mid-term Elections, 2006 and beyond

The Neo-Con Players - listed

The True Patriots

The <u>Bottom Line</u>, Again

Call to Action
        Our Legal Grounds
        Pulling out the Constitution

        "Operation American Freedom"

  Arrest Bush and Crew, the supreme court justices, and accomplices

  Rescind all of their Rules, Appointments and Regulations

  Get Out of Iraq ... and many other Countries

  Abolish the Electoral College, Reform the Court

  Amends for Blowback

  Pay Us All Back

  Change Course

Get Informed:
        Books & Documentaries
            Videos and Websites

        Appendix: Essays Wise and True - various authors

the concise story

Smoke & MiRRORS I

"Step right up!" invites the showman, "Come on into the Hall of Mirrors! Be amazed as we take you into a world that pulls at your perceptions, that tricks the brain and defies logic!"

Ah yes, a perfect introduction to modern American politics!   P.T. Barnum would recognize the scenario instantly. Smoke & Mirrors is about confusing the senses. It is the stuff of theater, of entertainment, of movies and magic shows. It also refers to that which is not real, a deception, or a clever manipulation.

This reference, and reality, to subterfuge, show, and magic is confronting us, the people of the United States of America, whether we are aware of it or not. The land that produced Barnum's *Greatest Show on Earth* -- and Las Vegas and Hollywood and the American Dream -- has become entwined, trapped, in a Matrix-like mass deception that is proving more dangerous and out of control with each passing year. We are collectively dealing with smoke screens, spin doctors, media managers, and public relations personnel who want us to see things they have created out of smoke and shadows. While investigative TV police shows take us into the world of forensic science and technological advances to help the hero investigators discover the crooks, our popular media obfuscates the real reality with reality shows. Pimp my country.
Bureaucratic and governmental crimes go uninvestigated while the love lives and new births of celebrity couples are churned around in a hundred ways for our "entertainment." Meanwhile, policy experts and talking heads are mirroring each other like franchises; and human parrots are reading their lines, repetitively, into our living rooms, and into our minds.

Any con artist knows that if the mark, or dupe, is to go for the ruse, he needs to be distracted, if not confused. Allow me, a stage hypnotist, to take you on a tour behind the political scenes.

Please follow the clues, and the inside mechanisms of sleight of hand and mis-representation, as we discover the *smoking* guns that tell a very different story than what we have been told. *Step right up* as we discover that in this overly-medicated and overweight land of plenty, consumerism is alive and un-well while our collective health, and the stability and sustainability of our natural resources, our rights, our education and our whole way of life are in grave jeopardy.

Lesson number one: **don't fall for the lines**.

One could analyze the stated politics, the platforms of the parties, and their policies, but that will take us away from the actual facts. Like the Wizard of Oz, discovered behind the curtains, the menacing figure of power and authority is not what we think it is in the USA. Unlike the Wizard, who turned out to be a congenial old man, the people behind this machine, behind the lights, buttons and levers, behind the smoke and mirrors, are unfortunately looking more like the cold machines of The Matrix.

Why am I referring to movies when introducing this subject of political intrigue, misconduct and criminal activity? Why, it's all about show, image, perception and belief. It's not real, but it is very real. Deadly real.

Take the Red pill and wake up.

Open the windows and let the fresh air blow away the smoke.

Break the mirrors.

Get yourself free.

Introduction

Who am I? An observer and citizen, like millions of others. As a fair-minded and philosophical progressive, I have been dismayed and alarmed by our recalcitrant and pugnacious US government for years. Make that decades. And then things went too far ...

Think back to the beginning of our present predicament. Let us go back to when George W. Bush took the helm.

To me, the 2000 election was amazing in its presentation, tactics and audacity. This was no ordinary "close race" and it was more than the media drama it was portrayed to be. It was more than an aggressive campaign to win; it was a *winner take all* onslaught more akin to a conglomerate hostile takeover than to a political election. It was outrageous, but the populace was not outraged. I followed the facts, and the flimsy rationales, peered through the smoke and made an uncomfortable conclusion: I saw it as a coup. Not an archetypal movie type of coup with military officers storming the executive offices, but a coup in business suits; lawyers looking defiant, Supreme Court Justices stepping in, talking heads explaining it to us, news anchors repeating the fuzzy facts like so many parrots, and finally a takeover of the presidency of the United States by the losers in the race.

At the time I was surprised others did not see the crime as I did. Oh, I knew that I wasn't alone in this "wild" conclusion – there were perhaps millions of individuals who saw through the deception and believed what they saw and heard and did not believe the interpretation of what occurred. While the majority were stunned, mollified, apathetic or medicated, thousands of protesters gathered at that first shameful inauguration – George W. Bush could not walk the traditional steps to office for fear of disruption by protesters. These brave souls were summarily ignored as "the usual fringe element," or even as dangerous un-American troublemakers. They were pepper-sprayed and aggressively pushed back. *They were spoiling the show.* To me, the usual conservative righteousness had taken on a new air of entitlement and royalty. What was happening to this country?

3

Surprised by the general apathy in the face of all of this criminal activity, I became more circumspect and looked more closely at "the way" the 2000 election was presented and described by the popular media and the corrupt politicians. I found that the whole storyline had been scripted years before the takeover, but not in the classic conspiratorial way.
The deceptions are now part and parcel of the presentation of the present government.
Read that last line again.

Did you read that line as suggested? You were directed there. Where else have you been directed? I hope to be your rights advocate: my desire is to aid you in becoming aware of the subtle and pervasive/ persuasive ways that we are influenced. As a hypnotherapist who has worked in hospitals, I am cognizant of how information can be worded or conferred to effect a desired outcome for patients. Creating an alternative view on appearances is termed *re-framing*, or allowing the patient to perceive that there are other ways to look at things. When this is done in a therapeutic environment, the suffering can find perspective, hope and relief. When done by a biased media, business or group, however, this is termed propaganda and brain-washing.

As a counselor and therapist, I have been trained to differentiate between what is true and what is desired, where one is and where one wishes to go, between fantasy and reality. When applied to society and politics, I can comprehend the Taoist paradox of a readied military in a peaceful world, as well as measured responses to the truth of the moment. This propensity to perceive the world in complex dynamics, I believe, has allowed me simultaneously to imagine wondrous possibilities and to recognize bullshit when I see it. This brings us to social ethics and how people deal with real life situations. In a crowded theater, one should be careful not to yell "Fire" to avoid a dangerous panic. In an emergency situation, some people go into denial, others become irrational. On the ignorant and greedy extremes of the human experience, there are examples of club owners in a burning building who lock the doors in order to collect the tabs.

On another extreme, some people rise to their greatness and become heroes. In writing this book I am seeking activists and heroes. Why?

There is a fire.

Can't you smell the smoke?

Politics and power have always attracted a mixed lot. Saints and sinners, eloquent educators and hot air. Like the old joke, "How do you know when a politician is lying? When his lips move.," – many people are cynical of *public servants* (an interesting description that should conjure up a sense of trust). Socrates warned us that a sure indicator of one's disqualification for public office is a desire to run for office. Having said that, there are some sincere people working in government. There are some well intentioned people doing their best.
And there are crooks.

As a student of comparative religions, I can get a detached perspective on George W. Bush and see him as a child of ordinary capabilities born into money and privilege. From a Buddhist view, his involvement with a baseball team in Texas could have been considered his "right livelihood" and I imagine he would have done relatively little harm there. The Peter Principle told us in the 1980s that some individuals create disharmony and havoc when they are promoted or advanced into a position that is beyond their skill or competence. I believe this is true of George "Dubya" Bush. With a good therapist, he could probably contribute in some positive way in his local community. As he is, he should not be in charge of major decisions concerning other people's lives, nor should he have any influence over the environment nor the economy. He especially should not be in charge of weapons of mass destruction. As a philosopher, veteran and therapist, I can tell you that George Dubya Bush is not qualified to lead.

Interestingly enough, his qualifications and competency are not the issues in this show. It is actually something quite different.

When we consider "Birds of a feather ..." and all that, Bush has surrounded himself with a bunch of limited people with short term, selfish views of the world. Some of them are extraordinarily acquisitive and ego-centric, some are aggressive and pugnacious, some righteous and condemning, most are biased and self-serving. Altogether, especially with positions of power and a huge military behind them, they are dangerous and should not be running things. There is a criminal element at their core, whether they rationalize it or not, and they do not have the American people's, nor the world's, interests at heart. Their PR handlers concocted an American values dream team packaged as compassionate conservatism. Have you seen much of that lately? I am surprised more people do not see them for what they are. Perhaps we are back to denial in that burning building, or wishful thinking, or even a naive trust that our American leaders will not harm us or bring bad things to us (more on 9/11 and Iraq later). Perhaps the *birds* metaphor is too lenient in describing this group; maybe we are looking at the *fox in the henhouse*, or perhaps wolves among sheep; The people presently in charge are definitely more predatory. Being cunning, they are actually quite adept at the tricks of the trade, using smoke and mirrors. Therefore, what you see is not what is.

In the huge melting pot of the US, there are many perspectives. We supposedly have a free press and many options and opinions should be reflected in public debates and governmental policies. What I take offense at, then, is the deliberate and manipulative lies in the form of official press releases, popular media and biased "news" that is dished out to us on a daily basis. An informed public needs to have information and ideas in order to conclude views and make decisions, but those views must be founded upon facts and not lies.

We are being lied to.

When I tell my friends and acquaintances that I am dumbfounded as to why citizens are not marching in the streets en masse, they look around and see no national outcry nor major signs of general discontent (I will tell you which part of the subconscious is at work there soon). Thus, they conclude, things must not be **that** bad. I remember the conversations I had with some of these hopeful people, right after the release of Michael Moore's "Fahrenheit 911" in the summer of 2004. Many of them shrugged, "Besides, with all of the exposés, documentaries and books showing what mediocre and deceptive leaders we have, surely they will be voted out in 2004" they told themselves.

"We'll just beat Bush in the upcoming elections," they said, confidently, **"Again**."
(OK, *that* didn't happen. Now what?)

"No," I said, during that election, "you are missing my point – Bush was not rightfully elected in the first place and has been occupying the Presidency (and ruining it and us) as an usurper and fraud for four years now. He's an impostor. He shouldn't have been on the election ticket in 2004. He should have been in jail." Even Ronald Reagan's son described Bush as "the man who occupies the White House." Reagan's son! Perhaps we are not alone after all.

Listen. If I saw a child being beaten, I would intervene. If I witnessed a robbery, or even a murder, it would be right that I should call for help – the police, emergency personnel, and doctors. If a building were on fire, I would sound the alarm. Ever since the events of the 2000 election were white-washed, I have been sounding the alarm. I raised my voice after the preemptive strike on a third world nation in early 2003 – partly for the fact that the hype and deception there was so similar to the crimes against the government *here* – and I am endeavoring to make my case clear within these pages. This little book you have before you started out as a discussion, and then a letter to the editor, then morphed into an article, and now into a documented alarm for action. *Yes, documented.* My purpose would be wasted if it were just my opinion – there are millions of opinions. No, what I am presenting here is a collection of facts, articles, research and exposés. Let us awaken from the dream; let us gaze beyond the smoke and mirrors, and deal with the facts.

I have a dedicated website which includes dozens of hyperlinks to groups and websites with even more facts, as well as several other internet links to hundreds of pages of evidence that I have collected over the years. What you have before you is the distillation of the collected evidence. Here's the site: http://www.culturefix.org/common_sense_revisited_treason/evidence

Throughout this book, you will note various tones, from outraged to ironic to imploring to angry. This is a collection of voices, several of them mine, many voices of investigative reporters, and some of them quotes by the perpetrators themselves. Thousands of people are talking, researching, writing and sounding the alarms. I am but one voice in the concerted chorus. Together, we are trying to reach as many people as possible – People of conviction and common sense. Brave people of action. Heroes.

Many of us are pinning our hopes on those individuals of conscience in positions of power who can and will stand for justice and do the right thing and arrest the perpetrators of the coup. Why should this be the preferred way to approach this situation?

Access.

To the vast majority of American citizens there are multiple barriers to the actual reins of power. There is a Berlin Wall between the common sense person on the street and the privileged leaders who call the shots, and order the shooting. Can we succeed? Yes. There can be alternate endings written for this show, as in other historical examples (some not long ago). Perhaps a sizable group of citizens will reach *critical mass* and topple this dangerous group in a popular movement. However it is done, we need to change things *and fast*; for things are deteriorating rapidly. We are collectively being herded, marched, to the right side of the concrete wall. History has also shown us that a well established group in power is more prone to stay and dig in for the long haul. This is how entrenched monarchies begin. This is what the Bush regime is pushing for – Domination.

8

This work is dedicated to Thomas Paine and the founders of this nation, who were reluctant to initiate radical solutions to a traditional governmental authority, but were pushed into strong actions due to a multitude of offenses by a tyranny. These United States are again confronted by an arrogant, self-serving and corrupt autocracy, and our experiment in democracy is in jeopardy.

Consider the facts and use your common sense.

Stephen Paine

January 2005, re-visioned in 2006 & 2007

"I see in the near future a crisis approaching that unnerves me and causes me to tremble for the safety of my country. ... corporations have been enthroned and an era of corruption in high places will follow, and the money power of the country will endeavor to prolong its reign by working upon the prejudices of the people until all wealth is aggregated in a few hands and the Republic is destroyed."

- U.S. President Abraham Lincoln, Nov. 21, 1864 (letter to Col. William F. Elkins) Ref: "The Lincoln Encyclopedia", Archer H. Shaw (Macmillan, 1950, NY)

Mesmerism and Hypnotism

My thesis about the state of the US in this first decade of the second millennium is based upon my many years of studies and experience of hypnosis. I have used this fascinating and misunderstood art successfully with private clients as well as with large groups, in medical settings and in entertaining stage hypnosis shows. It is an intriguing study all by itself, but when one views the larger world of societies and culture, it provides an important key in understanding why we do the things we do. I believe it is vitally important to know the basics of suggestibility and hypnosis for individuals to make their own decisions in life, to become aware and savvy consumers, and to be clear thinking citizens who can attain and maintain their freedom.

Thomas Jefferson warned us that "the price of freedom is an eternal vigilance." It would be ideal, but naive, to think this does not have to be the case.

Some people have been vigilant, my friends and fellow citizens, but the majority of them do not have access to your time and attention. Who does have access?

Who are in charge? Who owns and operates the programs (interesting word) we read, listen to and watch? Where do we get our collective views? Do not be deceived: there are individuals, businesses and groups of opportunists who would love to sway you to their way of thinking and behaving. They are showmen, salesmen, role-players, "experts" and influential officials. They have been fine-tuning the art of smoke and mirrors for generations. It is all hypnotic social conditioning.

Take this particular fact in: last year US marketing spent **$35 billion** advertising food. Food. Like we need to be reminded to eat. Like it isn't something we do every day. Of course it is more focused than that: billions spent on persuading us to buy *certain* food! Like children's food.... Sugar coated breakfast cereals with happy cartoons on the boxes.... throw away containers with colorful and alluring images. 35 billion dollars.

Every year. To sway you.
And your kids.

OK. Businesses have to tell you about their products. But just think; this is the tip of the iceberg. We are being sold a bill of goods in so many other areas it is incredible. Listen, we no longer go out to spend money on things, we *buy now to save!*
It is dumb-founding.

You need to know this. Knowledge is power in this regard, and I hope this review of the various means to your minds will be revealing, and ultimately liberating.

Dr. James Braid, an English ophthalmologist, coined the word **hypnosis** in 1842 after the Greek word for sleep. He thought the nerves were asleep. After he studied the phenomenon, he ultimately desired to change his definition, and the word hypnosis, but by then it was too late and the practice and popularity of this enigmatic art was being used by many people. Mesmerism had already been around and discussed for more than sixty years by this time, and there were many practitioners experimenting on their own, mostly in Europe but as far away as India. There was keen interest in the subject and therapeutic uses in France in the late 19th Century. Sigmund Freud was one of its many students at the time. German doctors used a form of hypnosis for their shell shocked troops of the First World War. Dr. Milton Erickson began his remarkable innovations after the Second World War, which he demonstrated and enhanced through the 1970s. Since the 1950s hypnosis has been used more and more in medicine, dentistry and psychology.

There have been those established nay-sayers and skeptics (they are always around!), but a determined and successful group of practitioners and researchers have utilized the tools and techniques of hypnosis to this present day. It is a mysterious and fascinating phenomenon and sparks awe, curiosity, suspicion and strong reactions in many people. If these suspicious (and hypnotized) individuals knew how broad and pervasive the various elements of hypnosis are in our everyday lives, they would have a cow.

How wide is the scope of *hypnotic* suggestion? Let me count the ways. ...
It is all around us, and affects everyone. It is my belief that *the majority of the world is hypnotized the majority of the time.* Consider the many ways that "suggestions" can be implanted into our unconscious minds; the variety of entryways into the passive mind are numerous and surprising:

First we need to understand the subtle mechanism itself. Essentially, when we relax our powers of discrimination, associated with our personal wills, and passively *allow* ideas and notions into our subconscious, we are open to suggestions or conditioning. This discriminating part of the mind is sometimes called the Gateway to the subconscious. This open gateway happens naturally and is most apparent, and useful, in the way children can quickly learn and adapt to their surroundings. This is an automatic occurrence and part of the learning process. This dynamic of "taking in" our surroundings is not necessarily bad. Our cultures, languages and civilizations are passed on this way. It is fast and fluid and probably vital for the survival of our species to "learn" things rapidly. Children are like sponges, we are told. We are delighted by this open and vital acceptance and curiosity of the world displayed by children. Interestingly enough, adults who maintain this open sense of wonder are labeled naive and gullible.

Children have never been very good at listening to their elders, but they have never failed to imitate them.
- James Baldwin

It is quite obvious, however, that, as children open their hearts and minds to their surroundings, sometimes erroneous or even damaging ideas are mixed in with good intentions and unexamined assumptions. Thus, this openness, sometimes termed the trusting mind (or naiveté), can be manipulated or programmed to unquestioningly follow the precepts of fairly narrow or negative people, families, groups, religions and nations.

In fairly well-adjusted adults, the faculty of the discriminating mind (the gateway) is developed, through guidance and encouragement, so that they can make good choices in life. This whole learning process actually parallels physical growth and we should be able to *make our way in this world* by our late teens or early twenties. Correspondingly, it is during this time of life that young people voice their own views and seek the deeper answers in personal studies and exploration. They question, and perhaps rebel against, the assumptions which they grew up with in their families and communities. This too is part of the natural process of individuation and maturity. They are at the age when they are using, exercising, their perceptual gateways, their capabilities to choose for themselves. The path of conscious persons is to examine their personal truths and to determine for themselves what they will adhere to *and* what they dismiss. This truth will set us free -- and may also put us at odds with our family, communities and nations.

> The postmodern mind has come to recognize, with a critical acuity that has been at once disturbing and liberating, the multiplicity of ways in which our often hidden presuppositions and the structures of our subjectivity shape and elicit the reality we wish to understand. If we have learned anything from the many disciplines that have contributed to postmodern thought, it is that what we believe to be our *objective* knowledge of the world is radically affected and even constituted by a complex multitude of *subjective* factors, most of which are altogether unconscious.

> - Richard Tarnas, ***Cosmos and Psyche****: Intimations of a New World View*, 2006, page 40 - emphases his (all quotes by this author are from this book)

To understand the mechanisms of this learning process is to delve into the very routes and by-ways of education and enculturation themselves. The forging of characters, the development of personalities and the socialization of behaviors are all intertwined in complex but understandable ways in which we assimilate our surroundings, attitudes and beliefs. We can easily state that the majority of personal views are inherited, and each succeeding generation drops and adds assumptions and popular truths in this very slow process of paradigm building. And this new input? - These new bits and pieces of information for our edification and progress? Nowadays we are bombarded with an over-whelming amount of news and information. It is easy to get confused in this fast-paced, technological, modern age; one of the resulting reactions to this complexity is a dumbing down or simplification of things to make things palatable or easier to assimilate, which implies *with not much analysis nor reflection*. Examples of this are the ubiquitous sound bites, or information bullets. A sound bite is, optimally, a clear summary of the larger context of a theme, but it can also be a particularly entertaining or cleverly worded (and quotable) statement that does *not* capture the essence of the issue but is manufactured to sell the idea--or to divert attention from the issue, or even to distort the truth. Sound bites are usually no more than 15 seconds, so they come quick and well packaged. Under the radar screen. This is just one thing to be aware of when you sit down to check out the news, or listen, absent-mindedly (interesting word) to the radio or TV in the background. Catchy jingles, clever phrases, photo-ops and well designed images and impressions are all part of the show.

Let me now take you behind the curtains of the show.

The gateway to the unconscious is open, or can be opened, in the following ways and situations.
... just follow the dots ...
... and look in the direction of the
arrows ...

$\longrightarrow$ 	 ↗

14

The Varieties of Hypnosis or "The 9 doors of suggestion"

* **authority** - a person, expert, boss, superior, or the Law. This first begins with parents, and then the "baton" is passed on to babysitters, teachers, principles, policemen, doctors and nurses, then politicians! For the most part ordinary citizens just go along with authorities, but remember, this is an automatic response and we are letting our guard down, or not using our own powers of choice and discrimination when we just *obey and follow* the authorities. Am I advocating not listening to authorities? Please don't get distracted. I am describing how suggestions are implanted in the sub-conscious mind.

* **repetition** ... let me repeat that. Ideas, notions, beliefs and even languages are "imprinted" when we hear things over and over again. When we hear something enough times, and from many persons repeating the same lines, we just *take it in* as normal, if not reasonable.

* **emotion** - when emotions are strong, thinking is not - "he was overcome with his feelings." "A crime of passion" is usually comprehended, understood or sympathized, and even a legal excuse in court cases (temporary insanity), ... "she was not in her right mind" - uh, *which* mind was she in?
"cool down and think about it." Obviously one way to get support for a war is to elicit strong feelings of fear, anger, revenge and battle excitement, among other emotions.

* **peers**; conformity, peer pressure; "fitting in" "being cool or hip"; We are all aware of this dynamic when we look back upon our school experiences. This is an innate survival mechanism and part of social systems: perhaps we are instinctually inclined to act in a pack; this would certainly make sense when we consider our evolutionary history of defending ourselves from stronger creatures. This *group-think* doesn't end with cavemen, nor with adolescence. Take the case of Dr. Barry J. Marshall and Dr. J. Robin Warren, who won the 2005 Nobel Prize for Physiology/ Medicine. Their discoveries of bacteria in the stomach were supposedly impossible (nothing could live in the acid stomach).

Their research was ignored for a long time by the medical establishment, their peers. Besides, they were from Perth, Australia. This is a backwoods, out of the way, area. Yes, prejudice is carried by peer groups and *the conformity principle*; Even scientists and medical doctors are guilty of this (who are authorities by the way). The pressure of peers, the conformity principle, is the glue that bonds us in communities and can be a uniting principle; it is also holding back progress in all levels of society when whole groups are stuck in recalcitrant and narrow-minded constructs and unexamined ideas.

* **tradition**: "because it's always been done that way!" "This is the way it is." I am editing this section right after Easter, the time of remembrance of Jesus, the resurrection, and the Easter Bunny. Where did the bunny come from? Carrying eggs in a basket? History, of course, will explain it to us, but that is not the point-- and the majority of people with children who delight in Easter baskets don't care: its tradition! "If it has been around this long, there must be something to it." "It has withstood the test of time." This is sometimes true, such as great pieces of art or music. But war has been around longer. Should we honor it too? Logic doesn't always play a part in establishing and following traditions. In America, the natives are called Indians, because Christopher Columbus got lost and thought he had arrived in the Indies. The mistake stuck.

* **linking** - complex, unconscious association with a person or group. This occurs when there is a link, or invisible threads of connection, to others. "You are just like your Dad!" "A chip off the old block." "You are a Jew - Catholic - Muslim," etc., or "You remind me of your mother, grandfather, dead aunt, etc." You are a Mexican, Russian, whatever nationality - *and now think about what this implies...* Those connections that our quick, facile minds make could *link* the person, group, religion or national character to emotions and associations like pride, suffering, guilt, persecution, neuroses, ingenuity, creativity, and so forth. It is all linked together in these "innocent" associations, sometimes by a casual reference. For instance, one could say to a child "you remind me of your Uncle George." This could be

merely seeing a physical resemblance. However, the child knows George likes to drink and then becomes violent. "Am I like that?" asks the child to himself. He looks in the mirror, "Maybe I am."

* **imagination** ... All things are possible! The mind instantly sets its analytical abilities aside in order to imagine! Visualization and stories and music and dreams all "arrest" our minds and allow us to imagine the possibilities! Here is a quick induction, or hypnotic opening, for children: "let's pretend!" The next thing we know, the child is talking to the butterfly and making plans for the fairy ball in the magic garden. How fun. Similarly the word *suppose* means to take for granted without proof; this is a workable definition and a clear description of imagination and how this is one way to by-pass our conscious gateway. New and imaginative suggestions create different possibilities. This helped us, in ancient times, to "picture" the enemy, or an untried approach or design, or a new group endeavor, I suppose.

* **role**; the position creates the notions and attitudes, "in the line of duty", a doctor's oath, "I'm the decider." Those who are married or have been married know that there are even palpable roles in the institution of marriage! There are those who get caught in the power or trappings of their positions. With this in mind, just think about the implications of "It comes with the job." "It was my duty!" "My job was just to follow orders." As we turn the pages of history, however, and view duty and roles at the Nürnberg trials in Germany, this "just following orders" excuse was not acceptable, The citizens of the world declared that there are higher authorities and laws to follow (which brings us back to making our own decisions!).

$ **Hypnosis** - using direct or known communication agreements - not unconscious or *just given* as a matter of course in our lives, therefore one of the most honest forms of suggestion and influence. Hypnosis may use all of the above ways to open up the sub-consciousness; the difference is that it is an agreed upon association between the hypnotist and the subject. This is a contract to change or improve something that is more than likely unconscious, like a habit or fear, and to aid the client to find peace, resolution and freedom.

Mass hypnosis is used, consciously and unconsciously, to urge, convince, persuade and to manipulate via large institutions and mass media. The alarm bells should be ringing. The manipulators use all of these doors to the unconscious to lull the crowd, and to get their way. Be aware.

There are various approaches, methods and *inductions*, by the way, to open the gateway hypnotically. An induction is the process, usually through words, that lowers the conscious mind's defensive autonomy. There are three main types of hypnotic inductions, and they are connected to the natural and ubiquitous list I have just given:

father/yang approach - authority, emotion, linking and repetition (direct commands, emotional directives)
mother/yin approach - emotion, imagination and linking (invitations to just go along and take it in)
indirect approach - imagination, linking, emotions, roles, and/or authority (don't think of the pink elephant). The psychiatrist and hypnotist Milton Erickson was a master of this form of induction. He ably used metaphor, stories and confusion techniques and, on occasion, included others in his therapy - actors playing parts or roles for the therapeutic process.

Note that all of these ways by-pass the critical or conscious mind. Also note that drama therapy, psycho-drama and expressive arts therapies utilize most all of these listed dynamics *plus* role playing and group dynamics, or the power of peers. When these techniques are constructively and consciously used, people can have amazing breakthroughs, revelations and healing. When used unconsciously by sleep-walkers or clever manipulators, or worse, when used consciously by opportunists, these by-ways into our unconscious minds can deceive and even enslave.

"Hypnosis, with its long and checkered history in medicine and entertainment, is receiving some new respect from neuroscientists," reports Sandra Blakeslee of the New York Times. "Recent brain studies of people who are susceptible to

18

suggestion indicate that when they act on the suggestions their brains show profound changes in how they process information. The suggestions, researchers report, literally change what people see, hear, feel and believe to be true." From -
THIS IS YOUR BRAIN UNDER HYPNOSIS
by Sandra Blakeslee, New York Times; November 22, 2005
http://www.nytimes.com/2005/11/22/science/22hypno.html

The exciting possibilities of this research is important, not only for healing and hypnosis, but to the very essence of what we perceive as reality. If you have seen and appreciated the innovative movie, "What the *Bleep* Do We Know," which deals with the meeting ground of theoretical physics, quantum mechanics and biological mechanisms, then the following ideas gathered by Blakeslee will definitely intrigue you. She continues:

> One area that [new research on hypnosis and suggestion] may have illuminated is the processing of sensory data. Information from the eyes, ears and body is carried to primary sensory regions in the brain. From there, it is carried to so-called higher regions where interpretation occurs.

> For example, photons bouncing off a flower first reach the eye, where they are turned into a pattern that is sent to the primary visual cortex. There, the rough shape of the flower is recognized. The pattern is next sent to a higher -- in terms of function -- region, where color is recognized, and then to a higher region, where the flower's identity is encoded along with other knowledge about the particular bloom.

> The same processing stream, from lower to higher regions, exists for sounds, touch and other sensory information. Researchers call this direction of flow feedforward. As raw sensory data is carried to a part of the brain that creates a comprehensible, conscious impression, the data is moving from bottom to top.

> Bundles of nerve cells dedicated to each sense carry sensory information. The surprise is the amount of traffic

the other way, from top to bottom, called feedback. There are 10 times as many nerve fibers carrying information down as there are carrying it up.

These extensive feedback circuits mean that consciousness, what people see, hear, feel and believe, is based on what neuroscientists call "top down processing." What you see is not always what you get, because what you see depends on a framework built by experience that stands ready to interpret the raw information -- as a flower or a hammer or a face.
The top-down structure explains a lot. ... If the top is convinced, the bottom level of data will be overruled."

Obviously, this is significant for understanding the role of hypnosis and positive suggestions in pain management, healing and recovery. When we really grapple with the implications of such brain interpretations, however, you know this has to effect what we believe reality to be. This top-down phenomenon is, furthermore, revolutionary in its implications for how we all "agree" to social customs, wide-spread conditioning, political propaganda, and commercial advertising. This is an important foundation in understanding the placebo effect, stage hypnosis, and those many interpretations of reality that marriage partners get lost in. Please grasp this: *our perceptions, that which we see and hear, can be over-ruled by our interpretation of what we Think is happening.*

Ah, but it gets trickier. There are very subtle images, sounds and impressions coming at us *below* the usual threshold of our senses, and we could be affected by these things too.

SHRINKS FIND BASIS FOR SUBLIMINAL LEARNING
Boston University / ScienceBlog, May 26, 2005
http://www.scienceblog.com/cms/node/8018

Watch out -- you may learn something and not even know it, says Takeo Watanabe, an associate professor of psychology at Boston University's Center for Brain and Memory. Watanabe and his team recently pinpointed the mechanism that makes subliminal learning work. Watanabe will present the team's findings at the American Psychological Society meeting in Los Angeles, May 27 and 28.

Long considered the realm of science fiction, subliminal learning occurs when individuals are influenced by a stimulus they are unaware of, like words played back below the threshold of hearing or images flashed on screen faster than the eye can perceive. Watanabe's recent findings grew out of his team's previous work in which they established that subliminal learning is real and that the brain is capable of learning without consciously focused attention.

In this latest research, Watanabe and his team uncovered the mechanism that primes the subconscious, enabling individuals to learn a task without actually realizing it. They also showed this type of learning is retained, giving a new interpretation to how long a learned behavior is retained in the visual cortex -- an area of the brain thought to be fixed very early in life.

...

Watanabe says that having subjects focus on letters [on a screen with subliminal images] activated an internal "reward" pathway in their brains, priming their subconscious to learn more efficiently.

According to Watanabe, the visual cortex, the area of the brain tested in his experiments, has long been considered unchangeable in humans past 6 months of age. Watanabe found it could be "changed" and that the changes could last for a considerable period....

"It's possible that other parts of the brain could work this way too," Watanabe says. "People might be able to improve their pronunciation of a new language, if it's presented simply, without paying attention. It's possible the brain could be changed without a lot of effort."

~ ~ ~

Hypnosis and Society

We are bombarded, especially in this fast paced, multi-media world of ours, with an over-whelming variety of options, visuals, ads, and impressions. As adults, ideally our reasoning minds make the correct choices with the possible options. Hopefully. With experience and maturity we can indeed decipher some of life's apparent mysteries and human confusions. Now think, however, of the ways that we could have had conflicting ideas and values implanted in us as children. How many Easter Bunny non sequitur traditions, illogical customs, habits and beliefs were handed down to us as children? The possibilities are astronomical, and the "road map" young individuals have to guide their way in the world could be confusing, if not downright erroneous. We can track many a neuroses back to an ingrained Belief System or an indirect and errant "guidance."

> It is hard to fight an enemy
> who has outposts in your head.
> - Sally Kempton

My sense is that for every negative suggestion inadvertently planted into one's psyche there are twice as many positive guides. Indeed, some encouraging or inspiring comment made at just the right moment could spark an epiphany. This brings another level to the sayings about "awakening" or "waking up to life," or even "born anew" or "born of the spirit." The light bulb goes on, or Helen Keller, born blind and deaf, comprehends that the word "water" tapped out on her palm is actually the fluid, water, *and* that *everything* has a word and moreover there is meaning or order to the world.

(As an aside, what we all know about Helen Keller is the cleaned up, white-washed version. When she started criticizing society, she was no longer the poor blind girl who was so easy to empathize with. Check it out.)

When we are aware of the various ways that we can be influenced, we can make better decisions about what we watch, what we read, and whom we listen to - and perhaps we should give a listen to the older, mature Miss Keller. This is the power of choice, of personal decision, and is vital to a well adjusted person, group, community and society.

~ ~ When "we" are asleep, however, ... we merely accept that which has been given or handed down. The result is what we see in our communities, in our societies, on the news. Many wonder, "How did things get so out of hand? So irrational and weird and frivolous and sad...?" What indeed.

The majority of the world is hypnotized the majority of the time.

This truism displays itself in hundreds of ways. Some things that we just take for granted are part and parcel of the unexamined lives we lead. The differences show up more clearly when we travel, when we visit other cultures and compare them with our own. Interestingly, minorities within cultures have this advantage of perceiving the contrasts and oftentimes are not pulled into the follies of their mainstream neighbors (they have their own familial ones!). So, let us now take a walk down *cultural conditioning* and enjoy the many ways humans have ordered their lives and arranged their realities around the world; let us look at cultural differences for clues to how this group hypnosis might work:

In Peru and other places in South America, to leave a little bit of food, wine, etc., says "I am full. You have fed me so well." It is a compliment to leave something on the table. In the USA, post Depression, you are to clean your plate to show your appreciation. "Don't waste your food!" It is funny that these two customs are connected to lands that have more want and poverty, Peru, while leaving food and drink, and in the land of plenty, the USA, where one needs to clean his plate. Traditions are not logical, of course.

You have a temperature? In Estonia, the thermometer goes under the arm, in the US it goes into the mouth, in Denmark it goes in the rectum. (A Dane read this and assured me that modern Denmark had switched; they now used a high tech device that poked in your ear.) Which is correct? They all work. They are all "choices" that are more like traditions.

"Give us a child till the age of seven and he's ours for life."
Jesuit Catholic saying

Saunas! Civilized!

In Northern Europe, but not in England, saunas are very popular (Was being comfortable with nudity separated by the Channel?). This is a great tradition, but history brings us an interesting, and tragic, story connected to peoples who used, or did not use, saunas. The race to the South Pole!
Why was it important to get there first? Nationalism played it's part then. National pride was at stake. (This was certainly better than nationalism leading to the First World War!) This race was between Roald Amundsen of Norway, and Robert Scott of Great Britain. Two explorers and national heroes... with different customs, or social suggestions on how to live.
Amundsen used sled dogs, Scott used ponies (which all died) Amundsen brought the sauna with him, and Scott froze to death.

When a particular incident turns into a local law, the result can be strange indeed. Long after the incident is forgotten, we have some laws to deal with. I remember reading about a local swimming hole that neighbor kids enjoyed. One day a child drowned there. The next week a fence was erected and signs from the local magistrate warned them, no, told them, that *swimming is forbidden*. An unfortunate accident turned into a blocked access to simple recreation and new laws of protection were on the books. Obviously it was well-intentioned and sought to protect children against a possible source of danger (that had been there for hundreds of years!). It lacked objectivity, however, for far more children are killed in traffic accidents, but cars are not forbidden. One can see the cause and effect of this particular local ruling, but sometimes we come across strange rules.

This reminds me ... Odd Laws from Minnesota:

It is illegal to sleep naked.
All men driving motorcycles must wear shirts.
Citizens may not enter Wisconsin (a neighboring state)
with a chicken on their head.

Yes, there are books written on odd laws of states and countries. This is sometimes funny but can take serious turns. I will return to the idea that hypnotized people create laws that are wrong or foolish or even criminal – and laws that *create* criminals.

Are certain emotions universal, or taught? People have committed "crimes of passion" if they have discovered their spouse having sex with another. The tribes of French Canadian Matis have an interesting custom of teaching sex. The young people can choose an adult to teach them about the ways of sex. The Canadian Mounties, the police, have been dealing with this *problem* for many years, for the predominant society's social codes consider this criminal. The native Hawaiians had a similar custom of teaching sex to their young. They also liked to surf naked. The Christian missionaries introduced modesty and shame into the culture and these terrible customs have been stopped, thank God.

Breathe

(Did you just breathe more deeply than usual? Just a suggestion.)

;-)

Ah, but this reminds me of a story:

"The Guru's Cat"

There was a guru that had a beloved cat in his ashram. When the guru gave talks, however, the cat would want to be in the center of things and crawled on him and meowed loudly. This wouldn't do, so the guru began to tie his cat to a column in the next room and then would proceed with his teaching. This routine continued for many years.
The guru became old and died.
He was followed by his loyal disciple, who became a guru in his own right. He continued the tradition of tying the cat up in the next room and then giving his talks. The cat eventually died too.

The ashram needed a cat, of course, so a new cat was adopted to take its place, and the custom of tying it up before giving talks continued.

This tradition of the guru tying up the cat before speaking became a sacred obligation, and continued for centuries. Learned men wrote interpretations of the divine meaning of the act, and scholars wrote treatises on the subject, which were handed down through generations.

Sacred Cows

This comes from the Hindu belief that the cow is sacred and revered in their scriptures and in their tradition. The god that protected cows, Krishna, is highly respected. Cows are seen, historically, as gentle creatures that give milk, pull carts, till land and fertilize crops; thus, they are valued and protected. This phrase has been used figuratively by Westerners since about 1900, and may also refer to a land who's people are hungry but do not kill the cows for food. Sacred cows are rules and customs one doesn't challenge, for they are part of the *group think* (peer pressure) *and* tradition *and* authority. Message: You leave the cows (concepts, beliefs, laws, traditions) alone! Do not mess with them! There is nothing to discuss. *Period.* People get very emotional about some of these beliefs, which then makes these ideas or notions especially ingrained – and defended. Let us take a look at sacred cows, or notions **not** to be reviewed nor criticized, historically and socially.

Divine Rights of Kings, blue bloods, superior birth, aristocracy ...

This notion of someone born aristocratic is found in many tales and in many lands. History usually peers behind the legends and describes events warts and all. Thus, historically, the vast majority of aristocrats initially achieved their privileged positions with aggressive, armed troops who were successful at conquering. Here was the origin of dynasties and the beginnings of royalty. Let's pretend, however, that this occurred in other ways. Use your imagination, now, in tales, *once upon a time* ... the noble family had a crisis, and a child was taken away and raised by "simple" people in the country, but this child was superior to all in his environment. He wasn't like the others. He was quicker, smarter, stronger, and ... lighter. Later, he grew up, had adventures, and made his way back to his natural place, the aristocracy, and married the princess. Ah, the imagination! Myth conceptions!

As various belief systems came into fashion, this persistent story of natural rulers continued or adapted to survive - somewhat like the evolution of species itself. When everything was God's Divine Will, then of course God knew who the king was (God knew everything); thus, the king had a divine right to rule and God placed him there. When he was bad or incompetent, well, the people must have deserved that. When the Age of Reason came along, these kings strove to be philosopher-kings, advanced and enlightened. When Darwin came along, his theories were adapted to prove that the ruling classes were naturally the fittest *by the fact* that they were at the top of the food chain. Logic bows to circuitous reasoning and imaginative rationale, *and the world is hypnotized*. Still.

Nationalism has been defended as patriotism and love of one's country. Millions died in world wars due to nationalism. To some, it is still a sacred cow. "My country right or wrong" is blind patriotism and often leads to chauvinist reactions, militant stances, and war. G. K. Chesterton's first book of essays, *The Defendant* (1901), had a chapter titled "A Defense of Patriotism": "'My country, right or wrong,' is a thing that no patriot would think of saying. It is like saying, 'My mother, drunk or sober.'" By the way, political theorists like George Orwell made a distinction between patriots who loved their ways and their country, and nationalists who wanted to export their superior culture, oftentimes with force.

From my country, the USA, we were often told "Our government has its flaws, but it is the best government in the world." If this piece of unexamined rationale was not sufficient to squelch national criticism, then the hypnotized patriots would go on the offensive - *America: love it or leave it*! or "Go back where you came from!" Uh, does this apply to Native Americans? ...

27

The logic is similar to a parent's "because I said so, that's why!" Here's the bad news: We are spoon fed misguided perceptions and outright misrepresentation *by those who play the parts of extended parents* in society.

Here's an item that will push buttons in the USA: CONSTITUTIONAL DO-OVER: Why a 1789 guide for a 2003 nation? by Ken Wheatcroft-Pardue, Fort Worth Star-Telegram, June 1, 2003
http://www.dfw.com/mld/startelegram/2003/06/01/news/opinion/5990986.htm

> ... it should come as no surprise that, according to a study by the Institute for Democracy and Electoral Assistance, the United States "ranks 139th in the world in average voter turnout in national elections since 1945." This widespread voter apathy is in reality an index of citizen frustration and alienation from a political system that just doesn't work.

> ... As for impeachment, we borrowed it from the British, who had the good sense to abandon it in the late 18th century because it was a clumsy and inefficient instrument for getting rid of the executive.
> Modern democracies don't impeach. If there is a conflict between the executive and legislative branches that cannot be worked out, new elections are called -- not a cumbersome, quasi-judicial proceeding but a political solution to a political problem.

> As for our last presidential election, regardless of whom you were for, it revealed clearly that we are not a modern democracy.
> Modern democracies do not have elections that remain in doubt for weeks, using ballots that are difficult to read, while at the same time allowing some votes to count more than others because of an arcane method of tabulating votes adopted because of a political compromise more than 200 years ago.

In modern democracies, the first-place vote-getter wins. Period. It is straightforward, transparent and clear, as every good government is and ours is not.

The fact is that our Constitution is not even particularly democratic. Consider the U.S. Senate, the least representative governing body in the Western world. The practice of having two senators per state is an outrage. In the Senate, less than 1 million Wyomingites have the same amount of representation as 35 million Californians. As Alexander Hamilton put it, "the practice of parsing out two senators per state shocks too much the ideas of justice and every human feeling." And he said that when the ratio between the most populous state and the least was near 10-to-1, not the obscene 69-to-1 that it is now.

We have put up with the patented absurdities of an unrepresentative Senate and the Electoral College for far too long. A constitution is only a plan of government. There is nothing sacred about it.

... At the very least, before we attempt to export democracy to the cradle of civilization, we should begin talking about the real deficiencies in our Constitution.

No one still wears white wigs and satin breeches, and no reason exists for us to continue to govern ourselves with an 18th-century document. Other countries with people no more capable than us have recently written new constitutions: Denmark in 1953, the Dutch in 1972 and 1983, and Portugal and Sweden in 1976. What stops us?

~ ~ ~

Modern medicine has surfaced in the last few centuries with its own "proven" approach and has left the superstitious days of folk remedies, where simple people would go out and pick herbs and dig up roots. Now we have modern pharmaceuticals (ground up and mixed herbs, formulated into pills) and has added mechanical and electronic devices to aid doctors and practitioners in the ancient art of healing. We are all living longer and healthier lives thanks to these improvements. This same modern medicine has gone through its own phases, from ridding itself of out-moded notions, to relying upon a mechanistic/biological view of the body, to having to adapt to a growing body of evidence that has been chipping away at our own Western cow: *science, or the scientific method, does not explain everything.*

Just within the last thirty years allopathic, or mainstream, Western medicine expanded into the "body-mind" model (even though there have been pioneers and advocates from the New Thought movement since the 1880s). The changes continue. For instance, just as society and politics had to deal with the revolutionary ideas of the 1960s, the medical establishment had to cope with paradigm shifts (changes in group or social perceptions) of what was true or acceptable (as compared with being told what was true by the new scientist-priests). Alternative therapies had arrived. Western medicine advocates had to control their tempers, and righteousness, when Asian medicine, such as acupuncture, became accepted and even earned financial recognition by health insurance providers. Other "quack" procedures such as chiropractic and homeopathy have made great strides forward in general acceptance.

J. Robert Oppenheimer, an important scientist in the development of the atomic bomb, had this to say:
"Science progresses funeral by funeral."
What was he talking about? A very old truism: the old must die before the new can be born. We are now coming to see a holistic model of medicine and healing that encompasses an expanded sense of who we are in the "body-mind-*spirit*" system.

America: the land of opportunity!
But will there be more opportunity for Bill Gates' kids? Presently, 2006, he is worth $51 billion, which equals the assets of the lowest 40% of Americans! This is 119 million citizens! The belief, or sacred cow (Hmm, perhaps it is a herd of cows), is that we are free individuals in a fair system with just laws; we are rewarded for hard work and initiative; the occasional aberration in

the free market will eventually correct itself, etc. Besides, everyone has an opportunity to make it! But statistics show they are not. There are *officially* 38 million Americans below the poverty line. The official numbers are published every August, by the way. The plot thickens, as thespians remind us:

US Poverty: Chronic Ill, Little Hope for Cure
by Bernd Debusmann - October 5, 2005, Reuters

"Every August, we Americans tell ourselves a lie," said David Brady, a Duke University professor who studies poverty. "The poverty rate was designed to undercount because the government wanted to show progress in the war on poverty. Taking everything into account, the real rate is around 18 percent, or 48 million people. Poverty in the United States is more widespread, by far, than in any other industrialized country."

So is America the land of opportunity? From that same article comes the capitalized statement:
U.S. POVERTY WORST IN INDUSTRIALISED WORLD ...
The hype of striking it rich and living the good life, however, is still so strong that thousands of illegal immigrants are fighting, and dying, to get into this land of milk and honey. They are probably not up on statistics. The latest news is that George Bush will be sending troops to guard the Mexican border. As we open up the boring history books, however, looking under "manifest destiny" and how the lands from Texas to California came into American possession in the first place, it is reminiscent of the myths and legends of how landed aristocracy came to govern. When will we ever learn?

My point? It is amazing how many poor people vote for rich Republicans, believing they will be represented by this oligarchic minority hanging out in plush country clubs and making vacation plans with private jet planes. Two worlds, one vote,... uncounted.

"This American system of ours ... call it what you like, gives to each and every one of us a great opportunity if we only seize it with both hands and make the most of it." – Al Capone

Hurricane Katrina and the televised pictures of some third world Blacks struggling for survival showed the ugly side of the sacred cow of the land of plenty. The have & have-not issue is way beyond the shores of America, however. According to the same article, "Poverty is a universal problem, as is inequality. The world's 500 richest people, according to U.N. statistics, have as much income as the world's poorest 416 million." Could this be true? This is when statistics come to life. Imagine this discrepancy. Take the pill of knowledge and ask yourself: is this fair? Equitable? Just? Or even charitable? Ah, but I suggested imagining, one of the ways to by-pass your critical faculties. Am I planting something? Perhaps, but remember this: *The majority of the world is hypnotized the majority of the time!* I am merely discussing sacred cows.

>>~o~<<

Professor Richard Tarnas, quoted previously, has put various pieces of the larger puzzle together and describes the maladies of a world paradigm, a social and scientific picture of how things are, that is devoid of the sacred. Our modern world view has been purged of enchantment, mystery and meaning; thus, it is disenchanted – and in serious trouble due to this Western dissonance and divisive paradigm:

> ... Since the encompassing cosmological context in which all human activity takes place has eliminated any enduring ground of transcendent values--spiritual, moral, aesthetic-- the resulting vacuum has empowered the reductive values of the market and the mass media to colonize the collective human imagination and drain it of all depth. If the cosmology is disenchanted, the world is logically seen in predominantly utilitarian ways, and the utilitarian mind-set begins to shape all human motivation at the collective level. What might be considered means to larger ends ineluctably become ends in themselves. The drive to achieve ever-greater financial profit, political power, and technological prowess becomes the dominant impulse moving individuals and societies, until these values, despite ritual claims to the contrary, supersede all other aspirations.

The disenchanted cosmos impoverishes the collective psyche in the most global way, vitiating its spiritual and moral imagination--"vitiate" not only in the sense of diminish and impair but also the sense of deform and debase. In such a context, everything can be appropriated. Nothing is immune. Majestic vistas of nature, great works of art, revered music, eloquent language, the beauty of the human body, distant lands and cultures, extraordinary moments of history, the arousal of deep human emotion: all become advertizing tools to manipulate consumer response. For quite literally, in a disenchanted cosmos, nothing is sacred. The soul of the world has been extinguished: Ancient trees and forests can then be seen as nothing but potential lumber; mountains nothing but mineral deposits; seashores and deserts are oil reserves; lakes and rivers, engineering tools. Animals are perceived as harvestable commodities, indigenous tribes as obstructing relics of an outmoded past, children's minds as marketing targets. At the all-important cosmological level, the spiritual dimension of the empirical universe has been entirely negated, and with it, any publicly affirmable encompassing ground for moral wisdom and restraint. The short term and the bottom line rule all. Whether in politics, business, or the media, the lowest common denominator of the culture increasingly governs discourse and prescribes the values of the whole. Myopically obsessed with narrow goals and narrow identities, the powerful blind themselves to the larger suffering and crisis of the global community.

In a world where the subject is experienced as living in--and above and against--a world of objects, other peoples and cultures are more readily perceived as simply other objects, inferior in value to oneself, to ignore or exploit for one's own purposes, as are other forms of life, biosystems, the planetary whole. Moreover, the underlying anxiety and disorientation that pervade modern societies in the face of a meaningless cosmos create both a collective psychic numbness and a desperate spiritual

hunger, leading to an addictive, insatiable craving for ever more material goods to fill the inner emptiness and producing a manic techno-consumerism that cannibalizes the planet. Highly practical consequences ensue from the disenchanted modern world view.
  - Richard Tarnas, pp 32, 33

Creating Criminals

I mentioned this briefly before, but let us examine a little more closely how Laws (authority + tradition) can "create" criminals:

Summer homes in Denmark: it is illegal to live in them year round. We in the US would look at such a restraint on our own private property and you and I know that *we* wouldn't stand for it. But it is an accepted law in that Scandinavian land.

Tobacco products are produced in some regions and packaged and distributed nationally and internationally. This is legitimate business. (OK, it is not a healthy business.) Simultaneously, cigarette smuggling occurs between states and nations. When the correct or legal system is followed, then we are discussing the transportation of products. If local or governmental laws or taxes or "duties" (interesting word) are ignored, then there is a crime being committed. If one does not follow the proper procedures and local laws, one is guilty of illegally transporting and selling tobacco products.

Slavery laws in the US: there were hundreds of laws to keep and maintain "private property" in the land of the free and the home of the brave, or slave. Those who helped free those slaves were criminals. The Supreme Court, the highest law of the land (note Big Authority), in 1857 tried to establish through the Dred Scott case the right of the institution of slavery. It so divided the country that there was a Civil War within three years. There was also a popular belief system at the time, which we would find ludicrous today but many took in earnest: Slave holders *believed*

that Negroes were not only inferior, but due to their simpleness, they needed white people to guide and direct them. This was the White Man's Burden.
Belief System = BS

> Our world view is not simply the way we look at the world. It reaches inward to constitute our innermost being, and outward to constitute the world. It mirrors but also reinforces and even forges the structures, armorings, and possibilities of our interior life. It deeply configures our psychic and somatic experience, the patterns of our sensing, knowing and interacting with the world. No less potently, our world view--our beliefs and theories, our maps, our metaphors, our myths, our interpretive assumptions --constellates our outer reality, shaping and working the world's malleable potentials in a thousand ways of subtly reciprocal interaction. World views create worlds.
> - Richard Tarnas, page 16

~ ~ ~

Let us recall The Prohibition in the 1920s and 30s in the US, when it was criminal to have a glass of beer or wine. The *belief* was that alcohol contributed to crime. Huge numbers of people were emotionally reacting to the horrors of the First World War. Ignoring the socially sanctioned factors to this and other wars, namely nationalism and imperialism, the Temperance advocates pushed for a change in the law to legislate morals. History and experience burst this erroneous belief behind Prohibition, for it was the *suppression* of alcohol that led to organized crime!

Side note: It was still illegal to brew beer privately until 1978 (changed by Jimmy Carter). Prior to that time only big operators produced beer and the watery, mass produced beer options were the result. Within a few years of legalization the micro-breweries emerged in the USA, now the envy of beer connoisseurs everywhere. This is a parallel tale, and a warning, about bland homogeneity and fewer options found in all markets when large business ventures, chain stores, franchises and even media are monopolized or when more innovative ideas and people are marginalized. But, back to Prohibition ...

History was not only ignored, but rewritten in America about this failed enforcement of morals. The whole "affair" was repackaged for future generations, and turned into a popular show! Without looking at the absurdity, and failure, of the law (written into the Constitution, no less), years later the enforcers of that wasted effort were turned into heroes! Elliot Ness and the Untouchables were mostly working for Prohibition, hunting down bootleggers (now called distillers, brewers and businessmen) and destroying bottles of whiskey, beer, and wine, or evil spirits. The focus of the smoke and mirrors TV show and movie was upon fighting those evil mobsters, like Al Capone, and ignoring the fact that this law unintentionally created the crime in the first place. Today the War on Drugs is our Prohibition II. Our courts, and our penitentiaries, are filled to the brim with these "criminals." There are more than 2 million US citizens in jail - this is more people than the whole state of New Mexico! (Could you imagine a huge fence around the state of New Mexico? No? But you could imagine a fence between the US and Mexico?!) Hold on now! Prohibition II. Take marijuana for instance; more than 10 states passed medical marijuana laws, but the federal government, led by *father knows best* authority types who did not read history, keep declaring these laws illegal. (But they are always fond of giving speeches about voting, democracy, and the rights of people to elect their representatives and to vote for laws.) Their BS? The *belief* is that drugs lead to crime. Pattern? Hypnotically asleep at the helm.

I am traveling this broad road of history and societies to share my perceptions of when and why and how beliefs (hypnotists say suggestions) that may not be true, or useful, or even desirable, are created and passed on to future generations. It is important to see the variety of ways that we have been influenced. This is also to declare that Bush and the neo-cons did not invent this (I'm not even aware they have a hypnotist on staff.), but they are masters of deception, of smoke and mirrors.

They and their friends and supporters "feed" the press, ar
"truth" is printed. Who owns the media, by the way? Pri·
individuals? Companies? Of course. Do they have biases?
Are they aligned with one particular party over the other?
It appears so. In fact, if you want to know which businesses are
giving money to which party, take a look at www.buyblue.org

So, please look at the news, and the national debates, with
an eye and an ear for signs of distraction, confusion and
manipulation. Mesmerized? You may never read the news the
same again.
Shall we open the papers? Turn on the TV?

In the USA, today, the people are still fighting about
Darwin. Or is it actually a rather small group of people ... who
have access to major media? Or is it media that would like us to
watch the left hand? Here's the news:

Evolution or Creationism. The Bible, of course, declares
that the world was made in six days, about 6,000 years ago.
Evolutionary science describes millions of years for things to
grow and develop. The belief, the Teaching, of many
fundamentalist Christians, is that the Bible is the Word of God
and thus literally true. I'm not sure what they say about dinosaur
bones, but The fight continues for the hearts and minds of our
children. Religious leaders (authorities), incite the congregations
(peers), via imagination, linking, repetition, and emotions. See
how this works?
Fundamentalists show up everywhere, by the way. An
offshoot of Social Darwinians believe that certain groups and
races are superior and will ultimately win in that natural selection.
Hitler followed his own skewed path on that one.

Hurricane Katrina: the winds of debate soon whirled
through America within days of this tragedy. The debate? - was it
God's wrath? Hurricane Katrina, which devastated the Gulf Coast
in September 2005, was God's judgment on sin, according to
Alabama state Senator Hank Erwin, a Republican. "Sadly,
innocents suffered along with the guilty. Sin always brings

suffering to good people as well as the bad." Is this illogical? Yes indeed, and it goes back to *that old time religion.* Churches and organized religions have successfully used indoctrination - or religious training - for centuries. On top of that, people with limited views have been using, or abusing, their own religions to justify their petty perceptions and prejudices. And the power of religion? Talk about the Really Big Authority! There is oftentimes a directive to "just believe" or "accept" the word of God (as interpreted by whichever group is teaching/preaching), which, in essence, is directly asking the listener to shut down or turn off the logical *gateway* or the door of discrimination. *Have Faith* (and follow us). Just Believe!

Hurricane Katrina struck a few days before the annual gay "Southern Decadence" celebration in New Orleans. Many religious groups put two plus two together. Aha!

But other religions knew the *real* truth: From Israel, it was because of the U.S. and its support of the Gaza evacuation. A prominent Rabbi stated: "No one has permission to take away one inch of the land of Israel from the Jewish people." Meanwhile, Muslim leaders were pointing at the US destruction from the hurricane and declaring that Allah was punishing the US for helping Israel and for invading Muslim countries. Fundamentalism is everywhere – and God seems to be siding with a whole lot of opposing groups.

Beliefnet.com, a website that tracks religious news, ran a poll in the fall of 2005 asking, "Does God have a role in natural disasters like hurricanes?"

6 percent answered, "Yes God is punishing us,"

12 percent checked "Yes, God is testing us."

29% agreed that "disasters are sent by God, but we don't know what the purpose was."

8 percent said God doesn't exist "and disasters like this are just forces of nature." When you look at these percentages, recognize that the population of the US is 297 million. Do the math.

Just to keep the record strait, I am an ordained minister from an interfaith church. I believe that all religions hold some truth and that if we eclectically choose the best ideas, practices and inspiration from these religions and philosophies, we will all benefit. There is a deeper complexity to religions of the world. Many belief systems that have grown into religious institutions started off with profound insights and clear perceptions of how life is on this planet. There are times when these religions clash as to truth and interpretation, such as with why God was chastising the US with hurricane Katrina. We collectively get into problems when we set one way/religion as the natural, superior, and right BS.

As the ancient Chinese sage advised, "The thing all men should fear is that they will become obsessed by a small corner of truth and fail to comprehend its over-all principles."
- Hsun Tzu (298 - 238 BC)

Jesus was pointing out the hypnotized when he said, "And so you have made the word of God invalid because of your tradition. You hypocrites, Isaiah aptly prophesied about you, when he said, 'This people honors me with their lips, yet their heart is far removed from me. It is in vain that they keep worshiping me, because they teach commands of men as doctrines.'" (Matthew 14:6-9)

In another mini-storm fallout from Katrina was the very generous offer by Cuba to send doctors and medicine to the hurricane ravaged southern US. There was a quicker response from this nation than from George Bush, by the way. Although the help was desperately needed, the official status of Cuba is "bad communist" - not good communist like China, and so the offer was ignored, then, a week later, rejected because of the red-tape excuse that the US did not have official relations with that country. It was pointed out that Taiwan was in the same category, but help was accepted there. This is a great example of national hypnosis, a governmental blind spot, an illogical stance that

cannot be explained rationally; therefore it is supported as another belief system: *Cuba is bad. They do bad things to people there. The people are not free in Cuba.*
What an ironic place to have an internationally condemned US prison, the infamous Guantánamo Bay.

Mass hypnosis in the news: Iraq
　　　Spin-meisters at work = propaganda
　　　Authority + emotions + repetition + linking
　　　There have been at least three official reports in the US declaring that there were no connections between the 9-11 attacks and Iraq. Plus, it has been proven that Iraq was not a danger to the USA and had no weapons of mass destruction. However, ...
Today, even after the publication of these reports, almost a quarter of Americans still believe that Saddam had ties to al Queda and that he had weapons (WMD) threatening the US. George Bush, Colin Powell and Condi Rice and other authority figures did their job of selling the war. Good smoke screen!

　　　By the way, what do you suppose will be on the people's minds after a few weeks of front and center news on particular themes? If there is a two week news blitz on employment, or immigration, or drugs, and then a poll is taken to find out what "the people" are concerned about, do you suppose that these very themes will be front and center in their concerns? The results of these polls are then brought out as proof that the aforesaid issues are of great concern to the citizenry. Repetition, authority figures, emotions ... and the show goes on!
... The smoke gets in my eyes.

　　　Just as criminals can be created by unjust and errant laws, entrenched individuals and groups can be protected and aided by laws, the government, and the system. Slave holders were examples of this dynamic in the past. We need look no further than our present government to observe numerous examples today. Since 2000 there have been numerous scandals, crimes and outrageous breaches of the law, but no one has gone to jail for any of it. A just society? Signs that the system is working? "Everyone is treated fairly in a court of law" is a sacred cow.

I wonder if every one of the 2 million Americans now in jail are fair examples of this system of ours?

Cultural Paradox

Cousin to the sacred cow: the cultural paradox. A paradox is an assertion, usually two-sided or contrasted by opposites, that is seemingly contradictory. For instance, comfortably lying naked in the snow. How can this be comfortable? Emerging from a hot sauna and cooling off in the white snow, that's how! Some paradoxes can co-exist, but unexamined and un-integrated belief systems can result in social or cultural schizophrenia, denial and irrational behaviors.

One sign of a faulty belief system, or implanted notions coming from unexamined cultural suggestions is *obsessiveness mixed with a pattern of ignoring inconvenient and contrary facts.*

We call this a "blind spot" in everyday psychology, but when whole groups exhibit a unified, and false, BS, then there are usually problems, suffering, injustices, and even war.

Some examples of co-existent paradoxes:
  wealth & asceticism
  efficiency & leisure
  private property & public ownership

When Belief Systems clash:
  sowing one's oats & whoring around (Oh, the old goose and the gander)
  rugged independence & obedience
  Aryanism & Zionism
  communism & fascism (the fascists hated those unChristian commies)
  christianity & capitalism (think about it)
  competition & cooperation
  patriotism & multinationalism

Some paradoxes in the USA:
   generous foreign policy vs world empire
   competitive markets vs stealing jobs (The *Buy American!*
   Campaign. And made in China!)
   Freedom of the Press vs National Security
   Exporting democracy vs nation building

Interestingly, in the same newspapers, magazines and shows that "inform and educate" us on world matters paradoxically also carry real bits of truth and facts. You will note familiar and mainstream media I have cited within these pages. However, one has to be vigilant to sift through the verbiage. Very similar to the adult who uses his powers of discrimination to choose what is acceptable and what is not, what he will accept into his consciousness and what goes in the dustbin, we need to make choices about what is true and what is not. How to sift through the facts and see through the smoke? One way to do this is to choose where we look for news and views.

Here is something from an alternative information source; a bit of news that confronts the American perception of superior attitudes and morals, especially compared to the atheistic commies: AMNESTY: CHINA, IRAN AND U.S. TOP WORLD EXECUTIONERS
By Robert Evans, Reuters / Common Dreams, April 6, 2004
   http://www.commondreams.org/headlines04/0406-10.htm

GENEVA - China, Iran, the United States and Vietnam were the world's top users of the death penalty in 2003, accounting for 84 percent of known executions, human rights body Amnesty International said Tuesday. ...

Yes, the US is #1. In so many ways we are *number one*. #1 in weapons, the military, using the world's resources per capita. (This Red pill is sometimes a drag, huh?) Truly living in reality is not as pretty and wholesome, and even a bit disturbing, but it is real, based on fact. Here is another #1 for the USA:

US NOTCHES WORLD'S HIGHEST INCARCERATION RATE
By Gail Russell Chaddock, The Christian Science Monitor,
August 18, 2003
http://www.csmonitor.com/2003/0818/p02s01-usju.html

WASHINGTON - More than 5.6 million Americans are in prison or have served time there, according to a new report by the Justice Department released Sunday. That's 1 in 37 adults living in the United States, the highest incarceration level in the world.

It's the first time the US government has released estimates of the extent of imprisonment, and the report's statistics have broad implications for everything from state fiscal crises to how other nations view the American experience.
If current trends continue, it means that a black male in the United States would have about a 1 in 3 chance of going to prison during his lifetime. For a Hispanic male, it's 1 in 6; for a white male, 1 in 17.

No, this isn't unpatriotic "pick on the USA" talk.

It is listing and declaring what the neo-cons have done to our country.

ℑmoke & MIRRORS II

Blinded by the Right

The Neo-Con Extremists

It is time to recognize that we are attending a very poorly done show. It is lowbrow and violent, with "plot-holes." We get restless and even anxious. We move to the side of the theater to peek behind the curtains. If we get past the CIA and the Secret Service, we can check out the people pushing the buttons and sounding the alarms.

"Shrouded in ambiguity and cloaked in deep secrecy, this administration continues to suddenly, and sometimes unexpectedly, drop its decisions upon the public and Congress, and expect obedient approval, without question, without debate, without opposition."
--West Virginia Democratic Senator Robert Byrd, West Virginia Gazette, June 29, 2002

Yes. First let us consider who we are dealing with. Many of these actors from this tragic farce you know from the foxy News *Shows*. The question you need to have before you is this: are these right wingers more than likely prone to, and capable of, carrying out the charges I present - a forced entry into the executive offices? Are these people righteous opportunists who could and would overlook the fact that they were committing a coup, because their eyes were on the prize? I have included within this study their policies and edicts concerning many and varied areas plus numerous examples to show that there is a consistency in their actions and behaviors that emphasize that they would indeed do anything to win and exert a dominating influence across the board - and the world. I have added an appendix that lists the characteristics of a certain brand of political extremism that is rather chilling when we contemplate the actions and beliefs of the Bush regime and the neo-cons. Check it out. Below are some thoughts about these interlopers by social commentator and best-selling author Kurt Vonnegut. He has gathered some wisdom in his eighty-some years and deserves a listen:

> Psychopathic personalities – hereinafter P.P.s – the medical term for smart, personable people who have no conscience. P.P.s are fully aware of how much suffering their actions will inflict on others but do not care.
> A P.P., should he attain a post near the top of our federal government, might feel that taking the country into an endless war with casualties in the millions was simply something decisive to do today.
> With a P.P., decisiveness is all. Or, to put it another way, we now have a Reichstag fire of our own.
>
> These people are around and they do rise. Women are attracted to them because they are so confident. They really don't give a fuck what happens, not even to themselves. But this is a serious defect and, no, we haven't been invaded and conquered by Martians. We have been conquered by psychopathic personalities who are attractive.
> (from Pathways Magazine, spring 2003)

In the infamous and embarrassing interview that Governor Bush gave in his 1999 campaign, when he could not name 3 out of 4 top leaders in international hot spots, he did give us an idea of what he *did* admire – a strong armed military takeover of one's own country:

"Bush: The new Pakistani general, he's just been elected – not elected, this guy took over office. It appears this guy is going to bring stability to the country and I think that's good news for the subcontinent." Washington Post, Nov 5, 1999

Although it is fairly common knowledge that Bush is not much interested in gaining knowledge -- relying on his staffers to tell him the news and read the various reports and "distill" the

information for him -- I am sure that this basic lack of curiosity about the larger world cannot be good for *any* public official, let alone the president. What is worse is that Bush will defend his position of ignorance by describing his gut reactions to things. The "decider" is going on instincts, my friends. On a 2001 trip to Italy George W. Bush was asked to explain himself. To the embarrassment of all thinking Americans, he told the assembled world leaders, "I know what I believe and I believe what I believe is right." And in 2002, Bush told a British reporter, "Look, my job isn't to nuance."
http://www.garlicandgrass.org/issue5/Kathleen_Maclay.cfm

Nuance is what the liberals do, and the conservatives make fun of or run over. We are not talking subtle with them, but black and white, unexamined extremes, and reactionary knee jerk militancy. This is present in world affairs, my friends, now and in the past. Any student of history can cite both foolish *and* intelligent people in prominent positions "calling the shots." The former are in the lead, for they do not appraise themselves but move forward to where the action is, while the latter find themselves leading due to their appraisal of their superior abilities and the will to win. I was, therefore, very intrigued when I came upon an article by Gregory Mott of the Washington Post, who reported that a study had been made on this very subject. (June 2, 2002); http://www.possibility.com/Misc/stupidity.html
He interviewed Robert Sternberg, director of Yale University's Center for the Psychology of Abilities, Competencies and Expertise (PACE), who edited "Why Smart People Can Be So Stupid" (Yale University Press)

> Sternberg, an expert in intelligence testing, contends that stupidness is not the opposite of smartness, but rather the opposite of wisdom ‹ defined as the ability to apply knowledge to achieve the common good.
> Sternberg recently took the time to answer some of our stupid questions.
> Q: What attracted you to the study of stupidity?
> A: The roots of the book were in my wondering about what's up with people who have very high intelligence in

the traditional sense, but seem to be out to lunch in another sense. How did Richard Nixon ever get involved in Watergate and the subsequent cover-up? What was Bill Clinton thinking when he kept repeating the same mistakes in his personal life? More recently, how did the intelligent people who ran Enron think they would get away with a shell game?

Q: Did any kind of unified theory of stupidity emerge from the research?A: I believe there are four main tendencies that lead us into this predicament:

» The egocentrism fallacy: We foolishly come to believe that because we are so smart, the world does and should revolve around us.

» The omniscience fallacy: We foolishly come to believe that part of the reason the world revolves around us is that we know much more than we do, or even all we need to know.
» The omnipotence fallacy: We foolishly believe this knowledge makes us omnipotent. We can do whatever we want and get away with it.

» The invulnerability fallacy: Then we foolishly believe we can get away with it because our intelligence makes us invulnerable to attack or even perhaps to criticism.

Q: Who is most likely to fall victim to these beliefs?
A: Oddly enough, the people most likely to succumb to the four fallacies are those who are very smart and those who are very stupid. The first group gets suckered out because they are so smart. The second group gets suckered out because they lack the cognitive capacity to realize how foolish these fallacies are.

> My fellow citizens, I am going to have to put George Bush in the second category. We are talking cognitive capacity. It is a safe bet that Bush is not acting alone. Some believe he

47

doesn't have the intelligence to act alone. In times of national crises, Dick Cheney is the one who is spirited off to safety and seclusion. Why? Is he the brains? Who is he anyway? Could he be the one in 1986 who opposed a call to release Nelson Mandela after 23 years in prison? Yes. He repeatedly opposed any sanctions against South African apartheid. Does he not have a heart? Well, it **is** faulty. And he's on the compassionate team? He makes money on weapons and war. Could this be a conflict of interest, especially if we look at the War on Iraq? He was there when young George Bush appeared before the 9-11 investigative Commission in 2004. Was it not out of some wild surrealist novel that Bush had Cheney sit with him during the important questioning!? As observers know well, they demanded total secrecy and hid behind the "national security" screen – their testimony was not recorded nor videotaped. Again, I didn't perceive any outcry at yet another instance of backroom dealing and obstruction of justice. Later, Bush described it as a pleasant experience. How nice.

But it has not been so nice for the rest of us.

William Rivers Pitt, teacher, author and activist, gave us some sobering perspectives and a rough outline of who we are dealing with in his "Greetings from Boston, Mr. Bush" (t r u t h o u t /Perspective, 1 October, 2002):

> There is no simpler way to put it: All hell has broken loose in the two years since Bush [took office]. The democratic ethic of American elections was torn to pieces in Florida, and by a Supreme Court that should never have gotten involved in the first place. A President was installed who lost an election but won a lawsuit. Upon arrival, he proceeded to fill the ranks of government with a rogues gallery of extremists and slick corporate CEOs:
> - Religious fundamentalist John Ashcroft became Attorney General after losing an election to a dead man;
> - Neo-conservative hawk Don Rumsfeld became Secretary of Defense, backed by appallingly dangerous men like Paul Wolfowitz and Richard Perle;

- Harvey Pitt became chairman of the SEC, institutionalizing the idea that conflicts of interest do not matter and that foxes are perfectly trustworthy when given a key to the henhouse;
- Former Enron vice president Thomas White was made Secretary of the Army, and when the Enron scandal exploded, we were told he knew nothing of it, he does not in fact know much about anything, his staffers call him 'Mr. Magoo' behind his back, and isn't that a heartwarming thought when one considers the control he has over our armed forces. News headline: Mr. Magoo is over-seeing the Army during the War on Terror. I doubt that will be on the GOP campaign literature in 2004.

OK, we are going to have to understand, on a deeper level, just who these people are. Whether one is playing some sport, or checking out the competition in business, or some other game or endeavor, it is important to analyze the other team. Who are we dealing with here? And, as a therapist looking to the inner and hidden dynamics of character, what psychological dynamics make these people tick? Let us look at the evidence.

RESEARCHERS HELP DEFINE WHAT MAKES A POLITICAL CONSERVATIVE
By Kathleen Maclay, UC Berkeley News, 22 July 2003
http://www.berkeley.edu/news/media/releases/2003/07/22_politics.shtml
BERKELEY - Politically conservative agendas may range from supporting the Vietnam War to upholding traditional moral and religious values to opposing welfare. But are there consistent underlying motivations?
Four researchers who culled through 50 years of research literature about the psychology of conservatism report that at the core of political conservatism is the resistance to change and a tolerance for inequality, and that some of the common psychological factors linked to political conservatism include:
- Fear and aggression
- Dogmatism and intolerance of ambiguity
- Uncertainty avoidance
- Need for cognitive closure

Of course there was much criticism, actually, name-calling and fist clenching, when this analysis was published. The reason? Faulty research methods? No. The researchers sifted through fifty years of studies. The neo-cons didn't like the conclusions, and they didn't want to be portrayed with these characteristics, even though they are true. Remember, the neo-cons have been carefully crafting their image for many decades now -- part of the smoke and mirrors show -- and, like other unpleasant facts that get in the way, you can bet that they will come out fighting to maintain the image. The ruckus is usually so loud and the fingers will be pointing in so many other directions that soon the report, analysis or investigation will be lost in the smoke, or fog, of confusion. It is a classic technique and used quite regularly. If this book gathers attention, there will be the same right wing reaction. You can bet on it.

If we can calmly review the results of this character analysis, however, we will see that the present government is acting exactly as described. *Exactly*. The acceptance of inequality fits into the belief system of *winners rise to the top*, thus they should be rewarded (with money, power and material goods) for their efforts. Of course, this overlooks the fact of inherited wealth, as well as the overwhelming evidence of ambitiousness often linked with very negative and even dangerous traits. History is full of such types. But these observations will be ignored due to another conservative characteristic of uncertainty avoidance. Things are black or white. You are for us or against us. There are good and evil people and nations (and we are good). Hell, as far as the neo-cons are concerned, there are good and bad elected representatives in Congress! The aggressive, bully boy tactics are not just for the average underling, but there are many examples of the righteous and closure oriented neo-cons backing Congressmen into corners. Here is but one example: June 10 2005 - When the republicans decided they did not want to hear anti-Patriot Act testimony in the U.S. House of Representatives, Chairman James Sensenbrenner (R-WI), suddenly and without warning, gavelled the special hearings to a close! Unilaterally, without debate, and in the middle of ongoing testimony. Father knew best. "Children! Shut up, behave, and go to your rooms!"

Welcome to government in a neo-con world!

You don't get harmony
when everybody sings the same note.
- Doug Floyd

After the disastrous Attorney General, John Aschcroft, stepped down, it was hard to imagine if it could get worse. It did.

It was Mr. Gonzales, after all, who repeatedly defended Mr. Bush's decision to authorize warrantless eavesdropping on Americans' international calls and e-mail. He was an eager public champion of the absurd notion that as commander in chief during a time of war, Mr. Bush can ignore laws that he thinks get in his way. Mr. Gonzales was disdainful of any attempt by Congress to examine the spying program, let alone control it.

The attorney general helped formulate and later defended the policies that repudiated the Geneva Conventions in the war against terror, and that sanctioned the use of kidnapping, secret detentions, abuse and torture. He has been central to the administration's assault on the courts, which he recently said had no right to judge national security policies, and on the constitutional separation of powers.
His Justice Department has abandoned its duties as guardian of election integrity and voting rights. It approved a Georgia photo-ID law that a federal judge later likened to a poll tax, a case in which Mr. Gonzales's political team overrode the objections of the department's professional staff.

The Justice Department has been shamefully indifferent to complaints of voter suppression aimed at minority voters. But it has managed to find the time to sue a group of black political leaders in Mississippi for discriminating against white voters.
- The Failed Attorney General, The New York Times | Editorial, 11 March 2007

One can easily state that security is a constant issue with conservatives. Unfortunately, when there is a "responsible" approach to money and security *mixed* with fear, aggression, dogmatism and intolerance (and inequality is fine, remember), how much security is one going to achieve? Strong armed tactics only bring reaction and a counter-force of resistance. Look at the reign of Ariel Sharon (as well as the War on Terror – especially focused upon Iraq): tough actions bring anger, revenge, armed resistance and more killing. Daily. This policy is creating terrorism in the Middle East. *Creating* enemies, making us all less secure. The conservative reaction? Get tougher. Don't admit mistakes (there's that ambiguity worry), and "stay the course" which means more troops, weapons and killing – and more terror and enemies. This will not end as long as they are in control.

> Donald Shields and John Cragan, two professors of communication, have compiled a database of investigations and/or indictments of candidates and elected officials by U.S. attorneys since the Bush administration came to power. Of the 375 cases they identified, 10 involved independents, 67 involved Republicans, and 298 involved Democrats. The main source of this partisan tilt was a huge disparity in investigations of local politicians, in which Democrats were seven times as likely as Republicans to face Justice Department scrutiny.

> **- Department of Injustice** by Paul Krugman, The New York Times, 09 March 2007

"When fascism comes to America, it will be wrapped in the flag and carrying the cross."
--- from "It Can't Happen Here" by Sinclair Lewis, 1935

When I first came across the following quote by Donald Rumsfeld concerning not finding weapons of mass destruction (WMD) in Iraq, I was simply surprised at the irrational connotations: "The absence of evidence is not evidence of absence." -- Note, however, that this is a clever phrase that puts one off center, a place of uncertainty, and open to suggestion... from an expert, like himself. Rumsfeld has had a long history of deception, double-speak and obfuscation. I recommend that you read activist and author Thom Hartmann detail his review of a very revealing documentary aired by the BBC titled **"The Power of Nightmares"** (Common Dreams - December 7, 2004). His article, HYPING TERROR FOR FUN, PROFIT - AND POWER, blows the lid off some paranoid and powerful neo-con players: http://www.commondreams.org/views04/1207-26.htm

Better yet, see the BBC documentary.
(As an aside, the amount of really good analyses, investigations and documentaries about the US that are made and distributed by other countries could be a good source of information for informed citizenry in *this* country, but the vast majority of these studies do not make it into the living rooms, or minds, of the American public. Of course, it begs the question - why are so many good documentaries about the US made and seen in Britain and elsewhere?! Makes you wonder why, huh? I smell smoke.)

In his report Hartmann goes into depth about the content of the documentary. It calls into question assumptions that we all grew up with... the Cold War fear and political stand-offs that held sway on so many levels for so many years. Remember, too, the character traits of conservatives and it all makes more sense. They are expressing their view upon the world, and creating the reality by their actions. BS creating reality – and fear, and war. Top-down interpretation, and we all were "guided" to join them in their hypnotic trance. Hartmann describes the documentary as myth-shattering; this is an equivalent appraisal of the hypnosis hypothesis I am presenting here. We can awaken from the myth, from the smoke and mirrors deception created by those who are either deluded in their firm and unshakable beliefs. It created by those who are opportunists who have a lot to gain by perpetuating their fearful worldview. Certainly their ever expanding net worth shows that they have benefited. I give you some quotes and some summations, in brackets [ ], within Hartmann's article, but please take the time to check out this BBC documentary yourself.

Thom Hartmann:

> What if there really was no need for much - or even most - of the Cold War?
> What if, in fact, the Cold War had been kept alive for two decades based on phony WMD threats?
>
> What if, similarly, the War On Terror was largely a scam, and the administration was hyping it to seem larger-than-life? What if our "enemy" represented a real but relatively small threat posed by rogue and criminal groups well outside the mainstream of Islam? What if that hype was done largely to enhance the power, electability, and stature of George W. Bush and Tony Blair?
>
> And what if the world was to discover the most shocking dimensions of these twin deceits - that the same men promulgated them in the 1970s and today?
> It happened.
> The myth-shattering event took place in England the first three weeks of October, when the BBC aired a three-hour documentary written and produced by Adam Curtis, titled "The Power of Nightmares"
> http://news.bbc.co.uk/1/hi/programmes/3755686.stm If the emails and phone calls many of us in the US received from friends in the UK - and debate in the pages of publications like **The Guardian**
> http://www.guardian.co.uk/terrorism/story/0,12780,13279 04,00.html are any indicator, this was a seismic event, one that may have even provoked a hasty meeting between Blair and Bush a few weeks later.
>
> [President Nixon, who fits the description of a person with a high IQ who made many dumb (and fateful) decisions, was experimenting with new foreign policy approaches, most notably finding common ground with Communist China. He tried to dismantle the dangerous Cold War with the Soviet Union before he had to resign in 1974. Then things were stalled. Two now very familiar men stepped in to save the day. Note they have not changed their tunes in 30 years!]

Rumsfeld and Cheney began a concerted effort - first secretly and then openly - to undermine Nixon's treaty for peace and to rebuild the state of fear and, thus, reinstate the Cold War.

And these two men - 1974 Defense Secretary Donald Rumsfeld and Ford Chief of Staff Dick Cheney - did this by claiming that the Soviets had secret weapons of mass destruction that the president didn't know about, that the CIA didn't know about, that nobody but them knew about. And, they said, because of those weapons, the US must redirect billions of dollars away from domestic programs and instead give the money to defense contractors for whom these two men would one day work.

...

The CIA strongly disagreed, calling Rumsfeld's position a "complete fiction" and pointing out that the Soviet Union was disintegrating from within, could barely afford to feed their own people, and would collapse within a decade or two if simply left alone.

But Rumsfeld and Cheney wanted Americans to believe there was something nefarious going on, something we should be very afraid of. To this end, they convinced President Ford to appoint a commission including their old friend Paul Wolfowitz to prove that the Soviets were up to no good.

According to Curtis' BBC documentary, Wolfowitz's group, known as "Team B," came to the conclusion that the Soviets had developed several terrifying new weapons of mass destruction, featuring a nuclear-armed submarine fleet that used a sonar system that didn't depend on sound and was, thus, undetectable with our current technology.

[Thus, even though there was no evidence, the B Team duped everyone around them into believing that there could be a danger that was not detectable with our present surveillance abilities. This must have been their "gut" instincts that told them this. Sound familiar? Here's another side to the theater: the Republicans were in disarray and disgrace after Nixon resigned; they needed to recreate their image as tough-minded saviors fighting the Commies. Ronald Reagan would ride into town dressed up in this costume within a few years. How perfect: recruit an actor to expand the smoke and mirrors *Tough Republicans to the Rescue* show!]

The moderator of the BBC documentary then notes: "... The CIA accused Team B of moving into a fantasy world."
.....
But, trillions of dollars and years later, it was proven that they had been wrong all along, and the CIA had been right. Rumsfeld, Cheney, and Wolfowitz lied to America in the 1970s about Soviet WMDs.
.....
But the neocons said it was true, and organized a group - The Committee on the Present Danger http://www.fightingterror.org/ - to promote their worldview. The Committee produced documentaries, publications, and provided guests for national talk shows and news reports. They worked hard to whip up fear and encourage increases in defense spending, particularly for sophisticated weapons systems offered by the defense contractors for whom neocons would later become lobbyists.
And they succeeded in recreating an atmosphere of fear in the United States, and making themselves and their defense contractor friends richer than most of the kingdoms of the world.
Similarly, according to this documentary, the War On Terror is the same sort of scam, run for many of the same reasons, by the same people. And by hyping it - and then invading Iraq - we may well be bringing into reality terrors and forces that previously existed only on the margins and with very little power to harm us. ...
Watching "The Terror of Nightmares" is like taking the

56

Red Pill in the movie The Matrix. ...
Get a pair of headphones (the audio is faint), plug them into your computer, and visit an unofficial archive of the Curtis' BBC documentary at the Information Clearing House website
http://www.informationclearinghouse.info/video1037.htm
(The first hour of the program, in a more viewable format, is also available here:
http://www.prisonplanet.com/articles/november2004/1211 04powerofnightmares.htm)

For those who prefer to read things online, an unofficial but complete transcript is on this Belgian site
http://www.acutor.be/silt/index.php?idW3

Masterminds (or is that mini-minds? Hey, they termed themselves the B Team, not A!) Cheney and Rumsfeld are definitely neo-cons to watch, but they are not alone. Bush's appointments for the Secretaries of the Air Force and the Navy are former executives for weapons companies.
Yes, the revolving door has been around for ages. This particular door squeaks. As for the Secretary of the Army? Why, we are back to an Enron man. Friends in America, these are some of the men giving advice and making decisions for you and I daily. There is an obvious conflict of interest in many of these choices. Money is being made, young people are dying, terrorists are multiplying, and the self-fulfilling prophecy of enemies of America is fulfilled ... which then requires more protection, surveillance, weapons and loss of civil rights. Look around you and you will see this is what has happened. Exactly.

Cheney and Rumsfeld were not acting alone, obviously. I've compiled a list of these perpetrators at the end of this exposé. Perhaps you could add a few felons-to-be. Please do.
Here's one:
How did John Bolton, a right winger at the State Department who intimidated intelligence analysts to support his hawkish views, get his important post at the UN? Bush had

bypassed the Senate in August 2005 by appointing him to the position when the lawmakers were in recess, avoiding the confirmation process and angering senators concerned that Bolton had a temper and would continue his aggressive style at the United Nations - just where we do not need it. He has continued to embarrass thoughtful Americans ever since.

Revolt of the Generals, by Richard J. Whalen - The Nation 28 September 2006

A revolt is brewing among our retired Army and Marine generals. This rebellion - quiet and nonconfrontational, but remarkable nonetheless - comes not because their beloved forces are bearing the brunt of ground combat in Iraq but because the retirees see the US adventure in Mesopotamia as another Vietnam-like, strategically failed war, and they blame the errant, arrogant civilian leadership at the Pentagon. The dissenters include two generals who led combat troops in Iraq: Maj. Gen. Charles Swannack Jr., who commanded the 82nd Airborne Division, and Maj. Gen. John Batiste, who led the First Infantry Division (the "Big Red One"). These men recently sacrificed their careers by retiring and joining the public protest.
In late September Batiste, along with two other retired senior officers, spoke out about these failures at a Washington Democratic policy hearing, with Batiste saying Defense Secretary Donald Rumsfeld was "not a competent wartime leader" who made "dismal strategic decisions" that "resulted in the unnecessary deaths of American servicemen and women, our allies and the good people of Iraq." Rumsfeld, he said, "dismissed honest dissent" and "did not tell the American people the truth for fear of losing support for the war."
...
The dissenting retired generals are bent on making Iraq this nation's last strategically failed war - that is, one doggedly waged by civilian officials largely to avoid personal accountability for their bad decisions. A failed war causes mounting human and other costs, damaging or

entirely destroying the national interest it was supposed to serve. ...

Retired Lieut. Gen. William Odom calls the Iraq War "the worst strategic mistake in the history of the United States" and draws a grim parallel with the Vietnam War. ...

The well-read retired Marine Lieut. Gen. Gregory Newbold wrote in a Time magazine essay: "I retired from the military four months before the [March 2003] invasion, in part because of my opposition to those who had used 9/11's tragedy to hijack our security policy." Newbold calls the Iraq War "unnecessary" and says the civilians who launched the war acted with "a casualness and swagger" that are "the special province" of those who have never smelled death on a battlefield.

... Rumsfeld publicly humiliated all who dissented, beginning with Army Chief of Staff Gen. Eric Shinseki, who was virtually dismissed the day he honestly gave his views to Congress. ...

Bureaucratic accountability comes hard and very slowly. According to a stark consensus of global terrorism trends by America's sixteen separate espionage agencies, * the US invasion and occupation of Iraq "helped spawn a new generation of Islamic radicalism and [expand] the overall terrorist threat." ...

America is a uniquely favored nation that redefines itself in each generation. But we have had a lifetime of embracing one democratic global war, and numerous presidentially inspired, politicized and secret smaller wars that have turned out badly. ...

* Did you get that? The USA has 16 separate espionage agencies! What the hell is going on here in this land of the free and the home of the brave?

~ ~ ~

Your tax dollars at work: gambling on destruction

There was a major uproar in Congressional halls when it became common knowledge just what another republican insider,

John Poindexter, * was conniving for Bush. Namely, placing bets on futures trading in assassinations and overthrows! Jeremy Kahn, writing for *Fortune* magazine (Feb & July 2003), incredibly, thought the idea useful:

> Earlier this year, the Defense Advanced Research Projects Agency (DARPA) gave a $1 million grant to startup Net Exchange to establish a futures market for political events in the Middle East. ... It would have allowed traders to place bets on events including whether Palestinian leader Yasser Arafat would be assassinated, or Jordan's King Abdullah II would be overthrown. Market participants could have remained anonymous, a fact that some senators critical of the program said raised the possibility that a terrorist could use the market to profit off his own attack. The plan, which FORTUNE first reported on in its March 3rd issue, was abandoned after Democratic senators assailed it as ghoulish, immoral, and absurd. Senator Minority Leader Tom Daschle of South Dakota claimed the program would provide a monetary incentive to those wishing to commit acts of terror. Senator Hillary Rodham Clinton (D-N.Y.) said the plan would have created 'a futures market in death.'

> The Policy Analysis Market was part of a larger Pentagon project called FutureMap (an acronym that stands for Futures Markets Applied to Prediction) that is run out of DARPA's Office of Terrorism Information Awareness. (This department was previously called the Office of Total Information Awareness but the Pentagon decided that that just sounded too Orwellian). The office is run by John Poindexter, who served as former President Reagan's national security advisor, and was a key figure in the Iran-Contra scandal. Earlier this year, Poindexter was forced to abandon a controversial plan to use the Internet to spy on average citizens in an attempt to prevent terrorist attacks after civil rights groups and federal legislators objected.

The Pentagon had asked for an additional $8 million for 2004, but the whole plan was terminated by late July 2003. What other schemes are underfoot and below the radar screen? Billions of the Pentagon budget is off limits to public – and even congressional – scrutiny. Why? National security, of course.

* By the way: Bush chose retired Admiral John Poindexter, who was convicted of lying to Congress, to lead the very Orwellian sounding Total Information Awareness Program, which is collecting vast amounts of personal information and intelligence about ordinary American citizens. Are we starting to get a basic personality profile on these "leaders"?

Nepotism

Dick Cheney's daughter is clumsily interfering in foreign aid with well paid jobs for her and her friends – all who lack important experience, diplomacy and wisdom it seems. Personnel at USAID and other foreign departments are reluctant to complain for fear of reprisal. Anyone who has observed hardball tactics by Cheney, Rumsfeld, and crew knows that complaining (foreign service or otherwise) personnel do have to worry about reprisal, job security, and very unpleasant repercussions. Is there an accounting? Isn't all of this adding up?

One can get a feeling for the extremist crew with the following piece, "**Where Did the Middle Go? How Polarized Politics and a Radical GOP have Put a Chill on Measured Debate**" by Theodore Roszak, San Francisco Chronicle, Oct 2004:

As a case in point, consider House Majority Leader Tom DeLay, R-Texas, whose remarkable career is the subject of Lou Dubose and Jan Reid's recent study **The Hammer: Tom DeLay: God, Money and the United States Congress**. There could be no better example of a "stupid white man" (to borrow Michael Moore's contemptuous label), provided one recognizes that a certain kind of stupidity is compatible with a certain kind of cunning. ... DeLay is a crafty strategist, no doubt about that. But how could any honest conservative fail to find DeLay an embarrassment to the country?

61

... here we have a major political leader whose world view is a bizarre stew of evangelical religion and Social Darwinist business values. Balance, moderation and discriminating intelligence play no role in his politics. This is a man who believes the Environmental Protection Agency is the equivalent of the Gestapo. And as Dubose and Reid make clear, DeLay has been as willing to target moderates for destruction as Democrats.

By DeLay's standards, even Newt Gingrich didn't qualify as a true conservative. After all, Gingrich called off the great government shutdown of 1995, which DeLay would have continued until hell froze over. In DeLay's eyes, Gingrich was a "think-tank pontificator and a flake" who never read the Bible. By the late 1990s, DeLay's take-no-prisoners political style was well along toward giving the Republicans permanent control of Congress. Today in Washington, DeLay and his colleagues govern with a winner-take-all ferocity, as if the Democrats simply didn't exist. They invite lobbyists to write legislation and give Democrats no chance to debate or amend.

The secret of their success? Covertly, they draw upon the racist fears of rednecks and blue collars, but overtly, they attribute their triumph to unswerving evangelical faith. DeLay, who faithfully attends Bible classes, is an ally of the Rev. John Hagee's Cornerstone Church in San Antonio, Texas. In this capacity, he fancies himself the congressional voice of "God's foreign policy," which calls for unstinting economic and military support for Israeli hard-liners from here to the Second Coming.

By the autumn 2004 DeLay had been indicted for various crimes (especially bad form for a moralistic Christian); however, his loyal (and fearful) fellow congressmen rallied around him, protecting his powerful post against the rules that state a Congressman under such investigation shall not remain in his position. But these guys are not much for rules and ethics, unless it helps them. Since those charges threatened his position (and ego), Tom Delay pressured many congressmen to make his case an exception to the law – a conviction against him should not stop him from leading the Congress as the majority leader. I remind you that if a Democrat were in his shoes, with his list of allegations, there would be no mercy. His campaign to save his skin was fought, but he had to bow to the greater outrage.

By early 2005 it was revealed that DeLay had large and suspicious payments being made to his family: his wife and daughter have been paid at least half a million dollars for "their services" just in the last few years! Nice family business, Tom. I'm sure it's all honorable.

The piece below is from Common Cause (January 2005):
> DeLay and his allies were successful pushing through a rule that by itself will likely gut the ethics process in the House.
> The Republicans call the change the "presumption of innocence rule." We call it the "party protection act," since no one will be investigated as long as Members vote along party lines. Under the old rule, if the Ethics Committee - a panel of five Republicans and five Democrats - deadlocked along party lines or otherwise, an investigation would automatically be triggered within 45 days. Under the new rule, the complaint is dropped in the event of a deadlock. This will allow either party to "veto" an ethics investigation. The ethics process should be premised on protecting the integrity of the House, not on party politics, party truces, and under the leadership of leaders like Tom DeLay who would violate House rules then try to bend the rules to suit his own political purpose.

~ ~ ~

Bill Moyers, a great voice of conscience for many years, shared his "Saving Democracy" in Feb 2006.
http://www.publicampaign.org/savingdemocracy/
On Tom DeLay and Jack Abramoff:
> DeLay was a man on the move and on the take. But he needed help to sustain the cash flow. He found it in a fellow right wing ideologue named Jack Abramoff.

Abramoff personifies the Republican money machine of which DeLay with the blessing of the House leadership was the major domo. It was Abramoff who helped DeLay raise those millions of dollars from campaign donors that bought the support of other politicians and became the base for an empire of corruption. DeLay praised Abramoff as 'one of my closest friends.' Abramoff, in turn, told a convention of college Republicans, 'Thank God Tom DeLay is majority leader of the house. Tom DeLay is who all of us want to be when we grow up.'

~ ~ ~

And let us not forget another key player in the crime. Writer John W. Dean gives us this: "In 1986, former Assistant United States Attorney James Brosnahan (today a noted San Francisco trial attorney) testified - based on an investigation the Justice Department had dispatched him to conduct - that as a young Phoenix attorney, Justice William Rehnquist had been part of conservative Republicans' 1962 efforts to disqualify black and Hispanic voters who showed up to vote. Brosnahan's testimony was supported by no less than fourteen additional witnesses. Rehnquist nevertheless became Chief Justice - thanks to the continued support of conservative Republicans."

Rehnquist Addicted to Painkillers for Years
By PETE YOST - AP

WASHINGTON (Jan. 5, 2006) - A physician at the U.S. Capitol prescribed a powerful sleep aid for William Rehnquist for nearly a decade while he was an associate justice of the Supreme Court, according to newly released FBI records.

The records present a picture of a justice with chronic back pain who for many months took three times the recommended dosage of the drug Placidyl and then went into withdrawal in 1981 when he abruptly stopped taking it. Rehnquist checked himself into a hospital, where he tried to escape in his pajamas and imagined that the CIA was plotting against him, the records indicate.

Although Rehnquist's drug dependency was publicly known around the time he was hospitalized in 1981, the release of the FBI records provides new details.

The justice was weaned off Placidyl in early 1982 in a detoxification process that took a month, according to the records. The hospital doctor who treated Rehnquist said the Capitol Hill physician who prescribed Placidyl for Rehnquist was practicing bad medicine, bordering on malpractice. Both doctors' names were deleted from the documents before they were released. [Notice that a doctor is blamed for the patient's addiction?]

The FBI documents were prepared in 1986 when Rehnquist - who began serving on the court on Jan. 7, 1972 - was nominated for chief justice, years after his problems with the drug had ended. They were released by the agency in response to requests under the Freedom of Information Act. The agency said one of the seven folders of Rehnquist documents could not be found.

A psychiatrist told the FBI that Rehnquist's family in 1981 noted "long-standing slurred speech which seems to coincide with administration of Placidyl," one FBI interview report stated. The psychiatrist also indicated that Rehnquist's chronic back pain led to his heavy use of such substances as Darvon and Tylenol 3, which the psychiatrist said also played a part in Rehnquist's condition.

An attending physician at the U.S. Capitol detailed Rehnquist's problems with Placidyl for the FBI, saying that prior to his seeing the justice in 1972, Rehnquist was prescribed the drug by another doctor for relief from insomnia. The attending physician told the FBI he continued to prescribe Placidyl for the entire 10-year period that he treated Rehnquist.

The physician said that Rehnquist had been prescribed 500 milligrams of Placidyl per evening, but that Rehnquist was actually taking 1,500 milligrams each night. ...

The physician indicated that he decided to discontinue the drug's use and to try another medication. Rehnquist said the new medication was not strong enough, an FBI interview report stated. The physician said he then prescribed a substitute and then another, at which point Rehnquist went into the hospital.

The hospital doctor who successfully weaned Rehnquist from the drug told the FBI that the toxicity of Placidyl causes blurred vision, slurred speech and difficulty in making physical movements. Once a patient stops taking the drug, the withdrawal symptoms of delirium begin, which is what happened to Rehnquist at the hospital.

~~ > What we had here, my fellow Americans, was a Supreme Court Justice who for at least ten years was addicted to prescribed drugs that slurred his speech and certainly impaired his thinking (what was he addicted to after 1982?). And how do conservatives deal with liabilities such as Rehnquist? Promote him! How many important Court cases did this blurry-eyed man make judgments on -- affecting our whole judicial system? What was he on when he decided the 2000 election?

Although he has passed on, his legacy is with us every day.

In the article previously mentioned, John W. Dean cites another pugnacious partner in the inner circle, Bush's political strategist Karl Rove. "A recent profile of Karl Rove in the November 2004 Atlantic Monthly, entitled 'Karl Rove In A Corner,' examines how Rove operates in a close race. While Rove has had only a few tactics, they are never pretty. ... The article describes 'Rove's power, when challenged, to draw on an animal ferocity that far exceeds the chest-thumping bravado common to professional political operatives' - and notes that 'Rove's fiercest tendencies have been elucidated in national media coverage.'"

 - **The Coming Post-Election Chaos** by John W. Dean, Oct 22, 2004
http://www.truthout.org/docs_04/102404V.shtml

By the summer of 2005 Karl Rove was pointed out as one of the informers (with Bush, Cheney and Libby all known accomplices) in a dangerous leak concerning internationalist Joseph Wilson and his wife. Wilson declared that the Iraqi invasion was unwarranted and ill-advised. The Bush regime did not like this opinion. Soon after, Wilson's wife, secretly working for the CIA, was exposed in the press. Rove is being protected; so far he gotten away with it. Perhaps the other neo-cons are afraid of him. Could it be that special prosecutor Patrick Fitzgerald is too? More on this indictable (and white-washed) offense later.

~ ~ ~

Bill Moyers delivered an inspiring address when he received an award in June of 2004 in Washington, DC. His speech was published as "This is Your Story - The Progressive Story of America. Pass It On." In it, he had some things to say about a very important advisor to George Bush:

> Their leading strategist in Washington – Grover Norquist – has famously said he wants to shrink the government down to the size that it could be drowned in a bathtub. More recently, in commenting on the fiscal crisis in the states and its affect on schools and poor people, Norquist said, "I hope one of them" – one of the states – "goes bankrupt."

Evidently, according to his skewed theory, when and if the US government goes bankrupt, it will be so minimalized that ordinary men (businessmen of course) could go about their lives without the busy-body government interfering. But that is not all on this anti-government opportunist. Terry Gross, public radio personality and host of "Fresh Air," interviewed Grover Norquist in October, 2003. Norquist is the head of Americans for Tax Reform and the reputed architect of President Bush's tax cuts.

Here's a piece from that interview [my comments too]:
> Terry Gross: Now the Bush tax cuts would cost us about $1.1 trillion over the next 10 years, and we're going to be hundreds of billions of dollars in debt. At the same time, the president wants $87 billion to rebuild Iraq and

Afghanistan. Do you think we're in a tough spot, needing a lot of money, to rebuild those two countries at the same time that we're cutting taxes?

[Grover Norquist used a diversion technique to put that complex conundrum on hold and instead told Terry that one had to distinguish between "we" the people and the "government" as two separate groups, and that we the people should have more money in our own pockets. This is classic neo-con financial reasoning, and we've heard as such from various speeches by Bush and friends, perhaps inspired by Norquist. Unfortunately, his sieve type mind doesn't get that the $87 billion special appropriation was coming from the evil government that wants to take our/his money. I mean, where would that huge amount come from if directly requested of we the people? - send an army of volunteers to every town with a collection plate for the military expenditure (and every other social or community expenditure? Evidently he never took political science 101.)? When discussing the estate tax, which is paid by people who leave over $2 million in inheritance (which affects only 2% of the wealthiest Americans), Norquist used the emotive "death tax" to address the subject. The following is his outrageous statement to Terry, and thus, his confused and disturbed reasoning]:

Grover Norquist: The argument that some who played at the politics of hate and envy and class division will say, 'Yes, well, that's only 2 percent,' or as people get richer 5 percent in the near future of Americans likely to have to pay that tax. I mean, that's the morality of the Holocaust. 'Well, it's only a small percentage,' you know. 'I mean, it's not you, it's somebody else.'

Terry Gross: Excuse me. Excuse me one second. Did you just ...
Grover Norquist: Yeah?

68

Terry Gross: ... compare the estate tax with the Holocaust?

Grover Norquist: No, the morality that says it's OK to do something to do a group because they're a small percentage of the population is the morality that says that the Holocaust is OK because they didn't target everybody, just a small percentage. What are you worried about? It's not you. It's not you. It's them. And arguing that it's OK to loot some group because it's them, or kill some group because it's them and because it's a small number, that has no place in a democratic society that treats people equally. The government's going to do something to or for us, it should treat us all equally. ..."

Terry Gross: So you see taxes as being – the way they are now – terrible discrimination against the wealthy, comparable to the kind of discrimination of, say, the Holocaust?

Grover Norquist: Well, what you pick – you can use different rhetoric or different points for different purposes, and I would argue that those who say, 'Don't let this bother you; I'm only doing it' – I, the government. The government is only doing it to a small percentage of the population. That is very wrong. And it's immoral. They should treat everybody the same. They shouldn't be shooting anyone, and they shouldn't be taking half of anybody's income or wealth when they die."

> Can you believe this man? While discussing the $87 billion used to forcibly occupy a foreign nation, Norquist is pointing his finger at our government and crying "they shouldn't be shooting anyone?" At the very least, this is not a deep thinker; however, his ideas are not only followed by the neo-con tax reformers, they have passed tax laws inspired by this idiot. If I understand his faulty reasoning correctly, the rich should not pay any more tax than someone making, say, $20,000 a year; to ask them to pay more would be discriminatory and "immoral." Now

That's skewed and terribly, selfishly biased. I am being polite when I say that he is obviously living in his own subjective world when he makes the comparison that the super rich paying estate taxes are like the Jews who faced the Holocaust. This is unbelievable! We can see, however, why the neo-con PR men are not giving this guy too much of a public profile. He works, however, behind the scenes, with many others.

~ ~ ~

On the hit list: I mean, this is someone who will hit first, and ask questions later: Michael Ledeen was involved in the Iran-Contra scandal during the Reagan Administration (and evidently got away with it), an adviser to Karl Rove and the Bush White House, and a fanatic who loves the cut-throat political theorist and proto-Nazi Machiavelli. This man is dangerous, and influencing our government right now. Some quotes from his personal philosophy:

"Paradoxically, preserving liberty may require the rule of a single leader—a dictator—willing to use those dreaded 'extraordinary measures, which few know how, or are willing, to employ.'"

"Moses created a new state and a new religion, which makes him one of the most revolutionary leaders of all time…The execution of the sinners was necessary to confirm Moses' authority."

"Good religion teaches men that politics is the most important enterprise in the eyes of God. Like Moses, Machiavelli wants the law of his state to be seen, and therefore obeyed, as divinely ordered. The combination of fear of God and fear of punishment —duly carried out with good arms—provides the necessary discipline for good government."

- Michael Ledeen, *Machiavelli on Modern Leadership: Why Machiavelli's Iron Rules Are as Timely and Important Today as Five Centuries Ago*

"It would be foolish for America's political strategists and congressional leaders to ignore Michael Ledeen and his interpretation of Machiavelli. Mr. Ledeen speaks from the cutting edge of a group of men and women who desire nothing more than to reconstruct America in their own image. This nation is in gre danger. Ledeen belongs to a group of men, including Harry Jaffa, Pat Robertson, Willmoore Kendall to Allan Bloom, who, according to Shadia Drury, scholar and author of *Leo Strauss and the American Right,* share "the view that America is too liberal and pluralistic and that what it needs is a single orthodoxy that governs the public and private lives of its citizens."

- Katherine Yurica, investigative writer and activist
http://www.yuricareport.com/Dominionism/MichaelLedeen.html

Right Web, an investigative online information source, is dedicated to naming the names and pointing out the right wing conservatives (and their organizations) who are pushing this country into more militarism and dangerous reactionary politics. You can find them on http://rightweb.irc-online.org/ In their description of Michael Ladeen, we see the slippery wordsmith turning definitions upside-down and re-inventing himself - while confusing and misleading the public. Note how he describes himself:

Michael A. Ledeen, who holds the Freedom Chair at the American Enterprise Institute, objects to being called a conservative. Instead Ledeen, a regular contributor to *National Review Online*, prefers the term "democratic revolutionary." What's more, Ledeen says that "most self-described leftists today are reactionaries, and have lost the right to describe themselves as people of the left."

http://rightweb.irc-online.org/profile/1261

~ ~ ~

Bishop John Shelby Spong felt strong emotions and expressed powerful and eloquent words in condemning the right wing racism masked as Christianity at the heart of the Republican Party. In his "Understanding The Christian Roots of My Political Depression," written after the Republican Convention in New York City (Sep 2004), Bishop Spong listed some grievances from past GOP election tricks, including George H. W. Bush's 1988 campaign that employed the Willie Horton ad against Michael Dukakis – implying that Dukakis "favored freeing black criminals to commit murder. Lee Atwater, mentor of Karl Rove, devised that campaign. The Willie Horton episode said to me that these people believed that no dishonest tactic was to be avoided if it helped your candidate to victory." Then came the George W. Bush's campaign in 2000, "when the patriotism of John McCain was viciously attacked. It appeared that five years as a prisoner of war in North Vietnam was not sufficient to prove one's loyalty to America. The third episode came when the operatives of this administration destroyed Georgia's Senator Max Cleland in 2002, by accusing him of being soft on national security, despite the fact that this veteran had lost three of his limbs in the service of his country." The recent attack against John Kerry's war record was also cited; and this accusation, he reminds us, is coming from a man who did not even serve in that same war. Bishop Spong continues:

> Then Senator Zell Miller, his face contorted with anger, recited a litany of weapons systems that he said Senator Kerry had opposed. What he failed to say was that most of these military cuts were recommended by a Secretary of Defense named Richard Cheney in the first Bush Administration! The last time I looked, the Ten Commandments still included an injunction against bearing false witness. Yes, other campaigns bend the truth but these tactics go beyond just bending, they assassinate character and suggest traitorous behavior. When that is combined with the fact that this party does this while proclaiming itself the party of religion, cultural values and faith-based initiatives is the final straw for me. I experience the religious right as a deeply racist enterprise that seeks to hide its intolerance under the rhetoric of super patriotism and "family values." For those who think that this is too strong a charge or too out of bounds politically, I invite you to look at the record.
>
> It was George H. W. Bush who gave us Clarence Thomas on the Supreme Court, calling him "the most qualified person in America." Thomas replaced Thurgood Marshall, who had been the legal hero to black Americans during the struggle over segregation. Clarence Thomas, the

opponent of every governmental program that made his own life possible, is today an embarrassment to blacks in America. .... Next one cannot help noticing the concerted Republican effort to limit black suffrage in many states like Florida where it has been most overt, and to deny the power of the ballot to all the citizens of Washington, D.C. Does anyone doubt that the people of Washington have no vote for any other reason than that they are overwhelmingly black?

... Are the leaders of this party the only educated people who seem not to know that their attitudes about homosexuality are uninformed? People no more choose their sexual orientation than they choose to be left-handed! To play on both ignorance and fear for political gain is a page lifted right out of the racial struggle that shaped my region. Racism simply hides today under new pseudonyms.

I lived in Lynchburg, Virginia, before Jerry Falwell rose to national prominence. He was a race baiting segregationist to his core. Liberty Baptist College began as a segregation academy. Super patriot Falwell condemned Nelson Mandela as a 'communist' and praised the apartheid regime in South Africa as a 'bulwark for Christian civilization.' I have heard Pat Robertson attack the movement to give equality to women by referring to feminists as Lesbians who want to destroy the family, while quoting the Bible to defeat the Equal Rights Amendment. The homophobic rhetoric that spews so frequently out of the mouths of these "Jesus preaching" right-wingers has been mentioned time and again as factors that encourage hate crimes.
...
I lived through the brutality that greeted the civil rights movement in the South during its early days. Congressman John Lewis of Atlanta can tell you what it means to be beaten into unconsciousness on a "freedom ride." I remember the names of Southerners who covered

their hate-filled racism with the blanket of religion to enable them to win the governors' mansions in the deep South: John Patterson and George Wallace in Alabama, Ross Barnett in Mississippi, Orville Faubus in Arkansas, Mills Godwin in Virginia and Strom Thurmond in South Carolina. I know the religious dimensions of North Carolina that kept Jesse Helms in the Senate for five terms. Now we have learned that Strom Thurmond, who protected segregation in the Senate when he could not impose it by winning the presidency in 1948, also fathered a daughter by an underage black girl. I know that Congressman Robert Barr of Georgia, who introduced the Defense of Marriage Act in 1988, has been married three times. I know that Pat Robertson's Congressman in Norfolk, Ed Schrock, courted religious votes while condemning homosexual people until he was outed as a gay man and was forced to resign his seat.

I know that the bulk of the voters from the Religious Right today are the George Wallace voters of yesterday, who simply transformed their racial prejudices and called them "family values." That mentality is now present in this administration. It starts with the President, embraces the Attorney General John Ashcroft and spreads out in every direction.

I have known Southern mobs that have acted in violence against black people while couching that violence in the sweetness of Evangelical Christianity. I abhor that kind of religion. I resent more than I can express the fact that my Christ has been employed in the service of this mentality. My Christ, who refused to condemn the woman taken in the act of adultery; my Christ who embraced the lepers, the most feared social outcasts of his day; my Christ who implored us to see the face of God in the faces of "the least of these our brothers and sisters;" my Christ who opposed the prejudice being expressed against the racially impure Samaritans, is today being used politically to dehumanize others by those who play on base instincts.

David Halberstam, in his book on the Civil Rights movement entitled The Children, quotes Lyndon Johnson talking with Bill Moyers right after the Voting Rights Act of 1965 had passed by large margins in the Congress of the United States. This positive vote followed the arousing of the public's consciousness by the Abu Ghraib-like use of dogs and fire hoses on black citizens in Alabama. Klan groups, under the direct protection of Southern State Troopers and local police, had also attacked blacks with baseball bats and lead pipes in public places, which had been seen on national television. Moyers expected to find President Johnson jubilant over this legislative victory. Instead he found the President strangely silent. When Moyers enquired as to the reason, Johnson said rather prophetically, "Bill, I've just handed the South to the Republicans for fifty years, certainly for the rest of our life times."

That is surely correct. Bush's polls popped after his convention. It is now his election to lose. The combination of super patriotism with piety, used in the service of fear to elicit votes while suppressing equality works, but it is lethal for America and lethal for Christianity. It may be a winning formula but it has no integrity and it feels dreadful to this particular Christian.

"Should any political party attempt to abolish social security, unemployment insurance, and eliminate labor laws and farm programs, you would not hear of that party again in our political history. There is a tiny splinter group, of course, that believes that you can do these things. Among them are a few Texas oil millionaires, and an occasional politician or businessman from other areas. Their number is negligible and they are stupid."

- President Dwight D. Eisenhower, 1954

RECLAIMING THE ISSUES: "KEEP GEORGE OUT OF JAIL"
By Thom Hartmann, Common Dreams; September 21, 2006
http://www.commondreams.org/views06/0921-28.htm

> On June 29, 2006, in the Hamden Case, the US Supreme
> Court ruled that Donald Rumsfeld and the Bush
> Administration had violated the Geneva Convention and
> other international treaties with regard to the treatment
> and prosecution of detainees in the so-called "war on
> terror."
>
> The logic of the decision could subject Bush, Cheney,
> Gonzales, and Rumsfeld -- along with those down the
> chain of command who followed their orders -- to
> prosecution as war criminals both in the United States and
> internationally. ..., they could be subject to lengthy
> imprisonment in the US for violating US laws, as well as
> being brought before the United Nation's International
> Court of Justice at The Hague, the same as Slobodan
> Milosevic.
> ...
> About six weeks later, on August 17, 2006, Federal Judge
> Anna Diggs Taylor ruled in Detroit that George W. Bush
> and his administration had committed numerous felonies
> with regard to wiretapping American citizens without a
> legal warrant, including violating the FISA act (which
> carries a 5-year prison term as the penalty for each
> violation) and violating the Constitution (which carries
> impeachment as its penalty).

[Thom Hartmann and other investigators are watching this
development. The crimes are much greater than this, of course,
but things are indeed adding up for the criminals. We will see if
there is justice in the USA. sp]

>>~o~<<

Here's a few right wingers pointing fingers:
*"The left promotes conflict. That is the tenet of communism and
of the environmental movement. I want to get the top national
scholars to dissect the environmental movement, identify who the*

left-wing leaders are, their political connections, how they get their funding, what tax laws they take advantage of, then change the game and attack them."

... Ladies and Gentlemen, meet the ethically challenged and eco-hostile Representative John Doolittle. The California Republican is just one in a rogue's gallery of "Two-Time Losers" profiled in the latest *Sierra.* These are legislators who have distinguished themselves not by their leadership, but rather with a stunning combination of corruption and environmental callousness. What's the connection? In a word: Money.
- This from August 2006, Sierra Club
  "It's vile. It's more sad than anything else, to see someone with such potential throw it all down the drain because of a sexual addiction."
- Former Florida Rep. Mark Foley, republican pedophile, referring to President Clinton during the Lewinsky scandal.

> As I was reading from the International Herald Tribune, Oct 5, 2006, I was struck by the hypocrisy of people like Foley. Somewhat reminiscent of pedophile priests protected by bishops who send them to other parishes, the scandal of republican Rep Mark Foley of Florida erupted in August of 2006. Foley, an alcoholic pedophile who solicited young intern boys by email, was busy compromising young pages for years. The republican speaker, Rep J. Dennis Hastert, knew about this at least by last spring and kept quiet. Pressure is on Hastert to resign, which he is righteously ignoring. Hastert lied about his knowledge of Foley's solicitations (with a 16 year old boy for one) in a cover up. Some leaders knew about this predator as of 2005. The plot thickens: NY rep Thomas Reynolds, who heads the National Republican Congressional Committee, told Hastert about Foley last spring. Foley contributed $100,000 to Reynold's congressional campaign committee [for telling Hastert? I think not.]. Reynolds didn't go public until Foley resigned and the scandal deepened. And how's this for G.O.P. morality: Foley was chair of a committee dealing with children's safety!

>>~o~<<

"Last week, Congress moved to suspend habeas corpus, one thing that distinguishes a civil society from a police state. Reaction was muted.

Then the Party of Family Values was revealed to have protected a sexual predator in its midst until finally a reporter asked some pointed questions and the honorable gentleman resigned and ran off to recovery camp: This level of hypocrisy takes a person's breath away. You thought that Abramoff, Norquist, Reed & DeLay had established new lows, but the elevator is still descending."

- from **Miracle drug of anger:** Raging against Republican hypocrisy is the tonic that keeps us old liberals forever young. By Garrison Keillor

http://www.salon.com/opinion/feature/2006/10/04/keillor/print.html

>>~o~<<

"Mr. President, you, and that advertisement of terror, are full of sound and fury - signifying (and competent at) nothing. Setting aside the fact that your government has done nothing else for these five years but pat yourselves on the back about terror, while waging pointless war on the wrong enemy in Iraq, and waging war on the cherished freedoms in America; just on this subject of counter-terrorism, sir, yours is the least competent government, in time of crisis, in this country's history! "These are the stakes," indeed, Mr. President."

- Keith Olbermann: Advertising Terrorism - www.truthout.com

~ ~ ~

Beyond DeLay: The 20 Most Corrupt Members of Congress (and five to watch):

Citizens for Responsibility and Ethics in Washington (CREW) **http://www.citizensforethics.org** released its second annual report on the most corrupt members of Congress on Sep 22 2006. This encyclopedic report on corruption in the 109th Congress documents the egregious, unethical and possibly illegal activities of the most tainted members of Congress. CREW has compiled the members' transgressions and analyzed them in light of federal laws and congressional rules.

78

Two members have been removed from last year's list of 13:

1) Rep. Randy "Duke" Cunningham (R-CA) is now serving an eight-year jail term for bribery and 2) Rep. Bob Ney (R-OH) has agreed to plead guilty to crimes that will likely result in a minimum two-year prison term.

CREW has also re-launched the report's tandem website, **www.beyonddelay.org**. The site offers short summaries of each member's transgressions as well as the full-length profiles and all accompanying exhibits.

In addition to Reps. Ney and Cunningham, former Majority Leader Tom DeLay (R-TX) has been indicted in Texas and is facing possible federal indictment in the Jack Abramoff scandal and Reps. William Jefferson (D-LA), Jerry Lewis (R-CA), Alan Mollohan (D-WV), as well as Sens. Conrad Burns (R-MT) and Bill Frist (R-TN) are now under federal investigation.

[Note that the vast majority of the criminals are republicans. Sp]

THE 20 MOST CORRUPT MEMBERS OF CONGRESS:

Sen. Conrad Burns (R-MT)
Sen. Bill Frist (R-TN)
Sen. Rick Santorum (R-PA)
Rep. Roy Blunt (R-MO)
Rep. Ken Calvert (R-CA)
Rep. John Doolittle (R-CA)
Rep. Tom Feeney (R-FL)

Rep. Katherine Harris (R-FL)
Rep. William Jefferson (D-LA)
Rep. Jerry Lewis (R-CA)
Rep. Gary Miller (R-CA)
Rep. Alan Mollohan (D-WV)
Rep. Marilyn Musgrave (R-CO)
Rep. Richard Pombo (R-CA)
Rep. Rick Renzi (R-AZ)

Rep. Pete Sessions (R-TX)
Rep. John Sweeney (R-NY)
Rep. Charles Taylor (R-NC)
Rep. Maxine Waters (D-CA)
Rep. Curt Weldon (R-PA)

DISHONORABLE MENTIONS:
Rep. Chris Cannon (R-UT)
Rep. Dennis Hastert (R-IL)
Rep. J.D. Hayworth (R-AZ)
Rep. John Murtha (D-PA)
Rep. Don Sherwood (R-PA)

"A government more dangerous to our liberty than is the enemy it claims to protect us from. We have accepted that the only way to stop the terrorists is to let the government become just a little bit like the terrorists."

- Keith Olbermann | National Yawn as Our Rights Evaporate - www.truthout.com

Okay, we have introduced the characters. Now the case.

I mean, ...

The Case

& Iraq as MIRROR of the Coup

There are so many terrible fallouts of the Iraq War. There are many activists who are rallying around some aspect of this deceptive and greedy oil grab and calling for Bush's impeachment. As far as I am concerned, the preemptive war and occupation of Iraq is not the main accusation here; it is just an egregious *example* of the Bush regime's tactics as usual. This regime will push, sue, manipulate, deceive, coerce, threaten and then initiate a strike to get what it wants, which is exactly how they came to rule in the first place. The basic indictable offense against the Bush contingent, their lawyers, and members of the Supreme Court, is the fraudulent election of 2000, focused upon Florida, with the aid and deceptions of Jeb Bush and Katherine Harris (the antiquated electoral college is definitely part of the problem, but that is another thing).

Before "we" take our liberating forces out into the world, toppling dictators who gained their power in coups, we need to clean up our own mess here at home. Those who yell that "the election is done, it has been decided", are part of the problem. They are accomplices to the crime, or, at the very least, self-serving apologists. They are using smoke and mirrors to have us all forget what happened, to put the past behind us and to move on (a favorite neo-con hypnotic maneuver which means "forget our breach of law/incompetency/crime" and let us move on and forget it.). Move on to what, however? More election frauds? More crimes? More wars?!

A crime was committed against the American people at the election polls. I am not referring to the 2004 election; no, while investigators and statisticians have reviewed that mess, we have a bona fide and **verifiable** stolen election several years before that one. Millions of people stood by in disbelief as opportunistic lawyers and judges intervened in the US election of 2000. We were shocked when the US Supreme Court, over-stepping its own bounds, overruled the Florida Supreme Court. And then, with a flimsy excuse but with the authority of the highest court in the land, the "supreme" court *selected* the next president of the United States for us. It was a **coup d'etat**, bloodless and arrogant. The debacle of the stolen election of 2000 was more than some clever political strategy.

Let us be very clear to people of common sense and observation:

Traitors have taken the government of the USA in a coup.

Yes. This means treason.

Thom Hartmann, investigative reporter and author of many books on democracy and participation, tells it like it was (Common Dreams, Nov 29, 2004) in his HOW TO TAKE BACK A STOLEN ELECTION
http://www.commondreams.org/views04/1129-26.htm

"On December 4, 2000, in time to change the outcome of the Electoral College vote, Greg Palast published an article in Salon.com http://www.gregpalast.com/detail.cfm?artidU&row=1, made into a BBC television documentary http://news.bbc.co.uk/olmedia/cta/progs/newsnight/palast.ram shortly thereafter, that laid out solid evidence of massive electoral fraud in Florida, perpetrated against the majority-Democratic-voting African American community by Katherine Harris and Jeb Bush. Without this fraud, Gore would have easily carried the state."

Did you get that? Information about the fraud was available **before** the supreme court stepped in. Remember this too: Clinton-Gore won Florida in 1996. What happened within those four years? Jeb Bush and the election poll purge. The case for the 2000 election is clear and well documented. Among many investigations, the October 2004 issue of Vanity Fair entitled "The Path To Florida" explains how the Republicans nullified and disqualified literally a *hundred thousand* Florida votes. Common sense would or should give us a clear duty and course of action to remedy such a thing. As stated by investigative reporter Greg Palast in his revealing book, *The Best Democracy Money Can Buy*: "I report from Europe, where simple minds think that the appropriate response to the discovery that the wrong man was elected would be to remove him from office." This simple solution wasn't even debated. The public outcry was dissipated, distracted, ignored. Why and How?

Since this initial crime against the people and the government of the United States, there are innumerable offenses by the aggressive Bush regime (so termed due to the takeover by this coup d'etat) against civil rights, the environment, and international law. Furthermore, this regime is corrupted by conflicts of interest, cronyism, international burglary, corporate cover ups, and, most dangerous to us all, by military force and threats of force. The regime is fanatically driven by its own narrow agenda. It does not represent the American people, nor does it even represent the majority of sincere Republicans. Throughout this indictment, I will use a small case "r" (republican) in describing these self-appointed leaders and their yes-men of that party.

The Country Betrayed

To make this very clear, George Bush and his belligerent team saw the prize, had only one intention – to take it, and thus preemptively attacked. Does this sound like Iraq? Same show, different episode. This is exactly what happened in the 2000 election. When the truth about Florida's fraud (overseen and executed by brother Jeb Bush) was about to be exposed, the neo-conservative troops ignored due process, forced the issue, and took the country. Conspirators within the supreme court - 5 people - "legitimized" the coup. The media - embedded from the start it seems - reported the debacle as a matter of course – not treason – and the deed was done.

"... most rank-and-file Democrats ... believe [Al Gore] was screwed—an experience with which they can identify."
 - Howard Fineman, "Unsettled Scores" *Newsweek,* Sept 17, 2001

"Well I would say that in the year 2000 the country failed abysmally in the presidential election process. There's no doubt in my mind that Al Gore was elected president."
[Applause]
"He received the most votes nationwide, and in my opinion, he also received the most votes in Florida. And the decision was made, as you know, on a 5-4 vote on a highly partisan basis by the U.S. Supreme Court; so I would say in 2000 there was a failure."
 - Jimmy Carter, Sep 19, 2005

This, then, is my conclusion: It was more than a failure of the system. Bush and crew took over the US government in 2000, fabricated a war to take an oil rich country, gave their rich friends and supporters a tax break on one hand and spent billions of average Americans' money on the other to enforce the Iraqi occupation (and make more money), and still had the time and gall to fix the 2004 election. That's chutzpah, if you want to give the scoundrels their underworld due, but I would rather call it **criminal in the extreme**.

Back away from the sacred cow that says such things don't happen here. Such things happen in South America. No, my friends, here. **We are an occupied country.**

No. This couldn't happen in the USA!? And why not? These preemptive war-hawks – chicken-hawks actually – have gotten away with everything so far. They became bolder after the very suspicious 2004 elections; it was a clear victory for George Bush and his expansionist cowboy views. Things got worse after that, if you can believe it. We can stay at home, turn up the TV, and ignore the obvious, but let us take a lesson from the brave Ukrainians of 2004 and do something to take back our own country.

You know as well as I how many outrageous things the Bush regime commits *weekly*. My aim is to uproot the problem at its most obvious, and vulnerable -- the Coup of 2000. If we can succeed in this, we would not only rid ourselves of the neo-con curse this year, but roll back all of their reactionary policies, appointments and regulations since early 2001. Can you imagine?

The Bush regime is liable for all of these transgressions and crimes against the citizens of the US – as well as against the world community ... not to mention the earth itself due to their anti-environmental policies. They must be stopped, and soon.

It is time to sign the arrest warrants. It is only right that when the usurping regime is arrested and removed from position, all of their injunctions, acts, laws and commands will be null and void. Justice and common sense demand this. This might look like "rolling back the clock," but actually we will be moving forward into our present century, perhaps even into our present millennium.

But I am making bold statements. Can I back them up? Read on.

Florida

Clinton-Gore won Florida in 1996.
"On election night [2000] Clinton homed in on Florida, according to [Newsweek's David A.] Kaplan's account. 'Why is it so f---ing close?' he asked. It was a good question then, and it has been haunting politics, in Florida and Washington, ever since."
- Howard Fineman, "Unsettled Scores" *Newsweek,* Sept 17, 2001

We begin our focus in the state of Florida. Al Gore won half a million more votes than Bush in the popular election. If ours were a democratically elected government, that would have been the end of the story. However, we are burdened by an antiquated 18th Century throwback called the Electoral College. It should be abolished and put into a museum where it belongs, but that argument comes later.

Jeb Bush promised to deliver Florida to his brother. He did. This was more than a campaign promise. It was or-castrated through fraud and manipulation. One way of winning was to keep black voters away, for they consistently vote 90 to 93% Democratic in Florida, according to investigator Greg Palast. Besides fixing the registers in various key counties, Jeb Bush used an 1868 law drafted by Confederates of the Civil War period to keep those "criminal Negroes" from voting. Jeb was no friend to blacks. He so outraged this group in his 1994 run for governor that they rallied en masse to vote against him in 1998. By then he had his computer list up and running. Suspiciously, he won that

election. I believe it was here that he and other right wingers began to see the use in "maintaining" the registry of voters and the behind the scenes use of computer technology. Later, through these manipulative and illegal efforts, tens of thousands of voters in Florida were denied the right to vote in 2000.
What am I saying?

Florida was fixed in George Bush's favor **before** *the November 2000 election.*

It is all spelled out with names, dates, references and interviews in Greg Palast's excellent book referred to above. In it he uncovers how the vote in Florida was fixed. Many of his articles and observations about the fraud were published *before* Bush was *selected* by the supreme court (hereby written in small case until the shame has been removed). Other reporters, journalists and writers, including Michael Moore, Thom Hartmann and William D. Hartung, have added their voices to the facts of the case. The minimizing and cover-up of the scandal must also go to numerous American media, who evidently planned to gain in the republican takeover. The profit motive, combined with fear of reprisal, more or less sedated the news organizations in America to publish only press releases and "canned stories provided by officials and corporation public relations operations." (Palast) In the Florida case, when a CBS reporter "investigated" Palast's claims, all she did was call up Jeb Bush's office. Guess what? The perpetrator of the crime and the brother of the candidate denied (read my lips: lied about) the charges. Duh?! This was the end of the CBS investigation. The British heard the real story on BBC. They heard it in England, we didn't. Is there something wrong here? This is a crime against free speech, fair elections, and democracy in the land that promotes, no, lectures the world about these rights.

As Greg Palast explains it, "In the months leading up to the November balloting, Florida Governor Jeb Bush and his Secretary of State Katherine Harris ordered local elections supervisors to purge 57,700 voters from registries on grounds they were felons not entitled to vote in Florida. As it turns out, these voters weren't felons, at most a handful. However, the voters on this 'scrub list' were, notably, African-American (about 54 percent) and most of the others wrongly barred from voting were white and Hispanic Democrats."

Palast asks: "Why wasn't the story printed? - the revelations in the story required a reporter to stand up and say the big name politicians, their lawyers and their PR people were freaking liars. It would be much easier, and a heck of a lot cheaper, to wait for the U.S. Civil Rights Commission to do the work, then cover the Commission's canned report and press conference." This is precisely what happened.

Palast proceeds to describe ballot machine fixing, disenfranchisement of thousands of extra voters (besides the 57,700 noted above), and damning evidence of criminal activity and corruption by Florida republicans, spear-headed by Jeb Bush and Katherine Harris and backed by a small contingent of determined reactionaries and profiteers. Let's follow their trail: it will be full of smoke and mirrors.

In 1998, the 'scrub list' for Florida was implemented by a private company with very close Republican ties, the DBT Online unit of Chasepoint Inc., of Atlanta, GA. No other state in the union had done this (although these virulent and flawed voting machines and others like them were used nationwide during the 2004 election. Do you feel comforted?). This was the same year that Jeb Bush suspiciously won his bid for re-election, remember. Are these brothers close or what? In May 2000, Harris' Florida office purged 8,000 names of felons *from Texas* given by DBT. *None* of the group was charged with anything more than misdemeanors. This is a 0% accuracy rate. Florida had to correct this glaring mistake, obviously. Thereafter the scrub list began to include actual felons. Although corrected, this was a warning of things to come.

"Loose matches" were used in the DBT database. This means sloppy in some parts of the country, but this was deliberate in this case. This created a wide net to purge tens of thousands from the voting list. This state-sponsored flaw created "false positives" - euphemism for wrong people - on the list. Some on this scrub list were convicted of their crimes in 2007 and in other future dates! No, this is not a science fiction plot. When this impossibility was brought to their attention, the republican response was to *delete* the conviction **dates** - 4,000 of them! Conclusion? *The Florida scrub list was a targeted list.* The vast majority of voters barred on election day were Democrats.

To refresh your memory, Bush "won" by 537 votes in that dramatic and infamous election. By another counting later, he could have won by 1500. **This is irrelevant when more than 90,000 voters, overwhelmingly Democrats, were illegally barred from voting.** Do you also remember thousands of Jewish voters voting for racist Pat Buchanan in Florida? - could there have been a mistake there too? Michael Moore, in his book concerning men of a particular color and intelligence, points out that if we were to simply look at the suspicious ballots collected in Jeb Bush's state, it was still a stolen election:

> All of these ballots violated Florida law, yet they all were counted. Can I say this any louder? *Bush didn't win! Gore did.* It has nothing to do with chads, or even the blatant repression of Florida's African-American community and their right to vote. It was a simple matter of breaking the law, all documented, all the evidence sitting there in Tallahassee, clearly marked without question—and all done purposefully to throw the election to Bush.
> - *Stupid White Men*

~ ~ ~

"Those who cast the votes decide nothing.

Those who count the votes decide everything."

- Russian Dictator Joseph Stalin

Freedom!
Everywhere *but here.*

Many democratically inclined readers are aware that the USA was involved with aiding the election process in the 2004 Ukraine election. Millions of dollars were spent to make sure that the elections were fair and that the right man would be acknowledged as the true winner. Millions of Ukrainians protested for weeks until the faulty election had been overturned. If only we had more democratic players here. Thom Hartmann, investigative reporter and thoughtful activist, not only tells us that apathetic Americans "allowed" the undemocratic and tragic outcome back in 2000, but he urges us to get up and do something. Now. Here he tells us (Common Dreams, Nov 29, 2004) HOW TO TAKE BACK A STOLEN ELECTION:

> Not only was the election of 2000 stolen by the Bush brothers, but it was proven by the later statewide recount that -- even after Jeb's knocking thousands of African Americans off the rolls -- Gore still would have won Florida had all the votes been counted.
>
> This was outrageous news, enough to bring people into the streets. And there were demonstrations -- loud and angry ones. But they were round-the-clock in front of Al Gore's VP residence in Washington DC (shouting with bullhorns "Get out of Dick Cheney's house!"), outside (and often within) vote-counting headquarters' in Florida, and entirely composed of Republicans.
> If Democrats and progressives had taken to the streets in mass numbers nationwide that November and December, it's entirely probable that the Supreme Court would have backed off and allowed a statewide recount to continue, and Al Gore would have been president for the past four years, instead of George W. Bush.
>
> Ironically, the Democratic Party knows how to highlight election fraud and start national movements to bring down administrations that try to steal elections. A Party-

affiliated group has helped do it four times in the past four years.
But not in Ohio, Florida, or anywhere else in the USA.

Instead, the National Democratic Institute for International Affairs http://www.ndi.org/ (Madeleine K. Albright, Chairman) has joined up with a similar organization affiliated with the Republican Party http://www.iri.org/ (the International Republican Institute -- John McCain, Chairman), other NGOs [non-governmental organizations], and US government agencies to support the use of exit polls and statistical analyses to challenge national elections in Ukraine, Serbia, Belarus, and the former Soviet republic of Georgia.

In three of those four nations they succeeded in not only mounting a national challenge, but in reversing the outcomes of elections.
...
As Ian Traynor -- one of the finest investigative reporters working in the world today -- notes in a 26 November 2004 article in The Guardian titled "US Campaign Behind the Turmoil in Kiev," http://www.guardian.co.uk/ukraine/story/0,15569,136023 6,00.html "the campaign is an American creation, a sophisticated and brilliantly conceived exercise in western branding and mass marketing that, in four countries in four years, has been used to try to salvage rigged elections and topple unsavory regimes."
...
The campaign to unseat corrupt regimes is funded by groups affiliated with both the Democratic and Republican parties, Traynor notes, as well as the US State Department, the US Agency for International Development, and non-governmental organizations including George Soros's Open Society Institute and ... Eleanor Roosevelt's organization Freedom House....
... Because in each of these nations the media – radio, TV, and newspapers – are either controlled by, beholden to, or

owned by supporters of the regime in power, the disparity between the exit polls and the official election result is trumpeted through non-traditional media like the internet, local activist groups, and mass rallies, until a critical mass is achieved, forcing the mainstream (regime-friendly) media to cover the story.

At the same time, nations who claim the ideal of free, fair, and transparent elections are encouraged to speak out, further inflaming the issue. This is no accident, of course -- Traynor reports that the US government itself invested over $44 million in challenging the results of the Serbian election, and is estimated to have put $14 million into supporting groups challenging the recent Ukrainian election.

Thus, we have the irony of US Secretary of State Colin Powell saying of the Ukrainian election: "We have been following developments very closely and are deeply disturbed by the extensive and credible reports of fraud in the election. ... We call for a full review of the conduct of the election and the tallying of election results."

Yes, we do need a concerted effort to change things here. We could wait to unravel and reveal the stolen *2004* election, but all of the work is done and the conclusions are clear about the **2000** Election. Furthermore, when the injustice of this coup is repaired and the criminals are prosecuted, all of the key players in the Bush regime would not have been eligible to run for 2004.

The 2000 election. There is more. Much more. Below are some salient points from the well-researched study *published during the election crisis* by Rich Cowan titled
13 MYTHS ABOUT THE RESULTS OF THE 2000 ELECTION

Actually, the recount issue is only half the story. There is mounting evidence that the State of Florida and hundreds of local voting precincts restricted the ability of thousands of non-white voters to vote. Violations were so widespread that the Justice Department may investigate this case.

-Ballots ran out in certain precincts according to the LA Times on 11/10/00.

-Carpools of African-American voters were stopped by police, according to the Los Angeles Times (11/10/00). In some cases, officers demanded to see a "taxi license -Polls closed with people still in line in Tampa, according to the Associated Press.

-In Osceola County, ballots did not line up properly, possibly causing Gore voters to have their ballots cast for Harry Browne. Also, Hispanic voters were required to produce two forms of ID when only one is required. (source: Associated Press)

-Dozens, and possibly hundreds, of voters in Broward County were unable to vote because the Supervisor of Elections did not have enough staff to verify changes of address.

-Voters were mistakenly removed from voter rolls because their names were similar to those of ex-cons, according to Mother Jones magazine.

-According to Reuters news service (11/8/00), many voters received pencils rather than pens when they voted, in violation of state law.

-According to the Miami Herald, many Haitian-American voters were turned away from precincts where they were voting for the first time (11/10/00)

-According to Feed Magazine (www.feedmag.com), the mayoral candidate whose election in Miami was overturned due to voter fraud, Xavier Suarez, said he was involved in preparing absentee ballots for George W. Bush. (11/9/00)

-Dan Rather reported that in Volusia County, Socialist Workers Party candidate James Harris won 9,888 votes possibly as the result of a computer error. He only won 583 in the rest of the state (11/9/00).
County-level results for Florida were at cnn.com.

-Many African-American first-time voters who registered at motor vehicles offices or in campus voter registration drives did not appear on the voting rolls, according to a hearing conducted by the NAACP and televised on C-SPAN on 11/12/00.

As most Americans may recall, in December 2000 the US supreme court **preemptively struck** the fair counting of votes, and then a week later overturned the Florida Supreme Court's ruling about recounting all votes that December 2000. Their flimsy excuses are outlined by Jamin B. Raskin, law professor at American University, in his revealing *Overruling Democracy: The Supreme Court vs. The American People.* They halted the counting at one point, and then declared later that there wasn't enough time to count the votes by a particular date! According to their definition of fair voting, there has never been a legal and fair election in the history of the United States!

The December 12, 2000, ruling by the supreme court essentially stated that a state recount of the votes was uncon-stitutional. What?! Re-counting votes unconstitutional?! When the absurdity of this biased decision was scrutinized as setting a very undemocratic *precedent*, the judges back-peddled and stated that this decision only pertained to the present situation. Is this crooked or what? Justice? No. The "justification" of a coup? Yes.

5 biased (and bought?) individuals on the supreme court - Antonin Scalia, Clarence Thomas, William Rehnquist, Anthony Kennedy, and Sandra Day O'Conner - essentially selected the US

President for the nation. They are pivotal culprits in the coup, and thus liable for sedition and complicity. The late "Justice" William Rehnquist declared at the time that there is no guaranteed right to vote. What?! These "justices" should be behind bars.

But that's against the Constitution! That is unprecedented, hysterically claim the defenders of the sacred cows. So these people wearing gowns are above the law? Bullshit, to hide behind the "sacred" US Supreme Court and the Constitution is nonsense. Look at the Constitution's origins and who created it. It was conceived and compromised by some high minded men, some slave holders, some lawyers, some businessmen, and some talkers. Let's face it, according to the original Constitution, a voter was a white man with money or position. A slave was considered 3/5 of a man, as far a state's representation was concerned. The Electoral College (a system which never states that a "winner take all" in voting by the way) was instituted as a carry-over from the British House of Lords, an aristocratic elite that is supposed to know better than the common people – but usually end up watching their own interests. This antiquated system is "constitutional" but undemocratic. This inviolate and cherished Constitution has been amended twenty seven times. That means that these sacred rules of law have been changed or compromised as it suited the legislators at the time. Public pressure forced several changes. The right to vote was extended from the privileged white male to blacks, then women, then native Americans, in that order. One amendment prohibited alcohol, and another one rescinded that foolish idea of uniform morality. No. Don't talk to me of our cherished US Constitution; especially if some Supreme Court Judges hide behind it for the purpose of selecting the President.

The supreme court ignored not only Florida law and precedence, but twisted federal law with their infamous intervention. Hypocritically, the justices pulled out the Fourteenth Amendment (written for equal protection for minorities under the law!) to defend poor white boy Bush. Long time observers of the court must have been outraged, for this conservative "justice" team is not fond of using this amendment

94

to protect minorities. Now strive to find the justice, logic and reason within the convoluted words of Antonin Scalia in his explanation of why the counting had to be halted:

"The counting of votes that are of questionable legality does, in my view, threaten irreparable harm to petitioner [Bush], and to the country, by casting a cloud upon what he [Bush] claims to be the legitimacy of his election." Excuse me? The *legitimacy of his election?* What gall! But see here, friends and Americans, they thus far have gotten away with it, so *it was* his election.

What most Americans may not know is that within weeks of this treasonous act, on January 10, 2001, the NAACP sued Florida's Katherine Harris, her co-conspirator Clayton Roberts, and DBT over the disenfranchisement of black voters. Was this not worthy of major coverage? Perhaps even more than the O. J. or Clinton trials*? Is a coup not newsworthy?* This lawsuit also outlines the crime. By the fact that they won the case should have been grounds to eject Bush out of office. But nothing happened to the regime. People, they have gotten away with murder.

In dealing with the supreme court, let us turn to their main document, the Constitution. Although it is referring to Electors in the Constitution, the winner should be obvious in an election. Nevertheless, in Article II., Section.1, Clause 3, we have *The Person having the greatest Number of Votes shall be the President...*
> Citizens of the United States, this is rather clear. This was not done; in fact, it was over-ruled with the aid of the supreme court itself.

Another excellent source of information is found in the documentary "Unprecedented: the 2000 Presidential Election" by Robert Greenwald, Joan Sekler, Richard Ray Perez and others. Please buy and distribute this revealing video at www.unprecedented.org. The following facts were collected from this well researched documentary:
- On the day of the election, the police had some work to do: Certain voters were getting in the way of the election. People were turned away. Police intimidation and tactics

included threats of arresting voters in line for loitering; elsewhere voters were required to show multiple identification. African-Americans were targeted to such an extent that they had a case against Florida within weeks.

- Besides outright tampering, the voting machines themselves were dirty, irregular and flawed. The famous "dimple" votes were due to uncleaned machines which wouldn't allow a complete punch-through. The confusing ballots and instructions created more miscounts, but these were probably due to bureaucratic bungling.

- Republican staffers were flown in to Florida to protest the recount process. They were loud and aggressive and made it into the news. What wasn't in the news is that these were paid republican protesters, aides from Tom DeLay's office in Washington DC! - *talk about a pre-emptive strike!*

- Overseas absentee ballots were counted *after* the election date deadline. The military stepped up the pressure to overseas personnel after the election and before the selection. (Were these soldiers ordered to vote by their superiors?) 680 of these votes were illegal, but certified by Katherine Harris' office. These illegal votes alone pushed Bush ahead in this ugly contest.

- "Voter intent" was not honored in Florida. The republicans wanted to stop the recount. They initiated legal proceedings to delay, denigrate and dismiss the manual counting process. Katherine Harris tried to circumvent the people's will many times, but was repeatedly overruled. (Her very position as a card carrying Republican made her biased to begin with.) In short, the votes were getting in the way of the election. Ironically, George Bush passed a more liberal recounting law in Texas in 1997. This too was ignored in this "special case."

- Bush and crew wanted the recount issue to be decided by the US supreme court. Why? They knew how it would go. They knew the court would vote Republican. "The supreme court is a political institution and we should be clear about that," said law professor Jamin Raskin.
- The professed "uniform standards" the US supreme court supported in their immoral decision, if applied throughout the US, would have invalidated most votes in all the states. To dance out of this dilemma of injustice, the justices decided that the Bush vs. Gore decision would only "apply to the present circumstances." *Their intervention basically meant that their decision was intended to elect Bush.* Can this get any clearer?

- Conflicts of interest:
Antonin Scalia's two sons were lawyers on the Bush team in the recount process. Eugene Scalia was a lawyer with the firm of Gibson, Dunn & Crutcher, which was the law firm representing Bush before the supreme court! Not surprisingly, one of the sons received a top level position in the Bush regime (Labor Dept.). The other is a top lawyer at the Energy Dept. (where Cheney is stonewalling the investigation concerning energy policy, the oilfields of Iraq, Enron, and Kenneth Lay). Hello?! Clarence Thomas' wife, Virginia Lamp Thomas, worked for the Heritage Foundation, a leading conservative think tank, *and had been hired by Bush* to review resumes for potential Bush appointees! This was a clear conflict. Sandra Day O'Conner was upset that Gore won (when it was believed he did), for she made it clear that she wanted to retire under a republican administration, which would have appointed a republican justice to replace her. Biased? Criminal?

> For all of these reasons these justices should have removed themselves from presiding. (Which would have kept the supreme court out of the affair altogether.) They did not. They broke the law. However, the irony is that since they *represent* the law, they got away with this illegal and biased intervention. Can you see

the hypnotic underpinnings here? Authority figures, a peer group of judges without peers, the highest court in the land, had decided *fairly*, for that is their job, to decide fairly. Right?
Far right.

> "In 'The Accidental President,' [*Newsweek*'s David A. Kaplan] unearths new details about backroom maneuvering and bitterness within the U.S. Supreme Court, which last Dec 12 ruled that the Florida recount was unconstitutional, effectively declaring Bush the winner. ... in an unusual display, Justice Stephen Breyer (in front of a delegation of Russian judges) castigated the conservatives' ruling as an 'indefensible' trampling of the people's will."
> – Howard Fineman, "Unsettled Scores" *Newsweek,* September 17, 2001

Excerpt from "The Accidental President" by David A. Kaplan:
> [Al Gore drafted an Op-Ed for the New York Times on Dec 12, 2000. He didn't know it then, but his piece, which assumed the court would vote in favor of the people and fair voting, would not be published, for the court had already secretly decided on that very day. Kaplan cites from this draft:]
> "Invoking Lincoln and Jefferson, he mused on the 'consent of the governed' and the 'wellspring of democracy.' Jefferson had justified revolution' because the people of the colonies had not given their consent. How could the U.S. Supreme Court justices 'claim for themselves' the right to determine the presidency? It was up to the people."

> [Post decision,] "... the justices were stewing. In particular, the dissenters—Justices Stephen Breyer, Ruth Bader Ginsburg, David Souter and John Paul Stevens— couldn't believe what their conservative brethren had wrought. How could the conservative Court majority decide to step into a presidential election, all the more so using the doctrinal excuse of 'equal protection'? *Equal Protection*? That's the constitutional rationale the *liberals*

had used for a generation to expand rights, and the conservatives despised it.

[In early January, 2001, the U.S. Supreme court hosted another meeting with their Russian counterparts. These exchanges were] ... an attempt by the most powerful tribunal in the world to import some of its wisdom to a sascent system trying to figure out how constitutional law really worked in a democracy t was by no means obvious. To outsiders, the idea that unelected judges who served for life could ultimately dictate the actions of the other two branches of American government, both popularly elected, was nothing short of unbelievable.
...
The Russians wanted to know how *Bush v. Gore* had come to pass—how it was that somebody other than the electorate decided who ran the government. That was the kind of thing that gave Communism a bad name. 'In our country,' a Russian justice said, bemused, 'we wouldn't let judges pick the president.' The justice added that he knew that, in various nations, judges were in the pocket of executive officials—he just didn't know that was so in the United States. It was a supremely ironic moment.
...
Bush v. Gore was so lean in its analysis, so unconvincing in its reasoning, that it led all manner of observers to wonder just where the Court had been coming from.
...
[Justice Stephen Breyer wrote his dissent of the infamous ruling]: "Congress, being a political body, expresses the people's will far more accurately than does an unelected Court. And the people's will is what elections are about." [Ruth Ginsburg, another dissenter, stated] "... here we're applying the Equal Protection Clause in a way that would de-legitimize virtually every election in American history."
[Justice Kennedy wanted to blame the ruling on Bush and Gore! He wrote] 'When contending parties invoke the process of the courts, it becomes our unsought

responsibility to resolve the federal and constitutional issues the judicial system has been forced to confront.' But that was theatrical nonsense. The justices refused to hear 99 percent of the appeals they were asked to take. ...

Nobody 'forced' Kennedy or four of his brethren to hear *Bush v. Gore*. In the very first instance, they had to choose who chose—whether the Court or Congress was the proper branch to settle the presidential dispute. The justices chose themselves."
- *Newsweek*, September 17, 2001

Almost four years later, law clerks spoke about what happened in the supreme court during that fated injustice. They were afraid of retaliation and condemnation, so they maintained anonymity for an article in the October 2004 issue of Vanity Fair magazine. Charles Lane, writing for the Washington Post / Fort Wayne Journal Gazette, (October 18, 2004), presented us with CLERKS SPILL BUSH V. GORE DETAILS:

"Most of the criticism in the Vanity Fair piece is aimed at Justices Antonin Scalia, Sandra Day O'Connor and Anthony Kennedy, all of whom voted in favor of Bush. Scalia is depicted bullying Justice Ruth Bader Ginsburg into watering down her dissenting opinion. O'Connor is described as emotionally fixated on stopping a recount and Kennedy as overly influenced by his right-wing clerks."
http://www.fortwayne.com/mld/journalgazette/news/nation/9949251.htm
Mr Lane could not get any supreme court justice to comment, and there was heated arguments from conservative clerks and lawyers angered that anyone spoke out at all. Have they not heard of an informed populace? Who are they working for? Citizens, if this is the climate of our "justice" system, we are all in great trouble.

We **are** in great trouble.

After the infamous ruling, "legal scholars across the country joined in the protest. In a full page ad in The New York Times, 554 law professors accused the high court of

100

'acting as political proponents' for Bush, and 'taking power from the voters.' Worse, the ad scolded, 'the Supreme Court has tarnished its own legitimacy.'

...

The critics contend the court should never have taken the case in the first place. It was a matter of state law, and should be left to state courts, as is the tradition, they argue.

...

The attacks are framed in unusually unflattering terms. Yale Law School's Bruce Ackerman: "A blatantly partisan act, without any legal basis whatsoever.' Harvard's Alan Derschowitz: 'The single most corrupt decision in Supreme Court history.' American University's Jamin Raskin: 'Bandits in black robes.'"

- How History Will View the Court by Stuart Taylor Jr., *Newsweek,* September 17, 2001

The Secret Vote That Made Bush President: The Untold Story of the Supreme Court's 5 to 4 Ruling,
by David A. Kaplan, excerpted from his book "The Accidental President"
- This was the title on the front cover of *Newsweek* in September 2001. Howard Fineman begins the lead piece, "Unsettled Scores," in the issue this way:
"Past as prelude: The economy's in trouble, Gore is stirring and in Florida the ghosts of 2000 are returning to battle anew."
Fineman tells us that rallys, marches and gatherings were planned to protest yet again the disputed outcome of the 2000 election. Activists were gathering in their united opposition, approaching the anniversary of the infamous supreme court vote. A case was building. The coverage, and the heat, was getting uncomfortably close to George Bush. This was the hotly debated theme on the cover of *Newsweek*, September 17, 2001.
Note this date. Magazines print and distribute their fare weeks before the date stated. By the time this issue—and the front page theme of Bush's suspicious *appointment* to president—the 9-11 disaster blew away the topic. The 9-11 timing was very favorable for Bush and the crew. The nation was bound and obligated to get

behind the chief executive in a national emergency. Discussion of his illegitimacy was almost unAmerican for the next several years.

Professor James K. Galbraith viewed the affair through his own ingenious and professional lens. In late December, 2000, he had the following to say, urging Americans to stage an on-going civic protest. This is from "Corporate Democracy; Civic Disrespect":

> With the events of late in the year 2000, the United States left behind constitutional republicanism, and turned to a different form of government. It is not, however, a new form. It is, rather, a transplant, highly familiar from a different arena of advanced capitalism. This is corporate democracy. It is a system whereby a Board of Directors-- read Supreme Court -- selects the Chief Executive Officer. The CEO in turn appoints new members of the Board. The shareholders, owners in title only, are invited to cast their votes in periodic referenda. But their franchise is only symbolic, for management holds a majority of the proxies. On no important issue do the CEO and the Board ever permit themselves to lose.

> The Supreme Court clarified this in a way that the Florida courts could not have. The media have accepted it, for it is the form of government to which they are already professionally accustomed. And the shameless attitude of the George W. Bush high command merely illustrates, in unusually visible fashion, the prevalent ethical system of corporate life.

> Al Gore's concession speech was justly praised for grace and humor. It paid due deference to the triumph of corporate political ethics, but did not embrace them. It thus preserved Gore for another political day -- the obvious intention. But Gore also sent an unmistakable message to American democrats: Do not forget.

It was an important warning, for almost immediately forgetting became the media order of the day. Overnight, it became almost un-American not to accept the diktat of the Court. Or to be precise, Gore's own distinction became holy writ: One might disagree with the Court, but not with the legitimacy of its decision. Press references from that moment forward were to President-elect Bush, an unofficial title and something that the Governor from Texas (President-select? President-designate?) manifestly is not.

The key to dealing with the Bush people, however, is precisely not to accept them. Like most Americans, I have nothing personal against Bush, Dick Cheney, nor against Colin Powell and the others now surfacing as members of the new administration. But I will not reconcile myself to them. They lost the election. Then they arranged to obstruct the count of the vote. They don't deserve to be there, and that changes everything.

~ ~ ~

Treason

Shall we look at treason itself? Although I will go into this further in my conclusions, the Constitution tells us in Article. III., Section. 3., Clause 1: *Treason against the United States, shall consist only in levying War against them, or in adhering to their Enemies, giving them Aid and Comfort. No Person shall be convicted of Treason unless on the Testimony of two Witnesses to the same overt Act, or on Confession in open Court.*

This begs the questions: Who are the enemies of the States? - those groups and corporations that weaken, deprive, destroy, pollute, and abuse? This description in the Constitution is rather broad. Good. I think we've got a case. We can easily find two witnesses; in fact, with much of the 2000 election fiasco beamed out to the American public, there were millions of witnesses. Adhering to their Enemies, giving them Aid and Comfort? My friends, the enemies of the States are the extremist neo-conservatives who put our country into danger internationally and corrupted the Constitution they were supposedly defending, plus their undermining of the Bill of Rights and other freedoms. The list of crimes are mentioned throughout this indictment.

How did this happen?

> "Behind the ostensible government sits enthroned an invisible government owing no allegiance and acknowledging no responsibility to the people. To destroy this invisible government, to befoul the unholy alliance between corrupt business and corrupt politics is the first task of the statesmanship of the day."
> - Theodore Roosevelt, April 19, 1906

Lulling the populace into acceptance has taken decades. This is the heart and soul of the smoke and mirrors deception, my friends. Just follow the career of J. Edgar Hoover and you will see the trail. Machiavelli offered advice on just how to accomplish this age-old rise to power and the maintenance of that power by any means. The ancient Romans recognized the political importance of "bread & circuses," or *keep the chumps entertained while we go about our business.* None of this is new in the world, nor new in this country.

> *A fool and his money are soon elected.*
> - Will Rogers

Brainwashed & bamboozled

As we can see bombarding us on all sides, age old systems of influence and coercion have been modernized and sanitized and, as James Galbraith eloquently described above, the corporate system of decisions and power has crossed over, again, into our government. This requires keeping the people in line: Let us not forget that our modern educational system was patterned after the efficient Ford automobile assembly line. Presently we are not turning out great scholars and innovators like we used to, but good workers, consumers, and kids who try hard to pass standardized tests. The kids who do not conform easily are fed medications, or drop out (and it is from this group, which ignores the dictates and the circus, we get the innovators and whiz kids advancing computing, technology and design!). We have a punitive, father knows best response for the trouble-makers: we have the highest number of prisoners per capita in the whole world. "Behave, and get with the program!" Result? Programmed kids,... and millions of children left behind. Follow the dots and you will see a pattern of conformity, passivity and blind obedience.

On with the Show.

Weren't we all entertained with the sensational 1990s trials of O. J. Simpson and Bill Clinton, in which the law – flawed, quirky, unjust – had the final ambiguous say in matters? Millions of TV and radio fans were created, passively privy to unfolding dramas in which they could not participate in but merely watched. These trials were popular reality shows. A new type of armchair observers were fashioned. This set the stage.

And then we watched politics. Like a soap opera, the American citizen had gotten used to seeing the Republicans on the offensive. From Reagan ignoring Congress and fomenting guerrilla warfare in Central America (and selling arms to Saddam Hussein), to Bush senior warring on his ex-pal Noriega in Panama (and selling arms and chemical weapons to Saddam Hussein), to Newt Gingrich and the "Contract on America," to 7 years of politically motivated investigations into Bill and Hillary Clinton's lives, Republicans were the aggressors, the party that played hardball. They were also the party that promoted itself as the one that won the war on communism, and the one that upheld the good, moral convictions of everyday citizens (which was untrue and never the case, but that is not what *sales* has to deal with – remember the ways to succumb to suggestions, smoke and mirrors.).

And the circus acts continued. Americans had also been exposed to big corporate mergers, hostile takeovers, and "necessary" downsizing and gutting of systems. Wall Street. The stock market. This was business. And what is the business of America? Business. What had the average Joe to do with major acquisitions and stock market regulations? Nothing. The behemoths of commerce moved separately from the wishes and desires of the little guy. We were all just passive onlookers in this far away game of Market Shares played by businessmen in fancy suits. The average Joe, if at all financially savvy, is actually watching the big market players and hoping to get some of the rewards by copying. Big-time tycoons and corporate executives are role models for financial, and life-style, success (ignoring the fact that many of the more visible ones are being indicted for illegal trading, accounting subterfuge, and unfair market manipulation, and many others are making their millions manufacturing weapons).

And what do we call those people who have the money and want to make sure the government gives them a better deal? Lobbyists – who bring something better than votes to Congress.

Lincoln (Weeps) by **Bill Moyers,** October 03, 2006 (more of this great essay is published in the appendix of this report) http://www.pbs.org/moyers/moyersonamerica/lincolnweeps.mp3

Once upon a time the House of Representatives was known as "the people's house." No more. It belongs to K Street now. That's the address of the lobbyists who swarm all over Capitol Hill. There are 65 lobbyists for every member of Congress. They spend $200 million per month wining, dining and seducing federal officials. Per month!

Of course they're just doing their job. It's impossible to commit bribery, legal or otherwise, unless someone's on the take, and with campaign costs soaring, our politicians always have their hands out. One representative confessed that members of Congress are the only people in the world

expected to take large amounts of money from s
and then act as if it has no effect on their behavic
...
The only way to counter the power of organized m ⌐ʊ
with organized and outraged people. Believe me, what
members of Congress fear most is a grassroots movement
that demands clean elections and an end to the buying and
selling of influence—or else! If we leave it to the powers
that be to clean up the mess that greed and chicanery have
given us, we will wake up one day with a real
Frankenstein of a system—a monster worse than the one
created by Abramoff, DeLay and their cronies. By then it
will be too late to save Lincoln's hope for "government of,
by, and for the people."

~ ~ ~

And the conditioning continued. Americans, once an
independent and resourceful aggregate of active players in
community and local decisions, have been "trained" to leave it to
the experts over the years. Soldiers and veterans all know of
hierarchy and the old motto "yours is not to reason why, yours is
but to do or die." The chain of command as concept and fact,
however, is promulgated everywhere. Listen through my
hypnotist-trained ears ... Here is what we are told: Everyone has
opinions (and in a democratic society, *you* are free to have them),
but the experts know. Local loudspeakers are ubiquitous and
clear: "Stay out of this! Let the doctor/ police/ boss/official/
administrator/general/ FBI/ authorities/lawyers handle this! –
"In an event, stay tuned to the emergency broadcasting system for
instructions!" – "Don't get involved! Call 911! ..."

You've got the picture. Add to this a fear of litigation or financial
or punitive reprisal, and you will keep millions "minding their
own business." Is it any wonder that people don't vote? Or don't
get involved? Apathy has been ingrained.

Here are simple examples of how we freedom loving and
equality-affirming Americans are taught, urged and forced to bow
our heads to "our betters": a policeman pulls you over in traffic. It

goes without saying that he is heavily armed and has radioed what he is doing and which vehicle he just pulled over. You have registered your vehicle and your name and address and police record are already known (a car theft specialist would already have changed license tags and carries a false ID). You will be very polite and will not make any quick moves, I assure you. When he tells you to do something, you better do it. When you go to the court, you Will Stand when the honorable judge steps into the room. Perhaps you will have a court appointed lawyer, who will tell you what to plead, how to talk and how to dress. You will be playing a role if you want the judge to favor you. Justice will be met, and *you will have your day in court* (there was no promise of fairness in these old statements, notice). Whether there was justice served is beside the fact. That's the law. Pay the fine and follow the rules. Now go home and pay your taxes.

In other words, you bow to authority. If you have the privilege of meeting the President, you will be watched (you have already been searched) and you will treat him with deference, or your special time will end immediately (maybe you will go to jail). If you wrote to the US Attorney General (before he retired), it would be addressed this way:

The Honorable John Ashcroft [then Gonzales!]
Attorney General of the United States
U.S. Department of Justice

Honorable indeed! Multiply all of this by 100. Or more! See it in your daily, weekly, monthly existence. Can you see that we have been conditioned to conform and to obey? Remember my list of suggestive doorways to the unconscious mind and you see the show is all set up. Here's the sad news: You, I, we, have our parts in the play, of course, but they will be merely cameos and non-speaking parts. But, ...
that's Showbiz!

But experts and highly trained or skilled individuals are needed, especially in our complex society, one may argue. OK, structure or organization and effective, informed decisions, systems and professionals are necessary in any society. There are

108

thousands of trained professionals who are very competent and responsible. All this is good and orderly. However, just as "political correctness" became a caricature of social sensitivity in the 1980s, the power handed over to experts and authorities has been over-done. TV pundits and loud mouthed know-it-alls have co-opted the civil discussion. How many times have you seen a debate or heard a speech on TV, which is immediately followed by experts who tell you what was just said? When an official report is produced that puts George and company in a bad light, talking heads like Condi Rice take the microphone and describe how this very report confirms what a great job they are doing (specific examples later). Spin-meisters, PR men and aggressive lawyers are all taking turns at the microphone, and we merely sit passively as the show goes on. Democracy and freedom are words used in speeches. Our present system is disabling our citizens.

In her excellent book, U.S. vs. George Bush, [http://www.amazon.com/United-States-George-Bush-al/dp/1583227563] Elizabeth de la Vega makes an unusual comparison. She compares the American body politic's response to Bush's criminal behavior to the Kitty Genovese case.

As you may remember, Kitty Genovese was a woman murdered in Queens in 1964 while thirty-eight neighbors watched and no one reported the incident to the police until it was too late. While the murder was widely seen as evidence of human callousness in modern society, a more sophisticated psychological assessment of the case reveals something quite different. According to psychologists Bibb Latane and John Darley, "When people are in a group, responsibility for acting is diffused. They assume someone else will make the call." So Kitty Genovese went unaided not in spite of everyone seeing it, but *because everyone saw it.*

As de la Vega points out, we Americans were all "bystanders" watching the crime take place, and now we must become witnesses. In order for the self-impeaching President to be actually impeached, it will take grassroots awareness and participation. But remember, the Bush presidency isn't a cause, it's a symptom. In the process, we must clearly understand and articulate to anyone we speak with that the entire impeachable system must be impeached. The egregious crimes of the Bush presidency are merely an expansion and escalation of what has been done in secret for sixty years. We can no longer pretend it's happening to someone else and we need not be involved. We are involved.

~ **The Self-Impeaching President** by Steve Bhaerman, January 15, 2007
http://www.wakeuplaughing.com/news.html

~ ~ ~

In front of the Boob Tube ... Measuring values and priorities in the USA:
"I could announce one morning that the world was going to blow up in three hours and people would be calling in about my hair!"
 - Katie Couric, *CBS Evening News* anchor woman and managing editor of a nightly news program

Americans, you have been bamboozled, brain-washed and distracted. Your government has been taken over by a small group of narrow-minded reactionaries with visions of 1954 (that has become actually closer to *1984*). Don't listen to the smooth-talking experts that shame you into obedience. Beware of TV. Get out of the country for a while and get a perspective, or view some of those international stations on your satellite dish, or subscribe to different magazines to get up to speed on what is really happening in this world. And don't you believe that if you have a contrary opinion then you are not a good American.

"Patriotism is the last refuge of a scoundrel."

Dr. Samuel Johnson, 18th Century

Now let us add "jobs" into the mix. Talk about supply *and demand*! Get out there! Compete! Get a job and stick with it! ... if you can. You Will follow suit, for there are no guarantees in the marketplace. Rugged independence, a free market, and blessed competition! That is what make Americans innovative, and great! Hey, you could be down-sized, or made obsolete, so don't complain (cry baby). Once you have some family and responsibilities, children to feed, paying for educations and comforts and that big mortgage, well, then *you know* you better not rock the boat. Keep the course. Steady as she goes (even if you don't like where she's going!).

Here's something many citizens don't know: One of the reasons why America is such a commercial powerhouse is that Americans work longer and harder than most. I guess we can start with that Puritan work ethic, then add to that comparatively fewer social services than in other Western countries (meaning that you are on your own), fewer days off (the average starting paid vacation in the US - 2 weeks; in Europe - 5). Then *some* Americans get lucky and get a raise and a salary (which is code for more hours of work). The story goes on. ... Do not underestimate the influence of millions of citizens keeping their collective noses to the grindstone. This also creates less energy to utilize elsewhere, and a tired conformity. The over-worked American is encouraged to buy all those goodies for your loved ones, starting with a huge mortgage (Which, when you add things up, means that you are paying 3 to 4 times the sale price of your home over 30 years. Sucker.). Thus, the average American just wants to rest, eat fast food for convenience, and watch a little telly. What's wrong with that?
Nothing.

"Americans will put up with anything provided it doesn't block traffic." — Dan Rather

~ ~ ~

Another "expert" in our very own brave new world is a machine. Although computers and technology have brought many amazing advances into our individual and social domains, they are not infallible. Years ago a popular reminder referring to software programs was "GIGO," or "garbage in, garbage out." It definitely depends on the programmers who write the codes.

Today we have given much of our inherent trust to our fast and efficient computers.

Not so fast! Here's an eye opening bucket of cold water on what has happened in the dusty electronic world of e-voting investigations:

HOW E-VOTING THREATENS DEMOCRACY by Kim Zetter for Wired (March 29, 2004)
http://www.wired.com/news/evote/0,2645,62790,00.html

In the article, we meet voting activist Bev Harris, who came up with some digital code concerning Diebold's electronic voting machines ... and their flaws. Harris has been e-publishing her revelations on BlackBoxVoting http://www.blackboxvoting.org/ ever since. Once the discoveries of a terribly insecure system began to interfere with Diebold Election Systems sales to counties and states, the cover-ups, cease and desist letters, threats and manipulation came fast and furious.

Harris inspired other researchers with technical backgrounds to dig deeper, like Stanford University computer scientist David Dill, who had served on a California task force on e-voting. He launched a nonprofit called VerifiedVoting.org http://www.verifiedvoting.org/ to educate people about the need for a voter-verified paper trail. All of this was known before the 2004 election, by the way. * Were these safeguards in place, especially because of the election 2000 "controversy?"
In a word, no.

* For the November 2006 election there was such wide-spread suspicion about uncounted or stolen votes that a movement, a website and a video campaign were created to motivate citizens to **video the election proceedings—for evidence!** The campaign was To *save our voting right*s:
- the video is on the popular website YouTube - Video the Vote 2006 -- http://www.youtube.com/watch?v=DaEECHjWptU

Then check out www.VideoTheVote.org
They sought volunteers on Nov 7th 2006 to video the voting processes. The whole process must be watched, and they asked

112

that people send in their own recordings/videos. Why? Videos are records of the "possible mistakes" that will surely come, *and did come.*

PR spokespeople on the right have been fighting the many "conspiracy theories" connected to the stolen elections for years. They have been pointing, of late, to the 2006 election as proof that it was all wild tales from the paranoid; after all, the Democrats did very well. Two things: 1) how well *could they have done* if the voting was really fair? And 2) wouldn't it be a wise thing to lay low for an election and then make the big push for the 2008 presidential election?! The neo-cons are strategists if nothing else. It is a safe bet that the elections of 2008, 2010, ... all need to be watched. Diligently.

Kim Zetter revealed that "In 2002, Congress passed the Help America Vote Act, or HAVA http://fecweb1.fec.gov/hava/hava.htm, which allocated $3.9 billion in matching federal funds to help states upgrade to new e-voting systems." Although this measure was the result of the disastrous 2000 election fiasco, I remind you that this was passed under Republican dominated executive and congressional approval and that the companies involved are right wing. Diebold's chief executive is a top fund-raiser for Bush, for instance. Be on the lookout for news concerning the largest voting firm, Election Systems & Software, or ES&S. Zetter writes:

> Up until 1995, Nebraska Sen. Chuck Hagel had been chairman of ES&S (then called American Information Systems) before quitting the company in March of that year two weeks before launching his Senate bid. ES&S, based in Omaha, Nebraska, manufactured the only voting machines used in the state in his election the following year. According to Neil Erickson, Nebraska's deputy secretary of state for elections, the machines counted 85 percent of votes in Hagel's race; the remaining votes were counted by hand.

Hagel, a first-time candidate who had lived out of the state for 20 years, came from behind to win two major upsets in that election: first in the primary race against a fellow Republican, then in the general race against Democrat Ben Nelson, the state's popular former governor. Nelson began the race with a 65 percent to 18 percent lead in the polls, but Hagel won with 56 percent of the vote, becoming the state's first Republican senator since 1972.

> Does this sound suspicious to you? Evidently, Hagel went to the same aggressive school that Bush and his chums attended. If you were to publicly state that all this looks suspicious, Sen. Hagel is quick to send an attorney to knock on your door. Is it a conflict of interest that Hagel still owns stock in the company that counts his votes? He would tell you no. This republican would **insist** that you leave it alone. He is running for President in 2008 by the way.

"The American way of dealing with dissent and with protest is certainly more advanced: why imprison dissidents when you can just let them shout into the wind to their heart's content?"

- from Surviving Peak Oil" (Lessons from the collapse of the Soviet Union) and the article <u>Closing the Collapse Gap</u> by Dmitry Orlov - http://energybulletin.net/23259.html

Thus, everything was perfect for the set up of Election 2000. Americans were over-worked and distracted. Some were getting some rewards in the Stock Market (Enron employees were looking at fat retirements!) -- and these small players would go with whatever kept things moving. Some Americans voted, others didn't. Apathy and ennui. The majority voted for Gore. The Republicans, who didn't like that, were being aggressive again, bending the rules to suit their agendas .... but that was normal. Then the legal system intervened, and the citizen spectators knew their past roles were to just watch TV and discuss it amongst themselves, just like with "those other trials". The *experts* appeared on television, contributing a cacophony of views to drown out reason – unconsciously creating a smoke screen while the backroom machinations were humming. Time passed, and the impatience factor came in -- make a decision. Any decision! This might adversely affect the market! Where's the umpire?

And then came the *coup de grace*, the final arbiter of the whole legal process (and be clear, it was no longer an electional, democratic process by December 2000, it was a partisan preemptive affront posing as a legal matter), the **supreme** court decided the outcome.

The verdict was in: **the man who came in second, and his party which manipulated the election process before the voting began, would be the next president of the land. The United States, which exports the ideas of freedom and democracy internationally, had been taken in a coup by men in suits and ties. A business deal.**
- SP

> Of course, we're all trying hard to forget about the moment when this ugly cultural shift hit critical mass and the Forces of Evil took over. I know what it is, you know what it is, even an idiot like Brit Hume knows what it is. It's that damn stolen election. Stolen, hijacked, abducted, and ripped from the very hands and hearts of the American people. There is absolutely NO DISPUTE over who got the most votes, and there's little question now about the shenanigans that took place in Florida; yet he who won is not the man we see playing Wiffle ball on the South Lawn this afternoon.
>
> - Michael Moore, telling it like it is in *Stupid White Men*
>
> >>~o~<<

Like the sleight of hand trick by a clever magician, the lawyers, media experts and government officials point towards their conclusions – in this case the *selection* of George W. Bush as president – and the trained populace acquiesced its voting rights and perceived the coup as a legal decision, or a business deal, or as a process beyond their power to do anything about. I can imagine there were some people who took in the whole affair exactly as they viewed some fictional show on bad TV.

> YOU DO NOT COUNT! It's a tough lesson to learn. And tougher still to discover that all the stuff you've always been told to do—vote, obey the law, recycle your wine-cooler bottles—doesn't really matter, either. You might as well pull the shades and take the phone off the hook, because you and your fellow Americans have just been declared irrelevant. *Your services as a citizen, we regret to inform you, are no longer required.*
> - Michael Moore, *Stupid White Men*

The results **are** in: The U.S. populace has been lulled, hoodwinked and conned into believing the 2000 election was "an unusual election, but the national mechanisms resolved the contested results." Smiling suits shook hands and congratulated themselves, and the media reported the outcome as fact. There are those who disagreed (like Vice President Gore) with the outcome but have been too timid to declare it for what it was – theft. To those law-abiding citizens of this nation (and consumers for the corporations), the only precedence set for overturning the national command was the Revolutionary War ... and any *laissez faire*, status quo, "believe the officials" kind of guy does not think in those terms. Such a thing happens in third world countries, not here!

Yes here!

And the pressure to conform and obey is on. We all feel it. The Patriot Act is but one of the flag waving books of regulations, written by expert right wing lawyers. We are being watched, scanned, monitored. And Big Brother is not afraid of anyone. Even duly elected US Congressional representatives are being forced to hold their tongues. On July 15th, 2004, Congresswoman Corrine Brown of Florida was censured by the House for raising questions about potential election fraud in her state. From her website:

CONGRESSWOMAN BROWN SPEAKS OUT ON THE HOUSE FLOOR
http://www.house.gov/corrinebrown/press108/pr040715.htm

(Washington, DC) "Striking my words from the House floor is just one more example of the Republican Party's attempt to try and cover up what happened during the 2000 election and of their activities this year in the state of Florida in preparation for stealing this year's election as well. What is the Republican Party so afraid of? Let me tell you what I'm afraid of: another stolen election and four more years of the Bush administration."

Here's a woman of power who is standing up and telling the truth. When she was told to shut up by the House of Representatives, but did you see the news coverage? Neither did I. She was right to be worried about the 2004 election. Here's a woman of power who is standing up and telling the truth. When she was told to shut up by the House of Representatives, but did you see the news coverage? Neither did I. She was right to be worried about the 2004 election. *

* Just ask legal activist Robert F. Kennedy, Jr., 2006:
"Republicans prevented more than 350,000 voters in Ohio from casting ballots or having their votes counted -- enough to have put John Kerry in the White House."
... and note this too: - AP-Ipsos polling, May 5, 2006: "Fewer voters today than in 2004 call themselves Republicans or Republican-leaning. In addition, 27 percent of registered voters were strong Republicans just before the 2004 election, while only

15 percent fit that description today." - If this is true, with only 27% admitting being strong Republicans before the 2004 election, then ... how did Bush win? But, back to the stolen 2000 election:

> So, let's see–a handpicked regime which spends most of its time giving out contracts and other favors to its corporate friends. That's a fair description of what's happening in Iraq, all in the name of democracy, George W. Bush style. But isn't that also a fair description of what's happening in America? We have a president who was selected for office by a partisan majority on the Supreme Court, despite the fact that his opponent received more votes, not only nation-wide, but even in Florida, the decisive state in terms of winning the majority of votes in the electoral college.
> - William D. Hartung (All of his quotes within this work come from his excellent *How Much Are You Making On the War, Daddy?* unless otherwise noted.)

Coming back to haunt us, on the 4th of July, 2004, the Miami Herald published QUESTIONS OVER FELON 'PURGE LIST' THREATEN BUSH by Marc Caputo, with staff writers Erika Bolstad, Lesley Clark, Gary Fineout, Jason Grotto and David Kidwell http://www.miami.com/mld/miamiherald/9076584.htm

> - From TALLAHASSEE - As thousands of Floridians learn that a state list could wrongly bar them from voting, Democrats have found a rallying point for the November elections and proof, they say, of long-held suspicions that Gov. Jeb Bush's elections machinery is rigged against them.

The article went on to remind readers that this is what "derailed" the 2000 election. The culprit? None other than that unrepentant brother Jeb Bush. The NAACP successfully sued Florida for disenfranchising black voters in that fraudulent election. Four years later, the purge list and the flaws in the system were still there, and that, my friends, is why George W. Bush is smiling today.

> This was surely another smoking gun - and on Independence Day no less. But have we seen anything about this since? Certainly not on the national scene, and more importantly, not in a courtroom. The next day, on July 5th, nine members of the House of Representatives officially requested that the United Nations send observers to monitor the November 2nd US presidential election to avoid a contentious vote like in 2000. These lawmakers were making a brave stand; were they on the evening news? They were derided as extremists by the majority republicans. By the time you read this, dear citizen, there have been thousands of other allegations of voting manipulations and registration fraud in the 2004 *and* 2006 elections.

"There's only one voter in this country: His name is Diebold."
-- Ken Pobo

Please note the irony, and hypocrisy, in the following quote by a man who has turned his back on his people:

> "We have been following developments very closely and are deeply disturbed by the extensive and credible reports of fraud in the election. ... We call for a full review of the conduct of the election and the tallying of election results."
> - Secretary of State Colin Powell on the *Ukrainian* election of Nov 2004

>>~o~<<

The media *slants* the message.

You have been noticing, no doubt, a pattern within these pages: not only have the republicans pretty much done whatever they like, but the media promotes them and their skewed agendas; at the very least the media takes them all at their word or apologizes for them. George Seldes, the journalist of conscience in America for generations, was correct – the public has been sold out for decades. Many people believe that the media has been representing the conservative right for only the past twenty years (although the "one note" clarion call of that right is the monotonous "liberal media" refrain). However, Mr. Seldes fought against this growing tide of biased news *since the 1930s.* Joe McCarthy brought him up against the House un-American Committee in the 1950s to silence him. By the time he died, at 104, in the 1990s, his cause was as relevant as ever. Think about it: what do wealthy individuals, groups or corporations do when a newspaper, radio or TV station publically criticizes or embarrasses them? Simple, and business-like! Buy them out and replace the miscreant and insolent journalists and editors! The media has been bought and sold years ago. We are merely consumers with a limited menu in a fast food, spoon fed, couch potato world.

Much can be said about the media involvement in this "selling of the White House." Many of these players tried to appear unbiased six months after the crime. But let's call it what it was: A cover-up was perpetrated on the American people with the appearance of an impartial review of the votes the following year, printed as "the end of the matter." The NY Times, L.A. Times, Washington Post, CNN and other news organizations made a show of legitimizing the Florida outcome by counting the lost votes themselves. These biased disinformation corporations ignored hand-written votes and circles around names (indicating the intent or will of the voter) while focusing upon chads. Volunteers in this effort were stymied and frustrated by the less-than-honest accounting (a popular pastime for republicans, it seems). This recounting completely ignored the 90,000 disenfranchised voters, which made the whole effort nil from the start. It was good PR, and a legitimization of the Bush *selection.*

In another effort at appearing fair, The Washington Post ran a story about the voter purge in June of 2001, having sat on the piece for seven months (they had this information *before* Bush was selected!). They decided it was safe to publish after the US Civil Rights Commission printed their report, confirming the fraud. Yes, the US Civil Rights Commission confirms all of this.

Again, Greg Palast: "In June [2001], an editor at one of the biggest newspapers in the US told me, 'The Committee has decided not to continue printing stories about the presidential vote. We think its over. We don't want to look partisan.'"

Stifling Truth for Patriotism

Pacifica Radio's *Peace Watch* in the US interviewed the British correspondent Robert Fisk for their program, which aired May 23, 2003. Fisk, who has been attacked by both sides of the Israeli-Palestinian dilemma as being biased, has been a brave voice of spirit for years: COVERING THE MIDDLE EAST: an Interview with ROBERT FISK, Znet, May 30, 2003 http://www.zmag.org/content/showarticle.cfm?SectionID=36&ItemID=3699

In discussing how American journalists censor themselves in order not to be accused of un-patriotic declarations, or, in the case of reports on Israel, not appearing anti-Semitic, Robert Fisk recalls how it was near impossible to speak out against the first Iraqi War in 1991. To do so was to be siding with the enemy. End of story. He continues:

Even worse was the reaction of September 11. I was actually crossing the Atlantic on 9/11 of course the plane turned around when the US closed its airspace. And from the satellite phone on my seat in the plane, I was on deadline, I realize this was a Middle East story, it must be Arabs, we didn't even know that then. And I wrote an 800 word story that said "so it has come to this. The lies of the Balfour declaration, the promises that we made, the lies, British to the Arabs, all the deceit of the decades, all the one sided peace process, all the suffering of the children of Iraq", I thought, and I said "seems to have produced this international crime against humanity", which is what it was. And the most extraordinary response to this, emails saying I was in league with the devil that I had a pact with Bin Laden. A Harvard professor went on Irish radio saying I was an evil dangerous liar, that to be anti American, and whatever that is, I suppose I was being accused of it was the same as being anti-Semitic. In other words to be opposed to Mr. Bush you become a Jew hater, a Nazi, a racist. An extraordinary attempt, even if you were British, to stop you from asking why.

American journalists, for example, could ask who and how they did it [9-11 Attack]. That was acceptable. It was alright to say they were Saudi Arabians, they were Arabs. Those were the countries they came from. But to then ask *what was wrong with the countries they came from* was absolutely forbidden, it was a no no, it was a taboo question. Not for us, we kept pushing it through the British press. But in America it was unpatriotic to ask that question because it meant you were giving credit to terrorists

...

Pacifica: Do you recognize a goal of objectivity; do you see a distinction between writing commentary and what a reporter thinks, and reporting facts?
Fisk: I think we are dealing here with a problem in American journalism school, which thank god we Brits don't go through. We do politics and history and other subjects at University. I think that the foreign correspondent is the nerve ending of a newspaper. My paper sends a correspondent to live abroad to tell us what happens there, not to tell us what two sides are saying, I can read that on the wire.

Over and over again for example, when I am in Jerusalem or Damascus, or Cairo, I talk to my American colleagues, who are just like me, same jobs - much better salaries of course, but the same role. And what they tell me is fascinating. They really have a deep insight, many of them, into what's happening in the region, but when I read their reports its not there. Everything they have to tell me of interest has been erased. When they want to put forth a point of view, they ring up some guy in America who has very little knowledge, usually, in one of the places I call the tink thanks, the think tanks, the Brookings

Institute, the Rand Corporation, and this guy blathers on for two paragraphs of bland prose, and this is put in as opinion. But I want to know what the reporter thinks, if you send a reporter to a region, if you send him there because you think he is an intelligent, fair, decent reporter; you don't have to ask him to give 50% of every paragraph to each side. I mean if you follow the rules that a journalist seems to have to follow in the Middle East, what do you do, say, if you cover the slave ship and the slavery campaign? Do you give the same amount of time to the slaves and the slave ship captain? Or what if you are covering the Second World War, do you give the same amount of time to prisoners and an SS guard? NO. You have to have some sense of morality, and passion and anger.

You know when I am at the scene, for example, the slaughter of Hamer in 1982, where the Syrian army crushed the people of Hamer, up to 20,000 dead, and destroyed their mosques in the old city. I managed to get in there, and my piece, if you read it now, drips with anger at the way in which this massive armed force, run by the then president's brother, was erasing a city and its history and its people. If you read my account of the Sabra and Shatila massacres carried out by the Israeli's allies in 1982 - as Israeli soldiers watched, the same thing happens. We should not be employed to be automatons - to effectively just be a voice for a spokesman. We should be out there telling it how it is; how journalism used to be.

Pacifica: But if a sense of passion, morality, and anger leads to a journalist like yourself being considered Pro Palestinian ...
Fisk: I'm not considered pro Palestinian

Pacifica: But do you ever hear that characterization, and does it undermine your credibility?

Fisk: Absolutely not. Of course Israelis who don't like to see their misbehavior narrated into the paper will say you're pro Palestinian, pro terrorist. Of course they do. And I have many times written about Arab misbehavior and immorality and immediately I am accused of being a Mossad agent. Indeed I appeared at a conference in Boston, called the Right of Return Conference, in which I criticized the corruption of Arab American groups, in which I criticized their total disassociation from the actual dirt and filth of the refugee camps.... and emails soon began to go around from various Arab students - around the United States - saying I had been judaized; this apparently based on the idea that I give a lecture once a year in Madison Wisconsin organized by a Jewish family, and that I was a member of Mossad. And you get it from both sides, and you have to take it. But, if you see, you want to be an uncontroversial journalist, and I am not a controversial journalist, I am a correspondent for a mainstream newspaper and I do my job, ... but if you are going to be frightened by people who are going to use this cheap language, if you are going to write so carefully so as not to offend anyone, then you are going to produce the path that appears in the American media now.

Pacifica: Governments tell us that they are protecting journalists by creating closed military areas, by restricting journalist access to battle zones; do you accept that?

Fisk: Well that is what the Soviets said when they labeled cities closed military areas in the Soviet Union. Look: during the Israeli occupation of Lebanon I learned very quickly that whenever the Israeli Army declared an area a *closed military area* it meant they were doing something which was meant to be hidden, and every time they did that I got into the town to see what they had been doing, and invariably there had been extra judicial executions, torture, or prisoners taken away and not being seen again, like what has happened here. Exactly the same happens in the West Bank. The moment they declared Bethlehem a closed military area, I am talking about the first of the reoccupation of the west bank by Sharon's soldiers, I went

124

straight into Bethlehem, and I did the same in Ramallah. Our job as journalists - when we hear the words closed military areas - is to go straight in, because that is where the story is. It has nothing to do with our protection. Indeed, in the case of the Israelis, they have shot so many journalists and wounded so many journalists the last thing I think they are interested in is the protection of journalists.

Pacifica: Have you ever written a story and looked back, and felt you jeopardized civilians or soldiers or anyone by reason of your story?

Fisk: No. I will give you a very practical example. And that is geography. It is very easy to do a *color piece*. "As we walked up the hill I saw a tank on my right." I always go through my copy, saying, have I identified that hill? because if I have I am giving a Palestinian, or an Israeli, or a Hezbollah, a chance to get that tank. Of course they [know] about it anyway, they know more about the military location than we do. But I am going to make sure *we* are not even open to the accusation. If, by reporting, for example, the massacre of Sabra and Shatila, we are accused of being anti-Semitic because we make people dislike Israel, well I am sorry, that is an argument I don't want to be involved in. Because my job is to report what I have seen. And of course, when a country, Syria at Hamer for example, Israel at the time of Sabra and Shatila, Iraq at Halabja,... when a nation uses its armed forces and behaves in a despicable way, that amounts to a war crime; well, it may be that our reporting makes people angry at the country; well tough luck, that country shouldn't have committed those war crimes.

Pacifica: There was great controversy in America when the entire tape of an Osama bin Laden broadcast was edited for American availability but was broadcast in full on Al-Jazeera. What is the role of the internet, of access to Al-Jazeera and other news sources, on Americans? and are people around the world getting a complete picture of what is going on?

Fisk: Well, we haven't fully understood yet the implications of the internet. Once the internet allowed Americans to tap into English language newspapers abroad, not just the Independent but the Guardian, the Financial times, the French press if they read French, or El Pais which is very good or is very good in Spain,... suddenly a new depth was given to them. They were not reading in the English press what they were reading in the New York Times. I could tell immediately, at the moment at almost a thousand letters a week, I am getting almost 50% from America. Now that is an indictment of the American media for a start. I should be getting 20% from America and 80% from the United Kingdom, But in fact more than half is coming from America, and many of them complain about what they refer to, as one did, of the lobotomized coverage in the American Press. Now what is the effect of this?

I think that more and more Americans are saying, "hold on, why can't we read this in our newspapers, why can't we watch this on our television" Yet again and again, even despite the fact, I don't think the American media realize the extent to which ordinary American citizens are looking at foreign publications, in itself an appalling reflection on the worth, or lack of it, in the American Media. Continually, still, American reporters hedge their bets. I was reading an article which was referring to Sabra and Shatila - which the Kahan Commission of Israel said that Ariel Sharon was personally responsible, page 93 I think it was. And the article in the Associate Press referred to him "allegedly facilitating the militias that went into the camp". A total cop out. *He was personally responsible*. He sent the militias into the camp, where 1,700 Palestinians were murdered. So I think what's happening with the internet,... there is a profound change coming among Americans interested in the region, or who have an

126

intellectual interest, in the Middle East. As for all the other Americans who are not interested in the Middle East I don't know. But certainly the internet is profoundly changing, not fast enough, but profoundly changing the way Americans look at regions that are not properly covered by their newspapers and television.

Pacifica: We call our program Clear and Present Danger. What, from your perspective, is the clear and present danger to free press in the United States?

Fisk: I will sum it up very briefly. The relationship of the press and television to government is incestuous. The State Department correspondents, the White House correspondents, the Pentagon correspondents, have set a narrative where instead of telling us what they think is happening or what they know is happening, they tell us what they are told by the spokesman. They have become sub-spokesmen. Spokesmen for the great institutions of state. When an American correspondent visits the Middle East, they turn up in Beirut, Damascus or Cairo, and where do they go? The first visit is to the American Embassy for a briefing with the ambassador, the economic advisor, the defense attaché and no doubt the CIA spook. Then they go and see an Arab Minister of information, who almost never knows any information about anything ever. Then they write a story. Now it's not always that bad, but that is the main theme which is followed. So what you have, I think, is a general consensus in America, which I hope is breaking up, that to challenge American foreign policy is in some way, not just insensitive, but unpatriotic. Especially foreign policy in the Middle East, which is still a taboo subject. You know, in America you can talk about Lesbians, Gays, and Blacks but not about the relationship with Israel and the US Administration or Congress. So I think it is this cozy, incestuous, dangerous relationship between press and administration, between sources and access, which causes many of these problems.

>>~o~<<

It looks to me, as I read news items in mainstream media, that the perspective is actually biased in favor of their employers, big business, or the right wing government. As a case in point, look at this: "CNN TO AL JAZEERA: WHY REPORT CIVILIAN DEATHS?" FAIR (Fairness & Accuracy In Reporting), April 15, 2004 http://www.fair.org/activism/cnn-aljazeera.html

> As the casualties mount in the besieged Iraqi city of Fallujah, Qatar-based Al Jazeera has been one of the only news networks broadcasting from the inside, relaying images of destruction and civilian victims -- including women and children. But when CNN anchor Daryn Kagan interviewed the network's editor-in-chief, Ahmed Al-Sheik, on Monday (4/12/04) -- a rare opportunity to get independent information about events in Fallujah -- she used the occasion to badger Al-Sheik about whether the civilian deaths were really "the story" in Fallujah.

> Al Jazeera has recently come under sharp criticism from U.S. officials, who claim the Iraqi casualties are 95 percent "military-age males" (AP, 4/12/04). "We have reason to believe that several news organizations do not engage in truthful reporting," CPA spokesman Dan Senor said (Atlanta Journal-Constitution, 4/14/04). "In fact it is no reporting." Senior military spokesman Mark Kimmitt had a suggestion for Iraqis who saw civilian deaths on Al Jazeera (New York Times, 4/12/04): "Change the channel to a legitimate, authoritative, honest news station. The stations that are showing Americans intentionally killing women and children are not legitimate news sources. That is propaganda, and that is lies."

> Acting as the substitute anchor on CNN's Wolf Blitzer Reports, Kagan began the interview by asking Al-Sheik to respond to those accusations, citing U.S. officials "saying the pictures and the reporting that Al Jazeera put on the air only adds to the sense of frustration and anger and adds to the problems in Iraq, rather than helping to solve them."

After Al-Sheik defended Al Jazeera's work as "accurate" and the images as representative of "what takes place on the ground," Kagan pressed on:
"Isn't the story, though, bigger than just the simple numbers, with all due respect to the Iraqi civilians who have lost their lives -- the story bigger than just the numbers of people who were killed or the fact that they might have been killed by the U.S. military, that the insurgents, the people trying to cause problems within Fallujah, are mixing in among the civilians, making it actually possibly that even more civilians would be killed, that the story is what the Iraqi insurgents are doing, in addition to what is the response from the U.S. military?"

CNN's argument that a bigger story than civilian deaths is "what the Iraqi insurgents are doing" to provoke a U.S. "response" is startling. Especially in light of official U.S. denials of civilian deaths, video footage of women and children killed by the U.S. military is evidence that needs to be seen.

...

Shame on the Press.
Or is shame enough?

This whole obeisance to the powers that be is killing truth. Who are journalists beholden to? Why, their employers, of course. Not to us, not to the truth, not to democracy in this land. This is not only a media scandal, it is a political betrayal. An investigation is in order. This points towards not only media corruption, but to specific culprits manipulating the press at the expense of democracy in the US. *

* To those who steer the media: there comes a time when biased accounts and short term greed must be weighed against the principles of what this country stands for, has stood for. Did you want your party, the Republican party, to win at all costs? Was that republican "victory" worth the cost of fair elections, public trust, and democracy itself? By putting "your men" in power, did you turn your

back on your fellow citizens, on fair elections, and on the democratic process? What price winning? What Faustian agreement did you sink into by backing up or apologizing for a coup? You have some accounting to do, and amending. If not, legally, what you (and especially the executives), the media, did are termed accessory to the crime, obstruction of evidence and justice, and fraud. In rectifying the harm done, will you now stand for the right thing, and not just "the right?"

One more thing - is there a journalist's union? Will news writers and commentators stand up and tell the truth, regardless of what their masters - um, employers dictate? Or are you hushed because you then "won't gain access" or won't add to your retirement account? - SP

American media has run under this ultraconservative onslaught for decades. They so control our media that all of their narrow-minded edicts seem normal, if not reasonable. This is exactly what people were worried about with the 2003 FCC (Federal Communication Commission) regulation changes: more stations in fewer hands is not good for diversity of opinion. Huge corporations like Clear Channel and Fox News are clear examples of how ultra-conservative media corporations, putting their own spin on the world, can negatively influence millions of Americans and broadcast biased news and views right into our homes... and minds.

NEW YORK - REPUBLICAN BIAS AT FOX NEWS DOCUMENTED IN NEW FILM, FEATURING FORMER EMPLOYEES – PRNewswire, July 2004
"At a New York press conference ..., four former Fox News employees will go on the record to expose Fox's persistent Republican partisan bias, while releasing internal memorandums from Fox News Channel showing executive level instructions to Fox on how to bias the news. The four Fox whistle-blowers appear, along with three others, in Robert Greenwald's new documentary **'Outfoxed: Rupert Murdoch's War on Journalism.'"**
> Greenwald, by the way, has produced other revealing documentaries, including "Unprecedented." He should be as well known as Michael Moore. He is a hero.

~ ~ ~

Leading up to the fall 2006 USA elections, a wealthy and influential foreigner, or should I rather say, an international citizen interested in money, did an strange thing: he publically endorsed Hillary Clinton, a Democrat who has been vilified by the far right for years. It was such news that it made news with other news media:

Murdoch's New York Post Endorses Hillary: Right-Leaning Tabloid Once Said 'Don't Run,' Now Backs Sen. Clinton For Re-Election

> NEW YORK, Oct. 30, 2006 - (CBS/AP) The New York Post endorsed Democratic Sen. Hillary Rodham Clinton for re-election on Monday, saying her Republican challenger, John Spencer, "isn't a credible alternative."
>
> The endorsement comes as a surprise given the right-leaning views of the Post, owned by media magnate Rupert Murdoch.
>
> Clinton won her Senate seat in 2000 despite a concerted effort by the Post to attack her candidacy. The Post even ran a pleading headline, "Don't Run!" before Clinton formally joined the race.
>
> During Bill Clinton's last year in the White House, the Post's news pages frequently referred to him as "horndog-in-chief."
>
> In addition to the Post, News Corp., the global media conglomerate controlled by Murdoch, owns Fox News and other television networks, as well as The Times of London and many other British and Australian newspapers.

>   Of course, this turn around might be due to Hillary making some conservative deal or promise; she did vote for the Iraq War and for giving Bush extended powers. My feeling is the rar right put the "fear of God" into her. But who is this man in the background, this person with un-due power over the media, and the minds, of citizens? It is worth a look:

131

Rupert Murdoch inherited a small Australian newspaper in 1952 and aggressively turned it into one of the biggest media corporations in the world, News Corp., a conglomerate that includes television, feature films, online services, newspapers and books. Over the years Murdoch acquired more and more media outlets all over the world, from Australia and Europe to the U.S. and China. Now one of the world's wealthiest men, he is frequently criticized for his political views and for "lowering the standards" of the publications and outlets he acquires. In the 1980s he became a U.S. citizen in order to meet requirements for owning TV stations. (Answers.com)

Freedom of the press? ...
> As far as I can tell, this is an opportunistic entrepreneur with an eternal eye on the bottom line – and the least common denominator, and thus ultimately with too much influence on American, and international, public opinion, elections and governments. We get more answers, and insights, from this online source of information:

In early 1985 Murdoch bought half of Fox for $250 million, and on May 6, 1985, Twentieth Century Fox bought Metromedia's seven television stations for $2 billion. By then Murdoch's assets were worth $4.7 billion, with annual revenues of $2.6 billion—but he was borrowing heavily to expand into the American television market. In the United States, only an American citizen could hold a majority interest in a television station, which meant the Metromedia stations could not be owned by Murdoch; Australia had a similar rule. Murdoch obtained an exception in Australia, and on September 4, 1985, he became a U.S. citizen. The rest of his family remained Australian citizens.

... In 1994 Murdoch dropped the BBC from Star Television amid protests that he was bowing to complaints from China's dictators, who said the BBC portrayed them badly. Murdoch's response was that he personally disliked the BBC, which was true; he regarded the BBC as an elitist organization that helped prevent the United Kingdom's society from becoming fully free and democratic. The accusation that he was unethically catering to China's dictators would return with more justification when in 1998 his book-publishing firm HarperCollins broke its agreement to publish the memoirs of the last governor of Hong Kong, Chris Patten, supposedly because Patten was overly critical of Chinese communists.

... By 2002 Murdoch owned more than 750 businesses in more than 50 countries. In December 2003 Murdoch made one of his most daring purchases when his News Corporation paid $6.8 billion for the controlling interest in DIRECTV, an American satellite-television service. This purchase would enable Murdoch to broaden the reach of his existing television services as well as to profit from the dissemination of other television services that would be required to pay him to carry their shows. ...

News Corporation was first incorporated in Australia; in 2004 Murdoch reincorporated his company, shifting it from Australia to the United States. By that year Murdoch's 35 American television stations reached 40 percent of America's population. Murdoch himself had come to be regarded by many as an extreme right-wing ideologue; he seemed to have changed his thinking about socialism, which he saw as a poison embodied in government regulatory agencies. He never escaped from bitter criticism that he published vulgar newspapers that demeaned society by emphasizing sex and mayhem at the expense of reasoned discussion. It was Murdoch's view that he was an entertainer, not an informer, and that he merely sold entertainment to his readers, most of whom were lower-class workers and middle-class women. He was unapologetic about his influence on public discourse. Amid complaints that Fox slanted the news in favor of government policies that he advocated, he insisted that he saw no such slant. (Answers.com)

> Thus, Murdoch is thriving in the USA because he makes money. The fact that he aids other republicans in their efforts to control and manipulate systems that promote big business is a mutual admiration society. This is how he continues to get "exceptions" to rules and benefits for his companies – which benefit the right wing business and republican interests. *Embedded* goes beyond the cozy relationship of certain journalists and the US military abroad. Yet another point that needs to be made: yellow journalism and scary stories of crime and mayhem, widely publicized, implants insecurity and fear into the minds of citizens. They will then vote for the party that is tough on crime and has a strong military. *The show continues.*

~ ~ ~

In May 2003 two top editors of the NY Times resigned over a scandal connected to a junior reporter's unresearched and made up stories. Shall we get our priorities straight? On the world scene, the theft of the 2000 election and its media reporting is a much greater crime. Where is the outrage here? Where is this journalistic ethic? Where is accountability here?

Does this high minded journalistic integrity reveal itself in the following quote?
"... a consortium of news organizations found and reported on the front page of The New York Times (and other papers) on 12 September 2001, that in Florida '...a statewide recount -- could have produced enough votes to tilt the election his [Gore's] way, no matter what standard was chosen to judge voter intent.' (The Times apparently chose to bury this fact -- that Gore actually won the 2000 election -- in the 15th paragraph and behind a misleading headline because the nation had been attacked on 9/11 the day before.)"
From Thom Hartmann, HOW TO TAKE BACK A STOLEN ELECTION (Common Dreams, Nov 29, 2004)

> American citizens, this is another smoking gun. The Truth of the 2000 election results printed under a misleading headline *the day after* the 9/11 attack – when no one was paying attention and nothing would be done due to the state of emergency! This was another hijacking! This crashed right into the White House. And

134

why was it printed on September 12th? So you can say that Yes you did print the truth but no one was listening? This looks like covering your ass, New York Times, not covering the biggest story in American political history! And who were you covering, who were you protecting? Mr. Bush, our fearless leader, the usurper and traitor? ... where was **he** the day before – *during* the attacks? Caught on tape and broadcast years later by Michael Moore in "Fahrenheit 9/11," this man you protected was a deer caught in the headlights, mind a-glaze while reading a children's book with kids in Florida. *He didn't know what to do. He was lost.* You set aside journalistic integrity, the Constitution, democracy, American values, truth, and international standards of the electional process, for this man?

It must have been money....

Many have witnessed cowardice, denial, and collusion by journalists, judges, media spokesmen, community leaders and congressmen. The Democrats, especially, have demonstrated cowardice in the extreme. Perhaps they were cowered and overcome by the republican barrage on the Clinton administration. President Bill Clinton, who was fairly elected, was investigated for seven years, at the cost to the American taxpayer of over $75 million. What did they find? His pants down. Impeached for adultery (do not be fooled by perjury and obstruction of justice). This was pure theater. The smoke was everywhere. Clever showmen contorted adultery into numerous other charges. It was a trick. And it worked. It was good practice for stories to come. The bully tactics of the far right, brandishing subpoenas and fear, routed the timid Democrats and soft spoken liberals. * There have been essays and editorials wondering how history would treat Bill Clinton after his impeachment. I wonder what great things he could have done had he not had a pack of jackals on his ass for 7 years. Do you think he was somewhat distracted? Harried? Set-up?

> * A note to fair-play liberals and followers of the democratic process: when confronted with armed fanatics, and pit-bull reactionaries, it is not the time to "play by the Marquis of

Queensberry Rules." When the enemy has a gun, you must defend yourselves. When our country and all that it stands for is under attack, you must be brave and courageous, matching strategy with superior strategy. - SP

If the media gets too liberal, there are other ways to enforce control. One common ploy of the neo-con show is to wrap themselves up in the moral flag while distracting the public from more important things, like high crimes and misdemeanors. Notice the smoke with the following:

CBS Fined $3.6M for 'Indecent' Programming
$550,000 Slap for Janet Jackson's 'Wardrobe Malfunction' Upheld by Jennifer C. Kerr, AP - WASHINGTON (March 15, 2006)

A government crackdown on indecent programming resulted in a proposed fine of $3.6 million against dozens of CBS stations and affiliates on Wednesday - a record penalty from the Federal Communications Commission.

> Can you believe all of the fuss over Janet Jackson and the accident that exposed one breast for a fraction of a second?! (In front of millions of American men watching football?! They loved it and wanted more.) And as this outrage to public decency "raged," the list of real crimes drops below the radar screen. Diversion? Misdirection? I believe this is purposely used by our government to redirect the focus. In the article there are references to the F word and the S word! Do these people know what music teenagers are listening too? Very tame utterances, my friends. According to the FCC judgments referred to above, teens are not to be shown having sex, especially in front of other teens (even though the TV program in question was making the point that parents needed to watch their kids). What a hypocritical stance, when the "lewd" and indecent behavior of lying executives fomenting war abroad, thus *killing* teens in foreign countries for oil profits, goes without comment! Who's slapping fines on *these* "programs?"

Politics is a dirty game, and both parties have unsavory characters. I'm not blindly Democratic; I am liberal and proud of it. It has the same root as liberate and liberty. We Americans

136

have been losing this liberty for years, and I am astounded to witness widespread apathy and even collusion with the criminal elements of the Bush - Cheney - Rumsfeld regime. The US, and the world, are paying for that crime daily.

Propaganda = Lies
... and smoke in the eyes

Dear friends of theater, mystery and imagination. Here is the section where we will view and preview the various "wordings" of this crew. This is where they make themselves appear other than what they are. Here is the arena of clever manipulations, careful posturing and posing. Their rhetoric and speeches are full of suggestive and imaginative smoke and mirrors. Read carefully, or you might miss what I have presented for you. You may wish to refer to the list of ways that we can be influenced as you read through these true examples. For instance, under imagination, recall that I had described an imaginative child talking to the butterfly and making plans for the fairy ball? Now picture this vision described by Condoleezza Rice before the War on Iraq: "We don't want the smoking gun to be a mushroom cloud." - A great example of an authority using persuasion, imagination and emotions to sell a product. (That was a great sound bite, guys! Sieg Heil!)

Once you get the slant, it is easier to see, and see through. It is imperative that we, as a united people and a progressive country, see through these lies and break out of their deceptions.

"In my name and over my signature, inaccurate, incomplete and unreliable statements were given to the committee, but I did not intend to mislead the committee."
- Newt Gingrich, 1996, on his ethics investigation

Why should the country espousing democracy most loudly have a well established propaganda machine? Wasn't that what the Soviets did? The Bush regime constantly uses lies and deceit to the world and to its citizens, on the floor of the UN and on the air in speeches. Vice President Cheney said that Iraq was "the geographic base of the terrorists who have had us under assault for many years, but most especially on 9/11." Even people who had no access to the CIA knew that Cheney was lying. I mean, the majority of the hijackers were from Saudi Arabia. The bipartisan 9/11 Commission found that Iraq had no involvement in the 9/11 attacks and no collaborative operational relationship with Al Qaeda. Does he think we can't read or think? Why isn't he a war criminal by now? I'll tell you why: he has been within the ranks of US governmental power since the 1970s and has profited from it. He is one of the types (from the Stupidity research quoted earlier) that is above it all and he is sure he will get away with it. So far, he has.

"Don't let the facts get in the way," the inner circle seem to say again and again. However, according to the Administration's handpicked weapon's inspector, Charles Duelfer, there was "no evidence that Hussein had passed illicit weapons material to al Qaeda or other terrorist organizations, or had any intent to do so." After the release of the report in September 2004, Bush retorted, "There was a risk--a real risk--that Saddam Hussein would pass weapons, or materials, or information to terrorist networks." Sources: New York Times, White House news release (with thanks to Judd Legum, who wrote "100 [UNSPUN and referenced] Facts and 1 Opinion: The Non-Arguable Case Against the Bush Administration" in The Nation magazine. http://www.thenation.com/doc.mhtml?i=20041108&s=facts). Notice the wording: by using the word "or," Bush - or his writers - combined weapons with merely information. Smoke. Not only did Bush and Cheney deny this significant report – that they commissioned! - but Condoleezza Rice immediately spun it **to vindicate** the assertions and decisions of her bosses! What gall! Those Republican spin-meisters are always at work.

That Condi is definitely always at work. Many months earlier, in her push to sell the Iraqi War to the American public, National Security Adviser Condoleezza Rice said that high-strength aluminum tubes acquired by Iraq were "only really suited for nuclear weapons programs," warning, remember, that "we don't want the smoking gun to be a mushroom cloud." However, the government's top nuclear scientists had told the Administration the tubes were "too narrow, too heavy, too long" to be of use in developing nuclear weapons and could be used for other purposes. (Source: New York Times) Dear readers, with Rice's background in Soviet Russia and the Cold War, she knew she was lying at the time. In another instance, implying that Americans cannot read or think for themselves, Condoleezza Rice interpreted the Kay Report on Iraq weapons findings and picked out pieces for her disinformation campaign in the fall of 2003. Kay specifically declared that there were no nuclear, biological or chemical weapons of any danger in the Iraqi arsenal. Rice lifted other citations out of context within the report as proof there were WMD and thus the invasion and occupation were justified. (Washington Post, 9 Oct 2003) I imagine next she is going to tell us there is no wind in tornadoes! Or the US never had slaves! She evidently believes Americans are illiterate idiots.

Notice, also, that all of these *public servants* state outrageous, illogical and audacious announcements on a weekly basis, with no accountability. After a while, they could easily assume that they could just go with their guts, make assumptions and make stuff up. It will be printed. Some may not like it. Nothing will happen. They will be well paid and people in meetings will applaud them. It is a recipe for heady stew for them. Their *roles* (remember that one?) seem to have some superman type protection that bounces bullets and deflects facts and criticism.

A Precarious State of the Union
By now Bush's lies about the Niger-Iraq uranium reference in his 2004 State of the Union address is well known. (It would be very enlightening to find out who forged the documents.) As this regime goes down, watch the finger-pointing – it will be quite telling. By the way, Bush told several lies in that war speech, uh, the State of the Union Address, not just one. But there is more to this than just lying – the Bush regime is corroding, if not attacking, another cherished American institution. The State of the Union address was created by the Founders of this country. This annual report was an early attempt

at what we call today transparency. It was created for a public suspicious of kings and their power. It was an opportunity for the leader to stand up before the people who elected him and tell them, the people, what he was doing. Like the supreme court itself, it has been a revered institution. Both are now sullied.

As many people know by now, US intelligence dispatched ex-Niger diplomat Joseph Wilson to find out the truth about the Iraq-Niger allegations. His report dismissed them as early as March 2002, according to *Time* magazine (July 21, 2003). Evidently the Bush team didn't like the truth, and ignored his report. On Jan 28, 2003, Bush lied to the American public about the Iraqi uranium plan. Only a week later, Powell, speaking before the UN Security Council, left this point out. Later, he said he made the omission because he didn't think it was solid enough "to present to the world." – not solid enough for the world, but just fine for the US public? Joseph Wilson was on record recommending a peaceful resolution to Iraq, a stance the White House did not like (I mean, where's the money and glory in that?). Many senior officials, including Condoleezza Rice, tried to imply that his report on the Niger connection only made it into the hands of low level staff. This, Wilson knew, was not true. "It was pretty clear that it had gotten to the right people," he said in an interview (printed in the *International Herald Tribune* Aug 8, 2003).

When Joseph Wilson started to talk openly of his mission to Niger and of his negative conclusions of the Iraq tie-in, the White House decided to shut him up. Why? He was an informed political professional who stated that the "facts" for attacking Iraq were made up. Conservative Washington columnist Robert Novak revealed that Wilson's wife was a covert CIA operative. The message from the regime? Keep quiet, one and all, for we can make life hard. As to the official threat, aimed at his wife, Wilson stated "it wasn't to intimidate me. Clearly this was to keep others from stepping forward." Their tactic, however, is coming back to haunt them. Leaking such inform-ation puts the operative in mortal danger. According to *The Hill*, 29 July 2003: "Under federal law, exposing the identity of an intelligence official is punishable by 10 years in prison." Sen. Charles Schumer is asking Robert Mueller, head of the FBI, to investigate "reports that two senior members of the Bush administration made the identity of an undercover Central Intelligence Agency (CIA) operative public." Rep. Alcee Hastings, a member of the House Intelligence Committee, stated "what happened is very dangerous to a person who may be a CIA operative. [The leak] came from the executive branch, in my view. Its intent is to stop other people like Joe Wilson, and I am going to insist on getting to the bottom of this in any way we can." Two years later Karl Rove was identified as one of the leaks. Was he immediately arrested for exposing an undercover agent and putting her in danger? No, he is one of the protected ones, above the law. It will be interesting how far special investigator Patrick Fitzgerald goes with this. So far he has caught Cheney's aid, Lewis Libby, who seems to be talking. Bush and Cheney are already implicated.

~ ~ ~

As Bush continues to lie about various things, one can't help but look back at the lie by President Clinton about his affair. The difference is telling, for no one died when Clinton lied. By 2007, Iraq is an ugly quagmire. Since the "official end" of the conflict, on May 1st, 2003, about sixteen Americans *per week* are being killed (and although American news media doesn't really care, way more Iraqis than that are dying every week). As of this writing, *more American soldiers and personnel have died in Iraq and the Gulf region than were killed on 9-11*, with more than twenty-four thousand casualties. Embarrassingly, a rather large proportion have died by *other* causes, reports the military. What other causes? Suicide, for one. "Friendly" fire is a monthly event. Here's something that will be in the news next year – and next decade: Gulf War Syndrome is complicated and underrated; one of the insidious culprits is DU, or depleted uranium casings (read: radiation), which gets into the body as shrapnel and inhaled in dust. More and more soldiers are being diagnosed with this dangerous radiation (not to mention hundreds of thousands of Iraqis). Here's just one article, not printed here but check it out: "Depleted Uranium: Dirty Bombs, Dirty Missiles, Dirty Bullets" http://www.truthout.org/docs_04/082304W.shtml

The military brass got bent out of shape in the spring of 2004 when pictures of coffins with American flags on them were published. Sending another strong message to the press, the newspeople who got these rather innocuous pictures out were fired (while the military ignored the fact that a similar picture was on an official website). That will keep other journalists from printing unpleasant things! As the Iraqi prison torture scandals escalates – with retaliatory beheadings videotaped by terrorists – I bet the military egg heads are now wishing for those peaceful days of draped coffins.

RED CROSS: IRAQ ABUSE WIDESPREAD, ROUTINE
By Alexander G. Higgins, Associated press, May 10, 2004

> GENEVA - Up to 90 percent of Iraqi detainees were arrested "by mistake," according to coalition intelligence officers cited in a Red Cross report disclosed Monday. It also says U.S. officers mistreated inmates at the notorious Abu Ghraib prison by keeping them naked in dark, empty cells.

> Abuse of Iraqi prisoners by American soldiers was widespread and routine, the report finds – contrary to President Bush's contention that the mistreatment "was the wrongdoing of a few."

IRAQ IS WORSE OFF THAN BEFORE THE WAR BEGAN, GAO REPORTS by Seth Borenstein for Knight-Ridder / Common Dreams, June 29 2004
http://www.commondreams.org/headlines04/0629-10.htm

From WASHINGTON, June 2004 - "In a few key areas - electricity, the judicial system and overall security - the Iraq that America handed back to its residents Monday is worse off than before the war began last year, according to calculations in a new General Accounting Office report released Tuesday:"
> http://www.gao.gov/new.items/d04902r.pdf

~ ~ ~

Slanting the News

The Bush team and the military are polishing the news for us. For instance, how about those midnight flights transporting thousands of Americans wounded, maimed and amputated? This is another piece of news the government doesn't want you to hear. The official number of wounded U.S. troops is 18,500 (by summer 2006) but the unofficial number varies between 20,000 - 48,000! Why? Evidently our military is hiding the numbers and playing with statistics; for instance, if a soldier dies on a plane leaving Iraq, then he is not counted as dying *in* Iraq. Can you believe that? Take a look:

WASHINGTON - "Nearly 17,000 service members medically evacuated from Iraq and Afghanistan are absent from public Pentagon casualty reports, according to military data reviewed by United Press International. The Pentagon said most don't fit the definition of casualties, but a veterans' advocate said they should all be counted."
- reported by Mark Benjamin, September 15, 2004
http://about.upi.com/exclusive/UPI-20040915-021124-6165R

~ ~ ~

If the Bush regime truly had its way, even more deceptions would be published as revised history (sound familiar?). Did you know that Donald Rumsfeld tried to change the Vietnam-era term "body bag" to the innocuous sounding "transfer tube?" Luckily there are still individuals and groups that fight such propaganda notions and word-cleansing. In the summer of 2004 a gloss-over by the Bush spinners had to be rescinded: "The State Department released a corrected version of its annual report 'On Worldwide Terrorism.' A previous report claiming that terrorist activity was at its lowest level for over 30 years had to be withdrawn amid much embarrassment. Over 3,600 people were wounded in terrorist acts last year, a big increase on 2002." http://www.economist.com/

Bush team scolded for disguised TV report
By Ceci Connolly, Washington Post | January 7, 2005

WASHINGTON – Shortly before last year's Super Bowl, local news stations across the country aired a story by Mike Morris describing plans for a new White House ad campaign on the dangers of drug abuse.
What viewers did not know was that Morris is not a journalist and his "report" was produced by the government, actions which constituted illegal "covert propaganda," according to an investigation by the Government Accountability Office.

In the second ruling of its kind, the investigative arm of Congress this week scolded the Bush administration for distributing phony prepackaged news reports that include a "suggested live intro" for anchors to read, interviews with Washington officials, and a closing that mimics a typical broadcast news sign-off.
...
"You think you are getting a news story but what you are getting is a paid announcement," said Susan Poling, managing associate general counsel at the Government Accountability Office. "What is objectionable about these is the fact the viewer has no idea their tax dollars are being used to write and produce this video segment."
In May, the Government Accountability Office concluded that the Department of Health and Human Services violated two federal laws with similar fake news reports touting the administration's new Medicare drug benefit. ....

Just like a Hollywood movie!

The Jessica Lynch story is now just a hazy memory in the American psyche; at the time it was a PR success. Too bad the heroics weren't true. Again, this is some chest-beating tactic that we accused the Soviets of doing. You remember the story: Young private Jessica was ambushed, fought hand to hand combat, was captured and sent to an enemy hospital until US troops stormed the dangerous place and saved her. The real story was released in July 2003; the military report stated the captain of Lynch's unit made a "single navigational error" (translation: he got lost). In defending themselves, the weapons jammed due to poor maintenance in the sandy conditions. Lynch evidently was not shot and stabbed, as was alleged at the time, but suffered wounds from the crash. The Iraqi soldiers left the hospital two days before the heroic rescue. Rumor has it that Jessica actually remembers a lot about what happened, but was ordered to keep quiet. Free speech violation for her or censorship imposed upon us? You choose. Thus, a relatively minor event was turned into a media show for public consumption... and propaganda. Was Hollywood involved? It would be quite clever of the neo-cons to publically deride liberal Tinseltown, all the while smiling, for they've had close ties since the Red Scare in the 50s; the most visible stars out of movieland are Ronald Reagan and Arnold the Governator. There must be others. Find out who attended the inaugural balls!

In short, the government and the military are creating a show for us on radio and TV. This is not news, these are not public announcements; this is propaganda and mind control. Many Americans are being duped in the process. Such brainwashing tactics should come as no surprise for people who have been following Bush over the years. Remember the subliminal ad campaign from the Bush campaign in the summer of 2000 calling the other party democ"**rats**"?

The African Bush?

Pandering to potential black votes while standing against affirmative action, Bush's tour of Africa in the summer of 2003 was another PR opportunity. Condoleezza Rice and Colin Powell followed the white chief around, evidently to imply support but in actuality it was Black subservience. An interesting anecdote is found in *Time* magazine about this trip: An advance White House team spent almost a week preparing a speech platform for Bush with the infamous structure called *The House of Slaves* displayed in the background. Not seen was an air conditioner at Bush's feet going at full blast in the African heat. He looked cool. Who paid for this stunt? You did. Good show!

145

Top Gun Bush

Real top guns and military personnel resented Bush being given the honorary title of a top gun at his photo-op on the aircraft carrier Eisenhower after the major hostilities were *officially* over in the spring of 2003. Why? He didn't earn it. His publicists loved it, and thought they would use it in his re-election campaign. (They also used 9-11 footage ... while Bush tried to stall the investigation!) The story the taxpayers should hear is this: the aircraft carrier was delayed from its arrival back to its home port in California, and then repositioned so that the San Diego skyline would not appear on TV. This stunt cost taxpayers $3.3 million and delayed our troops from going home.

Euphemisms of our times

Bush must have read George Orwell's *Animal Farm*, or its cliff notes. May I present Bushspeak:

The "Patriot Act" is a wonderful sounding initiative that sends us marching, as a nation, towards a police state. I imagine J. Edgar Hoover would be pleased, although he was accused many times of using Gestapo tactics in his ultra-conservative approach to national affairs.

"National Security" is used weekly as a reason for various proposals. It is also used to silence opposition and to keep backroom deals secret. Many right-wingers are very quick to use the term *terrorist* these days. I have cited many instances in this work. It is a term used against their enemies and is meant to silence criticism and objectivity. Who are their enemies? Well, essentially anyone who disagrees with them.

Have you noticed those digital highway boards on interstate highways? They officially warn about traffic jams ahead, but for some time now are urging drivers to "report suspicious terrorist activities on your cell phone ..." We have been on some alert, off and on, since the terrorist attacks. Perhaps the regime is humbly not reporting the caught terrorists during these various orange and red alert periods, and so we don't hear about them. Knowing this regime's love of photo-ops, however, I doubt much has been done during those alerts outside of keeping people in fear of those evil terrorists while trusting in their protector, George W. Bush.

Did anyone note that "Shock and Awe" are new terms for Blitzkrieg? The military has a long history of deception, misdirection and propaganda. All of this is probably as old as warfare itself. To be fair, sometimes such deception confuses the enemy and battles are won. On the other hand, once the struggle has ceased, it is time again for transparency, for truth and clarity. For instance, neither Afghanistan nor Iraq were illuminating examples of "precision" and "surgical" bombing and high technology of a flawless efficiency, as we were told. Missiles were aimed at Iraq and landed in Turkey and Kuwait, so the precision is questionable, to say the least. Americans found out just before the 2004 election that in April of 2003, right from under US military noses, 380 **tons** of explosives disappeared – 18 months before the 2004 election ... and all of that hoopla about winning the war in Iraq! Even though Americans knew that such a major military blunder occurred, millions of gullible citizens voted for this inept war leader. How many months had the military tried to cover-up this failure, no one knows, but there quickly came a media spin to protect Bush and the botched incident. They have been doing a good job so far, for in the last few years we have had stories of terrible attacks against wedding parties, hospitals, museums, schools, Canadian troops and other allies. Were these all done with "smart" bombs? And how many have died from *friendly fire?* Do Arabs count? Isn't it time for a candid accounting of the casualties on all sides?

The Bush regime's "Clear Skies" Initiative actually weakens most laws and regulations already covered by the Clean Air Act! (More on this later.) The "Healthy Forest Initiative" is also Bushspeak. The ludicrous plan of preventing forest fires by logging them is even more flawed than on the surface. To protect homes *near* forest land, measures are underway to allow the timber industry to log actually *far away* from private homes. "These large-scale, industrial logging operations not only will harm forest health, but could actually increase the risk of forest fires." (Joint statement by conservation groups, cited below.)

Bush's fine sounding Leave No Child Behind Act is already underfunded by $10 billion per year. (nwitimes.com) His generous international AIDS program? No money, no program. His Mars program will essentially scuttle many space exploration projects that have been operative for years, abandon the international space station, and take money away from more realizable studies and ventures by NASA and other programs.

The F.B.I. has been using powers it obtained under the Patriot Act to get financial, business and telephone records of Americans by issuing tens of thousands of "national security letters," a euphemism for warrants that are issued without any judicial review or avenue of appeal. The administration said that, as with many powers it has arrogated since the 9/11 attacks, this radical change was essential to fast and nimble antiterrorism efforts, and it promised to police the use of the letters carefully.

But like so many of the administration's promises, this one evaporated before the ink on those letters could dry. The F.B.I. director, Robert Mueller, admitted Friday that his agency had used the new powers improperly.
Mr. Gonzales does not directly run the F.B.I., but it is part of his department and has clearly gotten the message that promises (and civil rights) are meant to be broken.
- **The Failed Attorney General,** The New York Times | Editorial, 11 March 2007

~ ~ ~

In "What You See vs. What They See," *Time Magazine* compared the news as slanted east and west, between Muslim and Christian perspectives. (7 Apr 03) Their conclusion was that both sides were guilty of slanting things their way. Yes, American news is slanted or biased, especially in international issues, as most international observers know. It begs the question, however: Why is our news slanted? Don't we live in the United

States of America, the land of free speech, of truth and high principles?

"Universities Join the U.S. to Monitor Foreign News" by Eric Lipton (NYT) and reprinted in the International Herald Tribune, Oct 5, 2006:

"A consortium of major universities, with Homeland Security Department funds, is developing software that would let the government monitor negative opinions of the United States or its leaders in newspapers and other publications overseas. The 'sentiment analysis' is intended to identify potential threats to the nation, security officials said."

> Here's BushSpeak again! Doesn't *sentiment analysis* seem rather innocuous? Notice, too, that here criticism against Bush is the same as criticism, and a threat, against the US. And what to do once the government identifies newspapers, publishers and countries that dislike Bush? Pre-emptive attacks?

The universities: Cornell, U of Pittsburgh, U of Utah. And get this: the thrust of this multi-million dollar lunacy is to analyze the reaction to Bush's 2001 & 2002 references to "Axis of Evil," the handling of the prisoners at Guantánamo Bay, the global warming anti-position or denial, and the coup attempt against President Hugo Chavez of Venezuela. Right now $2.4 million is dedicated to this "research." The article continues: "Even the basic research has raised concern among journalism advocates and privacy groups, as well as representatives of the foreign news media. 'It is just creepy and Orwellian,' said Lucy Dalglish, a lawyer and former editor who is executive director of the Reporters Committee for Freedom of the Press."

Many Americans are fine with "Dubya" (a friendly name, no?) Bush because they haven't been told the truth, and they haven't seen past the lies. The news is being slanted, sold, bottled, and dispensed by many writers and commentators with little imagination and great self interest, such as ultra-conservative spokespeople Ann Coulter, Laura Ingraham and

149

their fellow jingoists Sean Hannity, Matt Drudge, Chris Matthews, Michael Savage, Charles Krauthammer, Rush Limbaugh,* Bill Kristol of the Weekly Standard, Fox News anchor Brit Hume, and then there is mean-spirited Bill O'Reilly (Bill stated that if no WMDs were found in Iraq, he would not trust Bush again. Well? Oh, and what a smooth PR move to quietly silence that woman who accused you of sexual harassment in the fall of 2004. Moral standards?). I am at a loss as to why people listen to them at all. For instance, rabid Ann Coulter offers advice on what to do about Muslim nations: "We should invade their countries, kill their leaders and convert them to Christianity." What?! Even more mainstream "authorities" like Tom Brokaw at NBC or Judith Miller of the NY Times show their partialities by what they don't report or choose to overlook ... all in Bush's favor.

> * Here's some vintage wisdom from Rush Limbaugh: "And now the liberals want to stop President Reagan from selling chemical warfare agents and military equipment to Saddam Hussein and why? Because Saddam 'allegedly' gassed a few Kurds in his own country. Mark my words. All of this talk of Saddam Hussein being a 'war criminal' or 'committing crimes against humanity' is the same old thing. LIBERAL HATE SPEECH! and speaking of poison gas... I SAY WE ROUND UP ALL THE DRUG ADDICTS AND GAS THEM TOO!..."
> November 3, 1988

>   These people are the propagandists of our day. They are either on the pay, deluded, stupid, uninformed, or sycophants of George Bush and the gang. For any of these reasons, they should not be "informing" the public as "experts" and should retire, if not be indicted themselves.

On the other hand, investigators like Keith Olbermann, Michael Moore and Greg Palast, and politically savvy humorists like Jon Stewart of *the Daily Show,* Bill Maher on *Real Time,* Garrison Keillor and Steve Bhaerman; plus conscientious entertainers such as Susan Sarandon, Tim Robbins, Tom Hanks,

Martin Sheen, the Dixie Chicks, Sean Penn, Jessica Lange, Renee Zellweger and others who have spoken out against the Bush regime or the Iraqi invasion have been ridiculed as naïve people who do not understand -- and should keep out of -- politics. However, entertainers who were pro-war were invited to speak at political rallies and fund raisers. This two-faced policy marginalizes dissent – supposedly an American right and very important for a voting public. Bush/war spokesmen like Dennis Miller and Kelsey Grammar don't seem too funny these days.

Here's something funny from the cartoon "Boondocks." Cartoonist Aaron Magruder has his character, a black youngster named Huey Freedman, say the following: "In this time of war against Osama bin Laden and the oppressive Taliban regime, we are thankful that OUR leader isn't the spoiled son of a powerful politician from a wealthy oil family who is supported by religious fundamentalists, operates through clandestine organizations, has no respect for the democratic electoral process, bombs innocents, and uses war to deny people their civil liberties. Amen."

Rumors: George Soros

Republicans are attacking George Soros, the activist who has spent untold millions promoting democracy around the world, because he is taking a similar stand in the United States by confronting George Bush and his neo-cons. As usual, the republicans are not interested in facts or truths. Innuendo works just fine. I hope these men have been sued for libel by now – and Mr. Soros has the clout to do it. I hope that voters and consumers remember these liars too. Read on:

"I don't know where George Soros gets his money, ... I don't know where - if it comes from overseas or from drug groups or where it comes from." - Dennis Hastert, the speaker of the House – third in line to the presidency (http://mediamatters.org/items/200409020005)

"[George Soros] wants to spend $75 million defeating George W. Bush because Soros wants to legalize heroin." - Newt Gingrich (http://mediamatters.org/items/200408310010)

"[George Soros] is a self-admitted atheist; he was a Jew who figured out a way to survive the Holocaust." - Tony Blankley, editorial page editor of The Washington Times (http://www.thenation.com/doc/20040705/alterman)

>   Mr. Soros is but one example of character assassination. Richard Clarke and Joseph Wilson are other prominent examples. Many good and honest people are targets. If this publication becomes popular, I will be a target too. Not only do these attacks remind one of Nazi and Soviet tactics – a scary thought in and of itself, but there are many people who are intimidated into silence by their threat.
Mission *accomplished.*

The Bush Regime

Fear is a powerful tool. It has been used successfully for thousands of years. Control freaks, repressive regimes and dictatorial despots readily use fear for their aims of mastery. As you have read, fear is a prime motivator of the conservative temperament. Fear is growing in this country, the USA. Fearful and compromised people are everywhere. Some individuals who were parading for the Iraqi conquest are afraid of contradicting the ruling party. Some marchers in this parade are in it for self gain. Others are deluded, convinced by propaganda. Some are merely afraid for their jobs, staying quiet because they have mouths to feed. Intimidation, pressure and fear are standard practices of this regime. As an example, in 2003 members of the Bush crew threatened Richard Foster, a top Health Dept. actuary, if he told the truth about the real (expensive) costs of the Bush Medicare plan to enemies of America, namely Democrats and the public. The nonpartisan GAO concluded the Bush Admin- istration created illegal, covert propaganda--in the form of fake news reports--to promote its industry-backed Medicare bill. Yes,

152

this comes right out of the General Accounting Office! With the false accounting numbers put before the congress, the faulty Medicare plan was passed – a coup for compassionate conservatism, but not for the elderly and poor. Only later, after the vote, were the actual figures known. There is an investigation now under way, but this only stalls the wise course. Why not just go to the source and relieve Bush of duty?

Defense Secretary Paul D. Wolfowitz lectured the US Army in October 2003, according to Washington Post writer Thomas E. Ricks. Evidently independent thinking – even from 3 and 4 star generals – is not welcomed by the controlling regime. Wolfowitz praised General Tommy R. Franks for submitting to the wisdom of Rumsfeld in the Iraqi War plans. Continued Wolfowitz, "Of course, he had an obligation, as all military leaders do, to listen to his civilian leaders, and in that case, it means listening a lot to my boss, Don Rumsfeld, and quite a lot to his boss, the president of the United States."
- If I take him literally, then the top military generals, who have sworn to protect the United States, should be listening to the popularly elected President of the United States, Al Gore.

Republicans are not all alike

Here's the truth: A relatively small group of despots, predominantly republicans, profiteers and war hawks, are brokers of fear to push their agenda and to silence dissent. There are many honest and sincere Republicans who have seen their party commandeered. Will you, members of the GOP, stand up against this wrong? Otherwise, this must be our conclusion: if Clinton was hounded and impeached for sexual indiscretion by the Republicans, and this same moral party was silent about Strom Thurmond's illegitimate interracial daughter (while being politically racist), protecting Trent Lott for his nostalgic hopes for segregation, looks the other way when Schwarzenegger's drug and sex past are revealed, keeping secret those dirty emails sent to young pages by Rep. Mark Foley, and when Rush Limbaugh becomes the poster boy for drug addiction, then Republicans are hypocrites and opportunists, attacking their opponents for political gain, not from some stance of moral superiority. Listen to some of your own conservatives:

Why I will vote for John Kerry for President

By JOHN EISENHOWER, Manchester Union Leader 09-29-2004
http://www.theunionleader.com/articles_showa.html?article=44657

As son of a Republican President, Dwight D. Eisenhower, it is automatically expected by many that I am a Republican. For 50 years, through the election of 2000, I was. With the current administration's decision to invade Iraq unilaterally, however, I changed my voter registration to independent, and barring some utterly unforeseen development, I intend to vote for the Democratic Presidential candidate, Sen. John Kerry.

The fact is that today's "Republican" party is one with which I am totally unfamiliar. To me, the word "Republican" as always been synonymous with the word "responsibility," which has meant limiting our governmental obligations to those we can afford in human and financial terms. Today's whopping budget deficit of some $440 billion does not meet that criterion.

Responsibility used to be observed in foreign affairs. That has meant respect for others. America, though recognized as the leader of the community of nations, has always acted as a part of it, not as a maverick separate from that community and at times insulting towards it. Leadership involves setting a direction and building consensus, not viewing other countries as practically devoid of significance. Recent developments indicate that the current Republican Party leadership has confused confident leadership with hubris and arrogance.

Many Republicans have been jumping ship. Again, it is very suspicious that so many conservatives and Republicans chose not to vote for Bush and Cheney in the last election. Therefore, who did? This is part of the e-voting scandal in the 2004 election. Below is yet another valiant stand from a prominent conservative writing in a classically conservative magazine. May Republicans see the truth in reactionary policies reminiscent of Soviet similarities (don't take my word for it, read on!).

Kerry's the One by Scott McConnell; The American Conservative - Nov 8, 2004 Issue (published October 23, 2004)

Unfortunately, this election does not offer traditional conservatives an easy or natural choice and has left our editors as split as our readership. In an effort to deepen our readers' and our own understanding of the options before us, we've asked several of our editors and contributors to make "the conservative case" for their favored candidate. Their pieces, plus Taki's column closing out this issue, constitute TAC's endorsement. - The American Conservative Editors

There is little in John Kerry's persona or platform that appeals to conservatives. ...Kerry is plainly a conventional liberal ...

But this election is not about John Kerry. ...

It is, instead, an election about the presidency of George W. Bush. ... Because he is the leader of America's conservative party, he has become the Left's perfect foil - its dream candidate. The libertarian writer Lew Rockwell has mischievously noted parallels between Bush and Russia's last tsar, Nicholas II: both gained office as a result of family connections, both initiated an unnecessary war that shattered their countries' budgets. Lenin needed the calamitous reign of Nicholas II to create an opening for the Bolsheviks.

Bush has behaved like a caricature of what a right-wing president is supposed to be, and his continuation in office will discredit any sort of conservatism for generations. The launching of an invasion against a country that posed no threat to the U.S., the doling out of war profits and concessions to politically favored corporations, the financing of the war by ballooning the deficit to be passed

155

on to the nation's children, the ceaseless drive to cut taxes for those outside the middle class and working poor: it is as if Bush sought to resurrect every false 1960s-era left-wing cliché about predatory imperialism and turn it into administration policy. Add to this his nation-breaking immigration proposal - Bush has laid out a mad scheme to import immigrants to fill any job where the wage is so low that an American can't be found to do it - and you have a presidency that combines imperialist Right and open-borders Left in a uniquely noxious cocktail.

During the campaign, few have paid attention to how much the Bush presidency has degraded the image of the United States in the world. ... In Europe and indeed all over the world, he has made the United States despised by people who used to be its friends, by businessmen and the middle classes, by moderate and sensible liberals. ... The poll numbers are shocking. In countries like Norway, Germany, France, and Spain, Bush is liked by about seven percent of the populace. In Egypt, recipient of huge piles of American aid in the past two decades, some 98 percent have an unfavorable view of the United States. It's the same throughout the Middle East.

Bush has accomplished this by giving the U.S. a novel foreign-policy doctrine under which it arrogates to itself the right to invade any country it wants if it feels threatened. It is an American version of the Brezhnev Doctrine, but the latter was at least confined to Eastern Europe. If the analogy seems extreme, what is an appropriate comparison when a country manufactures falsehoods about a foreign government, disseminates them widely, and invades the country on the basis of those falsehoods? It is not an action that any American president has ever taken before. It is not something that "good" countries do. It is the main reason that people all over the world who used to consider the United States a reliable and necessary bulwark of world stability now see us as a menace to their own peace and security.

156

These sentiments mean that as long as Bush is president, we have no real allies in the world, no friends to help us dig out from the Iraq quagmire. More tragically, they mean that if terrorists succeed in striking at the United States in another 9/11-type attack, many in the world will not only think of the American victims but also of the thousands and thousands of Iraqi civilians killed and maimed by American armed forces. The hatred Bush has generated has helped immeasurably those trying to recruit anti-American terrorists - indeed his policies are the gift to terrorism that keeps on giving, as the sons and brothers of slain Iraqis think how they may eventually take their own revenge. Only the seriously deluded could fail to see that a policy so central to America's survival as a free country as getting hold of loose nuclear materials and controlling nuclear proliferation requires the willingness of foreign countries to provide full, 100 percent co-operation. Making yourself into the world's most hated country is not an obvious way to secure that help.

.... Bush's public performances plainly show him to be a man who has never read or thought much about foreign policy.

The record, from published administration memoirs and in-depth reporting, is one of an administration with a very small group of six or eight real decision-makers, who were set on war from the beginning and who took great pains to shut out arguments from professionals in the CIA and State Department and the U.S. armed forces that contradicted their rosy scenarios about easy victory. Much has been written about the neoconservative hand guiding the Bush presidency - and it is peculiar that one who was fired from the National Security Council in the Reagan administration for suspicion of passing classified material to the Israeli embassy and another who has written position papers for an Israeli Likud Party leader have become key players in the making of American foreign policy.

But neoconservatism now encompasses much more than Israel-obsessed intellectuals and policy insiders. The Bush foreign policy also surfs on deep currents within the Christian Right, some of which see unqualified support of Israel as part of a godly plan to bring about Armageddon and the future kingdom of Christ. ...

...

George W. Bush has come to embody a politics that is antithetical to almost any kind of thoughtful conservatism. His international policies have been based on the hopelessly naïve belief that foreign peoples are eager to be liberated by American armies - a notion more grounded in Leon Trotsky's concept of global revolution than any sort of conservative statecraft. ... This election is all about George W. Bush, and those issues are enough to render him unworthy of any conservative support.

The American Conservative declared its voice, and choice, again in the next election two years later. The title of the piece urging conservatives to vote Democratic:

GOP Must Go, November 2006:

It should surprise few readers that we think a vote that is seen—in America and the world at large—as a decisive "No" vote on the Bush presidency is the best outcome. We need not dwell on George W. Bush's failed effort to jam a poorly disguised amnesty for illegal aliens through Congress or the assaults on the Constitution carried out under the pretext of fighting terrorism or his administration's endorsement of torture. Faced on Sept. 11, 2001 with a great challenge, President Bush made little effort to understand who had attacked us and why— thus ignoring the prerequisite for crafting an effective response. He seemingly did not want to find out, and he had staffed his national-security team with people who either did not want to know or were committed to a prefabricated answer.

As a consequence, he rushed America into a war against Iraq, a war we are now losing and cannot win, one that has done far more to strengthen Islamist terrorists than anything they could possibly have done for themselves. Bush's decision to seize Iraq will almost surely leave behind a broken state divided into warring ethnic enclaves, with hundreds of thousands killed and maimed and thousands more thirsting for revenge against the country that crossed the ocean to attack them. The invasion failed at every level: if securing Israel was part of the administration's calculation—as the record suggests it was for several of his top aides—the result is also clear: the strengthening of Iran's hand in the Persian Gulf, with a reach up to Israel's northern border, and the elimination of the most powerful Arab state that might stem Iranian regional hegemony.

The war will continue as long as Bush is in office, for no other reason than the feckless president can't face the embarrassment of admitting defeat. The chain of events is not complete: Bush, having learned little from his mistakes, may yet seek to embroil America in new wars against Iran and Syria.
Meanwhile, America's image in the world, its capacity to persuade others that its interests are common interests, is lower than it has been in memory. All over the world people look at Bush and yearn for this country—which once symbolized hope and justice—to be humbled. The professionals in the Bush administration (and there are some) realize the damage his presidency has done to American prestige and diplomacy. But there is not much they can do.
There may be little Americans can do to atone for this presidency, which will stain our country's reputation for a long time.

>>~o~<<

Glass, china, and reputation
are easily cracked,
and never mended well.

- Benjamin Franklin

A Republican Police State?

This strong fisted, reactionary regime made itself known from the beginning. During Bush's 2001 inaugural, on-duty police officers disguised themselves - one with a black ski mask - and pushed, shoved and pepper-sprayed protesters and bystanders at random. This was published two years later, in the Washington Post, 12 May 2003. In this same article, printed in the Style section(!), protests against Bush policies have included undue police aggression and illegal obstruction of peaceful protesters. The complaint, again and again, is that "the DC police collaborate with the FBI and other federal agencies to suppress dissent. And that the police engage in preemptive mass arrests, spying and brutality." (This was reported in the Style section, along with the TV review of the Three's Company movie! This should have been front page news. The media bias is blatant.) A "state secret" document at the Justice Dept. turned up to be merely a list of protest groups and activities. In the article, the DC police admitted they had infiltrated protest groups. One infiltrator suggested planting bombs on Potomac River bridges! This is just one city; it happens to be the capitol, so that makes it a special case. Are we moving towards unchecked control by a not-so-secret police?

"Without a countervailing grass-roots but national response, we'll continue to move toward a Stalinist type of state, with single-party rule, "purges" of the intelligence and law enforcement communities, increasing limits on civil liberties, and widespread cynicism about politics leading to increasing nonparticipation in the process."

- Thom Hartmann, HOW TO TAKE BACK A STOLEN ELECTION   (Common Dreams, Nov 29, 2004)

~ ~ ~

It is so ironic that the Republican Party, so loud and aggressive about fighting the communist Red Threat around the world, is now known connected to the US Red States and is steadily pushing towards a one party system of absolute control.

Is this eerie or what? It is rather scary, actually. They have become what they denounced. Whether we compare Soviet or Fascist systems (see appendix) to the present regime, what's to be done? And who's to blame for this outrage? Although it's standard procedure for Bush to pass the buck and choose fall guys as easily as he flubs spontaneous talks, we have no choice but to put blame where it belongs, on his own padded lap.

> It used to be that politicians would wait until they were in office before they became crooks. This one came prepackaged. Now he is a trespasser on federal land, a squatter in the Oval Office. If I told you this was Guatemala, you'd believe it in a heartbeat, no matter what your political stripe. But because this coup was wrapped in an American flag, delivered in your choice of red, white, or blue, those responsible believe they're going to get away with it.
> - Michael Moore, *Stupid White Men*

If it is not obvious by now, the Bush regime does not take criticism. I'm not saying they do not take criticism *well*, or that they get defensive when criticized. They do not take it. Period. "You are for us or against us" is not just Bush's message to the world on international terrorism; it is his message to anyone who disagrees with him, his policies, or his cronies. Criticism brings on immediate denial, retaliation, offensive actions, intimidation and threats. At every political and social gathering by Bush and the boys there will be guards, police, secret service agents and weapons. This is part of the show of force: *you Will have respect* is the message. If you say the wrong thing, or wear the wrong T-shirt, you will be firmly or forcefully escorted away from the royalty, and most probably for jail.

Bush is definitely the "war president," as he proudly says. Psychologically, all of these brown-nosed supporters, special agents, and heavily armed police are not-too-subtle signs of the not-too-bright but privileged boy who grows up angry and righteous and is not going to be pushed around anymore! Unfortunately, this reactionary, irrational boy-man has the FBI,

CIA, National Guard, and Marines to "sick" on you. This is scary. What does this mean to you, dear citizen? Well, if prominent people, four star generals, Congressmen, national officials, and leaders of nations are being pushed around and controlled, YOU – WE – are in trouble. Fear and intimidation are some of the ways that this team stays where they are and why there is not a lot of criticism.

"To announce that there must be no criticism of the president, or that we are to stand by the president, right or wrong, is not only unpatriotic and servile, but is morally treasonable to the American public."

Theodore Roosevelt, 1918

>>~0~<<

Let's let Senate Democratic Leader Tom Daschle give you a disturbing perspective in the following Floor Statement titled "Administration Attacking Good People for Telling the Truth," which he gave on March 23, 2004:

I want to talk this morning about a disturbing pattern of conduct by the people around President Bush. They seem to be willing to do anything for political purposes, regardless of the facts and regardless of what's right. I don't have the time this morning to talk in detail about all the incidents that come to mind. Larry Lindsay, for instance, seems to have been fired as the President's Economic Advisor because he spoke honestly about the costs of the Iraq War. General Shinseki seems to have become a target when he spoke honestly about the number of troops that would be needed in Iraq. There are many others, who are less well known, who have also faced consequences for speaking out. U.S. Park Police Chief Teresa Chambers was suspended from her job when she disclosed budget problems that our nation's parks are less safe, and Professor Elizabeth Blackburn was replaced on

162

the Council on Bioethics because of her scientific views on stem-cell research.

Each of these examples deserves examination, but they are not my focus today. Instead, I want to talk briefly about four other incidents that are deeply troubling. When former Treasury Secretary Paul O'Neill stepped forward to criticize the Bush Administration's Iraq policy, he was immediately ridiculed by the people around the President and his credibility was attacked. Even worse, the Administration launched a government investigation to see if Secretary O'Neill improperly disclosed classified documents. He was, of course, exonerated, but the message was clear. If you speak freely, there will be consequences.

Ambassador Joseph Wilson also learned that lesson. Ambassador Wilson, who by all accounts served bravely under President Bush in the early 1990s, felt a responsibility to speak out on President Bush's false State of the Union statement on Niger and uranium. When he did, the people around the President quickly retaliated. Within weeks of debunking the President's claim, Ambassador Wilson's wife was the target of a despicable act. Her identity as a deep-cover CIA agent was revealed to Bob Novak, a syndicated columnist, and was printed in newspapers around the country. That was the first time in our history, I believe, that the identity and safety of a CIA agent was disclosed for purely political purposes. It was an unconscionable and intolerable act.

Around the same time Bush Administration officials were endangering Ambassador Wilson's wife, they appear to have been threatening another federal employee for trying to do his job. In recent weeks Richard Foster, an actuary for the Department of Health and Human Services, has revealed that he was told he would be fired if he told Congress and the American people the real costs of last year's Medicare bill. Mr. Foster, in an e-mail he

163

wrote on June 26 of last year, said the whole episode had been "pretty nightmarish." He wrote: "I'm no longer in grave danger of being fired, but there remains a strong likelihood that I will have to resign in protest of the withholding of important technical information from key policymakers for political purposes."

Think about those words. He would lose his job if he did his job. If he provided the information the Congress and the American people deserved and were entitled to, he would lose his job. When did this become the standard for our government? When did we become a government of intimidation?

And now, in today's newspapers, we see the latest example of how the people around the President react when faced with facts they want to avoid. The White House's former lead counter-terrorism advisor, Richard Clarke, is under fierce attack for questioning the White House's record on combating terrorism. Mr. Clarke has served in four White Houses, beginning with Ronald Reagan's Administration, and earned an impeccable record for his work. Now the White House seeks to destroy his reputation. The people around the President aren't answering his allegations; instead, they are trying to use the same tactics they used with Paul O'Neill. They are trying to ridicule Mr. Clarke and destroy his credibility, and create any diversion possible to focus attention away from his serious allegations.

The purpose of government isn't to make the President look good. It isn't to produce propaganda or misleading information. It is, instead, to do its best for the American people and to be accountable to the American people. The people around the President don't seem to believe that. They have crossed a line-perhaps several lines-that no government ought to cross.

We shouldn't fire or demean people for telling the truth.

We shouldn't reveal the names of law enforcement officials for political gain. And we shouldn't try to destroy people who are out to make our country safer. I think the people around the President have crossed into dangerous territory. We are seeing abuses of power that cannot be tolerated. The President needs to put a stop to it, right now. We need to get to the truth, and the President needs to help us do that.

> Notice that even Tom Daschle is careful not to blame Bush directly. What he shared is informative and important, but how he puts the blame on "those around the president" is another sign that even a prominent Congressman is wary when it comes to crossing Dubya. Things are almost out of control. Almost?

Changing of the guard

There came a time in Rome's history when it ceased being a republic and became an empire. Are we there yet? We have 702 U.S. military installations scattered in 132 countries around the world. We just invaded a country on the other side of the world for its oil. When Bush wanted a "Coalition of the Willing" for that invasion, many small countries jumped at his command. Could it be that now that there is only one superpower, we/it can do as we please? Perhaps the old crew wants a totally new TV series? The Smoke and Guns Forevermore Show? Texas humorist and columnist Molly Ivins reminds us that the Bush team "don't want to govern, they want to rule."

One of the indicators of a "royal" change of state is hereditary succession. This is what Thomas Paine said of it in *Common Sense*, 1776:
"To the evil of monarchy we have added that of hereditary succession, and as the first is a degradation and lessening of ourselves, so the second, claimed as a matter of right, is an insult and an imposition on posterity. For all men being originally equals, no **one** by **birth** could have a right to set up his own family in perpetual preference to all others for ever, and though

himself might deserve **some** decent degree of honours and his contemporaries, yet his descendants might be far too unworthy to inherit them. One of the strongest **natural** proofs of the folly of hereditary right in kings, is, that nature disapproves it, otherwise she would not so frequently turn it into ridicule by giving mankind an **ass for a lion.**"
- emphases his.

Thomas Paine continues:
> But it is not so much the absurdity as the evil of hereditary succession which concerns mankind. Did it ensure a race of good and wise men it would have the seal of divine authority, but as it opens a door to the foolish, the wicked, and the improper, it hath in it the nature of oppression. Men who look upon themselves born to reign, and others to obey, soon grow insolent; selected from the rest of mankind their minds are early poisoned by importance; and the world they act in differs so materially from the world at large, that they have but little opportunity of knowing its true interests, and when they succeed to the government are frequently the most ignorant and unfit of any throughout the dominions.
> ... Of more worth is one honest man to society, and in the sight of God, than all the crowned ruffians that ever lived.

Hmm. Monarchy and succession. It is an old story. Many people like it today. No, maybe we are more closer to the ancient Roman first families: Those that rule, and jockey for position, amongst a finite group of families. Just in case it is not clear that we are being led by a privileged son of a powerful family who may not be as clever as his father would have liked, let me offer you a few gems from the hundreds of "Bushisms" collected from the public-speak of the leader of the free world:

> "I glance at the headlines just to kind of get a flavor for what's moving. I rarely read the stories, and get briefed by people who are probably read the news themselves."
> – Washington, D.C., Sept. 21, 2003

166

"One of the common denominators I have found is that expectations rise above that which is expected."
– Los Angeles; September 27, 2000

"Justice was being delivered to a man who defied that gift from the Almighty to the people of Iraq."
— Washington, D.C., Dec. 15, 2003

"Our enemies are innovative and resourceful, and so are we. They never stop thinking about new ways to harm our country and our people, and neither do we."
– Aug 5, 2004, at a signing ceremony for a $417 billion military spending bill.

"Actually, I - this may sound a little West Texan to you, but I like it. When I'm talking about - when I'm talking about myself, and when he's talking about myself, all of us are talking about me."
– Hardball; May 31, 2000

"I suspect that had my dad not been president, he'd be asking the same questions: How'd your meeting go with so-and-so?... How did you feel when you stood up in front of the people for the State of the Union Address - state of the budget address, whatever you call it."
 – Interview with the Washington Post; March 9, 2001

"As you know, these are open forums, you're able to come and listen to what I have to say."
— Washington, D.C., Oct. 28, 2003

"That's just the nature of democracy. Sometimes pure politics enters into the rhetoric."
– Crawford, Texas, Aug. 8, 2003

"Security is the essential roadblock to achieving the road map to peace."
 — Washington, D.C., July 25, 2003

"The ambassador and the general were briefing me on the - the vast majority of Iraqis want to live in a peaceful, free world. And we will find these people and we will bring them to justice." — Washington, D.C., Oct. 27, 2003

"I think if you know what you believe, it makes it a lot easier to answer questions. I can't answer your question." – In response to a question about whether he wished he could take back any of his answers in the first debate; Reynoldsburg, Ohio October 4, 2000

"This foreign policy stuff is a little frustrating." – As quoted by the New York Daily News; April 23, 2002

One could laugh, or cry. These quotes actually remind me of Dan Quayle, Bush Senior's VP; in fact, I have wondered if George Bush senior selected Quayle out of some unconscious fatherly feeling for his own son. It bewilders the mind. As for Dubya, if this were a regular guy out in a Texas field, we could smile more. Since, however, he is in charge of weapons of mass destruction – and not afraid to use them, that is another matter. He also has a poor memory – or does he just "spin" yarns all the time to make himself look good? On September 20th, 2001, Bush explained to the American public–with a straight face–that terrorists hate democratically elected leaders. He obviously didn't have anything to worry about. Wait, however. Was this a good sounding phrase for a speech, a flaw not to see the irony, or a deliberate statement/ hypnotic suggestion to reinforce his own legitimacy used during an emotional time -- just 9 days after the attacks? (This can be found at www.whitehouse.gov, where transcripts of various speeches and positions are published.) Would George be that clever? Karl Rove or Dick Cheney would.

Bottom line: Bush could not have done anything innovative, professional nor political without his family connections and people who prop him up. Outside of the obvious "who IS in charge?" and "why use Bush as a frontman anyway?" we are left with a serious national, ethical and leadership vacuum. Even if he had been fairly elected, he would be a disaster.

168

**"If ever time should come when vain and aspiring men
shall possess the highest seats in government, our country will
stand in need of its experienced patriots to prevent its ruin."**
-- Samuel Adams, US "Founding Father" & Patriot

~ ~ ~

Sister Joan Chittister, a Benedictine sister, has asked some
profound questions in her thought-provoking piece titled
"Is There Anything Left That Matters?" She has this to say
concerning Bush, the entitled king: "What may count most,
however, is that we may well be the ones Proverbs warns when it
reminds us: 'Kings take pleasure in honest lips; they value the
one who speaks the truth.' The point is clear: If the people speak
and the king doesn't listen, there is something wrong with the
king. If the king acts precipitously and the people say nothing,
something is wrong with the *people*."

Yes Ma'am. And We are the People. The Bush regime
can only remain in power when others are fooled into the deceit,
or cowed into silence.

Howard Zinn, a voice of conscience and truth for decades, also
asks us to do the right thing. In late February, 2003, he wrote:
There is a basic weakness in governments, however
massive their armies, however wealthy they are, however
they control the information given to the public, because
their power depends on the obedience of citizens, of
soldiers, of civil servants, of journalists and writers and
teachers and artists. When these people begin to suspect
that they have been deceived, and withdraw their support,
the government loses its legitimacy, and its power.

We have seen this happen in recent decades, all around the
globe. Leaders who were apparently all-powerful,
surrounded by their generals, suddenly faced the anger of
an aroused people, the hundreds of thousands in the streets
and the reluctance of the soldiers to fire, and those leaders
soon rushed to the airport, carrying their suitcases of
money with them.

The process of undermining the legitimacy of this government has begun. There has been a worm eating at the innards of its complacency all along -- the knowledge of the American public, buried, but in a very shallow grave, easy to disinter, that this government came to power by a political coup, not by popular will.

~ ~ ~

Now that this present regime has taken control, however, it has forced its will across the board, and across the world. The Peace Action Education Fund gives a few relevant points to contemplate concerning the Bush crew and world view: "During its tenure, the administration has blocked, or withdrawn from, many important international agreements. So far the administration has withdrawn from the Anti-Ballistic Missile Treaty; blocked enforcement of the Biological Weapons Convention; scoffed at the International Criminal Court; abandoned the Kyoto Protocol on global warming; and walked out of the Durban Conference on Racism."
(www.peace-action.org)

~ ~ ~

Not only do these various stances *decrease* national security, but shatters sixty years of concerted efforts at international cooperation, weapons controls, environmental regulations and world peace. Alarms really started sounding when a new belligerent phase in American policy was created – preemptive strikes. And this absurd and dangerous policy wouldn't have occurred had we not been attacked on September 11th, 2001, a fateful event that actually saved Bush's precarious position and squelched all the talk of his fraudulent claim on the White House. During the national crisis it would have been unpatriotic to divert our national attention from the real enemy, those evil terrorists abroad – not the cabal who took over our government. Thus, once again, lord Bush was saved by providence. But at what a cost. One would think he would have been more forthcoming and open about the terrible attack and how he was divinely positioned to help his people, but there is a

170

persistent reluctance to go into the attack details and to share the results with the American public.

... something is off here.

9/11

Something stinks at the bomb site.

Q: What is Bush hiding about 9-11? The National Commission on Terrorist Attacks in the United States was formed after the terrible attacks. *pResident* Bush opposed the commission's creation, but was forced to accept it later, due to pressure. To control the Commission, Bush then appointed Henry Kissinger to chair the panel. *Mr. Machiavelli himself?* After a public outcry, Kissinger resigned. In 2002, VP Dick Cheney reportedly asked congressional leaders to limit the investigation. They refused. The White House then decided to underfund the panel, offering only $3 million. Once again, they were forced to add more funds, bringing the total to $12 million. This should be compared to the tragic space shuttle Columbia's investigation budget of $50 million – and the 2nd inaugural festivities in January 2005 – $40 million. Do we have a pattern here? The Commission has been frustrated by lack of funding, non-cooperation, stonewalling and deception. There is obviously some concern by the Bush regime of what will be found in the rubble. We do know that the FBI and the CIA are looking very incompetent, which is "darn good" intelligence to Dubya. I believe it is deeper than this. I smell smoke.

By August of 2003, the government had censored many pages of the official report, keeping certain Saudi ties and other possible embarrassing facts from the public. Michael Moore has tracked the exodus of many members of the bin Laden family immediately after the 9-11 attacks and has asked some pertinent and embarrassing questions, so I don't need to go over them here. His basic challenge remains unanswered, however; specifically, why the secret military evacuation and protection of this family right after the attacks? In any other police investigation, such a coordinated maneuver to covertly hide possible suspects and witnesses would be hindering justice at the very least. It is quite obvious that the Bush family, James Baker, and many other plutocrats are protecting the Saudis; not because Saudi Arabia is democratic, for it is not, but because of money, oil ... and religion? The Saudis have not only heavily invested in the U.S. stock market, but also with key members of the Bush regime and their friends and family. The Seattle Times revealed that top Bush officials accepted $127,600 in jewelry and other presents from the Saudi royal family in 2003, including diamond-and-sapphire jewelry valued at $95,500 for First Lady Laura Bush. OK, it must be the money, for it can't be Religion! Although fundamentalist Christians know for a certain that Islam is *of the devil*, even the pugnacious Bush would not politically take on the land that holds two sacred Muslim cities – Mecca and Medina – for that would essentially be declaring war on all Muslims ... and that would be foolhardy indeed.

- See the articles posted on Common Dreams - www.commondreams.org: "US Ties to Saudi Elite May be Hurting War on Terrorism" and "Bush Advisors Cashed in on Saudi Gravy Train," by Jonathan Wells, Jack Meyers, and Maggie Mulvhill.;
... and see what Michael Moore reveals in his *Hey Dude, Where's My Country?*

     Yes, but Michael Moore is not to be trusted.

Well, how about a former President?

The heartfelt sympathy and friendship offered to America after the 9/11 attacks, even from formerly antagonistic regimes, has been largely dissipated; increasingly unilateral and domineering policies have brought international trust in our country to its lowest level in memory.
Jimmy Carter, Jan 2003

~ ~ ~

Daily Brief with Ray McGovern:
Bush, Tenet, Iraq, Conservatives, Vietnam and Sept. 11 through the eyes of a 27-year CIA analyst
by Nathan Callahan, February 20 - 26, 2004

When I ask Ray McGovern if the findings of President Bush's commission on intelligence failures in Iraq will give us answers—even if it doesn't get them to us until well after the November election—he has a one-word answer: "No."

McGovern is a measured man with a steady voice. For 27 years—from JFK to George H.W. Bush—he worked as a CIA analyst, chairing National Intelligence Estimates and preparing the president's Daily Brief. He's now co-director of Servant Leadership School in Washington, D.C., an inner-city school that provides training and other support for the poor.

...

"One would have thought that the raison d'être for the Central Intelligence Agency was to prevent another Pearl Harbor," McGovern says. "One would have thought that the person most responsible for this would have been cashiered on Sept. 12. Not so. So the question is: Why not so?"

"First of all, George Tenet warned the president of the United States about the threat of terrorism almost ad nauseam during the entire spring and summer of 2001. In the final analysis, the president had been warned often enough and long enough. He should have done something about it."

"Why didn't he?" I wonder.

"Because Bush didn't know what to do," McGovern says. "And Condoleezza Rice, his adviser on such things, didn't know a thing about terrorism. By her own admission, she hadn't opened the file that [Clinton National Security Advisor] Sandy Berger left behind that said, 'Read This File First.' She knew a lot about the Soviet Union and Eastern Europe but nothing about terrorism. The charitable explanation for why nothing was done is gross ineptitude and gross malfeasance."

"What about Tenet?"
"George Tenet no doubt has a little computer disc with the 27 or so warnings that he gave the president starting in spring and going right up until September 2001," says McGovern. "The president and his advisers in the White House, knowing this, didn't dismiss Tenet after Sept. 11 because it was too much of a risk. Were they to have dismissed Tenet on Sept. 12, they could not have been sure that he wouldn't have said, 'Wait a second. Let me print off some of these warnings. Let me show you what I told the president in the President's Daily Brief on Aug. 6, 2001.' So that's reason No. 1.
"Reason No. 2 is that Tenet is simply too useful of a guy to have around," McGovern continues. "He does what he's told. If he's told to do an estimate and told to make sure the conclusions come out the same as a Dick Cheney speech from the month before, he'll do it."

McGovern is referring to the National Intelligence Estimate that Tenet cranked out after Cheney's August 2002 WMD pep rally. It was a cart-before-the-horse exercise in policy-making: Cheney makes unsubstantiated claims in public. The intelligence agency fashions a report to cover his backside. According to an article penned by McGovern for TomPaine.com, "The conclusions of that estimate have now been proven—pure and simple—wrong."
The real reasons for the Iraq War, he says, are to be found online at the neo-conservative website the Project for the New American Century (newamericancentury.org). "And I would simply add, not as an afterthought but as a core part of this whole calculus, that this war was fought as much for Israeli strategic objectives as it was for American strategic objectives. As a matter of fact, the people running our policy toward Iraq have great difficulty distinguishing between the two."

174

As McGovern is speaking, I notice a slight rise in the pitch of his voice—an almost imperceptible quarter-step jump.

"If I'm sounding a little angry here," he says, "well, there's no word to describe it." There's a silence. "Outrage is just too pale a word to describe how we intelligence officials feel about George Tenet being so willing to prostitute our intelligence product, to cook it up to the recipe of high policy. That is the unpardonable sin of intelligence, and he's still doing it."

.... "I saw it in Vietnam," he says. "And usually it was the president himself or the White House that was responsible in the final analysis. Think Gulf of Tonkin."

On Aug. 5, 1964, intelligence officials told the media that North Vietnamese gunboats had attacked U.S. Navy destroyers in the Gulf of Tonkin. It was pure fiction, but it became Lyndon Johnson's rationale for escalating the U.S.'s involvement in Vietnam and cleared the way for a decade of war.

"We knew that there was no incident that night," McGovern says. "McGeorge Bundy [Johnson's National Security Advisor] knew that there was no incident that night. And yet LBJ, with his towering presence, his total power—corrupting totally—leaned over and said, 'McGeorge, are you going up to the Hill to sell this resolution?' Bundy [later] admitted on McNeil-Lehrer Newshour, one painful show: 'So I went. I went up, and I lied to Congress.'"

"So it's happened before," McGovern continues. "What's different this time is that we have a situation where, over a two-year period, an incredible, cleverly orchestrated campaign was waged to exploit the trauma of the American people, the trauma of Sept. 11, and to exploit it in such a way as to achieve the aims of the . . ."

McGovern stops to find the right word. "I don't call them neo-conservatives," he says, "because I'm conservative. I call them neo-fascists because that's what they are. And what these neo-fascists did was see Sept. 11 as a golden opportunity."

Neo-fascists? I ask McGovern if he's using Mussolini's definition of fascism. As Il Duce said, "Fascism should rightly be called corporatism, as it is the merger of corporate and government power." Think Halliburton, USA.

McGovern agrees but adds more. "I'm also talking about the measures that were taken in Nazi Germany after the fire that burned down the Reichstag, Germany's parliament building, in 1933. It was that fire that allowed Hitler to institute his own legislation."

McGovern draws a parallel between Sept. 11 and the Reichstag fire. After claiming that communists committed arson, Hitler used the incident to declare a state of emergency and suspend some of the constitutionally protected personal freedoms of German citizens. These rights included freedom of speech and assembly. "Very much like post-Sept. 11 legislation instituted here in this country to curtail civil liberties," McGovern says, "to make people feel that if they speak out against what is happening, they are unpatriotic."

...

How does the Arab world see us?

"It's really remarkable," McGovern says. "People like Donald Rumsfeld are intelligent, but it's embarrassing how they scratch their heads, and they say, 'I don't know what makes a suicide bomber. I don't know what makes people do that.'

"Well, if he watched Al Jazeera for a couple of nights, if he watched Israeli bulldozers knocking down Palestinians homes and he saw Israelis shooting up Palestinians in the occupied territories, then maybe he would get some sense as to why people of Palestinian or Arab or Islamic heritage — why they might look askance at the one country that they know makes this all possible. That's the United States of America."

When the Commission to study the 9-11 disaster reported their findings in the middle of June 2004, I thought this could be the smoking gun. The Commission declared that **there was no connection between the September 11th attacks and Iraq.** Bush and Cheney's reply? - "There was too!" This was either B Team talk or an instinctive reaction from their elementary school days!

> There were guns and smoke everywhere, actually. This really became evident when the following came out: "Bush Retains Attorney, Questioned in Oval Office" http://www.truthout.org/docs_04/062504A.shtml

~ ~ ~

It seemed ludicrous when Bush demanded from that same Commission that his testimony would not be recorded and that "Brains" Cheney go along with him for the talk. As usual, he got what he wanted. So far, he has escaped criminal charges for the 2000 coup, 9-11 incompetence, financial mismanagement, fraud and corruption, and now Iraqi war crimes. He has been lucky.... or is something else at play?

~ ~ ~

Mark Dunlea, writing for the Green Pages (Autumn 2004) had a list of questions the commission failed to reveal. But that was the plan, he stated in his piece titled "9/11 report fulfills political mission: Omissions save face for Bush." Mr. Dunlea's article deserves a read.

~ ~ ~

The bottom line on the 9/11 Commission is that when Bush and crew couldn't stop it or underfund it or minimize it, then they stacked it with friends who toned down the implications and honored the rights of executive privilege. It wasn't a coverup, it was plastic surgery. TruthOut.org also published an article on the findings and helped us read between the lines: "9/11 Report Attacks Patriot Act, Government Secrecy" http://www.truthout.org/docs_04/072304X.shtml

>>~o~<<

"How dare you, Mr. President, after taking cynical advantage of the unanimity and love, and transmuting it into fraudulent war and needless death, after monstrously transforming it into fear and suspicion and turning that fear into the campaign slogan of three elections? How dare you - or those around you - ever 'spin' 9/11? Just as the terrorists have succeeded - are still succeeding - as long as there is no memorial and no construction here at Ground Zero. So, too, have they succeeded, and are still succeeding as long as this government uses 9/11 as a wedge to pit Americans against Americans."

- Keith Olbermann: This Hole in the Ground - www.truthout.com

Blowback

The American people up to this point have been able to have it both ways. They've been able to take cover behind the various lies the Bush regime (and their enablers in Congress on both sides of the aisle) have perpetrated about why we invaded Iraq. They can now jump on the get-out-of-Iraq bandwagon for the wrong reason -- we aren't winning, and the Iraqi people are incapable of governing themselves. The real truth -- vividly exposed in Iraq but just as true during the Clinton years where corporate globalization continued to devour local autonomy throughout the world -- is that our economy as it exists today has become frighteningly dependent on death and destruction.

If you haven't done so already, go rent the DVD Why We Fight http://www.sonyclassics.com/whywefight/and invite a bunch of friends over to watch it with you. There you will see vividly the elephant (and its jackass fellow travelers) in the living room. Our entire house of cards economy is based on beating plowshares into swords, all for the benefit of a few. It's completely consistent and congruent that Vice President Cheney invited only the leaders of the oil industry into his conference to discuss energy policy nearly six years ago, and the ostensible conversation was how to divvy up the oil fields [http://www.judicialwatch.org/iraqi-oil-maps.shtml] of Iraq. For a more updated take on how the oil industry has already achieved its objectives, please see this article by Chris Floyd. - http://www.truthout.org/docs_2006/printer_010807A.shtml

The Self-Impeaching President by Steve Bhaerman, January 15, 2007
http://www.wakeuplaughing.com/news.html

~ ~ ~

The CIA has a term for the unexpected, negative reaction to US foreign policy: it is called "blowback." 9-11 was a blowback by a small group of Islamic fundamentalists who even gave a list of their grievances about our foreign policy. The US has a terrible history of international intervention, staging coups, and enforcing economic policies at gunpoint. Remember Ronald Reagan's "freedom fighters" in Central America? They turned out to be bullies and butchers who terrorized their own people... trained in the USA or in their own countries by our "experts." Add to America's past: nerve gas, the slave trade, giving smallpox-infected blankets to the native Americans. It goes back to the beginning: the British were shocked that an American colonist scalped a British soldier within the first months of the Revolutionary War. We have a violent history. Iraq is not our first unjust war; the difference, of course, is that we can do something about this one.

Think about this: The US government brokers weapons deals to many countries that our soldiers then have had to face, including Somalia, Haiti, Panama, Lebanon, the former Yugoslavia, Afghanistan and now Iraq. This may create a new category to our military dead and dying in these foreign lands, right next to "friendly fire."

The forces predicted in this complex snarl not only shattered national security on September 11, 2001, but put

America in the unusual position of the victim, with the corresponding outpouring of sympathy and compassion internationally. My hope is that the US shall become more reflective and form a foreign policy that truly provides justice for all. We will not achieve that with Bush and company, however. In the Washington Post (March 30, 2004), "A Dollop of Deeper American Values," Joseph S. Nye Jr. from Harvard details poor spending on public diplomacy. Apparently "the combined cost of State Department's public diplomacy programs and all international broadcasting in 2002 was just over a billion dollars - about the same amount spent by France and GB, countries one fifth of the size of the US." The author notes that it is 400 times less than what is spent on hard power, the military stuff, such as on the Bush regime's obsession with that super-costly Missile Defense Program. I doubt if the Bush crew are circumspect (or humble) enough to admit failings in foreign policy (Even if they were legitimately elected to decide such things.). The regime has shown its reactions to problems in general: shoot and ask questions later. Or is that shoot, bluff and cover-up? This is the exact recipe for blowback.

Staying the Course Until What? by Jane Smiley - 10.30.2006
www.huffingtonpost.com/jane-smiley/

...

Why, I ask myself, do I bang on about this? What does it matter if hundreds of thousands of people have died so that the oil companies can have the contracts they like? Isn't that the capitalist way? Isn't Capitalism the best of all economic systems in the best of all possible worlds? Doesn't the Iraq War demonstrate everything we need to know about Capitalism? Aren't we lucky to have a CEO president? Aren't we lucky to have two of them, in fact? And don't they constantly tell us how American they are, how patriotic, how Christian? Aren't we lucky that this means that to be American and Christian is to be a brutal, arrogant, narcissistic, money-mad, power-mad, ill-mannered, lying, cheating, war-crime perpetrating, Jesus-spouting, short-sighted boor? What is wrong with me that I can't accept that my job as a citizen is to nod happily while my tax dollars are being funnelled to big business, to hugely rich people, to those not in need? Here's some more numbers for you. According to Holland, Big Oil stands to profit to the tune of 194 billion dollars. That would seem like a lot until you realize that some experts put the cost of the Iraq war for American taxpayers at $2,000,000,000,000 (that's trillion). I see. For every extra dollar that the oil companies earn, we the taxpayers will have invested ten. Sounds like a bargain.

... We will not know how to get out of Iraq until we come clean about why we are there and what it means about who we are.
And of course, the ultimate irony is that our overuse of oil is destroying us. Americans use more oil more wastefully than anyone else on Earth. A car is simply a device for siphoning carbon out of the ground and into the atmosphere. Now that we know that, how stupid are we to keep doing it? To fight and kill in order to retain the right to do it? Bush maintains that "they envy our freedom", but I don't think so. I think it is more likely that they are appalled at our selfish license, our criminal indifference to others, and our apparently sadistic wish to have our way in all things. But so what? Stay the course!

~ ~ ~

No, there will be no circumspection under Bush, only more terrorism. The weird and convoluted thing about this is that then Bush and gang will say "See! Terrorists! We must increase our noble policy of fighting these evildoers!" See how they create a vicious cycle?

I believe the 9-11 attack not only warrants the investigation and prosecution of the hijackers and other terrorists, but also an investigation of those Americans in business and the military (and its covert brethren) creating ill will abroad, and then to stop those international activities that are now putting American citizens at risk. Think about it: the inquiry delving into the killings at Waco and Ruby Ridge in the 1990s found the FBI culpable of various mistakes in judgment and procedure. Isn't it fair to ask the same standard for international activities?

It is an old adage that before we start pointing elsewhere, we first need to look closer to home.

> Here are some enlightening, and sobering, books: *Killing Hope: US Military and CIA Interventions Since World War II* by William Blum. And *Perpetual War for Perpetual Peace: How We Got To Be So Hated* by Gore Vidal.

"Mr. Bush, you are accomplishing in part what Osama Bin Laden and others seek-a fearful American populace, easily manipulated, and willing to throw away any measure of restraint, any loyalty to our own ideals and freedoms, for the comforting illusion of safety."

- Keith Olbermann: "Have You No Sense of Decency, Sir?" www.truthout.com

It is obvious to people of common sense that the Bush regime will carry out the big club/ hidden stiletto diplomacy that created 9-11 in the first place. Bush and crew have now precipitated more blowback with their foolhardy and arrogant policy of preemptive strikes. This is a terrible scheme that truly endangers the world. Post Bush/Iraq, any country with a grudge or an agenda can attack another country, citing a potential danger. The USA has stamped its approval on that policy. We will all pay for that one.

>>~o~<<

Thus, it is imperative, for reasons of national security and international law, that the Bush regime be removed from office. By ridding ourselves of the coup, we are making, simultaneously, a statement to the world that Americans ultimately strive for justice and can achieve it at home and abroad. If we fail in this noble stance, we will continue to be seen as hypocrites and vulnerable to terrorists. Shall we begin to do the right thing, instead of the thing for the right?

Crimes

How shall we approach all of this regime's crimes? Let me count the ways....
Actually, many people are counting. Websites and newspaper columns are dedicated to the huge task. Backing up this article are hundreds of pages of information, research, and evidence. They are found on the web at ...
http://www.culturefix.org/common_sense_revisited_treason/evidence
There is an excellent reading list of books and revealing documentaries at the end of this work. Many illuminating, and damaging, articles and exposés are found on the TruthOut website: www.truthout.org

After the coup itself (no small matter), the next major crime is the fabrication and hidden agendas leading the United States of America into war with Iraq. This travesty is bound with the terrible policy of attacking potential enemies first, dismissing or bullying the United Nations and international allies, and deceiving and coercing the American public, as well as many other nations, into the invasion and occupation. We are talking war crimes; especially if we include the Iraqi prison scandals, the bombing of innocent women and children ("mistakes happen" they might say, but get this – we shouldn't be there making the mistakes in the first place!), and our very own prison camp on Cuba... that is a scandal all by itself. Now in the news are stories of our soldiers raping, killing and covering-up their crimes. As for those in charge, did I mention money, corruption and theft?

The pervasiveness of the mind-set
  The perverseness of the set-up

In the following pages I will relate many of the deceits, back-room schemes, little known incidents and damaging policies by this usurping cabal. One could become overwhelmed by all of the travail of this aggressive and controlling government, but I wish to list these transgressions because there is a clear pattern of greed, selfishness, callousness, and cronyism. I hope it will be clear that if this group of bully-boys could pull all of these other

outrageous "stunts," then it is very conceivable that they would initiate the coup in 2000. Patterns and imperiousness. It is unbelievable what they have done, what they are doing, and what they propose. It is just as amazing how they have gotten away with it all. If you feel that there is too much information presented, dear citizen, it is not exhaustive but only highlights gathered to make absolutely clear who and what we are dealing with; our whole system is in jeopardy.
The fire alarms are sounding.

Before we take a look at the crime called the Iraqi War, there is a little discussed first step just before the yelling began. Who remembers the matter of corporate scandals that were almost constantly in the papers prior to the first anniversary of 9-11? As far as I can see, the timing of the Iraqi propaganda campaign was not due to "suddenly" realizing that Iraq was an evil in the world. Yes, Iraq was next–and had been planned years before Bush came to office–but it was becoming uncomfortable in the White House for *other* reasons, and a Big diversion needed to happen. ...

Almost investigating those corporate scandals
By the spring of 2002, there were various corporate scandals making headlines. While the CEOs were getting huge benefit packages, thousands of employees were losing their retirements as well as their jobs. Several of these corporate scandals were inching ever closer to the White House, including the now familiar Halliburton company, led by Dick Cheney before he participated in the hostile takeover of the US Government. One of the most outrageous connections was with the now infamous Enron, a corrupt energy company head-quartered in Texas that manufactured black-outs in California for profit (that led to the pre-emptive attack on Gov. Davis, who was recalled and replaced by republican Arnold Schwarzenegger. Clever.). Just to bring back some of the items of the day, here are some points collected by Public Citizen (www.citizen.org):

- Enron Chairman Ken Lay, a longtime personal friend of George W. Bush, had his company give the biggest

184

campaign contribution, and then helped influence the national energy policy in Enron's favor. Dick Cheney was head of the energy task force. The notes of that important policy formation are still being kept from the public. This is big.

- Enron gave $61,000 to John Ashcroft's failed 2000 Senate campaign. [Do you suppose that this Attorney General would now bite the hand that fed him? Don't look for any serious investigations coming from his desk. - SP]

- Secretary of the Army Thomas White, a 10 year Enron executive who was involved in market manipulations and price gouging, sold off $12 million in company stock after Bush appointed him. [Was this due to avoiding conflict of interest, or did he know the state of his company?]

- U.S. Senator Phil Gramm of Texas pushed through legislation shielding Enron from government scrutiny, and later decided not to seek re-election in 2002. His wife, Commodity Futures Trading Commission chairwoman Wendy Gramm, pushed through a measure exempting Enron from federal oversight. After she resigned from that commission, she joined Enron's board of directors on the audit committee.

- Other consultants and aids to Bush who had strong ties to Enron: Marc Racicot, lobbyist, Lawrence B. Lindsey, advisor, Robert Zoellick, advisor, Spencer Abraham, Secretary of Energy, Patrick H. Wood III, chair of the Federal Energy Regulatory Commission, Alberto Gonzalez, White House counsel, Don Evans, Secretary of Commerce, Ralph Reed, GOP strategist and Enron consultant and former head of the Christian Coalition.

>>~o~<<

In 2006 Ken Lay was found guilty of many corporate crimes and cover-ups. Throughout, he used the classic defense of the neo-cons, which is offensive. "Ridiculous! Outrageous charges!" Talk about justice for all, when Ken Lay died of a heart attack in the summer of 2006, he was out enjoying a vacation in Colorado. When you have some time, take a look at

TruthOut.org, which publishes almost daily exposés of the Bush travesty. They published in June of 2004 a revealing piece titled **Enron Traders Caught on Tape: "Burn, baby, burn"** http://www.truthout.org/docs_04/060304A.shtml

In the meantime, political activist, author and true American William Rivers Pitt recognized the ruse early. "Greetings from Boston, Mr. Bush," (t r u t h o u t, 1 October, 2002):

> A trillion dollar tax cut was fobbed off on the American people as a boon to the common man, looting a budget surplus that turned out to be made up of smoke and mirrors - the surplus numbers had been based to a great degree on expected tax revenues from profitable super-companies like Enron and WorldCom. When their false profit reports came to light, the sudden realization that Bush tax cut had bitten through a negligible surplus and into the guts of the budget sent a shockwave through the economy.

> ... Humming underneath it all was the tension of dissolution. The Enron collapse had sabered the stock market through the guts, and there was blood on the trading floor every single day. A litany of catastrophe marched across the headlines: WorldCom, Dick Cheney's Halliburton, the shredders of Enron documents at Arthur Andersen, Global Crossing and a mob of other companies were forced to 'readjust' their profit reports and accept prosecution. Bush's umbilical connection to Enron became standard fare for a time, and journalists were even beginning to tickle the sordid details of his failed energy company, Harken Oil. It seems Mr. Bush played as fast and loose with the Harken numbers as his pal, Kenny-Boy.
>
> ...
>
> In August of 2002, Mr. Bush took a month off from his busy schedule - which included some 42% of his total time in office on vacation - to take a vacation at his ranch in Crawford, Texas. The following September, Bush

returned to work and prepared to unilaterally destroy the nation of Iraq, without consent from Congress or the international community. It seems America and the world had spent the month of August blithely unaware that the sword of Damocles was suspended above them. Saddam Hussein was preparing to unleash death and destruction upon the United States and the world, and Bush was going to put an end to that.

~ ~ ~

Assertive journalists, threats of investigations, and stories making these connections and others were growing by the summer of 2002. Bush, who was still not totally out of the clear for the 2000 election, needed some action *elsewhere*. Bombing Afghanistan (and not finding Osama bin Laden) was not helping his PR efforts. What happened next? Bush and crew then declared the War on Iraq their Number One priority near the first anniversary of 9-11 in 2002. The sympathy vote would be theirs, and it worked. The corporate scandals vanished into the news fog. Another successful preemptive strike in the form of a sleight of hand distraction.

And the American public fell for it.

Again.

"Our tone should be crazed. The nation's freedoms are under assault by an administration whose policies can do us as much damage as al Qaida; the nation's marketplace of ideas is being poisoned by a propaganda company so blatant that Tokyo Rose would've quit. Bill Clinton did what almost none of us have done in five years. He has spoken the truth about 9/11, and the current presidential administration."
Keith Olbermann: A Textbook Definition of Cowardice, 2006 - www.truthout.com

Iraq

"Why, of course the people don't want war....
But after all, it is the leaders of the country who
determine the policy, and it is always a simple
matter to drag the people along, whether it is a
democracy, or a fascist dictatorship, or a
parliament, or a communist dictatorship.... Voice
or no voice, the people can always be brought to
the bidding of the leaders. That is easy. All you
have to do is to tell them they are being attacked,
and denounce the pacifists for lack of patriotism
and exposing the country to danger."
 - Hermann Goering, Nazi leader, at the
Nuremberg Trials after World War II

Reasons for attacking Iraq:
- to defend the US from an imminent attack
- to eliminate weapons of mass destruction there
- to find and destroy chemical weapons
- to enforce various UN sanctions
- to punish Iraq for 9-11
(added later) - to liberate Iraq from the dictator Saddam Hussein

Please note the hypnotic/suggestible emotional and
imaginative words used here by THE authority figure in US
politics:

"The Iraqi dictator must not be permitted to threaten
America and the world with horrible poisons and diseases
and gases and atomic weapons."
George Bush, Oct. 7, 2002, in a speech in Cincinnati

*People never lie so much as before an election, during a
war, or after a hunt.*
 - Otto von Bismarck

>>~o~<<

Here is another article published about the ugly truth. I won't print it here, so take a look. Within months - and no horrible poisons and atomic weapons - the whole pretense was known:
10 APPALLING LIES WE WERE TOLD ABOUT IRAQ
by Christopher Scheer, AlterNet June 27, 2003
http://www.alternet.org/story.html?StoryID=16274

FYI: Keeping track of the dead and wounded in Iraq:
http://antiwar.com/casualties/

~ ~ ~

Years later, it is obvious to people of common sense that the conquest of Iraq wasn't about weapons of mass destruction, nor liberating its people altruistically. It was about oil, propping up the dollar, territory, profits, control, muzzling OPEC, defending Israel, and diverting everyone concerned from the corporate scandals that were coming too close to the White House by the summer of 2002. Don't take my word for all of this – high-profile officials, journalists, and activists have done their homework. Many world leaders and statesmen stood up to denounce the fraud.

~ ~ ~

"There was no reason for us to become involved in Iraq recently. That was a war based on lies and misinterpretations from London and from Washington, claiming falsely that Saddam Hussein was responsible for [the] 9/11 attacks, claiming falsely that Iraq had weapons of mass destruction. And I think that President Bush and Prime Minister Blair probably knew that many of the allegations were based on uncertain intelligence ... a decision was made to go to war."
- Jimmy Carter, March 2004

>>~o~<<

Arguments for war are paper thin and fall apart at the first touch. Weapons of mass destruction? Iraq may develop one nuclear bomb (though the UN inspectors find no sign of development) - but Israel has 200 nuclear weapons and the US has 20,000 and six other countries have undisclosed numbers. Saddam Hussein a tyrant? Undoubtedly, like many others in the world? A threat to world peace? Then how come the rest of the world, much closer to Iraq, does not want war? Defending ourselves? The most incredible statement of all. Fighting terrorism? No connection found between Sept. 11 and Iraq.
- Howard Zinn 2003

Here's the big news:

Iraq was set for an assault years before the coup.

Rumsfeld, Cheney, Wolfowitz, Jeb Bush and others on the neo-conservative right had targeted Saddam Hussein and Iraq since at least 1997. Yes, they had made their case long before September 11, 2001. They all belong to a "policy group" called the Project for the New American Century (PNAC) and called themselves (I kid you not) "the Vulcans" - a sinister name right out of a conspiracy theorist's notebook. They urged President Clinton to invade Iraq in January 1998. He declined. He paid. This group wrote to Newt Gingrich and Trent Lott in May 1998:

"We should establish and maintain a strong U.S. military presence in the [Middle East] region, and be prepared to use that force to protect our vital interests in the Gulf and, if necessary, to help remove Saddam from power."

Well, my fellow citizens, there it is in black and blood.

Iraq – a war planned in 1997, packaged in 2002, and executed in 2003.

After reviewing this group and its members, I rhetorically ask myself: Is this group a gang of international interventionist fanatical right-wingers or merely war hawks on a deluded mission to bring their brand of civilization to the world? Either way we lose. In this group's statement of principles, they declared that "... it is important to shape circumstances before crises emerge, and to meet threats before they become dire." Does that sound pre-emptive? Although their stated claims of world domination was referring to international nation building, I am arguing that by following this very policy they targeted enemies within this country (namely, those other than themselves) and pursued this aggressive takeover policy right here in the USA. They honestly (?) believe that the ideals of the Democratic Party are threats to *their* America, and thus it was important to "shape" the 2000 election, ignoring the popular vote, and intervening where they could in various elections, as in the whole state of Florida, governed by none other than Jeb Bush, obedient brother *and* member of The Project (The PNAC's website, which could be altered or scrubbed any day, is at www.newamericancentury.org).

Adrienne Larkin, writer and investigator, decided to poke around this project group's website, looking into its members and stated intentions. She almost couldn't believe what she found (2003):

> And the founding members of PNAC? If I told you, you would think I was lying, but I'll tell you anyway. Vice President Dick Cheney. Secretary of Defense Donald Rumsfeld. Paul Wolfowitz. Richard Perle. William Kristol, writer for one of Ruppert Murdoch's conservative rags. Elliott Abrams. And, of course, Jeb Bush. The membership roster of PNAC is a who's who of George Bush's right-wing political operatives.

> If you aren't persuaded that the PNACers are running the current "shock and awe" annihilation of Baghdad, you might be interested to know that Bush's proposed defense budget for 2003 matches to the nickel the amount pro-posed for military spending by PNAC in September of 2000.

Just in case you want a peek at what comes next, PNAC has a handy little statement on Post War Iraq on their website. The bottom line is: America is going to run the show over there for a long time. American forces will be there for years. And the democracy thing? Don't expect democratic "elections" over there within the next two or three years; wouldn't be prudent. And money? We will spend whatever it takes. America will run the rebuilding show, but you knew that already. Brown and Root, a subsidiary of Dick Cheney's Halliburton, has already inked the deal for beaucoup of your taxpaying bucks to build some bridges and roads.

Now that we know the principles in the great scheme to benefit *some* Americans, let us be on the lookout for those self-serving militants directing foreign policy. "It was [Richard] Perle and his DPB [Defense Policy Board] partner in crime R. James Woolsey who alleged links between Al Qaeda and Saddam Hussein. It was Perle and his colleagues at the DPB who suggested that Saddam Hussein's forces possessed nuclear, chemical, and biological weapons that posed an imminent threat to the United States."
- William D. Hartung

And so, not only the bogus reasoning for the US invasion of Iraq can be found in this Project group, but the methods and means of aggressive intervention and preemptive strikes are clearly stated many years before 9-11 and the Iraqi War of Occupation. The members of this Project are the main principles in the coup, coincidentally. We passive American citizens have heard it many times: This is a war for America, to keep our country safe. We had to attack them first, because they were planning to attack us (even though they couldn't defend themselves). Let's dig a little deeper: just what are our "vital interests" in the Middle East? Oil? Definitely. Israel? Probably. Maintaining those democratic governments in the region? There aren't any.

William Rivers Pitt gives us his wisdom and research in his SLAUGHTERGATE, t r u t h o u t | Perspective - Monday, June 23, 2003:

> It has become agonizingly clear that the Bush administration deliberately trumped up dire stories of Iraq's weapons capabilities in order to galvanize the American people behind war. They lied every day for months. Worse, the Bush administration deliberately used the horror of September 11 to justify war against a nation that posed no threat to American security. On June 15, former NATO Supreme Commander General Wesley Clark appeared on 'Meet the Press' with Tim Russert. A wretchedly revealing exchange came from the interview:

> GEN. CLARK: I think there was a certain amount of hype in the intelligence, and I think the information that's come out thus far does indicate that there was a sort of selective reading of the intelligence in the sense of sort of building a case.
> MR. RUSSERT: Hyped by whom?
> ...
> GEN. CLARK: Well, it came from the White House, it came from people around the White House. It came from all over. I got a call on 9/11. I was on CNN, and I got a call at my home saying, "You got to say this is connected. This is state-sponsored terrorism. This has to be connected to Saddam Hussein." I said, "But-I'm willing to say it but what's your evidence?" And I never got any evidence. And these were people who had-Middle East think tanks and people like this and it was a lot of pressure to connect this and there were
> a lot of assumptions made. But I never personally saw the evidence and didn't talk to anybody who had the evidence to make that connection.

Mr. Russert, predictably, did not follow up on this astounding claim during the interview. The import of these statements, however, is clear. General Clark was asked by the White House, and by those working for and with the White House, to connect Saddam Hussein and Iraq to the attacks of September 11. He was asked to do so on that terrible day, while people were still dying and while the buildings were still burning.

The tactic was effective. A poll by CBS and the New York Times taken just before the war began showed that 45% of the American people believed Saddam Hussein was "personally involved" in the attacks of September 11. A previous poll taken by Princeton Survey Research Associates showed that 50% of the American people believed that most of the 9/11 hijackers were Iraqis.

In a country with a news media that can provide data in an unrelenting stream 24 hours a day, millions of Americans believed in a connection that was completely and totally wrong. How can such a gap in comprehension be explained? Simply put, the Bush administration put forth a staggering array of lies and exaggerations, and the American media chose to repeat them ad nauseam instead of verifying the veracity of the claims. These poll numbers must be factored into those taken during and after the war which appeared to show American support for the attack.

General Clark was not the only expert to convince in the Iraq blitz, he is just one who would not make assumptions nor connections until he saw the evidence. In his book, "Against All Enemies: Inside America's War on Terror," (published March 2004) former national anti-terrorism adviser Richard Clarke wrote that Bush "launched an unnecessary and costly war in Iraq that strengthened the fundamentalist, radical Islamic terrorist movement worldwide." To their shame, Bush, Rumsfeld and Rice ignored Clarke's warnings about al Qaeda, ostensibly because Clarke had worked for the Clinton White House and thus couldn't be totally trusted, even though he was a Republican. Clarke told Bush there was no link between 9-11 and Iraq. "He came back at me and said, 'Iraq! Saddam! Find out if there's a connection,' and in a very intimidating way," Clarke said in an interview on CBS's 60 Minutes.

After Clarke's revelations of Bush and Rice's very deceptive manipulations (and incompetency), the White House launched a character assassination of the veteran security adviser – which will be hard to do, considering Clarke's top clearance and track record. So far he appears to have weathered the storm, for he continues to advise and write.

Salon's Mary Jacoby spoke with Senator Bob Graham (September 8, 2004) -
http://www.salon.com/news/feature/2004/09/08/graham/print.html

"In February 2002, Graham writes, Gen. Tommy Franks, then conducting the war against the Taliban in Afghanistan [and later to endorse Bush's candidacy at the Republican National Convention in New York], pulled the senator aside to explain that important resources in the hunt for Osama bin Laden, such as Predator drones, were being quietly redeployed to Iraq. * 'He told me that the decision to go to war in Iraq had been made at least 14 months before we actually went into Iraq, long before there was authorization from Congress and long before the United Nations was sought out for a resolution of support,'" In an action/vote that said a lot about what he knew about the truth, the Salon piece tells us that "Graham voted against the congressional war resolution authorizing force to topple Saddam Hussein." See what else Senator Graham has to say in his book, "Intelligence Matters: The CIA, the FBI, Saudi Arabia and the Failure of America's War on Terror."

- By the way, doesn't it sound menacing when a military General – Tommy Franks in this case – takes you aside and tells you that "Predator drones" are now deployed? I wouldn't know if he were warning me or kidding me.

Predator drones? I later found out that these are unmanned planes flown remotely by pilots who may be halfway around the world. Do you feel safer?

Soldier for the Truth by Marc Cooper, L.A. Weekly, April 2004

After two decades in the U.S. Air Force, Lieutenant Colonel Karen Kwiatkowski, now 43, knew her career as a regional analyst was coming to an end when -- in the months leading up to the war in Iraq -- she felt she was being "propagandized" by her own bosses.

With Masters degrees from Harvard in government and zoology and two books on Saharan Africa to her credit, she found herself transferred ... to a post as a political/military desk officer at the Defense Departmentís office for Near East South Asia (NESA), a policy arm of the Pentagon.

Kwiatkowski got there just as war fever was spreading, or being spread as she would later argue, through the halls of Washington. Indeed, shortly after her arrival, a piece of NESA was broken off, expanded and re-dubbed with the Orwellian name of the Office of Special Plans. The OSP's task was, ostensibly, to help the Pentagon develop policy around the Iraq crisis.

She would soon conclude that the OSP -- a pet project of Vice President Dick Cheney and Defense Secretary Don Rumsfeld -- was more akin to a nerve center for what she now calls a "neoconservative coup, a hijacking of the Pentagon."
Though a lifelong conservative, Kwiatkowski found herself appalled as the radical wing of the Bush administration, including her superiors in the Pentagon planning department, bulldozed internal dissent, overlooked its own intelligence and relentlessly pushed for confrontation with Iraq.

Deeply frustrated and alarmed, Kwiatkowski, still on active duty, took the unusual step of penning an anonymous column of internal Pentagon dissent that was posted on the Internet by former Colonel David Hackworth, America's most decorated veteran.

As war inevitably approached, and as she neared her 20-year mark in the Air Force, Kwiatkowski concluded the only way she could viably resist what she now terms the "expansionist, imperialist" policies of the neoconservatives who dominated Iraq policy was by retiring and taking up a public fight against them.

She left the military last March, the same week that troops invaded Iraq. Kwiatkowski started putting her real name on her Web reports and began accepting speaking invitations. "I'm now a soldier for the truth," she said in a speech last week at Cal Poly Pomona. Afterward, I spoke with her:

L.A. WEEKLY: What was the relationship between NESA and the now-notorious Office of Special Plans, the group set up by Secretary of Defense Rumsfeld and Vice President Cheney? Was the OSP, in reality, an intelligence operation to act as counter to the CIA?

KAREN KWIATKOWSKI: The NESA office includes the Iraq desk, as well as the desks of the rest of the region. It is under Deputy Assistant Secretary of Defense Bill Luti. ... The Office of Special Plans would take issue with those who say they were doing intelligence. They would say they were developing policy for the Office of the Secretary of Defense for the invasion of Iraq.
But developing policy is not the same as developing propaganda and pushing a particular agenda. And actually, that's more what they really did. They pushed an agenda on Iraq, and they developed pretty sophisticated propaganda lines which were fed throughout government, to the Congress, and even internally to the Pentagon -- to

try and make this case of immediacy. This case of severe threat to the United States.

... I was seeing around me ... an invasion of a sovereign country, an occupation, a poorly planned occupation. I was concerned about it; I was in opposition to that, and I was not alone. ...

LAW: There you were, a career military officer, a Pentagon analyst, a conservative who had given two decades to this work. What provoked you to become first a covert and later a public dissident?

KK: Like most people, I've always thought there should be honesty in government. Working 20 years in the military, I'm sure I saw some things that were less than honest or accountable. But nothing to the degree that I saw when I joined Near East South Asia.

... This was creatively produced propaganda spread not only through the Pentagon, but across a network of policymakers -- the State Department, with John Bolton; the Vice President's Office, the very close relationship the OSP had with that office. That is not normal, that is a bypassing of normal processes. Then there was the National Security Council, with certain people who had neoconservative views; Scooter Libby, the vice president's chief of staff; a network of think tanks who advocated neoconservative views -- the American Enterprise Institute, the Center for Security Policy with Frank Gaffney, the columnist Charles Krauthammer --.

So there was just not a process inside the Pentagon that should have developed good honest policy, but it was instead pushing a particular agenda; this group worked in a coordinated manner, across media and parts of the government, with their neoconservative compadres.

... There was a sort of groupthink, an adopted storyline: We are going to invade Iraq and we are going to eliminate Saddam Hussein and we are going to have bases in Iraq. This was all a given even by the time I joined them, in May of 2002.

LAW: You heard this in staff meetings?

KK: The discussions were ones of this sort of inevitability. The concerns were only that some policymakers still had to get onboard with this agenda. Not that this agenda was right or wrong -- but that we needed to convince the remaining holdovers. Colin Powell, for example.
There was a lot of frustration with Powell; they said a lot of bad things about him in the office. They got very angry with him when he convinced Bush to go back to the U.N. and forced a four-month delay in their invasion plans.

General Tony Zinni is another one. Zinni, the combatant commander of Central Command, Tommy Franks's predecessor -- a very well-qualified guy who knows the Middle East inside out, knows the military inside out, a Marine, a great guy. He spoke out publicly as President Bush's Middle East envoy about some of the things he saw. Before he was removed by Bush, I heard Zinni called a traitor in a staff meeting. They were very anti-anybody who might provide information that affected their paradigm. They were the spin enforcers.

And so everything was in place. There was sympathy for America after 9-11, there was momentum after Afghanistan, and there was the multi-year plan to take Saddam out and grab the region to "stabilize" it. CIA intelligence was slanted and the Pentagon was infiltrated with spin-meisters fabricating information and arm-twisting the hold-outs. Remember that, when we think Security in the USA we think of the intelligence gathering organizations and the highly trained people working in the Pentagon – see the authority figures manufacturing emotional and psychological phantoms to fight?

It was time to sell it to the Congress and to the American people. As for the rest of the world, well, if Texas thinks its true, then all should follow. Bush announced that he had initiated a war to "disarm Iraq, to free its people and to defend the world from grave danger." Who can see the irony, and hypocrisy, of this statement from the same speech?: "Our nation enters this conflict reluctantly -- yet, our purpose is sure. The people of the United States and our friends and allies will not live at the mercy of an outlaw regime that threatens the peace with weapons of mass murder." [Address to the Nation, 3/19/03]

Some representatives of truth saw the deceit way before the first shot was fired. (Too bad the media ignored Congressman Dennis Kucinich's bid for the presidency – he would have been refreshingly different; He is trying again for 2008. Do note, presidential hopefuls, that if the media ignores you, you don't get air play--and Americans do not get informed choices-- *they* get political popularity shows similar to American Idol programs. A lot of the choices have been made years before the actual election day.):

"At this point, frankly, the evidence does not suggest that Iraq was connected to 9/11, that there's any connection between Saddam Hussein and al-Qaeda, that there's any connection between Iraq and the anthrax attacks on this country. We don't hear from the CIA that Iraq has any usable weapons of mass destruction that they could deliver to the United States."
- Congressman Dennis Kucinich, Sept. 29, 2002

Senate Floor Speech - February 12, 2003 by SENATOR ROBERT BYRD (D-WVA):

This nation is about to embark upon the first test of a revolutionary doctrine applied in an extraordinary way at an unfortunate time. The doctrine of preemption -- the idea that the United States or any other nation can legitimately attack a nation that is not imminently threatening but may be threatening in the future – is a radical new twist on the traditional idea of self defense. It appears to be in contravention of international law and the UN Charter. And it is being tested at a time of worldwide terrorism, making many countries around the globe wonder if they will soon be on our – or some other nation's – hit list. High level Administration figures recently refused to take nuclear weapons off of the table when discussing a possible attack against Iraq.

This Administration, now in power for a little over two years, must be judged on its record. I believe that that record is dismal.

In that scant two years, this Administration has squandered a large projected surplus of some $5.6 trillion over the next decade and taken us to projected deficits as far as the eye can see. This Administration's domestic policy has put many of our states in dire financial condition, under funding scores of essential programs for our people. This Administration has fostered policies which have slowed economic growth. This Administration has ignored urgent matters such as the crisis in health care for our elderly. This Administration has been slow to provide adequate funding for homeland security. This Administration has been reluctant to better protect our long and porous borders.

In foreign policy, this Administration has failed to find Osama bin Laden. In fact, just yesterday we heard from him again marshaling his forces and urging them to kill. This Administration has split traditional alliances, possibly crippling, for all time, International order-keeping entities like the United Nations and NATO. This Administration has called into question the traditional worldwide perception of the United States as well-intentioned peacekeeper. This Administration has turned the patient art of diplomacy into threats, labeling, and name calling of the sort that reflects quite poorly on the intelligence and sensitivity of our leaders, and which will have consequences for years to come.

Calling heads of state pygmies, labeling whole countries as evil, denigrating powerful European allies as irrelevant – these types of crude insensitivities can do our great nation no good. We may have massive military might, but we cannot fight a global war on terrorism alone.

The war in Afghanistan has cost us $37 billion so far, yet there is evidence that terrorism may already be starting to regain its hold in that region.

Has our senselessly bellicose language and our callous disregard of the interests and opinions of other nations increased the global race to join the nuclear club and made proliferation an even more lucrative practice for nations which need the income?

In only the space of two short years this reckless and arrogant Administration has initiated policies which may reap disastrous consequences for years.

To engage in war is always to pick a wild card. And war must always be a last resort, not a first choice. I truly must question the judgment of any President who can say that a massive unprovoked military attack on a nation which is over 50% children is "in the highest moral traditions of our country". This war is not necessary at this time.

Even Bush's father had advised against it. In his memoirs, "A World Transformed," published in 1998 with Brent Scowcroft, George Herbert Walker Bush wrote the following to explain why he didn't go after Saddam Hussein at the end of the Gulf War:

"Trying to eliminate Saddam...would have incurred incalculable human and political costs. Apprehending him was probably impossible.... We would have been forced to occupy Baghdad and, in effect, rule Iraq....

There was no viable 'exit strategy' we could see, violating another of our principles. Furthermore, we had been consciously trying to set a pattern for handling aggression in the post-Cold War world. Going in and occupying Iraq, thus unilaterally exceeding the United Nations' mandate, would have destroyed the precedent of international response to aggression that we hoped to establish. Had we gone the invasion route, the United States could conceivably still be an occupying power in a bitterly hostile land."

If only his son could read.
If only the VP could remember:

> **Dick Cheney on Iraq, April 7, 1991** (During the first Iraqi War):
>
> "I think for us to get American military personnel involved in a civil war inside Iraq would literally be a quagmire. Once we got to Baghdad, what would we do? Who would we put in power? What kind of government would we have? Would it be a Sunni government, a Shia government, a Kurdish government? Would it be secular along the lines of the Ba'ath Party? Would it be fundamentalist Islamic? I do not think the United States wants to have U.S. military forces accept casualties and accept the responsibility of trying to govern Iraq. I think it makes no sense at all."
>
> - Dick Cheney on ABC
>
> >>~o~<<

Iraq: a war that has gone on longer than our involvement in World War II.

Point? Even to millions of conservatives, Iraq was a mistake. This point alone makes one wonders just who voted for George Bush in 2004. That fraud is being investigated. Stay tuned, (especially to Congressman John Conyers and to legal activist Robert F. Kennedy, Jr.). Otherwise, Bush junior created a major international catastrophe by invading Iraq – even his Dad would agree with that--politically and diplomatically, but not financially. Why? Both father and son have made a lot of money on this little venture. I'll let James Ridgeway of the Village Voice tell you about ...

The Spoils of War:
Be the First on Your Block to Make a Buck off Iraq
(VillageVoice.com | Mondo Washington, 9 October, 2002)
http://www.truthout.org/docs_02/10.12C.ridge.buck.htm

As they prepare to make war on Iraq, cowboy-in-chief George Bush and his cohorts have pulled out all the stops. They're trying to convince us that this act of pure aggression is a "preemptive" move that will allow Americans to sleep more peacefully in their beds, while the Iraqi masses cheer the conquerors who have starved them for a decade and then bombed them to smithereens. And that's just for starters. In the imaginations of Bush and his advisers, this Wild West approach to the Middle East stands to knock out Syria's despot, rein in the Saudi royal family, inspire the neighboring Iranians to their own pro-American putsch, banish the Palestinians to Jordan, and clear the way for Israeli settlers.

The doctrine of the preemptive strike is the perfect strategy for ushering in a new century of neocolonialism, unfettered by any need to respect sovereignty or self-determination. Better still, it's going to mean big bucks for whoever gets in on the ground floor. Before the war can begin, the movers and shakers in Washington and around the world have their eyes on divvying up the spoils.
...
Oil, clearly, is the commercial jackpot in this war. Even under the sanctions, Iraq provides us with 9 percent of our oil supply. Until this spring, we were buying half of all Iraq's oil exports. But oil is also the carrot the U.S. is holding out to potential allies.
...
At the recent Group of Eight summit in Canada, Russian president Vladimir Putin reportedly told Bush he couldn't care less whether Saddam got the heave-ho, as long as Russia got compensated for about $12 billion in outstanding loans to Iraq, and $4 billion owed them for transporting Iraqi oil. Meanwhile, the Russian oil

companies are scrambling to save their recent deals.
LUKoil, for one, signed an exploration contract in 1997.
...

... If there's war, the one man Bush will need is Abdullah
bin Abd al-Aziz, crown prince of Saudi Arabia. ... But by
all reports, al-Aziz is getting tired of being Our Man in
Riyadh, taking in billions in oil dollars and then
recirculating them back to the United States through
defense contracts. He wants a more independent policy.
...

Most important, the prince has reached out to Iran with the
goal of forging a common oil policy. A report last month
from the Petroleum Finance Company--a consulting firm
in Washington which works with Aramco, the joint U.S.-
Saudi oil company--pointed out that a united Saudi-
Iranian oil front would become the heartbeat of OPEC,
and would wield extraordinary power. Should either or
both of these two nations decide they've had it with Bush,
all they have to do is let the much-heralded free market
take over, flooding the globe with crude and sending oil
prices into a steep dive. Lower prices would wipe out not
only smaller international companies that have been
enticed into oil play by high prices, but could wipe out the
domestic oil companies in the United States, causing sheer
political hell for Bush in his little oil bastion of Houston.

>>~o~<<

The list of official reasons for attacking and occupying
Iraq is becoming thread-bare. What do our allies in Britain have
to say about the reasoning? We can't ask Tony Blair, for he will
just ask George for a good answer.
What have they dug up in the U.K.?

DIPLOMAT'S SUPPRESSED DOCUMENT LAYS BARE THE
LIES BEHIND IRAQ WAR
By Colin Brown and Andy McSmith, The Independent,
Dec 15, 2006 http://www.commondreams.org/headlines06/1215-06.htm
The [British] Government's case for going to war in Iraq
has been torn apart by the publication of previously

suppressed evidence that Tony Blair lied over Saddam Hussein's weapons of mass destruction.

A devastating attack on Mr Blair's justification for military action by Carne Ross, Britain's key negotiator at the UN, has been kept under wraps until now because he was threatened with being charged with breaching the Official Secrets Act.

...

The Foreign Office had attempted to prevent the evidence being made public, but it has now been published by the Commons Select Committee on Foreign Affairs after MPs sought assurances from the Foreign Office that it would not breach the Official Secrets Act.

It shows Mr Ross told the inquiry, chaired by Lord Butler, "there was no intelligence evidence of significant holdings of CW [chemical warfare], BW [biological warfare] or nuclear material" held by the Iraqi dictator before the invasion. "There was, moreover, no intelligence or assessment during my time in the job that Iraq had any intention to launch an attack against its neighbours or the UK or the US," he added.

Mr Ross's evidence directly challenges the assertions by the Prime Minster that the war was legally justified because Saddam possessed WMDs which could be "activated" within 45 minutes and posed a threat to British interests. These claims were also made in two dossiers, subsequently discredited, in spite of the advice by Mr Ross.

~ ~ ~

Well surely it was a great and noble thing to take out Saddam Hussein, right? I mean, he was an evil dictator. After Saddam Hussein was hung on Dec 30, 2006, journalist Robert Fisk had this to say:

A DICTATOR CREATED THEN DESTROYED BY AMERICA
By Robert Fisk, The Independent, December 30, 2006
http://news.independent.co.uk/world/fisk/article2112555.ece

Who encouraged Saddam to invade Iran in 1980, which was the greatest war crime he has committed, for it led to the deaths of a million and a half souls? And who sold him the components for the chemical weapons with which he drenched Iran and the Kurds? We did.

No wonder the Americans, who controlled Saddam's weird trial, forbade any mention of this, his most obscene atrocity, in the charges against him. Could he not have been handed over to the Iranians for sentencing for this massive war crime? Of course not. Because that would also expose our culpability.

...

I have catalogued his [Saddam's] monstrous crimes over the years. I have talked to the Kurdish survivors of Halabja and the Shia who rose up against the dictator at our request in 1991 and who were betrayed by us -- and whose comrades, in their tens of thousands, along with their wives, were hanged like thrushes by Saddam's executioners.

I have walked round the execution chamber of Abu Ghraib -- only months, it later transpired, after we had been using the same prison for a few tortures and killings of our own --

The Iraq Study Group was formed in 2006 to address the myriad Iraqi War problems and what to do about them. As many of the members were pro-war and pro-oil, the conclusions could have been slanted, to say the least. They did, however, suggest that US foreign policy take a more diplomatic approach to Iran and Syria. Bush ignored that recommendation, as well as whichever other ones he didn't like. An analyst of the report concluded that ...

It's Still About Oil in Iraq - *A centerpiece of the Iraq Study Group's report is its advocacy for securing foreign companies' long-term access to Iraqi oil fields.*
By Antonia Juhasz, The Los Angeles Times, 08 December 2006:

The U.S. State Department's Oil and Energy Working Group, meeting between December 2002 and April 2003, also said that Iraq "should be opened to international oil companies as quickly as possible after the war." Its preferred method of privatization was a form of oil contract called a production-sharing agreement. These agreements are preferred by the oil industry but rejected by all the top oil producers in the Middle East because they grant greater control and more profits to the companies than the governments. The Heritage Foundation also released a report in March 2003 calling for the full privatization of Iraq's oil sector. One representative of the foundation, Edwin Meese III, is a member of the Iraq Study Group. Another, James J. Carafano, assisted in the study group's work.

...

All told, the Iraq Study Group has simply made the case for extending the war until foreign oil companies - presumably American ones - have guaranteed legal access to all of Iraq's oil fields and until they are assured the best legal and financial terms possible.

We can thank the Iraq Study Group for making its case publicly. It is now our turn to decide if we wish to spill more blood for oil.

---- Antonia Juhasz *is a visiting scholar at the Institute for Policy Studies and author of* The Bush Agenda: Invading the World, One Economy at a Time.

We are running out of bona fide excuses for this immoral war. How about this popular one: The United States was aiding and enforcing UN sanctions by invading Iraq. Let's find out what the UN says about that: IRAQ WAR WAS ILLEGAL AND BREACHED UN CHARTER, SAYS ANNAN

By Ewen MacAskill and Julian Borger in Washington; The Guardian, September 16, 2004
http://www.guardian.co.uk/print/0,3858,5017264-103681,00.html

The United Nations secretary general, Kofi Annan:
"I have indicated it was not in conformity with the UN charter. From our point of view and from the charter point of view it was illegal."

Mr Annan has until now kept a tactful silence and his intervention at this point undermines the argument pushed by Tony Blair that the war was legitimised by security council resolutions.

...

The UN chief had warned the US and its allies a week before the invasion in March 2003 that military action would violate the UN charter. But he has hitherto refrained from using the damning word "illegal".
Both Mr Blair and the foreign secretary, Jack Straw, claim that Saddam Hussein was in breach of security council resolution 1441 passed late in 2002, and of previous resolutions calling on him to give up weapons of mass destruction. France and other countries claimed these were insufficient.

No immediate comment was available from the White House late last night, but American officials have defended the war as an act of self-defense, allowed under the UN charter, in view of Saddam Hussein's supposed plans to build weapons of mass destruction.
However, last September, Mr Annan issued a stern critique of the notion of pre-emptive self-defense, saying it would lead to a breakdown in international order. Mr Annan last night said that there should have been a second UN resolution specifically authorising war against Iraq.
Mr Blair and Mr Straw tried to secure this second resolution early in 2003 in the run-up to the war but were unable to convince a sceptical security council.

Mr Annan said the security council had warned Iraq in resolution 1441 there would be "consequences" if it did not comply with its demands. But he said it should have been up to the council to determine what those consequences were.

Could we say that we are in Iraq for the people and by the people there? In June of 2004 two scientific polls taken in Iraq stated that the majority of Iraqis wanted a US military withdrawal immediately. (http://www.fair.org/press-releases/iraq-democracy-polls.html) In other words, the reason for continued American presence there -- establishing democracy -- was ignoring the fact that US military forces were there against the wishes of the majority of its people! This should have been yet another reminder that Bush's nation building efforts were actually aggressive policies of self-gain, if not a crusade.

"Imperial Hubris" was published on July 15 2004 by "an anonymous longtime counter-terrorism official at the C.I.A. who previously ran the agency's unit that concentrated on Osama bin Laden. In his book and in subsequent interviews the author has said he believes that the war in Iraq has been a major distraction from the effort to fight Al Qaeda and that the war has also inflamed Islamic resentment against the United States while aiding Al Qaeda's recruitment among Muslims." Sounds like he knows something about blowback? Yes. Senior officials have told him to curb his interviews. So, it is not officially censorship if he is presently working for the government? Isn't there a national whistleblower law to protect him? Free speech was important at one time....
 - These facts came from "Agency Curbs War Critic Author" by James Risen of the New York Times.

Somehow we were sent to invade a nation because it was a direct threat to the American people, or to the world, or harbored terrorists, or was involved in the September 11 attacks, or received weapons-grade uranium from Niger, or had mobile weapons labs, or WMD, or had a need to be liberated, or we needed to establish a democracy, or stop an insurgency, or stop a civil war we created that can't be called a civil war even though it is. Something like that.

> Somehow our elected leaders were subverting international law and humanity by setting up secret prisons around the world, secretly kidnapping people, secretly holding them indefinitely, secretly not charging them with anything, secretly torturing them. Somehow that overt policy of torture became the fault of a few "bad apples" in the military.

- Kevin Tillman, brother and friend of Pat Tillman, killed in action; "After Pat's Birthday," Oct 19, 2006
http://www.truthdig.com/report/item/200601019_after_pats_birthday/=

As for other opinions on the inside, even from a purely military perspective, the War in Iraq was a mistake – and complicated by biased conniving. "Retired General Anthony Zinni is one of the most respected and outspoken military leaders of the past two decades," begins an article from CBS News 60 Minutes (May 21, 2004). "From 1997 to 2000, he was commander-in-chief of the United States Central Command, in charge of all American troops in the Middle East. That was the same job held by Gen. Norman Schwarzkopf before him, and Gen. Tommy Franks after." The name of the piece is GEN. ZINNI: 'THEY'VE SCREWED UP' and he has a lot to say, especially as an insider ...
http://www.cbsnews.com/stories/2004/05/21/60minutes/main618896.shtml (Well, as inside as an independent thinker could be.):

> Following his retirement from the Marine Corps, the Bush administration thought so highly of Zinni that it appointed him to one of its highest diplomatic posts – special envoy to the Middle East.
> But Zinni broke ranks with the administration over the war in Iraq, and now, in his harshest criticism yet, he says senior officials at the Pentagon are guilty of dereliction of duty – and that the time has come for heads to roll. Correspondent Steve Kroft reports.
> Zinni says Iraq was the wrong war at the wrong time - with the wrong strategy. And he was saying it before the U.S. invasion. In the months leading up to the war, while

211

still Middle East envoy, Zinni carried the message to Congress: "This is, in my view, the worst time to take this on. And I don't feel it needs to be done now."

But he wasn't the only former military leader with doubts about the invasion of Iraq. Former General and National Security Advisor Brent Scowcroft, former Centcom Commander Norman Schwarzkopf, former NATO Commander Wesley Clark, and former Army Chief of Staff Eric Shinseki all voiced their reservations.
Zinni believes this was a war the generals didn't want - but it was a war the civilians wanted.

Zinni says he blames the Pentagon for what happened. "I blame the civilian leadership of the Pentagon directly. Because if they were given the responsibility, and if this was their war, and by everything that I understand, they promoted it and pushed it - certain elements in there certainly - even to the point of creating their own intelligence to match their needs, then they should bear the responsibility," he says....

Zinni is talking about a group of policymakers within the administration known as "the neo-conservatives" who saw the invasion of Iraq as a way to stabilize American interests in the region and strengthen the position of Israel. They include Deputy Defense Secretary Paul Wolfowitz; Under-secretary of Defense Douglas Feith; Former Defense Policy Board member Richard Perle; National Security Council member Eliot Abrams; and Vice President Cheney's chief of staff, Lewis "Scooter" Libby. Zinni believes they are political ideologues who have hijacked American policy in Iraq.

"I think it's the worst kept secret in Washington. That everybody - everybody I talk to in Washington has known and fully knows what their agenda was and what they were trying to do," says Zinni.
...

Adds Zinni: "I know what strategy they promoted. And openly. And for a number of years. And what they have convinced the president and the secretary to do. And I don't believe there is any serious political leader, military leader, diplomat in Washington that doesn't know where it came from."

Zinni, who now teaches international relations at the College of William and Mary, says he feels a responsibility to speak out, just as former Marine Corps Commandant David Shoup voiced early concerns about the Vietnam war nearly 40 years ago.

"It is part of your duty. Look, there is one statement that bothers me more than anything else. And that's the idea that when the troops are in combat, everybody has to shut up. Imagine if we put troops in combat with a faulty rifle, and that rifle was malfunctioning, and troops were dying as a result," says Zinni.

"I can't think anyone would allow that to happen, that would not speak up. Well, what's the difference between a faulty plan and strategy that's getting just as many troops killed? It's leading down a path where we're not succeeding and accomplishing the missions we've set out to do."

60 Minutes asked Secretary Rumsfeld and his deputy Wolfowitz to respond to Zinni's remarks. The request for an interview was declined.

Is Iraq far away from the shores of America? Is it something to watch on the entertaining TV? No, it is very close to home, indirectly. The most immediate and tragic fact is the body bags coming back to our local neighborhoods (Hidden by the military, which does not want bad publicity - reality - obstructing their purportedly noble cause. Please note that suppression of such information is part of "forming public views", part of the Smoke & Mirrors show.). Think, however, about this: Hurricane Katrina has again clarified for all to see how inept George Bush is at running the government -- even if he were legitimately elected.

213

The terrible damage there is actually worse than it could have been: Bush and the neo-cons took millions of dollars out of the national defence program, FEMA, as well as from the Army Corps of Engineers (working on the levees) and transferred those necessary funds and personnel to Iraq -- a war that was fabricated and meant to steal oil and maintain domination of that foreign region. On top of that, the neo-con companies put in non-contested bids to help (themselves) in New Orleans and *that* region. (Exxon-Mobil made record profits off of this tragedy) Six months after the disaster the accounting books are looking very bad – untold millions lost! Corruption, mismanagement and suffering ... right here in the USA. Will the theft, the outrage, never end?

Meanwhile, back at the *Bush Ranch* East, Washington DC, once the weapons of mass destruction never materialized, it was time for the republican spin doctors to go into action. Saving Bush's ass once again, a Senate investigation (July 2004) blamed "poor intelligence" on the false claims that Iraq had dangerous weapons. Months before, officials were putting the blame on one lone Muslim informant. One guy! (The Bush Administration paid Iraqi-exile and neo-con darling Ahmad Chalabi $400,000 a month for intelligence, including fabricated claims about Iraqi WMD. It continued to pay him for months after discovering that he was providing inaccurate information. Source: MSNBC).

In July 2004 Richard Clarke wrote an insightful article about the 9-11 Commission Report, which had just been published. It was titled HONORABLE COMMISSION, TOOTHLESS REPORT in the New York Times. In it, Clarke criticized the bipartisan approach that squelched obvious con-clusions because it would look bad for Bush. He made his own conclusions:

"The Bush administration did little on terrorism before 9/11, and that by invading Iraq the administration has left us less safe as a nation. ... What the commissioners did clearly state was that Iraq had no collaborative relationship with Al Qaeda and no hand in 9/11. They also disclosed that Iran provided support to Al Qaeda, including to some 9/11 hijackers. These two facts may cause many people to conclude that the Bush administration focused on the wrong country. They would be right in thinking that."

>>~o~<<

The British publication, *The Economist*, displayed the intriguing title of their take on the official denial and termed it SINCERE DECEIVERS - "George Bush and Tony Blair said it was right to have invaded IRAQ even though no weapons of mass destruction have since been found there."
http://www.economist.com/displayStory.cfm?story_ID=2920850

Are we getting closer to George Orwell's political world-view yet? Or is this mere insanity? This may be Animal Farm to some comedians, but it is 1984 my friends, and that is not as entertaining. It is time to lay the blame where it lies, at the foot of the White House steps, and within the homes and offices of the usurpers and their cohorts. There is smoke ... and a fire.

Who is in charge? - A tiny, unelected group, supported by powerful, unrepresentative minorities, wrote the late professor Edward Said (early 2003):

> The Bush administration's relentless unilateral march towards war is profoundly disturbing for many reasons, but so far as American citizens are concerned the whole grotesque show is a tremendous failure in democracy. An immensely wealthy and powerful republic has been hijacked by a small cabal of individuals, all of them unelected and therefore unresponsive to public pressure, and simply turned on its head. It is no exaggeration to say that this war is the most unpopular in modern history. Before the war has begun there have been more people protesting it in this country alone than was the case at the height of the anti-Vietnam war demonstrations during the 60s and 70s. Note also that those rallies took place after the war had been going on for several years: this one has yet to begin, even though a large number of overtly aggressive and belligerent steps have already been taken

by the US and its loyal puppy, the UK government of the increasingly ridiculous Tony Blair.

>>~o~<<

There is so much written and distributed on the internet concerning all of this that it is amazing – and immensely important for an informed populace. Here are a few more to consider:
"10 Appalling Lies We Were Told About Iraq"
http://www.truthout.org/docs_03/062903G.shtml
 and "C.I.A. Official Alleges Retaliation for Not Faking WMD Evidence" (Dec 2004):
http://www.truthout.org/docs_04/121004W.shtml

>>~o~<<

Bush promoted the war like a wily salesman (which is what he is). He cajoled, vented, fumed, postured and lied for his personal cause. He deliberately misled the nation for his own agenda. The lies he used during his State of the Union address in January 2003 were just one of many examples. Blaming CIA director George Tenet just shows what he will do to cover his ass.... not to mention leaking CIA operatives to teach a lesson (Joe Wilson), and character assassination for public disloyalty and criticism (Paul O'Neill and Richard Clarke). Bush is venomous when you get on his wrong side. How many will die because of this liar and bully? Thousands have so far. The US is now in a prolonged guerrilla war with Iraq. Was it a mistake based on wrong information? With what I have presented thus far, it is not. Would Bush admit it if it were a mistake? Never.
BUSH DEFIANT AMID WMD REPORT
- CBS News / Associated Press, October 7, 2004
http://www.cbsnews.com/stories/2004/09/16/iraq/main643989.shtml
Faced with a harshly critical new report
http://www.cbsnews.com/htdocs/pdf/wmdfinalreport.pdf,
President George W. Bush conceded Thursday that Iraq did not have the stockpiles of banned weapons he had warned of before the invasion last year, but insisted that "we were right to take action" against Saddam Hussein.

...
> Mr. Bush spoke one day after Charles Duelfer, the American weapons hunter in Iraq, presented to the Senate and the public a report that Saddam's weapons of mass destruction programs had deteriorated into only hopes and dreams by the time of the U.S.-led invasion last year. The decline was wrought by the first Gulf War and years of international sanctions, the chief U.S. weapons hunter found.

> As we peruse the article, it is now familiar to see the denial and defiance. Taking no responsibility for erroneously sending in troops, destroying lives, killing Iraqi women and children as well as our own soldiers, Dubya stated, "Much of the accumulated body of our intelligence was wrong and we must find out why." Oh yes, it was the other George – Tenet! (Demonstrating to the world what Bush thinks about friendship and loyalty, George Tenet was indeed the fall guy, having stepped down in June 2004 for "personal reasons." My sense is that he has been paid to keep quiet about the truth and will be living the good life - with a sullied reputation - or he will be writing his own book soon, which will be revealing.)

All of this is adding up.

Also see Chalmers Johnson: "How to Create a Worthless Intelligence Agency" http://www.truthout.org/docs_04/112504Y.shtml

Ignoring the huge amount of anti-American sentiment and the quagmire that is creating terrorists daily, Bush defiantly declared at the time "America is safer today with Saddam Hussein in prison." Notice the Smoke & Mirrors sound bite in this misleading statement, made by a powerful authority figure (who, when the smoke clears, will be found to be a war criminal)? Why aren't more people protesting in the streets? Here's my take: They have been trained that it is a waste of time, that's why. Dozens of protests, and hundreds of thousands of protesters, have rallied around the issues of the stolen election, the war in Iraq (before and after it happened), and other fascist policies by this government. Nothing happens, nothing changes.

The media ignores it all.
Read on:
TACTICS BY POLICE MUTE THE PROTESTERS, AND THEIR MESSAGES by Michael Slackman and Diane Cardwell, with Steven Greenhouse, Marc Santora and William K. Rashbaum, New York Times, September 2, 2004:
http://www.nytimes.com/2004/09/02/politics/campaign/02protest.html

> As the Republican National Convention approached its final evening tonight, nearly 1,800 protesters had been arrested on the streets, two-thirds of them on Tuesday night alone. But for all the anger of the demonstrations, they have barely interrupted the convention narrative, and have drawn relatively little national news coverage.

> Using large orange nets to divide and conquer, and a near-zero tolerance policy for activities that even suggest the prospect of disorder, the New York Police Department has developed what amounts to a pre-emptive strike policy, cutting off demonstrations before they grow large enough, loud enough, or unruly enough to affect the convention.

> The NY police have adopted a pre-emptive strike policy! Why did the media ignore this and other protests? Ted Koppel, who put on some fatigues to get the news in Iraq (read: embedded) was also quoted in this article, saying that it was not "Chicago 1968." Ted, get a grip. This government is prepared that such a thing would never happen. There are more police, more surveillance, more infiltration of all of those un-American and "suspicious" groups than in the 1960s. Yes, the government and military learned the lessons of Vietnam: nip the problem of protest in the bud and monitor the news. Infiltrate protest groups, hide the body bags, arrest the protesters "just in case," feed official news to the journalists, and repeat the same lines time and again. Ted, the protest groups are marginalized and muffled.

The whole thing is covered – except the News!
... even a party is covered!

"Just in Case: Funds ready for Iraq Victory" News item published in the NYT, republished in the International Herald Tribune, Oct 5, 2006: "Tucked away in fine print in the military spending bill for this past year was a lump sum of $20 million to pay for a celebration in the nation's capital 'for commemoration of success' in Iraq and Afghanistan."

> Can you believe this? Republicans in Congress are planning a victory party -- after nothing but bad news, failures and international scandals. This party money could be called "stay the course despite reality" party. What could your community do with $20 million? SP

The *Inside* Story

So, were there any honest reasons why Bush got us in this war? There *was* more in this war for Bush than the obvious oil and profits. Unfortunately for us all, I believe that to George W. Bush, war on Iraq may have offered more personal reasons: the insecure boy with below average verbal and executive skills wanted to show the world that he could do something better than his dad. Junior knows that if it weren't for his dad, he wouldn't be the player he is. "Dubya" spent the first half of his life ignoring his inadequacies by joking and drinking; then the second half of his life desperately trying to outdo his dad – which won't happen. In Iraq, however, perhaps young George thought he could do what his dad didn't do – oust the evil Saddam Hussein ("who tried to kill my Dad" Dubya has declared from time to time.). Here's another clue: Socially and intellectually, young George has distanced himself from his Yale and Harvard schoolmates and that liberally educated and privileged group. Why? He probably felt out-classed and inadequate around "those elitist intellectuals," and he has said as much. Junior's autocratic style, which demands obedience and secrecy, automatically promote policies which are meant to keep those unfriendly critics away. On the PR front, Mr. Bush strives to promote a folksy chumminess; however, behind the stone buildings of Washington and the Pentagon, he is known to be pushy, controlling, belligerent, and secretive. He speaks of "loyalty" but means "blind obedience." When we combine his god-certain righteousness, his unwillingness to admit mistakes, and a seeming lack of compassion for the thousands of people killed by his decisions, a disturbing picture emerges of a remorseless character out of some Gothic novel. He asserts himself through fear and intimidation. Such a psychological complex appears psychopathic. The sycophants he surrounds himself with know the lines to mimic and when to applaud to keep on his good side. Thus, by surrounding himself with yes-men and subordinates, Dubya is the big, wealthy man in the Texas (and now DC) countryside! Yeehaw! Now we're gettin' some respect!

There have been various psychiatric and psychological analyses of George Bush published. One in particular paints a realistic and disturbing picture of the man who has led this superpower into a pit:

Bush and the Psychology of Incompetent Decisions, by John P. Briggs, MD, and J.P. Briggs II, PhD
t r u t h o u t | Guest Contributors, 18 January 2007
I won't print it here, but it is online:
http://www.afterdowningstreet.org/node/17439

~ ~ ~

Investigative reporter Russ Baker had an interesting story in his **Why George Went To War**, June 2005:

"... there's evidence that Bush not only deliberately relied on false intelligence to justify an attack, but that he would have willingly used any excuse at all to invade Iraq. And that he was obsessed with the notion well before 9/11—indeed, even before he became president in early 2001. ...
"He was thinking about invading Iraq in 1999," said author and *Houston Chronicle* journalist Mickey Herskowitz. "It was on his

mind. He said, 'One of the keys to being seen as a great leader is to be seen as a commander-in-chief.' And he said, 'My father had all this political capital built up when he drove the Iraqis out of Kuwait and he wasted it.' He went on, 'If I have a chance to invade…, if I had that much capital, I'm not going to waste it. I'm going to get everything passed that I want to get passed and I'm going to have a successful presidency.'"
http://www.tompaine.com/articles/2005/06/20/why_george_went_to_war.php

>>~o~<<

Let's look at this objectively. Even if such a flawed man had been fairly elected, the United States of America should not have an emotionally and psychologically impaired person at the command of vast weapons and troops. History is full of similar men in power, and the world has suffered. Is this mad king George assaulting our American shores yet again? An interesting parallel continues, especially as we look at the similarity between the Tories and the British interests of 1776 and the arch-conservative republicans and the Bush traitors of 2000. Think of *pResident* George and King George of the UK as Thomas Paine describes Britain:

> Alas, we have been long led away by ancient prejudices, and made large sacrifices to superstition. We have boasted the protection of Great Britain, without considering, that her motive was **interest** not **attachment**; that she did not protect us from **our enemies** on **our account**, but from **her enemies** on **her own account**, from those who had no quarrel with us on any **other account**, and who will always be our enemies on the **same account**.
> - emphases his

Some of the similarities are spooky. The man who gathers the votes of the red states; and the king who marshaled the Redcoats. Both men of privilege seemingly out of touch with their "subjects." Living the wealthy good life while taxing the poor. Sending troops far far away to enforce policy. Is history

221

repeating itself? Or is it spiraling out of control? Or are we talking about a variation on a theme, or myth, or story? Or maybe a totally different story from the Revolutionary period: G. W. Bush is a red state Benedict Arnold.

The British did not defeat the Americans in that War. It took an insider 224 years later to do it. Neo-con businessmen and political opportunists took the country. King George is back? If so, where are the patriots?

From my preface on hypnosis you understand that we can all be manipulated by the power of suggestions. You may recall that one of the dynamics of hypnotic suggestibility is the Role itself. There is a certain power in professional and executive positions. I am not referring to the normal power associated with this - the capability to exert power over others - but the *role* having power *over* the possessor of the position, or in this case, the office of the President. In the very revealing interview titled "Nothing Prepared Me for Bush", by Onnesha Roychoudhuri, AlterNet (28 April 2006), the author interviews professor and journalist Robert Scheer, who "has reported on every administration since Richard Nixon. But as he says in this interview, he never expected the lies and cynicism of Bush II." Sheer wrote a book titled "Playing President" and this interview is rather revealing. He first describes the candidate entering into the election process:

> RS: The process itself is so debilitating, so controlling, that it really doesn't matter who these guys are or what they start out with. Even with the best of intentions, even when they're very smart and knowledgeable - as opposed to George W., who is neither - it doesn't seem to matter. All they are proving is their ability to manipulate, to think superficially, and to exploit national security issues rather than deal with them.
> OR: Can you explain the title of the book?
> RS: "Playing President" is an attempt to capture what it's really all about. Trying out for the role becomes the dominant experience, and by the time you get into office,

222

you've been shaped by it and keep playing out the part. What you've learned to do in the process is to be superficial, to suspend more profound thoughts, to silence your own doubts and your own serious thinking.

OR: Why does that happen?

RS: It's built into our political process, particularly in a mass society with a mass media with a large owning bloc of almost 300 million citizens.

> It is certainly thought-provoking to realize that the *role* of President can exert an influence upon whomever holds the office. If one is basically noble, one could rise to greatness. The more flawed, confused or irrational one is, however, the office could magnify and intensify the basic character flaws of the individual. It has said that "power corrupts,....." I don't believe it. There are many examples of wise rulers throughout history. On the other side, I believe that a powerful position can bring out the dark side of weaker or contorted individuals. Tsar Ivan the Terrible of Russia comes to mind. Modern examples are various dictators, like Joseph Stalin (our ally in WWII), Pol Pot, famous for the "killing fields" of Cambodia (and supported by the US), and Saddam Hussein, dictator of Iraq and sometime friend of the US. Please do not assume that I am comparing Bush with other dictators. I am referring to powerful influences upon people in positions of power.

>>~o~<<

Is Saddam Hussein a villain? Of course. Not only did the US know this for decades, but none other than Donald Rumsfeld, operating as a special US presidential envoy to the Middle East (under Reagan and Bush in the 80s) had several pictures taken of him shaking Saddam's hand. These ignoble photo-ops occurred while that dictator was using chemical weapons. It gets uglier: Michael Dobbs of the Washington Post reported that the Reagan-Bush administration authorized the sale to Iraq of poisonous chemicals and deadly biological viruses, such as anthrax and bubonic plague. No wonder that "Dubya" Bush was convinced that Saddam had chemical weapons – his daddy sold it to him. According to William D. Hartung, who runs the Arms Trade

Resource Center (a project of the World Policy Institute), between 1985 and 1990, or during the Reagan & Bush I administrations, $500 million worth of militarily useful equipment and supplies were sold to Saddam Hussein, including chemical weapons.

Bush the elder, of course, responded to Saddam's Kuwait invasion with a consolidated, internationally sanctioned retaliation against Iraq. This could now be termed Gulf War I (1991). Then came the economic and political sanctions, no-fly zones enforced by air patrols, and multi-year bombings of Iraq (with depleted uranium - *radioactive!* - casings) during what could be called Gulf War II (1991-2003). Now we are looking at Gulf War III (2003 - ?). Essentially, the US has been at war with this country since 1991, or sixteen years and counting – something to consider. The number of Iraqi deaths since Dubya's War? ... - And this coming from the desire for revenge of 9/11 that killed less than 3000 people ... which the Iraqis had nothing to do with?! Would you believe 100,000?! http://www.newscientist.com/news/news.jsp?id=ns99996596 Since 1991? - half a million Iraqis?!

Check it out yourself: www.iraqbodycount.org

>>~o~<<

The War Itself

Within a month the Iraqis had been beaten, again. Jubilation for the liberators – with a strong desire to overlook the obvious: There was no retaliation with weapons of mass destruction. Thus, there were none, or none capable of firing. Believe me, if Saddam had such weapons he would have used them against the evil Americans attacking his country. He didn't. He didn't have any. More than a year later it was official: **there were no weapons of mass destruction**. This means that the whole rationale for attacking this dangerous enemy was bogus, false, a big lie.

Had the multinational inspection team been given enough time, they would have concluded, there is no doubt, that there was no threat. Hans Blix, the chief inspector of the international team, has publically declared that his efforts were colored and slanted by the British and American governments. The ugly truth is that the Bush regime did not want the real facts of Iraq to come forth. To stop this, Bush heightened the rhetoric, lowered his tone, and preemptively attacked.

Throughout all of this, we were witness to Bush and crew's hammering style. This regime tried to legitimize their desire for oil and strategic land by false evidence, bribes, coercion, sensationalism, belligerence and backroom arm-twisting. *The US was caught spying on UN security council members*, evidently to find out how they would vote on the impending war. These tactics were not new to sophisticated observers both here and abroad. When doubting nations decided to oppose the bullies (thank you Germany, France and Russia, among others), the world experienced the true fascist colors of the Bush regime. When the UN wouldn't bend to US will, the Bush regime tried to shame the international community for their lack of resolve and timidity. Out of this came the infamous PR jibes against France, including the silly "freedom fries" for French fries, and so forth. This would have been merely embarrassing to conscientious Americans, but then Bush showed he was a Texas Ranger wanna-be: Catching even Tony Blair by surprise, the Bush regime attacked Baghdad on its own. Hypocrisy has many faces.

Who uses chemical weapons? Why, we do! Please note in the following article how the Pentagon tells "little white lies" when asked questions. *Why, you must be precise* in your language when asking questions! J. Edgar Hoover used this all the time. When asked if the FBI were spying on a particular person or group - when not directed to - he would, on occasion, stop the surveillance, then make an official statement or offer in an interview that *indeed* the FBI was not eavesdropping on ____ (Martin Luther King, for instance), which would then be true. Later, the spying would continue. That was in the 50s and the 60s. Have we not become yet more sophisticated in our lies since then?

Look for the mirrors, smell the smoke in the following:

US ADMITS IT USED NAPALM BOMBS IN IRAQ
by Andrew Buncombe, Washington, The Independent, Aug 10, 2003

http://news.independent.co.uk/world/americas/story.jsp?story=432201

American pilots dropped the controversial incendiary agent napalm on Iraqi troops during the advance on Baghdad. The attacks caused massive fireballs that obliterated several Iraqi positions.

The Pentagon denied using napalm at the time, but Marine pilots and their commanders have confirmed that they used an upgraded version of the weapon against dug-in positions. They said napalm, which has a distinctive smell, was used because of its psychological effect on an enemy.
A 1980 UN convention banned the use against civilian targets of napalm, a terrifying mixture of jet fuel and polystyrene that sticks to skin as it burns. The US, which did not sign the treaty, is one of the few countries that makes use of the weapon. It was employed notoriously against both civilian and military targets in the Vietnam war.
The upgraded weapon, which uses kerosene rather than petrol, was used in March and April, when dozens of napalm bombs were dropped near bridges over the Saddam Canal and the Tigris river, south of Baghdad.

"We napalmed both those [bridge] approaches," said Colonel James Alles, commander of Marine Air Group 11. "Unfortunately there were people there ... you could see them in the [cockpit] video. They were Iraqi soldiers. It's no great way to die. The generals love napalm. It has a big psychological effect."
At the time, the Pentagon insisted the report was untrue.
"We completed destruction of our last batch of napalm on 4 April, 2001," it said.

226

The revelation that napalm was used in the war against Iraq, while the Pentagon denied it, has outraged opponents of the war.

"Most of the world understands that napalm and incendiaries are a horrible, horrible weapon," said Robert Musil, director of the organisation Physicians for Social Responsibility. "It takes up an awful lot of medical resources.
It creates horrible wounds." Mr Musil said denial of its use "fits a pattern of deception [by the US administration]".
The Pentagon said it had not tried to deceive. It drew a distinction between traditional napalm, first invented in 1942, and the weapons dropped in Iraq, which it calls Mark 77 firebombs. They weigh 510lbs, and consist of 44lbs of polystyrene-like gel and 63 gallons of jet fuel.

Officials said that if journalists had asked about the fire-bombs their use would have been confirmed. A spokesman admitted they were "remarkably similar" to napalm but said they caused less environmental damage. But John Pike, director of the military studies group Global-Security.Org, said: "You can call it something other than napalm but it is still napalm. It has been reformulated in the sense that they now use a different petroleum distillate, but that is it. The US is the only country that has used napalm for a long time. I am not aware of any other country that uses it." Marines returning from Iraq chose to call the firebombs "napalm".
Mr Musil said the Pentagon's effort to draw a distinction between the weapons was outrageous. He said: "It's Orwellian. They do not want the public to know. It's a lie."

~ ~ ~

Our military is looking pretty bad these days. Casualties, AWOLs (absent without leave, or desertions), *friendly fire, innocent* killings, scandals, torture and assassinations. The Left is wisely careful to distinguish between the errant policy of creating the unlawful war in the first place and not blaming the soldiers in the field following orders. I was touched by the erudition and compassion shown by journalist and activist, Bill Moyers, when he addressed the military academy, West Point, right after the 2006 elections. He shows a lot of wisdom as he weaves history, philosophy and justice in his... **Message To West Point** by Bill Moyers, TomPaine.com - 29 November 2006

http://www.truthout.org/cgi-bin/artman/exec/view.cgi/67/24346

...

In the months leading up to the invasion [Rupert] Murdoch turned the dogs of war loose in the corridors of his media empire, and they howled for blood, although not their own. Murdoch himself said, just weeks before the invasion, that: "The greatest thing to come of this to the world economy, if you could put it that way [as you can, if you are a media mogul], would be $20 a barrel for oil." Once the war is behind us, Rupert Murdoch said: "The whole world will benefit from cheaper oil which will be a bigger stimulus than anything else."

Today Murdoch says he has no regrets, that he still believes it was right "to go in there," and that "from a historical perspective" the U.S. death toll in Iraq was "minute." "Minute." ...

I said earlier that our founders did not want the power of war to reside in a single man. Many were also dubious about having any kind of regular, or as they called it, "standing" army at all. Standing armies were hired supporters of absolute monarchs and imperial tyrants. The men drafting the Constitution were steeped in classical and historical learning. They recalled how Caesar in ancient times and Oliver Cromwell in more recent times had used the conquering armies they had led to make themselves dictators. ...

Not until World War II did the Army again take part in such a long, bloody, and fateful conflict as the Civil War had been, and like the Civil War it opened an entirely new period in American history. The incredibly gigantic mobilization of the entire nation, the victory it produced, and the ensuing 60 years of wars, quasi-wars, mini-wars, secret wars, and a virtually permanent crisis created a superpower and forever changed the nation's relationship to its armed forces, confronting us with problems we have to address, no matter how unsettling it may be to do so in the midst of yet another war.

...

Let me cut closer to the bone. The chickenhawks in Washington, who at this very moment are busily defending you against supposed "insults" or betrayals by the opponents of the war in Iraq, are likewise those who have cut budgets for medical and psychiatric care; who have been so skimpy and late with pay and with provision of necessities that military families in the United States have had to apply for food stamps; who sent the men and women whom you may soon be commanding into Iraq understrength, under-equipped, and unprepared for dealing with a kind of war fought in streets and homes full of civilians against enemies undistinguishable from non-combatants; who have time and again broken promises to the civilian National Guardsmen bearing much of the burden by canceling their redeployment orders and extending their tours.

You may or may not agree on the justice and necessity of the war itself, but I hope that you will agree that flattery and adulation are no substitute for genuine support. Much of the money that could be directed to that support has gone into high-tech weapons systems that were supposed to produce a new, mobile, compact "professional" army that could easily defeat the armies of any other two nations combined, but is useless in a war against nationalist or religious guerrilla uprisings that, like it or not, have some support, coerced or otherwise, among the local population. We learned this lesson in Vietnam, only to see it forgotten or ignored by the time this administration invaded Iraq, creating the conditions for a savage

229

sectarian and civil war with our soldiers trapped in the middle, unable to discern civilian from combatant, where it is impossible to kill your enemy faster than rage makes new ones.

And who has been the real beneficiary of creating this high-tech army called to fight a war conceived and commissioned and cheered on by politicians and pundits not one of whom ever entered a combat zone? One of your boys answered that: Dwight Eisenhower, class of 1915, who told us that the real winners of the anything at any price philosophy would be "the military-industrial complex."

...

There is yet another way the chickenhawks are failing you. In the October issue of the magazine of the California Nurses Association, you can read a long report on "The Battle at Home." In veterans' hospitals across the country - and in a growing number of ill-prepared, under-funded psych and primary care clinics as well - the report says that nurses "have witnessed the guilt, rage, emotional numbness, and tormented flashbacks of GIs just back from Iraq." Yet "a returning vet must wait an average of 165 days for a VA decision on initial disability benefits," and an appeal can take up to three years. Just in the first quarter of this year, the VA treated 20,638 Iraq veterans for post-traumatic stress disorder, and faces a backlog of 400,000 cases. This is reprehensible.

...

I know the final rule of the military Code of Conduct is already written in your hearts: "I am an American, fighting for freedom, responsible for my actions, and dedicated to the principles which made my country free..." The meaning of freedom begins with the still, small voice of conscience, when each of us decides what we will live, or die, for.

IRAQ VETS LEFT IN PHYSICAL AND MENTAL AGONY
By Aaron Glantz, Electronic Iraq, IPS, January 4, 2007
http://electroniciraq.net/news/printer2793.shtml

SAN FRANCISCO - On New Year's Eve, the number of U.S. soldiers killed in Iraq passed 3,000. By Tuesday, the death toll had reached 3,004 -- 31 more than died in the Sep. 11 attacks on the World Trade Centre and the Pentagon.

But the number of injured has far outstripped the dead, with the Veterans Administration reporting that more than 150,000 veterans of the Iraq war are receiving disability benefits.

... [A doctor just returned from US military hospitals in Germany stated that] an extremely high number of wounded soldiers are coming home with their arms or legs amputated. Imbascini said he amputated the genitals of one or two men every day.

...

Pentagon studies show that 12 percent of soldiers who have served in Iraq suffer from post-traumatic stress disorder. The group Veterans for America, formerly the Vietnam Veterans of America Foundation, estimates 70,000 Iraq war veterans have gone to the VA for mental health care. ...

On Christmas, for example, Army Reservist James Dean barricaded himself in his father's home with several weapons and threatened to kill himself. After a 14-hour standoff with authorities, Dean was killed by a police officer after he aimed a gun at another officer, authorities told the Washington Post.

Veterans for America's Robinson told IPS that Dean, who had already served 18 months in Afghanistan, had been diagnosed with PTSD. He had just been informed that his unit would be sent to Iraq on Jan. 14. ...

Robinson says his organisation has also documented the existence of at least 1,000 homeless veterans of the Iraq war.   ~ ~ ~

There have been some far-reaching and very negative fall-out from the Iraqi War, beyond the obvious bombs and killings, beyond the not-so-obvious war vets who are wounded emotionally, psychologically and physically. There is an international political and strategic fallout. George Bush has almost singlehandedly dismantled NATO because of his war. The North Atlantic Treaty Organization, NATO, mostly concentrated on Europe and including the USA and Canada, all agreed after World War II to unite militarily to a common enemy, the Soviet Union. If one were attacked the others would come to their defense. When Bush promoted and pushed for the Iraq War he also called upon our NATO allies to help him. Many of them balked because Iraq did not attack the US, and the idea of a pre-emptive strike was against everything the treaty stood for. It was actually a total turn-about of the principles, a farce and an imposition, and to be herded into this trumped-up war because of NATO agreements was insulting, and illegal. There is now open opposition, internal debates and even a total re-thinking of the relevancy of NATO. It may fall apart.

Thanks, George, you did it again. Making us all safer, are you?

If you think that is an eye opener, then take a look at this, found on the internet on Wikipedia, the online evolving encyclopedia:

> The International Criminal Court (ICC) was established in 2002 as a permanent tribunal to prosecute individuals for genocide, crimes against humanity, and war crimes, as defined by several international agreements, most prominently the Rome Statute of the International Criminal Court. The ICC is designed to complement existing national judicial systems; however, the Court can exercise its jurisdiction if national courts are unwilling or unable to investigate or prosecute such crimes, thus being a 'court of last resort,' leaving the primary responsibility to exercise jurisdiction over alleged criminals to individual states.
>
> The ICC's definitions are very similar to those of the Nuremberg trials. Supporters of the ICC argue that the

states which object to the International Criminal Court are those which regularly carry out genocide, war crimes and crimes against humanity in order to protect or promote their political or economic interests.

The United States has not ratified the treaty creating the court, and has stated it does not intend to do so. The country's main objections are the interference with their national sovereignty and a fear of "politically motivated prosecutions.

> I am sure that Bush's repeated claims the the UN is irrelevant is behind the present policy. When the most powerful nation refuses to accept any review or criticism of its policies and actions, then it unfortunately undermines the potential good such a court can do for international human rights. However, Machiavelli would see the prudence in staying legally clear of such a court if one was the largest weapons manufacturer & most aggressive nation--with various critics and enemies.
More from the Wikipedia article:

In 2002, the U.S. Congress passed the American Service-members' Protection Act (ASPA), which contained a number of provisions, including prohibitions on the U.S. providing military aid to countries which had ratified the treaty establishing the court (exceptions granted), and permitting the President to authorize military force to free any U.S. military personnel held by the court, leading opponents to dub it 'The Hague Invasion Act.' The act was later modified to permit U.S. cooperation with the ICC when dealing with U.S. enemies, but not anything the U.S. would do [clever].

The U.S. has also made a number of Bilateral Immunity Agreements, or so-called 'Article 98' agreements, with a number of countries, prohibiting the surrender to the ICC of a broad scope of persons including current or former government officials, military personnel, and U.S. employees (including non-national contractors) and nationals.

> Talk about covering your ass! Can you imagine such an agreement in *any* situation? In a marriage, business, law, and especially in a war? "I want you to sign this legal document forgiving me for **anything** I and my friends might do in the future!" This is a pre-emptive strike against any and all future misdeeds and a clearing of all responsibility! What a cool deal for predators and opportunists, however. On the other end, who, or which countries, would even agree to such a preposterous thing? Hmm ... perhaps those countries who want foreign aid, membership in NATO, a favor owed by the number one superpower, or simply weapons?

Who says it's not the oil?

What do militarily powerful countries, which are dependent on oil, do when the end of the oil is near? The world is running out of this slick commodity. We will peak, or go over the crest and see limited production levels, between 2007 and 2017. Luckily, we have Bush and his oil friends to guide us through this difficult period. And what great connections! Bush and his buddies have been in the oil business for years! What a happy coincidence! Even the academic one, Condoleezza Rice, has a tanker named after her by Chevron. And that honor because she was on their board of directors for a while. Do all board directors get this honor?

"The U.S. is running out of energy. Natural gas is in scarce supply. Crude-oil production is winding down. The last nuclear power plant was ordered in July 1973. No meaningful alternative fuels exist. In short, Americans are heading toward their first major energy crunch since the 1970s."
Time, 21 July 2003

>>~o~<<

There are many investigative journalists out there putting all the dots (or slime) together on this oil grab. Let me simply say that the evidence has been collected and we, the free and democratic people of the United States – through our great leader president Bush – have invaded an oil rich country under false pretenses and now control a huge amount of crude oil that will aid us, the greatest nation in the world, to maintain our advantages well into this century. Via Iraq we also can influence the evil OPEC, which tries to make too much money on oil. It would be too long to include the revealing information within these **Smoke & Mirrors** pages, but the article "Crude Dudes" by Linda McQuaig of the Toronto Star, is an eye opener.

Below is just a portion of the report; the full article online at: http://www.thestar.com/NASApp/cs/ContentServer?pagename=th estar/Layout/Article_Type1&call_pageid=971358637177&c=Arti cle &cid=1095545411401

> There's something almost obscene about a map that was studied by senior Bush administration officials and a select group of oil company executives meeting in secret in the spring of 2001. It doesn't show the kind of detail normally shown on maps ‹ cities, towns, regions. Rather its detail is all about Iraq's oil.
>
> The southwest is neatly divided, for instance, into nine "Exploration Blocks." Stripped of political trappings, this map shows a naked Iraq, with only its ample natural assets in view. It's like a supermarket meat chart, which identifies the various parts of a slab of beef so customers can see the most desirable cuts .... Block 1 might be the striploin, Block 2 and Block 3 are perhaps some juicy tenderloin, but Block 8 ‹ ahh, that could be the filet mignon.
>
> The map might seem crass, but it was never meant for public consumption. It was one of the documents studied by the ultra-secretive task force on energy, headed by U.S. Vice-President Dick Cheney, and it was only released under court order after a long legal battle waged by the public interest group Judicial Watch.
> Another interesting task force document, also released under court order over the opposition of the Bush administration, was a two-page chart titled "Foreign

Suitors for Iraqi Oilfields." It identifies 63 oil companies from 30 countries and specifies which Iraqi oil fields each company is interested in and the status of the company's negotiations with Saddam Hussein's regime. Among the companies are Royal Dutch/Shell of the Netherlands, Russia's Lukoil and France's Total Elf Aquitaine, which was identified as being interested in the fabulous, 25-billion-barrel Majnoon oil field. Baghdad had "agreed in principle" to the French company's plans to develop this succulent slab of Iraq. There goes the filet mignon into the mouths of the French!

The documents have attracted surprisingly little attention, despite their possible relevance to the question of Washington's motives for its invasion of Iraq ‹ in many ways the defining event of the post-9/11 world but one whose purpose remains shrouded in mystery. Even after the supposed motives for the invasion ‹ weapons of mass destruction and links to Al Qaeda ‹ have been thoroughly discredited, talk of oil as a motive is still greeted with derision. Certainly any suggestion that private oil interests were in any way involved is hooted down with charges of conspiracy theory.
Yet the documents suggest that those who took part in the Cheney task force ‹ including senior oil company executives ‹ were very interested in Iraq's oil and specifically in the danger of it falling into the hands of eager foreign oil companies, rather than into the rightful hands of eager U.S. oil companies.

As the documents show, prior to the U.S. invasion, foreign oil companies were nicely positioned for future involvement in Iraq, while the major U.S. oil companies, after years of U.S.- Iraqi hostilities, were largely out of the picture. Indeed, the U.S. majors would have been the big losers if U.N. sanctions against Iraq had simply been lifted. "The U.S. majors stand to lose if Saddam makes a deal with the U.N. (on lifting sanctions)," noted a report by Germany's Deutsche Bank in October 2002. *   →

* This article was adapted from *It's The Crude, Dude: War, Big Oil, And The Fight For The Planet*, by Linda McQuaig, 2004. It looks like she has done her homework.

~ ~ ~

Here's another oily tidbit from *EarthRights International* (July 28, 2003). Bush made yet another Executive Order when the nation was focused upon casualties of the war (No draped coffins by order of the US military however!):

> Executive Order 13303, issued on May 22, 2003, claims to be essential to Iraqi reconstruction efforts. A cursory reading of the Order indicates that its real purpose is to protect oil companies by giving virtual impunity for any activities undertaken relating to Iraqi oil.
> ...
> Under this Order, an oil company complicity in human rights violations, or one that causes environmental damage, would be immune from lawsuits. The language of the Executive Order is so broad that it might as well have been written by lawyers for Halliburton, ExxonMobil and ChevronTexaco.
> ... EO 13303 offers a wide range of protections to certain persons, entities and assets associated with the Iraqi oil industry. The document is apparently intended as a sweeping grant of immunity to individuals, corporations, agencies and others involved in Iraqi oil sales, marketing, or other oil-related activities.

~ ~ ~

Just in case you are still not convinced, let a specialist give you the low down. Michael Klare is a professor of peace and world security studies at Hampshire College in Amherst, Mass., and the author, most recently, of ...

Blood and Oil: The Dangers and Consequences of America's Growing Petroleum Dependency (The American Empire Project, Metropolitan Books). Here's what he had to say the end of 2004:

"No Escape from Dependency: Looming Energy Crisis

237

Overshadows Bush's Second Term"
by Michael Klare, December 8, 2004 (TomDispatch.com):

The onset of this new energy crisis was first signaled in January 2004, when Royal Dutch/Shell – one of the world's leading energy firms – revealed that it had overstated its oil and natural gas reserves by about 20%, the net equivalent of 3.9 billion barrels of oil or the total annual consumption of China and Japan combined. Another indication of crisis came only one month later, when the New York Times revealed that prominent American energy analysts now believe Saudi Arabia, the world's largest oil producer, had exaggerated its future oil production capacity and could soon be facing the wholesale exhaustion of some of its most prolific older fields. Although officials at the U.S. Department of Energy (DoE) insisted that these develop-ments did not foreshadow a near-term contraction in the global supply of energy, warnings increased from energy experts of the imminent arrival of "peak" oil -- the point at which the world's known petroleum fields will attain their highest sustainable yield and commence a long, irreversible decline.

How imminent that peak-oil moment may in fact be has generated considerable debate and disagreement within the specialist community, and the topic has begun to seep into public consciousness. A number of books on peak oil -- **Out of Gas** by David Goodstein, **The End of Oil** by Paul Roberts, and **The Party's Over** by Richard Heinberg, among others -- have appeared in recent months, and a related documentary film, **The End of Suburbia**, has gained a broad underground audience. As if to acknowledge the seriousness of this debate, the Wall Street Journal reported in September that evidence of a global slowdown in petroleum output can no longer be ignored. While no one can say with certainty that recent developments portend the imminent arrival of peak oil output, there can be no question that global supply shortages will prove increasingly common in the future.

Bush's Petro-Cartel Almost Has Iraq's Oil, Part I & II
by Joshua Holland, AlterNet, 16 October 2006

It's clear that the U.S.-led invasion had little to do with national security or the events of September 11. Former Treasury Secretary Paul O'Neill revealed that just 11 days after Bush's inauguration in early 2001, regime change in Iraq was "Topic A" among the administration's national security staff, and former Terrorism Tsar Richard Clarke told 60 minutes that the day after the attacks in New York and Washington occurred, "[Secretary of Defense Donald] Rumsfeld was saying that we needed to bomb Iraq." He added: "We all said ... no, no. Al-Qaeda is in Afghanistan."

On March 7, 2003, two weeks before the U.S. attacked Iraq, the UN's chief weapons inspector, Hans Blix, told the UN Security Council that Saddam Hussein's cooperation with the inspections protocol had improved to the point where it was "active or even proactive," and that the inspectors would be able to certify that Iraq was free of prohibited weapons within a few months' time. That same day, IAEA head Mohammed ElBaradei reported that there was no evidence of a current nuclear program in Iraq and flatly refuted the administration's claim that the infamous aluminum tubes cited by Colin Powell in making his case for war before the Security Council were part of a reconstituted nuclear program.

In February of 2001, just weeks after Bush was sworn in, the same energy executives that had been lobbying for Saddam's ouster gathered at the White House to participate in Dick Cheney's now infamous Energy Taskforce. Although Cheney would go all the way to the Supreme Court to keep what happened at those meetings a secret, we do know a few things thanks to documents obtained by the conservative legal group JudicialWatch. As Mark Levine wrote in The Nation ($$):

... a map of Iraq and an accompanying list of "Iraq oil foreign suitors" were the center of discussion. The map erased all features of the country save the location of its main oil deposits, divided into nine exploration blocks. The accompanying list of suitors revealed that dozens of companies from thirty countries - but not the United States - were either in discussions over or in direct negotiations for rights to some of the best remaining oilfields on earth.

...

Levine wrote, "It's not hard to surmise how the participants in these meetings felt about this situation." According to The New Yorker, at the same time, a top-secret National Security Council memo directed NSC staff to "cooperate fully with the Energy Taskforce as it considered melding two seemingly unrelated areas of policy." The administration's national security team was to join "the review of operational policies towards rogue states such as Iraq, and actions regarding the capture of new and existing oil and gas fields."

At the State Department, planning was also underway. Under the auspices of the "Future of Iraq Project," an "Oil and Energy Working Group" was established.

...

But the execs from Big Oil didn't just want access to Iraq's oil; they wanted access on terms that would be inconceivable unless negotiated at the barrel of a gun. Specifically, they wanted an Iraqi government that would enter into Production Service Agreements (PSAs) for the extraction of Iraq's oil.

PSAs, developed in the 1960s, are a tool of today's kinder, gentler neocolonialism; they allow countries to retain technical ownership over energy reserves but, in actuality, lock in multinationals' control and extremely high profit margins - up to thirteen times oil companies' minimum target, according to an analysis by the British-based oil watchdog Platform (PDF).

As Greg Muttit, an analyst with the group, notes:

Such contracts are often used in countries with small or difficult oilfields, or where high-risk exploration is required. They are not generally used in countries like Iraq, where there are large fields which are already known and which are cheap to extract. For example, they are not used in Iran, Kuwait or Saudi Arabia, all of which maintain state control of oil.

In fact, Muttit adds, of the seven leading oil producing countries, only Russia has entered into PSAs, and those were signed during its own economic "shock therapy" in the early 1990s. A number of Iraq's oil-rich neighbors have constitutions that specifically prohibit foreign control over their energy reserves.

PSAs often have long terms - up to 40 years - and contain "stabilization clauses" that protect them from future legislative changes. As Muttit points out, future governments "could be constrained in their ability to pass new laws or policies." That means, for example, that if a future elected Iraqi government "wanted to pass a human rights law, or wanted to introduce a minimum wage [and it] affected the company's profits, either the law would not apply to the company's operations, or the government would have to compensate the company for any reduction in profits." It's Sovereignty Lite.

The deals are so onerous that they govern only 12 percent of the world's oil reserves, according to the International Energy Agency. Nonetheless, PSAs would become the Future of Iraq Project's recommendation for the fledgling Iraqi government. According to the Financial Times, "many in the group" fought for the contract structure; a Kurdish delegate told the FT, "everybody keeps coming back to PSAs."

...

With a Constitution cooked up in DC, the stage was set for foreign multinationals to assume effective control of as much as 87 percent of Iraq's oil, according to projections by the Oil Ministry. If PSAs become the law of the land - and there are other contractual arrangements that would allow private companies to invest in the sector without giving them the same degree of control or such usurious profits - the war-torn country stands to lose up to $194 billion vitally important dollars in revenues on just the first 12 fields developed, according to a conservative estimate by Platform (the estimate assumes oil at $40 per barrel; at this writing it stands at more than $59). That's more than six times the country's annual budget.

To complete the rip-off, the occupying coalition would have to crush Iraqi resistance, make sure it had friendly people in the right places in Iraq's emerging elite and lock the new Iraqi government onto a path that would lead to the Big Four's desired outcome.

Part II

With 140,000 U.S. troops on the ground, the largest U.S. embassy in the world sequestered in Baghdad's fortified "Green Zone" and an economy designed by a consulting firm in McLean, Virginia, post-invasion Iraq was well on its way to being a bonanza for foreign investors.
[But Bush and friends had to deal with the international debt that Saddam amassed. This debt was taking money from future profits. James Baker was sent around the world to ask for financial forgiveness for the poor Iraqis - a strategy liberal groups used aiding poor countries. By the way, Baker's law firm, Baker Botts, is representing the Saudi Arabian monarchy in a suit brought by the families of the victims of 9/11.]

The largest chunk of debt, $120 billion, was owed to the Paris Club, a group of 19 industrialized nations. Baker negotiated a deal whereby the Paris Club would forgive 80 percent of Iraq's debt, but the catch - and it was a big one - was that Iraq had to agree to an economic "reform" package administered by the International Monetary Fund, an institution dominated by the wealthiest countries and infamous across the developing world for its painful and unpopular Structural Adjustment Programs. [SAP]
...
Among a number of provisions in the IMF agreement, along with privatizing state-run companies (which resulted in the lay-offs of an estimated 145,000 Iraqis),

slashing government pensions and phasing out the subsidies on food and fuel that many Iraqis depended on, was a commitment to develop Iraq's oil in partnership with the private sector. Then-Finance Minister Adel Abdul Mehdi said, none too happily, that the deal would be "very promising to the American investors and to American enterprise, certainly to oil companies." The Iraqi National Assembly released a statement saying, "the Paris Club has no right to make decisions and impose IMF conditions on Iraq," and called it "a new crime committed by the creditors who financed Saddam's oppression." And Zaid Al-Ali, an international lawyer who works with the NGO Jubilee Iraq, said it was "a perfect illustration of how the industrialized world has used debt as a tool to force developing nations to surrender sovereignty over their economies."

The IMF agreement was announced in December of 2005, along with a new $685 million dollar IMF loan that was to be used, in part, to increase Iraq's oil output. The announcement came a month after Iraqis went to the polls to vote for their first government under the new Constitution. The timing, according to the Washington Post, was meant to spare Iraqi "politicians from voters' wrath." That was a wise idea; immediately following the agreement's signing gas prices skyrocketed and Iraqis rioted.

The icing on the cake is that the deal James Baker negotiated with the Paris Club refers to Iraq as an "exceptional situation"; no precedent was set that would allow other highly indebted countries saddled with odious debt from their own past dictators to claim similar relief.

...

In an investigation for The Nation, Naomi Klein discovered that Baker had pursued his mission with an eye-popping conflict of interest. Klein learned that a consortium that included the Carlyle Group, of which Baker is believed to have a $180 million stake, had contracted with Kuwait to make sure that it was paid the money it was owed by Iraq. When Baker met with the Kuwaiti Emir to beg forgiveness for Iraq's odious debt, he had a direct interest in making sure he didn't get it.

...

Immediately after the invasion, Phillip Carroll, a former Chief Executive with Royal Dutch-Shell, and a 15-member "board of advisors" were appointed to oversee Iraq's oil industry during the transition period. According to the Guardian , the group's chief executive "would represent Iraq at meetings of Opec." Carroll had been working with the Pentagon for months before the invasion - even while the administration was still insisting that it sought a peaceful resolution to the Iraq crisis - "developing contingency plans for Iraq's oil sector in the event of war." According to the Houston Chronicle, "He assumed his work was completed, he said, until Defense Secretary Donald Rumsfeld called him shortly after the U.S.-led invasion began and offered him the oil adviser's job." Carroll, in addition to running Shell Oil in the U.S., was a former CEO of the Fluor Corporation, a well-connected oil services firm with extensive projects in Saudi Arabia and Kuwait and at least $1.6 billion in contracts for Iraq's reconstruction. He was joined by Gary Vogler, a former executive with ExxonMobile, in Iraq's Office of Reconstruction and Humanitarian Assistance. After spending six months in the post, Carroll was replaced by Robert McKee, a former ConocoPhillips executive. According to the Houston Chronicle, "His selection as the Bush administration's energy czar in Iraq" drew fire from Congressional Democrats "because of his ties to the prime contractor in the Iraqi oil fields, Houston-based Halliburton Co. He's the chairman of a venture partitioned by the ... firm."

The administration selected ChevronTexaco Vice President Norm Szydlowski to serve as a liaison between the Coalition Provisional Authority and the Iraqi Oil Ministry. Now the CEO of the appropriately named Colonial Pipeline company, he continues to work with the

Iraq Energy Roundtable, a project of the U.S. Trade and Development Agency that recently sponsored a meeting to "bring together oil and gas sector leaders in the US with key decision makers from the Iraq Ministry of Oil."

... The same day that the UN legitimized the occupation, George Bush signed Executive Order 13303 providing full legal immunity to all U.S. oil companies doing business in Iraq in order to facilitate the country's "orderly reconstruction."

... Iraq's new government is faced with what may prove to be an insurmountable crisis of legitimacy based largely on the fact that it's seen as collaborating with American forces. Overwhelming majorities of Iraqis of every sect believe the U.S. is an occupier, not a liberator, and are convinced that it intends to stay in Iraq permanently.
...

What is clear is that the future of Iraq ultimately hinges to a great degree on the outcome of a complex game of chess - only part of which is out in the open - that's playing out right now, and oil is at the center of it. It's equally clear that there's a yawning disconnect between Iraqis' and Americans' views of the situation. Erik Leaver, a senior analyst at the Institute for Policy Studies in Washington, told me that wrangling over the distribution of Iraq's oil wealth is "definitely causing problems on the ground" but the entire topic is taboo in polite DC circles. "Nobody in Washington wants to talk about it," he said. "They don't want to sound like freaks talking about blood for oil." At the same time, a recent poll asked Iraqis what they believed was the main reason for the invasion and 76% gave "to control Iraqi oil" as their first choice.

Bush Cites Oil As Reason to Stay in Iraq
By Peter Baker, The Washington Post; 05 November 2006

Greeley, Colo.- During the run-up to the invasion of Iraq, President Bush and his aides sternly dismissed suggestions that the war was all about oil. "Nonsense,"

Defense Secretary Donald H. Rumsfeld declared. "This is not about that," said White House spokesman Ari Fleischer.

Now, more than 3 1/2 years later, someone else is asserting that the war is about oil - President Bush. As he barnstorms across the country campaigning for Republican candidates in Tuesday's elections, Bush has been citing oil as a reason to stay in Iraq. If the United States pulled its troops out prematurely and surrendered the country to insurgents, he warns audiences, it would effectively hand over Iraq's considerable petroleum reserves to terrorists who would use it as a weapon against other countries.

"You can imagine a world in which these extremists and radicals got control of energy resources," he said at a rally here Saturday for Rep. Marilyn Musgrave (R-Colo.). "And then you can imagine them saying, 'We're going to pull a bunch of oil off the market to run your price of oil up unless you do the following. And the following would be along the lines of, well, 'Retreat and let us continue to expand our dark vision.' "

Bush said extremists controlling Iraq "would use energy as economic blackmail" and try to pressure the United States to abandon its alliance with Israel. At a stop in Missouri on Friday, he suggested that such radicals would be "able to pull millions of barrels of oil off the market, driving the price up to $300 or $400 a barrel."

> More scare tactics, Mr Bush? Of course, if you and your friends had a little more self-reflection, you would see that there is now a dangerous extremist in charge of the oil in that country -- you.

>>~o~<<

The Race for Iraq's Resources: *Will Iraq's oil blessing become a curse?* by Joshua Gallu, Der Spiegel (republished on TruthOut), 22 December 2006

Oil is central to Iraq's reconstruction and economic recovery, and the U.S. government is urging Iraq to develop the sector quickly. The recent Iraq Study Group report recommended the US help Iraq "prepare a draft oil law" to hasten investment. The report estimates Iraq could raise oil production from 2 million to 3 or 3.5 million barrels per day over the next three to five years.

Critics say the US is leaning on the IMF and World Bank to push Iraq into signing oil contracts fast, so western firms can secure the oil before Chinese, Indian and Russian firms do. An IMF official told SPIEGEL ONLINE that "passage of a hydrocarbon law is not a condition for financial support from the IMF."

Nevertheless, Iraqi authorities found it necessary to promise the IMF a draft petroleum law by the end of this year - this in the same letter that says "we will take whatever steps are necessary to ensure that the program remains on track."

The IMF sets the conditions for Iraq's debt relief from the so-called Paris Club countries. Eighty percent of that debt has been wiped clean, and the final 20 percent depends on certain economic reforms. With the final reduction, Iraq's debt would come to 33 percent of its GDP - but if the reforms are not made, debt would climb to 57 percent of GDP, according to an IMF report.

Criticisms have also been levelled against the World Bank, where former US deputy defense secretary Paul Wolfowitz is in charge. Wolfowitz has been accused of pushing a US agenda after opening a World Bank office in Baghdad.

~ ~ ~

"In the meantime, the Bush Administration's privatized approach to rebuilding Iraq, which activist groups like Global Exchange and the Institute for Southern Studies have called the 'second invasion' – the **corporate** invasion – of Iraq, is proceeding apace."
- William D. Hartung

Pigs at the Trough

And let us be clear about this: money is being made on this war by Bush and friends. Perhaps the original plan was simply to divide up the oil revenues, but so far U.S. taxes are being funneled there. My bet is that the various countries who were owed money by Iraq are being paid off. When that huge debt/hush money is paid, the US businesses will have a majority rights to the oil. Who wins? Not the taxpayers, and not national security. Besides Bechtel, DynCorp is making money there, and Vinnell, a subsidiary of Northrop Grumman, and Chevron .... the list goes on. More will be said about Halliburton and the Carlyle Group later. Here's one small example of what's draining our economy (and our reputation): Congress has pushed forward a no-win financial deal for American tax-payers; the Air Force will pay $100 billion to lease Boeing 747s for use as refueling planes. Looking deeper – the ailing airline industry can't afford to buy as many planes now. Interestingly enough, if the military merely bought the planes outright, it would be much cheaper. Senator John McCain described this as "war profiteering."

"At least 32 top officials in the Bush administration served as executives or paid consultants to top weapons contractors before joining the administration."
- William D. Hartung

One can say that weapons and military products, the corporations that manufacture them, and the individuals who make a living from such things are aiding national security. It is not that simple. If they are selling to both sides of a conflict, which is done, then that is definitely unethical. If they promote their cause, and products or services, by private political deals,

248

unfair legislation, no-bid contracts and other clever stratagems, that is also unethical (but not necessarily illegal in our areas of grey national policies and expedient commerce). If, however, they promote war (and those who initiate war) just for profit, this goes beyond ethics and steps into criminality.

Check out The Center for Corporate Policy's **The Top Ten War Profiteers of 2004** (31 December 2004):

1. AEGIS: a UK firm whose founder was once investigated for illegal arms smuggling. Awarded a $293 million contract.

2. BEARING POINT: the former consulting division of KPMG, BP received a $240 million contract to help develop Iraq's "competitive private sector." Bearing Point spent five months helping USAID write the job specifications.

3. BECHTEL: multi-million $ contracts. Many insiders here.

4. BKSH & ASSOCIATES: Chairman Charlie Black is an old Bush family friend and prominent Republican lobbyist whose firm is affiliated with Burson Marsteller, the global public relations giant. BKSH clients with contracts in Iraq include Fluor International - contracts worth up to $1.6 billion.

5. CACI: Maj. Gen. Antonio Taguba reported in an internal Army report that two CACI employees "were either directly or indirectly responsible" for abuses at the [Abu Ghraib] prison, including the use of dogs to threaten detainees and forced sexual abuse and other threats of violence. In August the Army gave CACI another $15 million no-bid contract to continue providing interrogation services for intelligence gathering in Iraq.

6. CUSTER BATTLES: the Defense Department suspended Custer Battles (the name comes from the company's two principle founders - Michael Battles and Scott Custer) and 13 associated individuals and affiliated corporations from all federal contracts for fraudulent billing practices involving the use of sham corporations set up in Lebanon and the Cayman Islands.

7. HALLIBURTON: multi- $$ billions. There are multiple criminal investigations into overcharging and kickbacks. In nine different reports, government auditors have found "widespread, systemic problems with almost every aspect of Halliburton's work in Iraq, from cost estimation and billing systems to cost control and subcontract management." Bunnatine Greenhouse, a top contracting official, says that when the Pentagon awarded the company a 5-year oil-related contract worth up to $7 billion, it pressured her to withdraw her objections.

8. LOCKHEED MARTIN: $21.9 billion in Pentagon contracts in 2003 alone. With satellites and planes, missiles and IT systems, the company has profited from just about every phase of the war except for the reconstruction. E.C. Aldridge Jr., the former undersecretary of defense for acquisitions and procurement, gave final approval to begin building the F-35 in 2001, a decision worth $200 billion to the company. He soon left the Pentagon to join Lockheed's board. ... Not only are Lockheed executives commonly represented on the Pentagon various advisory boards, but the company is also tied into neoconservative networks. For example, Lockheed VP Bruce Jackson (who helped draft the Republican foreign policy platform in 2000) is a key player at the neo-conservative planning bastion known as the Project for a New American Century.

9. LORAL SATELLITE: Loral Space & Communications Chairman Bernard L. Schwartz is very tight with the neoconservative hawks in the Bush administration's foreign policy ranks, and is the principal funder of Blueprint, the newsletter of the Democratic Leadership Council.

10. QUALCOMM: Two CPA officials resigned this year after claiming they were pressured by John Shaw, the deputy undersecretary of defense for technology security to change an Iraqi police radio contract to favor Qualcomm's patented cellular technology. Shaw's efforts to override contracting officials delayed an emergency radio contract, depriving Iraqi police officers, firefighters, ambulance drivers and border guards of a joint communications system for months. Shaw says he was urged to push Qualcomm's technology by Rep. Darrell E. Issa, a Republican whose San Diego County district includes

Qualcomm's headquarters. Issa, who received $5,000 in campaign contributions from Qualcomm employees from 2003 to 2004, sits on the House Small Business Committee, and previously tried to help the company by sponsoring a bill that would have required the military to use its CDMA technology. The DoDefence's inspector general has asked the FBI to investigate Shaw's activities.

~ ~ ~

Pigs requesting Pork

Perhaps the Bush regime assumed that occupied Iraq would indeed be a "cakewalk" and the oil refineries would be pumping money back into various pockets in short order. This did not happen. Or, should I say, the money did not flow back into the US government – it has gone elsewhere. When the oil revenues did not flow freely, the Bush team quickly tapped into another well, the American taxpayer. As we all know, $87 billion was requested by Bush–and granted by congressional yes men– in the fall of 2003. Adding this to previous requests, we are looking at $280 billion in expenditures for Iraq *and counting* ... which is on top of $4 billion *a month* for the military operation itself. These extra "emergency appropriations" (as if such expenditures weren't budgeted into a military venture of this size!) actually ran out by August 2004; Bush did not plan on making another request for billions more until *after* he won the election in November. Suspiciously, let us not forget that Bush signed the huge $417 billion military annual budget in August of 2004 – was it padded to hide another "appropriation" just prior to the election? Although he knew he would win the election, pushing the average American too far too fast would not have been good campaigning. Maybe he *does listen to* the American public.

Nah.

Let's get out our trusty magnifying glass and look at this money thing. Just a small portion of that "special appropriation" $87 billion went towards the following:
- o - $100 million for building seven "model communities,"

complete with houses, schools, roads and clinics. Could this be tried in the U.S.?

o - $400 million for two 4,000 bed prisons. (Well, this **is** being tried in the U.S. In fact, the prison industry is one of the top employers in the land of the free.) And we know how those prisons are being used. Abu Ghraib should be in our consciousness for years (but we do have an expert spin team working on it).

o $100 million to hire 100 experts at $100,000 each for 6 months to assist in prison construction. You do the math on that one!

If you would like to keep up on these numbers on Pentagon spending, check out:
- Center on Strategic and Budgetary Assessments at www.csbaonline.org
- National Priorities Project at www.nationalpriorities.org

It is no coincidence that the lucrative Iraqi rebuilding contracts were "awarded" to Bush's family, friends, and supporters. Enriching his friends by stealing from a third world country, with American troops.... What a clever business plan. So this is what the son of an ex-CIA director plans with an MBA! May I present the following points:

Of the $4 billion sucked up in Iraq per month, about a third of it is going to private contractors. Some of the big players: - Bechtel, with many connections to the *right* people, contracted with Iraq in 1988 to build a chemical plant. Who was President then? This war company is presently enjoying a bigger contract with the new leader of Iraq, George W. Bush. The plan is simple, if brutal: severely bomb Iraq, secure the oilfields, and use US tax money, plus oil profits, to pay Bush's friends to rebuild the country *for democracy*. If we look closer, I'll bet the companies awarded the Iraqi business have stockholders in the Bush regime. The bottom line? April 2003: Bechtel is awarded $680 million deal for reconstruction. Surprise? That was just the beginning for them.

252

- Halliburton, Dick Cheney's old company,* was awarded an uncontested, lucrative contract *before* Iraq was invaded. As of the end of August, 2003, Halliburton had been awarded $1.7 billion dollars since Bush-Cheney stole office. In the fall of this same year, their uncontested contract had been extended again. So much for competition. By the end of 2004 this company passed the $10 billion mark.

* Here's some intriguing background: In 1992, while Cheney was the Defense Secretary under Bush the 1st, Halliburton was awarded a US Army contract to plan international contingency operations for the military. (Isn't this what the well-paid personnel at the Pentagon are supposed to be doing?) This was *after* Halliburton was paid $3.9 million to ascertain if such a plan could be done by a private company! Another $5 million was awarded to this enterprising company to study *more specific* logistical possibilities (and the Republicans scream about wasted money by the Democrats!). In other words, Halliburton was paid to create a job that it was highly qualified for, applied for it, and won the contract! A pattern emerges, for not only was this the company that Cheney would lead to huge governmental profits as CEO, but he used a similar strategy for himself:
While being paid by candidate George Bush in 2000 to search for a possible running mate, Cheney conducted the study, interviewing more than 80 possible candidates, and then decided that **he** was the best man qualified! Dick Cheney created the V.P. Job for himself as a business plan. The plot just thickened.
Back to Halliburton: guess who wrote the contingency plans for the War on Iraq? And who got the no-bid, no-contest contract? That's right. Way right. By the way, Cheney made $26.4 million his last year as CEO of Halliburton, and (last I checked) holds $46 million in this company's stock. It behooves him to nurture that company, and this company is very grateful to Cheney. Conflict?

"As of this writing (2003), Cheney is still on Halliburton's payroll, receiving roughly $150,000 per year in deferred compensation while holding stock options on over 400,000 shares of the company." stated William D. Hartung, who also had the following story to report:

> Due to pressure by [congressman] Waxman and other critics, the Pentagon finally agreed to re-bid the second phase of the Iraqi oil contract, to give other contractors a chance to work on the non-emergency elements of the job. But just one month after holding a major bidders' conference in Dallas to brief companies on the scope of work for the phase two Iraqi oil industry rebuilding contract, the Army Corps of Engineers accelerated the scheduled work so that the bulk of it would have to be done by Halliburton *before* a new contractor could take over. As a result of that administrative sleight of hand, what looked like a contract for $1 billion or more was cut back to a contract worth about $176 million. Bechtel, itself a well-connected firm in Republican circles, cried foul and withdrew from the bidding. (When even an influential firm like Bechtel cries foul, you *know* the fix is in.)

> And who advised the Army Corps of Engineers to accelerate things? That *had* to come from headquarters. Another scandal.

Just to be fair: My point is not that individuals who have worked in the military-industrial complex should be exempt from working in government–there are natural ties and expertise here–but that when a bogus war is pawned onto the American public and young people are dying for this sham while members of an administration (and their friends and family) are profiting from it *is criminal.*

>>~o~<<

Greg Palast, writing before the 2000 election, had more to say not only about Halliburton, but the Carlyle Group, another recipient of republican greed. This defense contract investment firm, the Carlyle Group, is filled with political insiders on its payroll, including none other than ex-president George H. W. Bush. From *The Nation* magazine, August 21-28, 2000, he writes:

Undoubtedly, one reason Cheney was so indulgent of folks like [head of Carlyle Group Frank] Carlucci who cashed in on their government service (James Baker and Dick Darman are now also on the Carlyle payroll) is that he planned to do the same thing himself. When Cheney became CEO of Halliburton in 1995, the energy conglomerate did only a third of its business abroad. Building on the relationships he knitted at Defense, particularly during the Gulf War, Cheney has aggressively expanded Halliburton's foreign operations to more than 70 percent of its $14.9 billion annual business, boosting the company's stock value more than 100 percent. Cheney nearly tripled Halliburton's spending on federal lobbying (not counting the millions it has ladled out to a host of conservative business and trade associations). No surprise, then, that with Cheney in charge Halliburton has doubled its government contracts, to $2.3 billion. The company's latest annual report lists its Brown & Root Services Division's "two largest customers" as the US Defense Department and the British Defense Ministry. Halliburton has also raked in $1.5 billion in US government loans from the Export-Import Bank and the Overseas Private Investment Corporation, up from $100 million in such loans before Cheney took over. That's a lot of "compassion" for these phony fiscal conservatives, and it explains why the Center for Public Integrity has branded Cheney's company a "corporate- welfare hog."

- There's more to be said about Carlyle. Activist Eric Francis writes about those business partners "just trying to make a living" February, 2003:

Those partners include former secretary of defense Frank Carlucci, former secretary of state James Baker III, former British Prime Minister John Major, and other former heads of state. They include people who have served both Democratic and Republican presidents.

The Guardian, a highly-respected UK newspaper, called the firm The Ex President's Club. "Since the start of the 'war on terrorism', the firm -- unofficially valued at $3.5 bn -- has taken on an added significance," the newspaper reported in an October 2001 article. "Carlyle has become the thread which indirectly links American military policy in Afghanistan to the personal financial fortunes of its celebrity employees, not least the current president's father. And, until earlier this month, Carlyle provided another curious link to the Afghan crisis: among the firm's multi-million-dollar investors were members of the family of Osama bin Laden."

~ ~ ~

"Carlyle is as deeply wired into the current administration as they can possibly be. George H. W. Bush is getting money from private interests that have business before the government, while his son is President ... George W. Bush could, some day, benefit from his father's investments ... that's a jaw-dropper."
- Chuck Lewis, Director, Center for Public Integrity, March 2001

Much more can be found in Dan Briody's *The Iron Triangle: Inside the Secret World of the Carlyle Group* (2003). Let me just add that this group gave $358,000 to the Bush campaign in 2000 and $70,000 to Gore. We can see which way they're leaning.

~ ~ ~

Richard Perle is definitely one pig at the trough. He has been publically reprimanded (not by Bush) for repeatedly having conflicts of interest. While privy to the inside story at the war room, he created a consulting firm called Trireme to advise people on how to profit on the new terrorist climate. I'd like to see his financial books. I'm sure Mr. William D. Hartung would too:

> Trireme was only incorporated in November 2001, **after** Perle was appointed chairman of the DPB [Defense Policy Board *] by Rumsfeld and **after** the September 11th terror attacks set the stage for massive increases in military and security spending.

See also "Did Richard Perle Loot $5.4 Million from Hollinger?" http://www.truthout.org/docs_04/090504X.shtml

* By the way, 9 out of 30 DPB members had relationships with weapons contractors.

~ ~ ~

William D. Hartung had this to say about another suspicious character in the Iraqi takeover: on the appointment of Jay Garner, retired general, to head the U.S. occupation of Iraq, by Douglas Feith and Donald Rumsfeld:

> Appointing a retired general affiliated with a firm that has profited from U.S. intervention in the Middle East to run post-invasion Iraq was bad enough. But to appoint a retired general and war profiteer who *also* has affiliated himself with an organization like JINSA [Jewish Institute for National Security Affairs], which is on record in support of the Israeli occupation of the West Bank and *against* the Oslo Accords, was breathtaking in its stupidity.

~ ~ ~

Still following the money ...

Another underlying reason for taking over Iraq: there was a huge international debt owed by this country – over $100 billion to Kuwait alone, and more than $400 billion altogether. So it is easy to see that other companies and countries were waiting for their promised billions. In the meantime, there were several countries lining up to do business with Iraq once the UN sanctions were lifted – and Saddam Hussein was certainly not going to do business with Bush Junior and the evil United States. It was looking like a matter of time until the US grip changed hands. The neo-cons knew that. It was time for action if the US wanted to play in the oil. This was good business and part of "Realpolitik." In the real-time arena, though, we find ourselves in an ugly guerrilla conflict that doesn't look like it will end soon. As far as I can tell, young people in uniform are being killed for a profit motive. As old as history? Yes. Outrageous? Yes. Here in the good ol' USA? Yes. What's being done? Nothing, so far.

Note to investigators: find out who was owed – and who was going to get the US occupation contracts – and you will find more motives for the aggression. What happens to Iraqi oil is of interest to many countries and corporations, including Saudi Arabia, Russia, China, Israel, Turkey, and, oh yes, the United States.

~ ~ ~

"Spending On Iraq Sets Off Gold Rush" ran the headlines in the Washington Post on October 9, 2003. Jonathan Weisman and Anitha Reddy reported that management fees for a police training proposal would be "$26 million a month, while 1,500 police trainers would cost $240,000 each per year, or $20,000 each per month. DynCorp of Reston [VA] is likely to get the contract."

The reporters interviewed Deborah D. Avant, a political scientist at George Washington University, who informed them that perhaps 20,000 contractors were in Iraq and Kuwait, which was a group larger than any other foreign military presence - other than the US military itself. From their article:

> The Iraqi gold rush has raised concerns on Capitol Hill that the administration may be losing control of the taxpayers' money. As the task of rebuilding shifts from government employees to for-profit contractors, members of Congress are worried that their oversight will diminish, cost controls will weaken and decisions about security, training and the shape of the new Iraqi government will be in the hands of people with financial stakes in the outcome. Avant calls it 'the commercialization of foreign policy.'

The reporters quoted Henry A. Waxman (D - CA), a leading critic of Bush's handling of the Iraqi War:

"What we're seeing is waste and gold-plating that's enriching Halliburton and Bechtel while costing taxpayers billions of dollars and actually holding back the pace of reconstruction in Iraq."

See also William Rivers Pitt (Dec 2004): 'Kickbacks Involving Halliburton Contracts'   http://www.truthout.org/overview.htm

And Waxman (Dec 2004): "Halliburton Iraq Contracts Pass $10 Billion Mark"
http://www.truthout.org/docs_04/121004A.shtml

~ ~ ~

If the Bush regime lies about most everything it does, it is not a big stretch to wonder if the top dogs are getting pay-offs to Swiss bank accounts, or to fictitious names or companies, and that these funds will be in their pockets soon after they leave office. I would suggest auditing their books for the next 10 years, but who would take on such a bookkeeping project – all the top accounting agencies are under investigation.

Behind Our Backs

So many terrible things are being done quietly and out of sight of public scrutiny. This alone is a national scandal. The Bush regime has restricted all executive directives and papers from 1980 (Reagan & Bush senior) to the present. In 2004 the Bush regime spent $6.5 billion creating 14 million new classified documents and securing old secrets – the highest level of spending in ten years. This means that this government spent $120 classifying documents for every $1 it spent declassifying documents. (www.openthegovernment.org) National security? They are fond of unwrapping *that* flag. Obviously, there are skeletons in those closets. We may be talking here of obstruction of justice....Yet again. Perhaps we will find out more about the Reagan-Bush ties to Saddam? Things are being hidden. Are papers and tapes being destroyed at this moment?

Secrecy and behind-the-scenes coercion is the order of the day. In their efforts to keep their plans from the public, Bush & Cheney have refused to divulge who advised their energy policy (Enron, etc.). Paul Krugman, one of the few brave writers from the New York Times, had this to say about the republican wheeling and dealing in his **"Crony Capitalism, U.S.A."** (January 15, 2002):

> But the Bush administration, with its sense of entitlement, seems unconcerned by even the most blatant conflicts of interest like the plan of Marc Racicot, the new chairman of the Republican National Committee, to continue drawing a seven-figure salary as a lobbyist. (He now says he won't lobby but he will still receive that salary.)
>
> The real questions about Enron's relationship with the administration involve what happened before the energy trader hit the skids. That's when Mr. Lay allegedly told the head of the Federal Energy Regulatory Commission that he should be more cooperative if he wanted to keep his job. (He wasn't, and he didn't.) And it's when Enron helped Dick Cheney devise an energy plan that certainly looks as if it was written by and for the companies that advised his task force. Mr. Cheney, in clear defiance of the law, has refused to release any information about his task force's deliberations; what is he hiding?

~ ~ ~

Remember the fanfare concerning the trial of Saddam Hussein in the summer of 2004? Once the trial got underway, however, we didn't hear too much about it or him. There was renewed attention on him and his temper early in 2006, but nothing about what he said came to the public forum. Wonder why? – especially since he was such an evil man, and Americans seem to love watching trials? International journalist Robert Fisk, writing from Iraq, tells us about it ... and other things
(The Independent/ Arab News, August 2, 2004)
http://www.arabnews.com/?page=7&section=0&article=49292&d=2&m=8&y=2004

BAGHDAD - The war is a fraud. I'm not talking about the weapons of mass destruction that didn't exist. Nor the links between Saddam Hussein and Al-Qaeda which didn't exist. Nor all the other lies upon which we went to war. I'm talking about the new lies.

For just as, before the war, our governments warned us of threats that did not exist, now they hide from us the threats that do exist. Much of Iraq has fallen outside the control of America's puppet government in Baghdad but we are not told. Hundreds of attacks are made against US troops every month. But unless an American dies, we are not told. This month's death toll of Iraqis in Baghdad alone has now reached 700 ‹‹ the worst month since the invasion ended. But we are not told.

The stage management of this catastrophe in Iraq was all too evident at Saddam Hussein's "trial". Not only did the US military censor the tapes of the event. Not only did they effectively delete all sound of the 11 other defendants. ... But don't think we're going to learn much more about Saddam's future court appearances. Salem Chalabi, the brother of convicted fraudster Ahmad and the man entrusted by the Americans with the tribunal, told the Iraqi press two weeks ago that all media would be excluded from future court hearings. And I can see why. Because if Saddam does a Milosevic, he'll want to talk about the real intelligence and military connections of his regime ‹‹ which were primarily with the United States.

Helping Israel

There is obviously some confusion by the Bush regime of national priorities, international ethics, with whom America aligns itself, and what our allies do and promote. Forgetting both US weapons stockpiles and similar Israeli caches – as well as the military history of both of these nations, Bush (in his guise as TV kid show Mr. Rogers) stated, "See, free nations are peaceful nations. Free nations don't attack each other. Free nations don't develop weapons of mass destruction." (Milwaukee, Wisconsin, Oct. 3, 2003) I guess the USA is not a free nation. Neither is Israel.

Aluf Benn, writing for *Haaretz Daily*, on February 19, 2003, wrote a revealing article with the caption SHARON SAYS U.S. SHOULD ALSO DISARM IRAN, LIBYA AND SYRIA

> Prime Minister Ariel Sharon said yesterday that Iran, Libya and Syria should be stripped of weapons of mass destruction after Iraq. "These are irresponsible states, which must be disarmed of weapons of mass destruction, and a successful American move in Iraq as a model will make that easier to achieve," Sharon said to a visiting delegation of American congressmen.
> Sharon told the congressmen that Israel was not involved in the war with Iraq "but the American action is of vital importance."

>   If the US does eventually intervene in these other Muslim countries -- and Iran is certainly being eyed, then it will be clearer just how wrapped up the neo-cons are with their right wing brethren in Israel. The $3 billion a year in military and economic aid is just the tip of the iceberg in US financial support, according to a column in the Christian Science Monitor, which is known for being rather open in its news and views (contrary to what one might think from the title of the publication). David Francis's "Economic Scene" published in Dec 2002, was a condensed report on aid to Israel by economist Thomas Stauffer - and commissioned by the US Army War College. It created a thunderstorm. http://www.csmonitor.com/2002/1209/p16s01-wmgn.html

Then we have this: **Rights group urges US to cut Israel aid**, by Laila El-Haddad in Gaza, 04 January 2006:

"Israel has been the largest annual recipient of US foreign assistance since 1976, and the largest cumulative recipient since World War II, according to a report published by the

262

Congressional Research Service (CRS) in Washington DC. .... US direct aid to Israel was nearly $2.6 billion in 2005, with an additional $3 billion provided by way of loan guarantees."

Evidently these loans are regularly forgiven (meaning not paid back). Who pays? You. Could you imagine what the US populace would do if this were either common knowledge, or voted upon by referendum? Especially if we consider that the USA has almost 38 million Americans below the poverty line?! Israel, by the way, has been re-selling American weapons (at a very nice profit) to countries that the US cannot or will not sell to, such as to Turkey. As Rabbi Michael Lerner of *Tikkun* magazine has said, this blind agreement of official Israeli policy is detrimental to US security here and abroad. Listen to someone fighting for justice: "... at a meeting with Jewish leaders last year, [George] Soros offered his opinion that Israeli foreign policy is in significant measure responsible for increasing anti-Semitism around the world." - 2004
http://www.thenation.com/doc/20040705/alterman

By stating the facts of oppressive and right wing policies of Israel, I will undoubtedly be called anti-Semitic: this is the label thrown at anyone who dares criticize a Jew, an Israeli, or the country of Israel. Am I anti-American because I criticize the US? No. This is a manipulative tactic aimed at stifling any discussion about the inconsistencies, unethical behaviors, and even criminal activities of individuals, or of this nation. Sacred cows, or muzzling criticism? There are many conscientious Jews who know that such a gag policy is detrimental to growth and trust. Sharon is Israel's Bush, and he and his belligerent actions are black eyes to international good will towards Israel. Although he has stepped down, the strong armed contingent is alive and un-well today. The outrageous attacks in the summer of 2006, aimed at southern Lebanon again (which Israel illegally occupied for years), is but the latest show of ugly force. More terrorists being created – that America will need to face.

Here is an egregious example of this blind aid (below). In the much condemned assault on Lebanon in the summer of 2006 the official word from Washington was neutral. What was really happening, however, was total support for this onslaught – with the Muslim world watching ... while the people of the United States were completely in the dark:

U.S. Speeds Up Bomb Delivery for the Israelis

By David S. Cloud and Helene Cooper

New York Times [with comments from yours truly, pointing out the inherently dangerous policies and double-speak that obscures the truth. SP]

WASHINGTON, July 21, 2006 — The Bush administration is rushing a delivery of precision-guided bombs to Israel, which requested the expedited shipment last week after beginning its air campaign against Hezbollah targets in Lebanon, American officials said Friday.

The decision to quickly ship the weapons to Israel was made with relatively little debate within the Bush administration, the officials said. Its disclosure threatens to anger Arab governments and others because of the appearance [the appearance?] that the United States is actively aiding the Israeli bombing campaign in a way that could be compared to Iran's efforts to arm and resupply Hezbollah. [which would be hypocrisy]

The munitions that the United States is sending to Israel are part of a multimillion-dollar arms sale package approved last year that Israel is able to draw on as needed, the officials said. [nice deal, and the cost?] But Israel's request for expedited delivery of the satellite and laser-guided bombs was described as unusual by some military officers, and as an indication that Israel still had a long list of targets in Lebanon to strike.

Secretary of State Condoleezza Rice said Friday that she would head to Israel on Sunday at the beginning of a round of Middle Eastern diplomacy. The original plan was to include a stop to Cairo in her travels, but she did not announce any stops in Arab capitals. [Do you think this might have been another slight to the Arabs?! Favoritism, perhaps?!]

Instead, the meeting of Arab and European envoys planned for Cairo will take place in Italy, Western diplomats said. While Arab governments initially criticized Hezbollah for starting the fight with Israel in Lebanon, discontent is rising in Arab countries over the number of civilian casualties in Lebanon, and the governments have become wary of playing host to Ms. Rice until a cease-fire package is put together.
To hold the meetings in an Arab capital before a diplomatic solution is reached, said Martin S. Indyk, a former American ambassador to Israel, "would have identified the Arabs as the primary partner of the United States in this project at a time where Hezbollah is accusing the Arab leaders of providing cover for the continuation of Israel's military operation." [Yes, we must never look like we would have the Arabs as primary partners. Like the US ever sides against Israel!]
The decision to stay away from Arab countries for now is a markedly different strategy from the shuttle diplomacy that previous administrations used to mediate in the Middle East. "I have no interest in diplomacy for the sake of returning Lebanon and Israel to the status quo ante," Ms. Rice said Friday. "I could have gotten on a plane and rushed over and started shuttling around, and it wouldn't have been clear what I was shuttling to do." [Good confusion talk, Condi. This is classic smoke.] ...

The new American arms shipment to Israel has not been announced publicly [don't explain it to the US public? And why?!], and the officials who described the administration's decision to rush the munitions to Israel would discuss it only after being promised anonymity [like one cannot talk openly in our society?]. The officials included employees of two government agencies, and one described the shipment as just one example of a broad array of armaments that the United States has long provided Israel. [well, that says a lot. A lot.]

One American official said the shipment should not be compared to the kind of an "emergency resupply" of dwindling Israeli stockpiles that was provided during the 1973 Arab-Israeli war, when an American military airlift helped Israel recover from early Arab victories. [here's a bit of recent history that some folks might find revealing. Yes, the US helped, covertly, Israel win that war. The oil crisis came out of that, and more anti-American hatred.] David Siegel, a spokesman for the Israeli Embassy in Washington, said: "We have been using precision-guided munitions in order to neutralize the military capabilities of Hezbollah and to minimize harm to civilians. As a rule, however, we do not comment on Israel's defense acquisitions." [good diplomat-speak. unfortunately there have been 10 times the number of Lebanese killed to Israelis thus far, so we could either say that the strategy to minimize harm to civilians was not successful, or this diplomat is simply lying.] ...

Pentagon and military officials declined to describe in detail the size and contents of the shipment to Israel, and they would not say whether the munitions were being shipped by cargo aircraft or some other means. But an arms-sale package approved last year provides authority for Israel to purchase from the United States as many as 100 GBU-28's, which are 5,000-pound laser-guided bombs intended to destroy concrete bunkers. The package also provides for selling satellite-guided munitions. [we are talking a lot of fire-power... and enemies for the USA.]

>>~0~<<

Right-wingers and fanatics are found everywhere and in every nation. No group is immune. The list of offences, outrages, and crimes within this book is proof positive of what happens when the wrong people are in charge. The focus of this book is the United States, but injustice and sorrow can be found wherever the short sighted and selfish congregate, and that includes Israel. They are doing their own Smoke & Mirror show. 9-11 was a blowback attack, and biased US policies towards Israel was partly to blame.

~ Let us see if Israeli justice is quicker or braver than the USA version: see what is happening with their own 2007 presidential scandal in the appendix.

Please find the logic, or the diplomatic finesse, in the following:

> Israeli media reported that hardline deputy prime minister, Avigdor Lieberman, told Rice that the Israeli Army will have to re-enter the Gaza Strip at some point, and that 30,000 U.N. troops are needed to secure the chaotic Palestinian territory on Israel's southern flank.

> Lieberman has in the past said Israel should assassinate Hamas' leadership, ignore the moderate Palestinian president and walk away from international peace efforts. His ideas do not necessarily carry weight, but Rice defended the decision to meet with him.

> "I'm going to enlist the support of anybody I can to try and move forward a Palestinian state living at peace side by side with Israel," Rice said. "That is the goal here."
> - http://www.msnbc.msn.com/id/16606866/

> Mr. Lieberman does look like the conservative counterpart to Rice and Bush, but any Palestinian or Arab will more than likely immediately reject any recommendations that this hardball fanatic has to offer. Thus, a poor choice to meet with him publicly, and further proof to the Muslim world that they have few friends or objective officials in the present US government. My educated guess is that such talks will be useless and lead nowhere.

So much for the road to peace.

No, we are heading to a broader road to expanded war:

A POLITICAL BOMBSHELL FROM ZBIGNIEW BRZEZINSKI EX-NATIONAL SECURITY ADVISER WARNS THAT BUSH IS SEEKING A PRETEXT TO ATTACK IRAN

By Barry Grey in Washington DC; wsws.org, February 2, 2007
   http://www.wsws.org/articles/2007/feb2007/brze-f02_prn.shtml
~ ~ ~ You can read the above article online; below is from another
article that describes the bigger picture – alarm bells should be ringing:

THE U.S.-IRAN-IRAQ-ISRAELI-SYRIAN WAR
   By Robert Parry, consortiumnews.com, January 12, 2007
   http://www.consortiumnews.com/2007/011107.html

In his prime-time speech, Bush injected other reasons to anticipate a wider war. He used language that suggested U.S. or allied forces might launch attacks inside Iran and Syria to "disrupt the attacks on our forces" in Iraq.

"We will interrupt the flow of support from Iran and Syria," Bush said. "And we will seek out and destroy the networks providing advanced weaponry and training to our enemies in Iraq."
...
On Jan. 4, Bush ousted the top two commanders in the Middle East, Generals John Abizaid and George Casey, who had opposed a military escalation in Iraq. Bush also removed Director of National Intelligence John Negroponte, who had stood by intelligence estimates downplaying the near-term threat from Iran's nuclear program.

... Bush reportedly has been weighing his military options for bombing Iran's nuclear facilities since early 2006. But he has encountered resistance from the top U.S. military brass, much as he has with his plans to escalate U.S. troop levels in Iraq.

As investigative reporter Seymour Hersh wrote in The New Yorker, a number of senior U.S. military officers were troubled by administration war planners who believed "bunker-busting" tactical **nuclear** weapons, known as B61-11s, were the only way to destroy Iran's nuclear facilities buried deep underground.

A former senior intelligence official told Hersh that the White House refused to remove the nuclear option from the plans despite objections from the Joint Chiefs of Staff. "Whenever anybody tries to get it out, they're shouted down," the ex-official said. [New Yorker, April 17, 2006] By late April 2006, however, the Joint Chiefs finally got the White House to agree that using nuclear weapons to destroy Iran's uranium-enrichment plant at Natanz, less than 200 miles south of Tehran, was politically unacceptable, Hersh reported.

"Bush and [Vice President Dick] Cheney were dead serious about the nuclear planning," one former senior intelligence official said. [New Yorker, July 10, 2006]

Delegating to Israel
But one way to get around the opposition of the Joint Chiefs would be to delegate the bombing operation to the Israelis. Given Israel's powerful lobbying operation in Washington and its strong ties to leading Democrats, an Israeli-led attack might be more politically palatable with the Congress.
Israeli Prime Minister Ehud Olmert also has called the possibility of an Iranian nuclear bomb an "existential threat" to Israel that cannot be tolerated.

Bush's tough talk about Iran also comes as Israel is reported stepping up preparations for air strikes against Iran, possibly including the use of tactical nuclear bombs, to destroy Natanz and other Iranian nuclear facilities.
The Sunday Times of London reported on Jan. 7 that two Israeli air squadrons are training for the mission and "if things go according to plan, a pilot will first launch a conventional laser-guided bomb to blow a shaft down through the layers of hardened concrete [at Natanz]. Other pilots will then be ready to drop low-yield one kiloton nuclear weapons into the hole."

The Sunday Times wrote that Israel also would hit two other facilities -- at Isfahan and Arak -- with conventional bombs. But the possible use of a nuclear bomb at Natanz would represent the first nuclear attack since the United States destroyed Hiroshima and Nagasaki in Japan at the end of World War II six decades ago.

...

Without doubt, Bush's actions in the past two months -- reaffirming his determination to succeed in Iraq and warning about a possible regional explosion if he fails -- suggest that his future course is an escalation of the conflict, not some "graceful exit."

>>~o~<<

In April 2004, Bush promised Sharon portions of the West Bank, which was a decision that totally ignored the needs and wants of the second-class Palestinian people. Bush has done nothing to stop the wall being built, which has touched off international alarm (the last such similar project occurred in Soviet occupied East Germany!). And all that great talk about voting, democracy and the voice of the people – until you don't like what the people voted for, namely, the Palestinians elected Hamas, an organization that Bush was told was a terrorist group. But this is not the first time that Bush has ignored an election result, right?! Such policies are creating more anti-American fervor amongst Muslims the world over. Why? Because the US always sides with Israel. Check all the UN resolutions that aimed at censuring, criticizing or warning Israel in the last 50 years and you will find a close protective connection. Mr. Bush, you are among a long list of rubber-stampers for this aggressive country, and you are creating terrorists by following suit.

But Bush isn't listening. Why? Because he is ...

hearing voices

George Bush talked of his special connection to God, as quoted by *Haaretz* in Israel, June 2003: "God told me to strike at al-Qaida and I struck them, and then He instructed me to strike at Saddam, which I did, and now I am determined to solve the problem in the Middle East. If you help me, I will act, and if not, the elections will come and I will have to focus on them."

Bush, like other fundamentalists, does not listen to reason nor to opposition. He is deluded not only with his own limited vision of God, but when mixed with his family privilege and position thrown in, we are getting warily close to a revised Divine Right of Kings doctrine. When the weak-willed Democrats ignored the "religion thing" and made Bush's fundamentalism a non-issue in the 2000 presidential campaign, perhaps they thought they were being "politically correct" (such a passive effeminate tendency would not occur to Bush). What were they thinking? Don't get me wrong, I am a very spiritual person. Furthermore, being religious, especially in America, is part of the fabric of this nation, but fundamentalism is famous for blind righteousness, intolerance, and narrow-mindedness. Things are not negotiable for these fanatics; they, as a group, are not known for subtleties and compromise. To them, as a group, things are black or white, right or wrong, good or evil. Sound familiar? Al Gore's 2000 campaign was too gentlemanly, urbane and polite (undoubtedly viewed as frail and unmanly by the republicans; not "strong on war" – I mean defense!). John Kerry's 2004 campaign was similarly thoughtful and nuanced. A loser.

I am not afraid of a Christian Republican, although that particular combination could be seen as very conservative. It has been years since a decent Republican has been directing high minded ideals for their party and for this nation (and there has always been a racist, controlling and righteous element on the sidelines).

Here's a reminder from a fair minded pragmatist who probably understood the words of Jesus better than most:

> **"Every gun that is made, every warship launched, every rocket fired, signifies in the final sense a theft from those who hunger and are not fed, those who are cold and are not clothed."**
> - Dwight D. Eisenhower

~ ~ ~

Meanwhile, compassionate conservatism (remember that?) reared its dubious head in postwar Iraq when Bush suggested universal health care to the conquered nation. When it was pointed out that he was against this generous entitlement at home, the promise disappeared in a government fog.

There is more than entitlement or righteousness here; Bush and his ilk will not stop with what they have planned so far. Robert Higgs published on February 18, 2003, "George Bush's Faith-based Foreign Policy" (AlterNet):

> The administration's faith in preemptive warfare currently expresses itself in the plan for military conquest of Iraq, a country that has not threatened the United States and does not possess the means to do so effectively in any event (in part because the United States has been waging low-level warfare and enforcing an economic embargo against it for some 12 years). The Cheney-Rumsfeld-Wolfowitz-Perle coterie evidently has faith that the United States can conquer Iraq quickly and then turn it into a showcase of stable, flourishing democracy. The sheer preposterousness of this expectation suggests that it is fueled more by quasi-religious zealotry than by logic and evidence. When the administration released its "National Security Strategy" to Congress last summer, the grandiosity of the intentions expressed in the document stunned many observers - as Mises Institute historian Joseph Stromberg noted, "it must be read to be believed." The strategy amounts to an enormously presumptuous agenda for domination of the entire world, not only overweening in the vast scope of the specific ambitions enumerated but also brazen in the implicit assumption that the president of the United States and his lieutenants are morally entitled to run the planet.

> It takes a lot of faith in one's own rectitude to declare, among other things, that "our best defense is a good offense" (I am not making this up; it's in the document). Small wonder that George Bush closes his introduction to the document by resorting to religious metaphor, referring to his foreign policy as "this great mission."

...

"As a matter of common sense and self-defense, America will act against . . . emerging threats before they are fully formed," the president declares in that same introduction. In disturbingly Orwellian rhetoric, he affirms that "the only path to peace and security is the path of action" - the path, that is, of launching unprovoked military attacks on other countries. This ongoing pre-emption, supported by the administration's faith that it can identify the threats correctly even before they blossom, will be, the president warns, "a global enterprise of uncertain duration." ...

Finally, the Bush administration has faith that it can continue to drag the American people down the path of perpetual war for perpetual peace and endless nation building. Maybe it can: for the most part, the people certainly have rolled over and played patsy so far, especially if we judge by the actions of their pusillanimous representatives in Congress, who hastened to pass a resolution unconstitutionally delegating to the president their power to declare war against Iraq.

To Bush and his religious cohorts, millions of protesters worldwide were "fringe fanatics," including the following irreligious who spoke out against the war: the Dalai Lama, the Pope, Bishop Desmond Tutu, Bishop Spong, Nelson Mandela, Rabbi Michael Lerner, Dennis Kucinich, James K. Galbraith, and Jimmy Carter -- not to mention hundreds of other public figures and celebrities. Fringe fanatics? No, voices of spirit.

"All across the country -- not just the great metropolitan centers, like Chicago, but places like Bozeman, Montana, Des Moines, Iowa, San Luis Obispo, California, Nederland, Colorado, Tacoma, Washington, York, Pennsylvania, Santa Fe, New Mexico, Gary, Indiana, Carrboro, North Carolina -- fifty-seven cities and counties in all -- have passed resolutions against the war, responding to their citizens."
- Howard Zinn, Feb 27, 2003

And we do need those positive American voices. Bush and his bulldozers are tarnishing the international good will of all Americans. According to a poll of Europeans from the fall of 2002, international opinion of American foreign policy is very low. Andrew Osborne in Brussels wrote in *The Guardian* on March 5, 2003 that "Anxiety about America and the way it projects its global power was exposed yesterday when an European commission opinion poll showed that half the union's citizens see Washington as a danger to world peace rather than a force for good."

The article continues: "Citizens in all 15 member states believe it does more harm than good when it comes to promoting world peace, fighting poverty in the developing world and protecting the environment." Millions of Europeans were disappointed that Bush won the 2004 election. Those that are not too cynical cannot believe that the American voters are that dumb or gullible.

>>~o~<<

It is an understatement to say that Bush and crew have polarized citizens, groups and nations. In the late spring of 2003 Colin Powell publicly reflected upon how France will be punished for its stance on Iraq. The blundering Bush "leadership" is disappointing our own international diplomats and represent-atives. The following is a few paragraphs of the famous text of John Brady Kiesling's letter of resignation to Secretary of State Colin Powell. Mr. Kiesling was a career diplomat who had served in United States embassies from Tel Aviv to Casablanca to Athens. In February of 2003, during the buildup to the Iraq invasion, he could not with good conscience serve under George W. Bush:

> The policies we are now asked to advance are incompat-ible not only with American values but also with American interests. Our fervent pursuit of war with Iraq is driving us to squander the international legitimacy that has been America's most potent weapon of both offense and defense since the days of Woodrow Wilson. We have begun to dismantle the largest and most effective web of international relationships the world has ever known. Our

current course will bring instability and danger, not security.

The sacrifice of global interests to domestic politics and to bureaucratic self-interest is nothing new, and it is certainly not a uniquely American problem. Still, we have not seen such systematic distortion of intelligence, such systematic manipulation of American opinion, since the war in Vietnam. The September 11 tragedy left us stronger than before, rallying around us a vast international coalition to cooperate for the first time in a systematic way against the threat of terrorism. But rather than take credit for those successes and build on them, this Administration has chosen to make terrorism a domestic political tool, enlisting a scattered and largely defeated Al Qaeda as its bureaucratic ally. We spread disproportionate terror and confusion in the public mind, arbitrarily linking the unrelated problems of terrorism and Iraq. The result, and perhaps the motive, is to justify a vast misallocation of shrinking public wealth to the military and to weaken the safeguards that protect American citizens from the heavy hand of government. September 11 did not do as much damage to the fabric of American society as we seem determined to so to ourselves. Is the Russia of the late Romanovs really our model-- a selfish, superstitious empire thrashing toward self-destruction in the name of a doomed status quo?

The status quo was found internationally in the "Coalition of the Willing," which is the official term to the countries that backed the US Iraq War. Shame on them. Or am I being too harsh? Here's the reality: Their backing helped legitimize the oil and land grab. Perhaps quietly many of these sycophant countries disagree with the whole affair, but they are undoubtedly saying to themselves that they are realists playing ***real politics***. Some of them are opportunists and so, like countries throughout history, they have sold out ethics for some silver. Several European nations were coerced into joining, especially if they wanted to either join NATO or stay on America's good side, including getting those economic goodies. As "prudent" as it was to join Bush the conqueror, their participation has simultaneously helped the United Nations to become irrelevant, just as he said it was. I've already pointed out that NATO was now in a quagmire, its very existence in doubt. The March 2004 train bombing in Madrid, Spain, which killed 200 people and wounded many more, gave another spin to the Coalition. The ousted Spanish prime minister ignored the fact that 90% of Spaniards were opposed to the war. He chose to follow George W. Bush instead. Remember, oh members of the willing, that faith-based Bush does not give a whit about your inferior, un-American country. He would enjoy giving France a good whipping, I'm sure. Hell, he would probably like to invade Massachusetts with a Texan brigade. He is not listening to you; he doesn't care. Well, if you are Christians, he'll probably pray for you.

In the meantime, this is what you have gotten from your alignment with Bush's oil grab: young men and women from 17 countries (other than the US) have died in Iraq as of July 2006. Tens of thousands wounded. The list grows day by day. Here is the Iraq Coalition body count site: http://icasualties.org/oif/

Here's something else you have received with your open support for George and his policies: secret US prisons in your own backyards. In "stern" magazine (45/2006) we find an article detailing a German citizen who was kidnapped and sent to "Eagle Base" in Tuzla, Bosnia; officially a US-NATO installation but now revealed to be a secret prison camp. The man in question, who was beaten and illegally held for months, was later found to be quite innocent. Sorry.

note: this mistaken identity thing, which seems to happen too often, is a primary reason these "detainees" should be treated humanely: they may be innocent. After kidnapping, mishandling, beatings and torture, an apology is just not enough.

Of course, apologies come from people who admit mistakes. Some question if this band of zealots are deluding themselves (see below); if so, then we should ask if we wish

276

deluded rulers making decisions - even if they were fairly elected, which they were not.

>>~o~<<

Let's hear from someone religious *and* thoughtful. Sister Joan Chittister calls us to consider all the implications of Iraq in her excellent **"Is There Anything Left That Matters?"**:

It matters that it was destroyed by us under a new doctrine of "preemptive war" when there was apparently nothing worth pre-empting.

It surely matters to the families here whose sons went to war to make the world safe from weapons of mass destruction and will never come home.

It matters to families in the United States whose life support programs were ended, whose medical insurance ran out, whose food stamps were cut off, whose day care programs were eliminated so we could spend the money on sending an army to do what did not need to be done.

It matters to the Iraqi girl whose face was burned by a lamp that toppled over as a result of a U.S. bombing run.

It matters to Ali, the little Iraqi boy who lost his family - and both his arms - in a U.S. air attack.

It matters to the United Nations whose integrity was impugned, whose authority was denied, whose inspection teams are even now still being overlooked in the process of technical evaluation and disarmament.

It matters to the reputation of the United States in the eyes of the world, both now and for decades to come, perhaps.

And surely it matters to the integrity of this nation whether or not its intelligence gathering agencies have any real intelligence or not before we launch a military armada on its say-so.

And it should matter whether or not our government is either incompetent and didn't know what they were doing or were dishonest and refused to say.

The unspoken truth is that either as a people we were misled, or we were lied to, about the real reason for this war. Either we made a huge - and unforgivable - mistake, an arrogant or ignorant mistake, or we are swaggering around the world like a blind giant, flailing in all directions while the rest of the world watches in horror or in ridicule.

If Bill Clinton's definition of "is" matters, surely this matters. If a president's sex life matters, surely a president's use of global force against some of the weakest people in the world matters. If a president's word in a court of law about a private indiscretion matters, surely a president's word to the community of nations and the security of millions of people matters.

There is the matter of the unpopular war itself. As is quite clear by now, a non-military option was possible. (It was not for the US to unilaterally implement in any case; there was no connection with al-Qaeda and 9-11. In fact, there are more links of these sorts to our "ally" Saudi Arabia.) Keep in mind that this is essentially a 15 year siege; since the Gulf War of 1991 Iraq has been starved, set apart, burdened, and bombed. This is not counting the 8 year war they had against Iran in the 1980s, which Reagan-Bush encouraged. And it looks like the US will be there for a long time: Rumsfeld has promised us a **permanent war** as early as October 2001 (www.defenselind.mil).

How to Create Terrorists: *a recipe*

Yet another reminder that the wisdom of Ronald Reagan is near and dear to the neo-cons, Rumsfeld and his military Neanderthals are bringing back a nostalgic piece of policy from the good old days of death squads in Central America. Michael Hirsh and John Barry from Newsweek (08 January 2005) give us the details on **The Salvador Option**: *The Pentagon may put Special-Forces-led assassination or kidnapping teams in Iraq:*

What to do about the deepening quagmire of Iraq? The Pentagon's latest approach is being called "the Salvador option"- and the fact that it is being discussed at all is a measure of just how worried Donald Rumsfeld really is. "What everyone agrees is that we can't just go on as we are," one senior military officer told Newsweek. "We have to find a way to take the offensive against the insurgents. Right now, we are playing defense. And we are losing." Last November's operation in Fallujah, most analysts agree, succeeded less in breaking "the back" of the insurgency-as Marine Gen. John Sattler optimistically declared at the time-than in spreading it out.

Now, Newsweek has learned, the Pentagon is intensively debating an option that dates back to a still-secret strategy in the Reagan administration's battle against the leftist guerrilla insurgency in El Salvador in the early 1980s. Then, faced with a losing war against Salvadoran rebels, the U.S. government funded or supported "nationalist" forces that allegedly included so-called death squads directed to hunt down and kill rebel leaders and sympathizers. Eventually the insurgency was quelled, and many U.S. conservatives consider the policy to have been a success-despite the deaths of innocent civilians and the subsequent Iran-Contra arms-for-hostages scandal. (Among the current administration officials who dealt with Central America back then is John Negroponte, who is today the U.S. ambassador to Iraq. Under Reagan, he was ambassador to Honduras.)

Following that model, one Pentagon proposal would send Special Forces teams to advise, support and possibly train Iraqi squads, most likely hand-picked Kurdish Peshmerga fighters and Shiite militiamen, to target Sunni insurgents and their sympathizers, even across the border into Syria, according to military insiders familiar with the discussions.

...

> THAT was a direct example of a covert program that will be sure to create more terrorists (Yes, say the top brass, but they will be ours!). Now on to the *indirect* mode. We are losing this war

279

on the human front. James Ridgeway wrote a revealing piece in his article "Guerrillas in the Midst: Death Hits Mr. Rumsfeld's Neighborhoods" (Mondo Washington, July 29th, 2003):

> Consider the story of little Mohammad al-Kubaisi, as Amnesty International described it last week. On June 26, Mohammad was carrying the family bedding up to the roof, where they slept each night. As he climbed, Mohammad saw American soldiers searching nearby houses. He stopped to watch. Across the street, an American soldier spotted the boy and raised his gun. An Iraqi standing near the soldier said something about "that baby." But the soldier said, "No baby," and shot the boy.
>
> When his mother heard Mohammad had been hit, she raced home and saw that he was still alive and scooped him up, but American soldiers searching the house "kicked her aside," offering no medical treatment. Two neighbors rushed the boy to the hospital. But the road was blocked by an American tank, and when one of the neighbors tried to explain to an interpreter what was going on, the soldiers "handcuffed them behind their back and threw them face down on the ground." After 15 minutes, the Iraqis were allowed to get up and told to go home because the curfew had begun. It was too late for little Mohammad. He had died.
>
> So goes the battle for the hearts and minds of Iraq.

The bad news continued. "U.S. Reportedly Kills 40 Iraqis at a Wedding Party"
http://www.truthout.org/docs_04/052004B.shtml

>>~o~<<

War is ugly and fearsome, sometimes bringing out the worst in people. As the Iraqi occupation turns into a prolonged guerrilla war, with American casualties daily, US military officers are giving their troops free reign to protect themselves. Although this seems natural and even necessary in this war climate, remember that "we" are officially in Iraq for reasons of *our* national security, and *their* liberation. When our troops rough up or kill the natives, even accidentally, anger and hatred for all Americans will be the result. Muslims the world over are hearing stories of American brutality, torture, and killing. Below are some telling quotes from that conservative publication, *Time*, during the first month of the war, dated April 7, 2003:

"We are slaughtering them."

"Man, sometimes I wish we didn't have the Geneva Convention. You see what they did to our guys?"

"Tell them if they shoot one bullet, we will shoot 2,000 bullets back."

"The war ultimately will boil down to how many of our soldiers we are willing to sacrifice to keep dead Iraqi civilians off al-Jazeera," says a Navy officer at the Pentagon.

And then things got ridiculous: On fratricide, or friendly fire, from a Brave New World voice: "We have so overwhelmed our enemies that the ratio has climbed," says Lieut. Colonel Chris Hughes of 101 Airborne. "It is a direct reflection of the fact that our enemies have not been able to inflict serious damage on us." This preposterous statement was quoted without comment. This is right out of Bedlam.

The scariest thing was found in a poll in that issue: If the US troops in Iraq are hit with chemical weapons (remembering that we have used napalm on them), should the US use nuclear weapons?

> It was applauded, no doubt, that 62% of the respondents said No. However, 34% said Yes! How many millions of Americans would this be? I know statistically that 23% of the voting public sided with Bush in 2000; which we now know is less than the number willing to use nuclear weapons in a third world country. (This points to a failure of the American education system, but that's another story.) These millions of Americans don't get the real goal of this war. Our religious fundamentalists would gladly nuke the godless Muslims, but the land is valuable, you see. The military, of course, had the right stuff in their orders: get the oil. Thus, it was no surprise to the followers of the Iraq War that the oil fields were captured and *secured* quickly and efficiently.

>>~o~<<

By the summer of 2006 the social and political landscape looked quite differently. The troop reactions to scary situations and "misjudgments that led to fatalities" were seeming like the good old days. Stories of revenge, planned killings or assassinations, women and children wounded and killed, and even massacres were in the news. Former Marine and decorated Vietnam Vet, Pennsylvania Congressman John Murtha, declared that U.S. troops killed innocent civilians "in cold blood." A revenge-driven rampage burst upon the Iraqi town of Haditha in November of 2005, was reported in *Time* magazine in March 2006, and slowly became an issue months later. Murtha, who of course had more information due to his position, claimed that it was "much worse than reported." (*Time*, May 29, 06)

In another story, four GIs were under investigation for the rape and killing of a young Iraqi woman, plus the killing of her family, evidently to leave no witnesses. (This happened in March 2006 and was reported in late June 2006.) These US soldiers then torched the house to hide the evidence. The main ringleader was actually arrested in North Carolina, because he was discharged early from the Army due to a personality disorder. Is this appalling? http://news.aol.com/topnews/articles/_a/soldier-gets-100-years-for-iraq-rape/20070223070909990001?ncid=NWS00010000000001

People, our sweet and patriotic boys and girls are evidently turning into trigger happy killers. They will continue to lose the War on Terror by their very actions, then they will be discharged and come home, warts, rage and all. I understand that there is a psychological system in place to deal with these kids (and let me be clear here – these are indeed teens and young twenty-somethings who may have had good intentions before they got into a war zone, but they are victims of Bush, Cheney and Rumsfeld way up the *chain* of command.), and I hope this social therapy will help integrate these youngsters back into good lives. Post Traumatic Syndrome and radiation poisoning are ugly additions to a general sense of betrayal. And, as the rest of the governmental support system is suspect, I can only imagine what we, as a society, will be facing in the next decades. Oh, and the next generation will be footing the bill. The neo-con fall-out is everywhere. Everywhere.

Posing with Prisoners

The Abu Ghraib prison scandal erupted in the spring of 2004, with American boys and girls shown posing in front of humiliated, abused and tortured Iraqis. What might be drifting into the fog of memory is that Bush then clumsily addressed the Arab peoples, mumbling something about an investigation is underway, but "our justice system" assumes someone is innocent until proven guilty. This was not a good time to lecture a people on justice – especially by a man that ignored international consensus and the United Nations when he chose to send troops to their country. As you may recall, Donald Rumsfeld used a photo opportunity to take responsibility for the prison "problem," and within days Dick Cheney was praising him as the best Defense Secretary we've ever had. Donald Rumsfeld then embarrassed our nation when he "philosophized" and described the torture of Iraqi citizens at Abu Ghraib as "the excesses of human nature that humanity suffers." Is this too much or what? Wait, there's more. In an audacious move, behind the scenes, Bush's dream team tried a "protecting the guilty" ploy, which thankfully did not work on the international front: *The Economist* informed us "America was forced to withdraw a Security Council resolution that would have exempted American UN-peacekeeping troops from prosecution by the INTER-NATIONAL CRIMINAL COURT. It had won immunity in previous years, but the prisoner scandal at Abu Ghraib strengthened opposition from other members of the council." http://www.economist.com/

> Can you believe that?! Of course, bi-lateral agreements were made to some very stupid countries, as reported earlier.

All of these devious ploys will backfire, as even simple non-Christians can look at the Abu Ghraib photographs and figure out who the culprits are. Obviously, Middle Eastern Muslims are not used to dealing with the US justice system, in

which the man who came in second can win the election with some clever lawyers. Our American brand of justice was at work months before the prison scandal broke. During the first week of June, 2004, TruthOut.org published for public consumption: "Administration Lawyers Approved Torture"
http://www.truthout.org/docs_04/060804A.shtml

By July 2004 The New York Times, Newsweek, The Washington Post and The Wall Street Journal published or referred to official memorandums that discussed fine points of distinction on whether one was torturing or not. To this date no high ranking person has been reprimanded for this scandal.

Here's another revealing article:
"Prison Chief: Rumsfeld Authorized Torture, Israelis Involved"
http://www.truthout.org/docs_04/070504A.shtml

Former Attorney General John Ashcroft, who was being questioned by the Senate Judiciary Committee in early June 2004 about the prison torture scandal, not only protected the president (was this perjury?) but defended his less-than-ethical lawyers for con-cluding the following: "inflicting pain in interrogating people detained in the fight against terrorism did not always constitute torture."

Ashcroft repeatedly stated that the president had broader powers than normal because the US was in a state of war. I would like to point out here that we are in a war with Iraq that was *manufactured by* Bush and his oil and weapons buddies. Ah, the smoke and mirrors show does not end.
I'm getting a bit tired of it.

Marjorie Cohn, professor of law, concluded the following: "It's all falling into place. The Wall Street Journal has revealed that Bush's lawyers told him he can order that torture be committed with impunity. It is now official that George W. Bush is above the law. ... Torture is sanctioned policy that comes from the top." (http://www.truthout.org/docs_04/060904A.shtml)

See also "Army Report: Gen. Sanchez Approved Torture at Abu Ghraib" http://www.truthout.org/docs_04/082804Y.shtml and "U.S. Bars U.N. from Alleged Torture Centers" http://www.truthout.org/docs_04/082304B.shtml and "Rumsfeld Gave Torture 'Marching Orders' in Memo" http://www.truthout.org/docs_04/121804X.shtml

Gitmo

Do we have our own concentration camp? I'm sure anti-Castro activists are pleased that there is a strong and imposing US military presence on the island of Cuba. But Guantánamo Bay will backfire in the propaganda wars if we consider that the U.S., representing the free world alternative to communism, has imprisoned people that Donald Rumsfeld and other officials did not declare prisoners of war. Why? Because then these "enemy combatants" would have rights under the Geneva Convention. *Quid pro quo* - Guantánamo Bay, besides putting more equipment and troops on the *evil* island of Cuba, quickly showed the punitive US leaders *why there was* a Geneva Convention. Once they used this legalese ploy of not declaring the captives "prisoners of war," when US troops were captured and mistreated in Afghanistan and Iraq following the same logic, the Rumsfeld brigade changed their position... somewhat. (They don't like to retract or admit mistakes, you see.) These guilty detainees, Rumsfeld declared, are more than criminals, they are dangerous terrorists and must be treated differently. The dangerous criminals imprisoned in "Gitmo", as it is affectionately called, range in ages 13 - 70. Come on! The most dangerous people on the planet? Unfortunately, since more than sixty-five have been released as of October 2004 (and dozens more by 2006), perhaps they weren't so dangerous after all. Although the thirteen year old does need watching, to be sure.

Broad Use of Harsh Tactics Is Described at Cuba Base
by Neil A. Lewis; The New York Times; 17 October 2004:

Washington – "Many detainees at Guantánamo Bay were regularly subjected to harsh and coercive treatment, several people who worked in the prison said in recent interviews, despite longstanding assertions by military officials that such treatment had not occurred except in some isolated cases. …"

In the summer of 2004 it was discovered that there was an *official hiding of prisoners from the International Red Cross.* Is this the United States? This prison is an international black eye on this country and its stated principles. Here's another chilling headline published the end of November, 2004:
Red Cross Finds Torture at Guantánamo
http://www.truthout.org/docs_04/120104Z.shtml

And another: GUANTÁNAMO'S LONG SHADOW
By Anthony Lewis, New York Times, June 21, 2005:
> When Vice President Dick Cheney said last week that detainees at the American prison camp in Guantánamo Bay, Cuba, were treated better than they would be "by virtually any other government on the face of the earth," he was carrying on what has become a campaign to whitewash the record of abuses at Guantánamo.

> This article goes into some unpleasant and even revolting detail about what goes on at this prison. Check out the article yourself:
http://www.nytimes.com/2005/06/21/opinion/21lewis.html
>>~o~<<

The Wall Street Journal (May 20 2006) gave us this news: "A U.N. Panel Urged the U.S. to close its prison in Guantánamo Bay":
> The Committee Against Torture also said Washington should disclose the existence of any secret detention facilities, should end all forms of torture and shouldn't send suspects to nations where they might be tortured. The panel's report came on the same day as the military disclosed prisoners wielding broken light fixtures, fan blades and pieces of metal clashed with guards trying to stop a detainee who was pretending to commit suicide. Six prisoners were injured.

The military transferred 15 Saudi detainees to their country, leaving about 460 prisoners at Guantánamo.

- note: evidently the suicide attempt was real. During the first week of June three prisoners were dead.

>>~o~<<

The United Nations took a huge step in standing up to the US neo-cons in the spring of 2006. They issued a report that listed the ugly details about the Guantánamo Prison Camp and declared that it should be closed. *Time* (May 29, 2006) reported the reaction in **Gitmo Comes Under Fire**. The US response to the UN declaration?

"The White House response came swiftly. Spokesman Tony Snow insisted that all prisoners in U.S. custody are treated 'fully within the boundaries of American law.'"

> This is a scary thought for the rest of us, but within a month he was seen as yet another liar for the regime: In June 2006 the supreme court ruled that the whole process of artificially defining prisoners and using secret and biased military "justice" was unconstitutional and defied international law. Bush responded with his typical pose of the "don't back down" tough guy, declaring to the American populace that he was not going to endanger them by releasing these dangerous criminals.

>>~o~<<

One would think that with all of the negative press about Abu Ghraib and Guantánamo that someone at headquarters might want to tone things down or at least to appear as if there was some humanitarian concerns discussed or even promoted at the White House. So who does Bush choose to replace the right of right John Ashcroft? In January 2005 the US Senate debated Alberto Gonzales' nomination to become Attorney General, replacing Herr Ashcroft. MoveOn.org informed us of this unsavory option and urged Americans to contact their Senators. Do email campaigns like this work? Not yet. This is what they wrote: "Gonzales is the White House counsel notorious for opening the door to torture at Abu Ghraib and Guantánamo Bay prisons." Senators should have viewed the Gonzales nomination very skeptically, given his reactionary history. MoveOn.org initiated an unsuccessful campaign during the debates to call on Senators to ask Gonzales to unequivocally renounce torture as an instrument of American policy.

Law professor Marjorie Cohn then took the next logical step in dealing with this torture scandal and the larger issues present. She tried to tell our Congress, and the American people, the truth about: **"The Gonzales Indictment"** t r u t h o u t | Perspective (19 January 2005):

> Alberto Gonzales should not be the Attorney General of the United States. He should be considered a war criminal and indicted by the Attorney General. This is a suggested indictment of Alberto Gonzales for war crimes under Title 18 U.S.C. section 1441, the War Crimes Act. ...
> Defendant ALBERTO GONZALES wrote, in a memorandum to President George W. Bush dated January 25, 2002, that the war against terrorism is a "new paradigm" that "renders obsolete Geneva's strict limitations on questioning of enemy prisoners and renders quaint some of its provisions."
> Defendant GONZALES wrote that the Third Geneva Convention should not apply to members of the Taliban and Al Qaeda who were captured after the United States invaded Afghanistan in October 2001. Defendant GONZALES also advised President Bush in that memorandum that he could avoid allegations of war crimes under The War Crimes Act by simply declaring that the Geneva Convention does not apply to members of the Taliban and Al Qaeda. Defendant GONZALES wrote that a determination of the inapplicability of the Third Geneva Convention would insulate against prosecution by future "prosecutors and independent counsels."
>
> In apparent reliance on the advice in Defendant GONZALES' memorandum, and notwithstanding the requirement of Article 5 of the Third Geneva Convention that a "competent tribunal" determine the status of

288

prisoners, President George W. Bush issued an order on February 7, 2002, specifying that the United States would not apply the Third Geneva Convention to members of Al Qaeda, and that as commander-in-chief of the United States, he had the power to suspend the Geneva Conventions regarding the conflict in Afghanistan, although he declined to suspend them at that time.

~ ~ ~

> Please note, my fellow Americans, such underhanded and unethical maneuvers are common with this regime. Bush and the gang, of course, ignored opposition and appointed Gonzales anyway. They always get what they want. They always get what they want.

... And this is what *we* get, and got, in early 2007:

> For now, the nation's focus is on the eight federal prosecutors fired by Attorney General Alberto Gonzales. In January, Mr. Gonzales told the Senate Judiciary Committee, under oath, that he "would never, ever make a change in a United States attorney for political reasons." But it's already clear that he did indeed dismiss all eight prosecutors for political reasons - some because they wouldn't use their offices to provide electoral help to the G.O.P., and the others probably because they refused to soft-pedal investigations of corrupt Republicans.

> In the last few days we've also learned that Republican members of Congress called prosecutors to pressure them on politically charged cases, even though doing so seems unethical and possibly illegal.

> The bigger scandal, however, almost surely involves prosecutors still in office. The Gonzales Eight were fired because they wouldn't go along with the Bush administration's politicization of justice. But statistical evidence suggests that many other prosecutors decided to protect their jobs or further their careers by doing what the

289

administration wanted them to do: harass Democrats while turning a blind eye to Republican malfeasance.

- **Department of Injustice** by Paul Krugman, The New York Times, 09 March 2007

When do we collectively stop this onslaught on world justice?

How many noticed the media coverage of the cheering in the streets of Iraq when Donald Rumsfeld resigned in the autumn of 2006? People on the street were interviewed. They hated him and were glad to see him go. Well, I can understand their anger and contempt for him, but this news coverage also brought up a few questions for Americans to think about; namely, why do the American people have to wait until a top White House /Pentagon Chief resigns to find out what people think of him in "our" occupied territory, Iraq? Do they know something about him that the average American Joe doesn't? And what do they, and perhaps more broadly, what do the people of other nations, think about our *other* leaders, like Condi Rice, Dick Cheney and George Bush? I personally think it would be useful information. (I also know that there is a vociferous minority that would yell "What the fuck do we care about what other countries think of us?!" They are the redneck followers, pre-programmed stooges, of the neo-cons and the first to shriek "America is Number One!" Their ignorant and reactionary belief is that Whomever dares to criticise this sacred trust of domination is un-American and should be shot. Yes, strongly worded. I believe that their dangerous bullying stifles debate and self-reflection in this country.)

A last Hurrah from out-going Defense Secretary Donald H. Rumsfeld: Just before he resigned he wrote a confidential memo to George Bush, sharing more of his wisdom. Notice the Father Knows Best stance is still proudly and doggedly displayed, and also notice, from this report, his disdain for the American people, who can be led through PR; and then note an antiquated patriarchal stance towards the Iraqi people:

Rumsfeld Memo Proposed 'Major Adjustment' in Iraq by MICHAEL R. GORDON and DAVID S. CLOUD, The New York Times, WASHINGTON (Dec. 2, 2006)

... To limit the political fallout from shifting course he suggested the administration consider a campaign to lower public expectations.

"Announce that whatever new approach the U.S. decides on, the U.S. is doing so on a trial basis," he wrote. "This will give us the ability to readjust and move to another course, if necessary, and therefore not 'lose.' "

"Recast the U.S. military mission and the U.S. goals (how we talk about them) - go minimalist," he added. ...

The memorandum sometimes has a finger-wagging tone as Mr. Rumsfeld says that the Iraqis must "pull up their socks," and suggests reconstruction aid should be withheld in violent areas to avoid rewarding "bad behavior." [This first remark was later expanded:] ...

One option Mr. Rumsfeld offered calls for modest troop withdrawals "so Iraqis know they have to pull up their socks, step up and take responsibility for their country." ...

Taking a leaf out of Mr. Hussein's book, Mr. Rumsfeld seemed to see some merit in the former dictator's practice of paying Iraqi leaders. "Provide money to key political and religious leaders (as Saddam Hussein did), to get them to help us get through this difficult period," one option reads.

Tight security? Or the public on a leash?

If we didn't have blowback, we wouldn't have had 9-11; if we wouldn't have had that attack, "we" wouldn't have given Bush the expanded powers he has today. Not only has he exercised that license internationally in numerous and aggressive actions, but he has used his expanded war powers to cover his tendency for secrecy and control at home. We are being spied upon, videoed, finger-printed and recorded. We are losing our rights daily. Many examples are to be found in the provisions in the Patriot Act (implying that anyone who questions it must not be patriotic), which include the following:

> - the authorization of unconstitutional searches and wiretaps.
> - the Attorney General can classify groups as domestic terrorist organizations without judicial review. *It is scary to think of this important power in the reactionary hands of John Ashcroft, and now Alberto Gonzales.*
> - detention up to seven days without charges.
> - surveillance of all Americans at libraries or booksellers. Security geeks are pressuring librarians to notify them if anyone checks out certain suspicious books. Furthermore, librarians are prohibited from telling you that you are being watched. Makes you wonder who's on the suspicious book list? Michael Moore? Noam Chomsky? either Clinton? Henry David Thoreau? Thomas Paine?

> - Sounds like Brave New World?!

>>~o~<<

"Before the smoke had cleared in Washington and New York, the Bush administration had decided that the best possible way to defend freedom was to restrict it as much as possible. The PATRIOT Anti-Terror Act was drafted - the original version carried a provision from Ashcroft to suspend habeas corpus indefinitely, but was wisely deleted by the Senate - and in its core lay the tools of a new, fearful domestic statecraft. Americans could be detained without access to attorney or trial for an indefinite period. Access to attorneys would be monitored and recorded. Searches of private homes could be performed without notification. Religious and political groups could be put under surveillance with no justification. Mr. Ashcroft proclaimed to Congress in public testimony in December of 2001 that anyone who disagreed with these new policies was aiding terrorism, or were terrorists themselves."
- William Rivers Pitt, "Greetings from Boston, Mr. Bush," (t r u t h o u t, 1 October, 2002)

Thousands are standing up to this Patriot Act, including cities, counties, and states. And with good reason. If unchecked, we will become another oligarchy, plutocracy or police state, and our freedoms and civil rights will be merely words in nationalistic speeches. Let us, however, refer to the Constitution itself. Certain provisions in the Patriot Act, the actions of Attorney Generals Ashcroft and Gonzales, and the activities of Guantanamo and other prisons are unconstitutional!

- Article I., Section. 9., Clause 2: *The Privilege of the Writ of Habeas Corpus shall not be suspended, unless when in Cases of Rebellion or Invasion the public Safety may require it.*

Also note: Bill of Rights, Article [IV.] *The right of the people to be secure in their persons, houses, papers, and effects, against unreasonable searches and seizures, shall not be violated, and no Warrants shall issue, but upon probable cause, supported by Oath or affirmation, and particularly describing the place to be searched, and the persons or things to be seized.*

- The US Constitution

All this is rather clear, but I don't recall the supreme court standing up to intervene on our behalf, do you? No one is immune at this point. The Bush regime has threatened US congressmen for allowing "leaks" to the public. Does this not alarm you? Even the elected representatives of this country are being monitored and threatened! For the rest of us, well, we'll be speaking in whispers soon. Below we have an eye-opening observation from the San Francisco Chronicle (January 6, 2002):

THE PRESIDENT didn't ask the networks for television time. The attorney general didn't hold a press conference. The media didn't report any dramatic change in governmental policy. As a result, most Americans had no idea that one of their most precious freedoms disappeared on Oct. 12, 2001. Yet it happened. In a memo that slipped beneath the political radar.

Attorney General John Ashcroft vigorously urged federal agencies to resist most Freedom of Information Act requests made by American citizens.

Passed in 1974 in the wake of the Watergate scandal, the Freedom of Information Act has been hailed as one of our greatest democratic reforms. It allows ordinary citizens to hold the government accountable by requesting and scrutinizing public documents and records. Without it, journalists, newspapers, historians and watchdog groups would never be able to keep the government honest. It was our post-Watergate reward, the act that allows us to know what our elected officials do, rather than what they say. It is our national sunshine law, legislation that forces agencies to disclose their public records and documents. When coupled with President Bush's Nov. 1, 2001 executive order that allows him to seal all presidential records since 1980, the effect is positively chilling.

Notice how a neo-con, and someone who as Attorney General was supposed to protect all Americans from legal tyranny, uses great sounding phrases to reconstruct himself and his cronies as the saviors of the people. What he is saying, of course, is keep silent, obey orders, and let us tap your phones and look into your clothes closet. If you complain, you must be siding with the enemy.:

> "To those who scare peace-loving people with phantoms of lost liberty, my message is this:
> Your tactics only aid terrorists, for they erode our national unity and diminish our resolve. They give ammunition to America's enemies, and pause to America's friends. They encourage people of good will to remain silent in the face of evil."
> -- US Attorney General John Ashcroft, in his testimony before the Senate

~ ~ ~

"So, Mr. Bush, Mr. Cheney, and Mr. Ashcroft, we who dissent are not anti-American. We are not disloyal. We most definitely are not traitors. We are not causing your problems. We merely want some answers. We have the liberty given to us by our founding fathers to disagree with you and to ask probing

questions. When you attempt to take away that liberty, it is you who have become the traitors in our midst. It is you who are anti-American. It is you who are responsible for eroding our national unity. Leaders who have nothing to hide have no problem answering questions."
- Rebecca Knight, *Memorial Day*, 2002

Arianna Huffington, who used to be friends with Newt Gingrich, is now an outspoken critic of George Bush. She has written many pieces on the various activities of this outrageous regime. Below are some observations from just one of her writings, entitled, "White House Chutzpah" (Dec 2002):

On the environment: Not satisfied with just gutting the Clean Air Act, the White House chose to announce its polluter-friendly decision in the most dismissive, least accountable way possible, delivered not by the president or EPA head Christie Whitman but by a low-level administrator, on a Friday afternoon leading into a holiday week, and with no cameras allowed. In your face, people who like fresh air!

On stealing from the poor to give to the rich: In an act of reverse Robin Hood effrontery, the president helped defray some of the cost of his non-stop campaigning with an accounting trick that allowed him to dip into the coffers of the Office of Family Assistance by piggy-backing campaign appearances onto trips ostensibly made to talk about welfare reform. That's right, money meant to assist poor families was used to help elect politicians who believe that, even with all the problems facing this country, cutting taxes for the rich should be job No. 1. These, of course, are the same Scrooges who did nothing to stop the unemployment benefits of 800,000 workers from expiring during the midst of the holiday season. Ho, ho, ho, poor people!

On sucking up to special interests: I guess that the back channel passage of that tailor-made -- and White House approved amendment to the Homeland Security Bill protecting Eli Lilly, maker of the questionable vaccine preservative Thimerosal, from billions in potential lawsuits just wasn't enough of an insult to democracy. To pour salt in that fresh wound, the administration has asked a federal claims court to block public access to documents unearthed in over a thousand Thimerosal-related lawsuits. Take that, suffering parents of autistic children!

On political patronage: At the same time the White House was moving to scale back pay increases for career federal employees, it was also secretly doling out big buck bonuses to political appointees -- a practice banned during the Clinton presidency because of abuses during the last Bush administration. Who was it again who was going to restore integrity to the White House?

On fighting the war on terror: A majority of Americans have a negative view of Saudi Arabia. As well they should, given the desert kingdom's two-faced attitude, the money that ended up in the pockets of 9/11 hijackers, its telethons for suicide bombers, its refusal to let U.S. planes targeting the Taliban take off from Saudi soil, and the not insignificant fact that most of the 9/11 hijackers were Saudi, as are most of the suspects being held in Guantánamo. In spite of all this, the White House continues to treat the spoiled princes of the House of Saud as bosom brothers, ...

Bottom line, my fellow Americans: George Dubya Bush is a liar and war monger ... which has led to national in-security, inter-national distrust, tons of bombs and thousands dead. Where is the moral outrage when lies lead to deaths, and the profits on those deaths? The Smoke & Mirrors show is slowly turning into a very scary movie. But it is real.

"No man thinks more highly than I do of the patriotism, as well as abilities, of the very worthy gentlemen who have just addressed the house. But different men often see the same subject in different lights; and, therefore, I hope it will not be thought disrespectful to those gentlemen if, entertaining as I do opinions of a character very opposite to theirs, I shall speak forth my sentiments freely and without reserve. This is no time for ceremony.

"Should I keep back my opinions at such a time, through fear of giving offense, I should consider myself as guilty of treason towards my country, and of an act of disloyalty toward the Majesty of Heaven, which I revere above all earthly kings.

"Is life so dear, or peace so sweet, as to be purchased at the price of chains and slavery? Forbid it, Almighty God! I know not what course others may take; but as for me, give me liberty or give me death!"
-- Patrick Henry, US "Founding Father", Gentleman, and Revolutionary

~ ~ ~

There are many voices in this chorus against the mad king George. Many of them are quoted within these pages. The Bush regime has shown enough corruption, arrogance and contempt that they should be impeached en masse. Although it is the belief of this writer that such a procedure would imply their legitimacy, there is a movement and a website dedicated to that end. See the website www.votetoimpeach.org. Former US Attorney General Ramsey Clark is doing good work there and elsewhere. My slant and advice is to play hardball with them; otherwise they will walk all over you -- or have you disappear. I have addressed the legal ramifications of calling for arrests for treason and other crimes in my Call To Action section. Read all about it!

Many people voted for Bush and Cheney because they portray themselves as good, financially conservative pragmatists. That show is a bust too.

Let's check the take at the box office:

Economy: Con, Cash-in & Cripple

> Paul Krugman ... was describing Bush's approach to politics and economic policy as crony capitalism, American-style. As a trained economist, he was able to see from the outset that the Bush budget and tax plans were based on such bogus numbers that administration officials had to be lying, and had to know they were lying.

> - William D. Hartung

Some sobering facts:

- Total annual **world** military expenditures - 2003: $794 billion! Bush signed record US military budget in August 2004: $417 billion! People, we of *the land of the free and the home of the brave* are the world's number one supplier, buyer and distributor of weapons. How much did you get back from the tax break last year? $300? $400? $800? Well, with 110 million taxpayers, each of you taxpayers then spent $3,791.00 on the military.... Last year! and it will only go up next year. (Not counting "special appropriations.") Look at the numbers: our annual military budget is larger than the rest of the world <u>combined</u>! Do we need that much national security? These figures are not common knowledge (although they are published for all to read), and if any elected representative is "soft on national defense" then there will be some name calling and finger pointing. This is irrational when confronted with the facts.

I repeat, the U.S. annual military budget is larger than the rest of the world **combined**.

This is the budget of a huge pit bull, a two ton guerrilla, or dare I confront a sacred cow - an imperialist power!
The United States of America is an Empire?!
Yes. One of the ugly realizations after one wakes up and looks around is that the hysterical calls for **defence** in Congress is actually to maintain an international American Empire.

"We have 702 U.S. military installations scattered in 132 countries around the world."
 - Former Air Force officer Mikey Weinstein, former JAG [judge advocate general]; a lawyer for Ronald Reagan in the West Wing, and Ross Perot's former general counsel; 2006

And **you** are paying for it. Although this section is dealing with the financial side, the scary side of this is that the majority of Americans don't know that their country is an imperial power. They know it is the only Superpower, but that may spark an image of a comic book character, not the reality of a conquering nation with a huge military backing up its foreign policies; not the reality that some people, maybe millions of people, might resent this imposing and overbearing military-corporate-government; not the reality that we Americans are hated to the extent that some extremists would take over civilian airplanes to fight back. This is blowback. What price empire?!

The following numbers are *what is happening to your money*; but please do not forget how terrorists are created ... partly with your funds.
Here are the figures for our US economic mess:
– The annual US deficit is $412 billion (interestingly, about the same amount that is spent on the military annually). Guess that's another $3,745.00 per taxpayer per year. (To break even.)

– The national debt as of Halloween, 2006:
$8,573, 415,489, 400.00 - yes, that is 8.57 trillion! * This is adding up at $1.62 billion per day! About half is paper debt to

social security (So that's where it went! And what is Bush planning on doing to make up that money to give back to the Social Security fund so that retirees can live - cheaply? Why, invest it in a safe place for our elderly – the stock market!); the other half of this huge debt is owed to mostly foreigners (Treasury-bills), by the way. Soon, especially for you All-Americans that want to buy American and shop American and live in American homes ... well, it ain't going to be American for long!   * This up to the minute counter is found at http://www.brillig.com/debt_clock/
– The War in Iraq Cost the United States $338 billion (end of October 2006)
       That's $338 billion ... and counting ...

– America is racking up a staggering $665 billion in additional foreign debt every year — that's $5,500 for every U.S. household!

       Now that you are hot under the collar, let's do some more math: There are 110 million taxpayers in the US ... so to break even on the national debt at this time we are looking at about $70K apiece! Once you factor in social security and these annual expenditures/debts, we are sweating about $350K per taxpayer. Some statistics make things look somewhat nicer, like only a $30,000 debt ... for *each* American, not each taxpayer. Lower number, but now we include children in the numbers -- who will ultimately be faced with this mess when they are grown. Now you know what all the fuss is about: Bush and the wreaking crew are saddling you, and your children, with enormous debt. And how much tax rebate did you get again?

See where your tax dollars go:
http://nationalpriorities.org/auxiliary/interactivetaxchart/taxchart.html

    Lest we forget, Bush inherited a **$236 billion** national surplus from the Clinton administration.

– The Government Accountability Office released a report that found that Bush's economic policies "will result in massive fiscal pressures that, if not effectively addressed, could cripple the economy, threaten our national security, and adversely affect the quality of life of Americans in the future." Dec 2004

- The Bush regime installed as top officials more than 100 former lobbyists, attorneys or spokespeople *for the industries they oversee.* (commondreams.org) It is well known that the disgraced Enron CEO Ken Lay -- a close friend of President Bush -- helped write our US energy policy – which aided him and his company. (Source: MSNBC)

During the flag-waving police-with-automatic-weapons RNC (Republican National Convention) in the summer of 2004, many critics tried to get the facts out to the American people about what this man and his crew were doing to the economy.

Here is an excerpt from one piece called "BUSH IN NYC: WATCH OUT, THE 'REFORMER WITH RESULTS' IS BACK" by Arianna Huffington, 31 Aug 2004

> Since he took office, 1.2 million people in America have lost their jobs, bringing the total to 8.2 million.
> The number of Americans living below the poverty line has increased by 4.3 million to 35.9 million - 12.9 million of them children.
> The number of Americans with no health insurance has increased by 5.8 million - with 1.4 million losing their insurance in 2003. The total now stands at 45 million.
> Forty percent of the 3.5 million people who were homeless at some point last year were families with children, as were 40 percent of those seeking emergency food assistance.
>
> Median household income has fallen more than $1,500 in inflation-adjusted terms in the last three years, and the wages of most workers are now falling behind inflation. Average tuition for college has risen by 34 percent, while 37 percent of fourth graders read at a level considered "below basic."

One third of the president's $1.7 trillion in tax cuts benefits only the top 1 percent of wealthiest Americans.

~ ~ ~

But tax cuts are needed to stimulate the economy, hysterically repeats Dubya. "This is about jobs, about America, about our troops, and about freedom." - yet another opportunity for Bush to wrap himself up in the flag while offering his wealthy friends tax advantages. Mr. Bush, wasn't your MBA days also your drinking daze? Any accounting student will tell you that to increase spending in a war economy while offering tax cuts is lunacy. When we look at the fine print, however, we see the thief at work again. The cuts are for the rich. Dividends for wealthy stockholders, capital gains savings for big property owners. Essentially, salaried Americans (those who are working!) will be paying the taxes, while those who have inherited wealth or who are profiting from stocks and investments will be protected and spared undue taxation. Clever.

In 2000, candidate George W. Bush said "the vast majority of my tax cuts go to the bottom end of the spectrum." He passed the tax cuts, but the top 20 percent of earners received 68 percent of the benefits. (Sources: cbpp.org, vote-smart.org) This is just one example that earned George the term "liar" in so many articles and books.

"The Bush Administration relentlessly pushed an energy bill containing $23.5 billion in corporate tax breaks, much of which would have benefited major campaign contributors." (Sources: taxpayer.net, Washington Post)

As major corporate scandals rocked the nation's economy, the Bush Administration reduced the enforcement of corporate tax law – conducting fewer audits, imposing fewer penalties, pursuing fewer prosecutions and making virtually no effort to prosecute corporate tax crimes. (iht.com) Meanwhile, tax audits for the working poor increased. (www.theolympian.com)

Let's lift ourselves out of the morass for a moment and remember this: US corporations paid around 60% of taxes in 1960. Today they pay around 20%. Obviously corporations have been successful lobbyists in the last forty years. Who has taken up the slack? You, my friend. It can get worse: The Bush regime gave Accenture a multibillion-dollar border control contract even though the company moved its operations to Bermuda to avoid paying taxes! (New York Times, cantonrep.com)

The fox is in the henhouse, and he's painted red, white and blue!

This habit of making everything patriotic and nationalistic is part of the show. Will Durst, in his *Working for Change* column, had a few things to say about it:

> Speaking in front of the Orlando Chamber of Commerce on the necessity of passing the President's proposed tax cut, Treasury Secretary John Snow said: "We can not afford to fail the American people, especially our troops overseas."
>
> That's right, it's no longer a job-creating tax cut necessary to jump start the economy – now, it's the red, white and blue tax cut and the only people lined up against it are un-American Saddam-loving commie pinko yellow rat bastards.
>
> Now, I know it's politics. And I know posturing is part of the game. And I even know you run with your strengths, and obviously the President's strength right now is waving Old Glory and shooting flares into munitions sheds. But for crum's sake, how freaking devious, not to mention obvious, can you get? A tax cut for the troops? Who's buying this?
>
> 90% of the benefits of this tax cut are going to the top 10% of American wage earners. It's like trying to sell an extra boardroom bathroom by citing it as a major benefit to the janitors. Yeah, sure, some guys in uniform might get to trod the marble floors, but only to clean up executive crap.

Fiscally Irresponsible

Let's talk economics in a free market. Customarily, a certain portion of any profitable (big) business goes to the stockholders, as well as to lobbyists, bonuses and even kickbacks. Should we guess that a 10% profit is conservative here? Let's be conservative – just to show how its done. Let's take a fictional amount, say, $87 billion as a special appropriation. Ten percent of that means that $8.7 billion will be skimmed off the top to re-apportion or to distribute to stockholders. Another hefty amount would go directly to CEOs and other executives and directors as salaries, bonuses and stock options. Let's say this could be $1.3 billion, just to make a round figure of $10 billion. Do I have this right? I mean, this is how successful, private companies operate, right? Could you imagine Bush being honest about that?

"I address the American people, the greatest people in the world, and the freest," I imagine Dubya saying, "I am asking for $10 billion of your tax dollars to give directly to the wealthy, but patriotic, citizens involved with our military industries. That will get them going. That will motivate them to supply the goods and services out there in that heathen land so that your sons and daughters can fight. God bless America!"

This privatization of governmental duties, according to Republican philosophy, is supposed to stream-line our government, create a more efficient service industry, and save us tax dollars. Have I got that right? However, if taxes are collected to go towards such profits as described above, we are merely shifting social services to private businesses and paying more for less (Yes, less; for profitable businesses must cut corners, economize, push employees, and have a clear bottom line. This means a portion goes directly to the stockholders and executives, as outlined above. The sacred cow BS says that private businesses do things more efficiently than government. Has anyone been taking notes on businesses in Iraq and Hurricane Katrina relief? Not efficient. Not consistent. Not value.). Who are winning here? This looks like a confidence game to me, and I'm not buying it.

304

The ethical stakes are higher than this, however. Republicans pride themselves (or is that PR/advertise themselves?) on their conservative fiscal policies of government spending and taxpayer breaks. But if the present regime is cutting social programs and funneling off increased tax dollars to their friends in the private sector on a bogus war, this is nothing but theft; when applied to the Gulf region, we have grand theft and war crimes. Here's the truth:

'STAGGERING AMOUNT' OF CASH MISSING IN IRAQ
By Emad Mekay, IPS, August 20, 2004
http://ipsnews.net/interna.asp?idnews=25168

> WASHINGTON - Three U.S. senators have called on Defence Secretary Donald Rumsfeld to account for 8.8 billion dollars entrusted to the Coalition Provisional Authority (CPA) in Iraq earlier this year but now gone missing.
> In a letter Thursday, Senators Ron Wyden of Oregon, Byron L Dorgan of North Dakota and Tom Harkin of Iowa, all opposition Democrats, demanded a "full, written account" of the money that was channelled to Iraqi ministries and authorities by the CPA, which was the governing body in the occupied country until Jun. 30.

... whatever became of this outrageous story? ...

~ ~ ~

Paul Richter of the Los Angeles Times (September 26, 2004) tells us the lowdown in the title of his article:
COSTS WHITTLE FUNDS TO IRAQIS - MUCH OF THE U.S. AID FOR REBUILDING ISN'T ENTERING THE ECONOMY, DRAINED BY THE INSURGENCY, PROFITS FOR CONTRACTORS AND SALARIES FOR FOREIGNERS:

Where are your US tax dollars going? Richter tells us that "some government analysts said those costs might eat up half or more of the rebuilding aid. However, private analysts estimated that the 'Iraq premium' meant that up to 75% of U.S. spending in the country provided no direct benefit for Iraqis. *

Richter goes on to introduce Frederick Barton, co-director of the reconstruction studies program at the Center for Strategic and International Studies, a Washington think tank, and a former Clinton administration official in the U.S. Agency for International Development, who has studied the problem/feeding frenzy. "Barton and his organization estimate that less than 30% of the money spent reaches Iraqis. Another 30% appears to be going to security, about 10% to U.S. government overhead, 6% to contractor profits, and 12% on insurance and foreign workers' salaries. The rest, perhaps 15%, may be lost to corruption and mismanagement, they estimate."

 * What a clever sounding euphemism, "Iraq premium," to describe a massive rip-off of Billions of US funds. I'll bet that Bush and Cheney personally know some of the benefactors from these funds, uh, your funds. And can you imagine what insurance *cost* in a war zone? Are "acts of God" in the fine print?! I mean, which insurance company would enter into such a high risk contract? – unless the legalese were stated in such a way that only premiums would be paid but no or little payments to the insured? Now That would be a cool and safe insurance for a company to entertain. This would be an arena to investigate.

>>~o~<<

The National Priorities Project has given us THE COST OF WAR, explained below: http://www.nationalpriorities.org/ NPP's Latest Publication: "Americans Pay High Cost for War" http://nationalpriorities.org/issues/military/iraq/highcost/index.html

> Here you will find State-by-state data on the number of soldiers killed and wounded, the dollar cost, and the number of reservists and National Guard troops on active duty – presented in the context of worsening conditions in Iraq as well as expert opinions on national security policy. NPP decribes their work: "War affects everyone, not just those directly involved in the fighting. This webpage is a simple attempt to demonstrate one of the more quantifiable effects of war: the financial burden it places

on our tax dollars." And then they offer directions in using their web site: [To the right you will find a running total of the amount of money spent by the US Government to finance the war in Iraq. This total is based on estimates from Congressional appropriations. http://costofwar.com/index.html Below the total are a number of different ways that we could have chosen to use the money. Try clicking on them; you might be surprised to learn what a difference we *could have* made.]

Bottom line? ...
> Currently, the Cost of War is **$421 billion** (end of April 2007) and continues to advance at $6 billion per month. This comes to $1403 for each man, woman and child in the USA, and adding up daily. If you are in a family of four, then that is $5612.00 and counting. Again, how much tax refund did you get?

This is mind boggling. George Bush senior's famous "Read my lips: no new taxes," was classic fudging. He did not introduce *new* taxes, he just raised existent taxes. Promise kept! Public fooled. Here was Bush junior (read my lips better) trying to out-do his dad again. **The federal government is cutting taxes while spending more.** The fall guys are the state governors, who have to tax more to compensate for the decreased federal aid. (Governor Gray Davis of California was recalled because of it. The Iraq War had cost California $26 billion, and don't get me started on what Enron did; I'm sure this wasn't mentioned in the Schwarzenegger fiasco.)
These "cut tax and spend" Republicans are not new. This is the worst deficit since Ronald Reagan trickled down twenty five years ago.

There are many investigators who believe that the illogical spending spree by incumbent republicans actually points to a policy of bankrupting the US government; the right wing "reasoning" behind this apparently inane, self-destructive policy would be to sling the US government into a merely survival mode, "freeing" citizens, or businessmen, from the yoke of an intruding government. Certainly there is a long history of conservative and libertarian ideology that touts *less government*, but I am uncertain that the present regime has this agenda. Having stated that, this fanatic bunch of despots have other delusional ideas, so why not this one?

>>~o~<<

The latest on the Oh-so-American company that has used so many billions of US taxpayers' money to grow into the giant it is? Look at this outrageous "pragmatic" business & tax decision:
Halliburton to Move Headquarters to Dubai
  by Mohammed Abbas and Anna Driver – Reuters, 12 March 2007
  http://money.aol.com/news/articles/_a/halliburton-to-move-headquarters-to/20070312063809990001?ncid=NWS00010000000001

Internationally recognized writer, professor and journalist Edward Said asks, and answers, some important questions in his **"Who is in charge?"**:

> Every one of the 500 congressional districts in this country has a defense industry in it, so that war has been turned into a matter of jobs, not of security. But, one might well ask, how does running an unbelievably expensive war remedy, for instance, economic recession, the almost certain bankruptcy of the social security system, a mounting national debt, and a massive failure in public education?
>
> ~ ~ ~

What would Thomas Paine say? "... As parents, we can have no joy, knowing that this government is not sufficiently lasting to ensure any thing which we may bequeath to posterity: And by a plain method of argument, as we are running the next generation into debt, we ought to do the work of it, otherwise we use them meanly and pitifully. In order to discover the line of our duty rightly, we should take our children in our hand, and fix our station a few years farther into life; that eminence will present a prospect, which a few present fears and prejudices conceal from our sight."

~ ~ ~

Find out who benefited the most in the two major Bush tax cuts. Who made the most in this bogus war? Who contributed the most for his election campaigns? Follow the money, my friends, just follow the money.

In this section I am focusing upon the economic loss and financial ruin of our once rich country, but there are other costs always in our collective consciousness: the mental and emotional health of our own young people serving our country, believing they are doing the right thing. There are 133,000 American troops in Iraq (Jan 2007), and plans are underway to increase that number. (This is not counting Afghanistan and other mid-east countries, nor the hundred thousand or so who already served and returned home.) Fighting has increased, tempers are hot, and anti-American Muslim "patriots" are increasing their attacks on all nationalities in the occupied country. Some soldiers are choosing not to go to war. These conscientious objectors will be tracked down and prosecuted. Others are coming back home physically whole but suffering from panic attacks, nightmares and post distress syndrome. What price empire?

Let's go back a little bit: In April 2003 the White House projected that it would cost 2 billion a month to maintain a US military presence in Iraq. Just two and a half months later that figure had doubled. (Great time for a tax cut, Dubya!) But there's more. We are finding out – from our social services network – how Bush is saving money:
Wounded Soldier to Get Refund - Army Had Demanded Payment for Bloodied Body Armor by ALLISON BARKER, AP - CHARLESTON, W.Va. (Feb. 8, 2006):

> A former soldier injured in Iraq is getting a refund after being forced to pay for his missing body armor vest, which medics destroyed because it was soaked with his blood, officials said Wednesday.
> First Lt. William "Eddie" Rebrook IV, 25, had to leave the Army with a shrapnel injury to his arm. But before he

could be discharged last week, he says he had to scrounge up cash from his buddies to pay $632 for the body armor and other gear he had lost.

Rebrook, who graduated from West Point with honors, said he was billed because a supply officer failed to document that the vest was destroyed as a biohazard. He said a battalion commander refused to sign a waiver for the vest, saying Rebrook would have to supply witness statements to verify the vest was taken from him and burned.

"When that vest was removed from my bleeding body in Iraq, it was no longer my responsibility," Rebrook said Wednesday.

> Good thing he could eventually prove his case and defend his irresponsible behavior. Evidently there were 21 similar cases.

Then we have the following, which you can look up:
Homeless Iraq Vets Showing Up at Shelters
http://www.truthout.org/docs_04/121004Y.shtml

I imagine compassionate George saying, "Sorry about those vets. We had to cut corners somewhere! Now, pass the barbecue sauce!"

It was estimated in 2005 that it would take another $10 billion just to get the Iraqi power grid up and operating... if there are no saboteurs. No doubt we will soon learn of new items and expenses. (And let us not forget Afghanistan, where *one billion dollars a month* is quietly being spent. The price tag there was $60 billion by inauguration day 2005.) Is it possible to audit this huge outlay of money? It will be very revealing just where it is all going.

It is simply not possible to have a multi-billion-dollar, multi-year tax cut, a Pentagon budget that will top $500 billion by the end of this decade, a seemingly endless string of wars for 'regime change' that are paid for through emergency appropriations over and above the Pentagon's massive annual spending, plus massive new expenditures for intelligence and homeland security, and

still expect the government to meet its traditional responsibilities in the areas of education, income security, transportation, health care, housing, environmental protection, and energy development.
 - William D. Hartung

Meanwhile, out on the world scene, after snubbing and deceiving UN and NATO allies before the war, a financially concerned but still proud Bush regime was *calling for* financial and military support for the occupation. Many countries, including France, Germany and India, are not impressed with the hypocrisy. In essence, these countries are saying, "You left us out of the decision, and now you call for our aid in the occupation?"

As an interesting aside: Bush's arrogant and immature policy against those who opposed his invasion of Iraq came back to bite him when he visited France as part of a celebration of D-Day's 60th anniversary in 2004: A French poll there overwhelmingly wanted John Kerry for US President. Later in that month, displaying his diplomatic skills for all to see, George Bush urged the European Union to "open membership talks with Turkey." France's Jacques Chirac "retorted testily that this was none of America's business." http://www.economist.com/

What did the Bush team do when they decided that the various intelligence organizations weren't cooperating with each other? The Office of Homeland Security is another *cut tax and spend Republican scheme*. Instead of insisting that the various military, security and intelligence arms of the US government communicate and coordinate with each other, Bush created a huge *new* bureaucracy of redundancy, surveillance and checks. Or is that cheques? Billions are being lost in this ill conceived venture. It is another strain on the economy at a time when we can least afford it. What special service can Homeland list in it's accomplishments? Money was used from it to build bleachers and other non-security outlays for the $40 million 2005 inaugural party for Bush and the boys. Way to go, Tom Ridge! Let's sing! 'Old Home(land) on the range!'

Compassionate Conservatism?

First, allow me to bring back for your nostalgic recollection the "humble" promises of this man who wants to rule us; compassionate conservatism. Nice sound to it. It got votes. Then, I offer you the following list of items that are more compassionate for businesses and war than for you or I. Let's start with the devious overview, shall we?

OUT OF SPOTLIGHT, BUSH OVERHAULS U.S. REGULATIONS
By Joel Brinkley, New York Times, August 14, 2004
http://www.nytimes.com/2004/08/14/politics/14bush.html

WASHINGTON - April 21 was an unusually violent day in Iraq; 68 people died in a car bombing in Basra, among them 23 children. As the news went from bad to worse, President Bush took a tough line, vowing to a group of journalists, "We're not going to cut and run while I'm in the Oval Office."

On the same day, deep within the turgid pages of the Federal Register, the National Highway Traffic Safety Administration published a regulation that would forbid the public release of some data relating to unsafe motor vehicles, saying that publicizing the information would cause "substantial competitive harm" to manufacturers.

As soon as the rule was published, consumer groups yelped in complaint, while the government responded that it was trying to balance the interests of consumers with the competitive needs of business. But hardly anyone else noticed, and that was hardly an isolated case.

Allies and critics of the Bush administration agree that the Sept. 11 attacks, the war in Afghanistan and the war in Iraq have preoccupied the public, overshadowing an important element of the president's agenda: new regulatory initiatives. Health rules, environmental regulations, energy initiatives, worker-safety standards and product-safety disclosure policies have been modified in ways that often please business and industry leaders while dismaying interest groups representing consumers, workers, drivers, medical patients, the elderly and many others.

>>~o~<<

Guns for sport?
Bring back those good ol' Uzis.

Tom Delay and the Bush regime had no intention of extending the ban against assault weapons. What else could happen when John Bolton was appointed Assistant Secretary of State for Arms Control? His background? Ex- VP of neo-con AEI (American Enterprise Institute), rabid NRA advocate, pushing for assault weapons for the sportsman. * Are hunters using machine guns on wild animals these days? Is that sporting? The recurring fact that most apologists overlook is that automatic weapons are used only on humans. Is there anything more to say?

Oh yes, this: Arms manufacturers gave $190,000 to the Bush campaign – four times as much as they gave to Gore.
  * Is this the Mr. Bolton that Bush appointed to watch the UN? There will be a show down, of course, at the not-OK corral.
    This sacred cow of weapons mirrors the international scene, unfortunately, as our soldiers are confronting American-made weapons in the Middle East, from assault rifles to land mines to radioactive dust and shrapnel from depleted uranium encased bombs. When will we ever learn?

While members of the National Rifle Association spends millions on lobbying for the right to bear arms, hysterically pointing to the Bill of Rights in their defense, they have totally forgotten why they should have the right to bear arms. King George of England wanted to take away the guns of American Colonists and leave them defenseless when his Royal troops squelched tax revolts, or started a war, or pushed Americans around. We are supposed to have an armed militia to defend America from national threats. Where were you, oh defenders of the realm, when we had a coup? The authors of the Bill of Rights weren't thinking "sports hunting" when they included that right onto parchment. You totally blew the only reason our forefathers wanted American citizens to have arms!

To refresh your memories: Bill of Rights, Article II.:
A well regulated Militia, being necessary to the security of a free State, the right of the people to keep and bear Arms, shall not be infringed.

>>~o~<<

Women and their "Choices"

In 1994, the US signed on to the Cairo Accord, which aimed at improving women's health and slowing down world population growth, essential for sustainable living. Who was President then? Bush refused to affirm this support at the meeting of Asian and Pacific nations in Bangkok. His "faith initiative" strikes again, displaying his own fanaticism and lack of perspective: no support for ideas and programs that might counsel pro-choice options – while US planes and missiles are bombing children in Iraq and Afghanistan. Hello?!

Received on the internet, Jan 2003 - too late to influence the appointment of a right wing fundamentalist doctor. This advisory committee was a governmental born again dream come true, and don't you know Saint George took up the lance.:

President Bush has announced his plan to select Dr. W. David Hager to head up the Food and Drug Administration's (FDA) Reproductive Health Drugs Advisory Committee. The committee has not met for more than two years, during which time its charter has lapsed. As a result, the Bush Administration is tasked with filling all eleven positions with new members. This position does not require Congressional approval. The FDA's Reproductive Health Drugs Advisory Committee makes crucial decisions on matters relating to drugs used in the practice of obstetrics, gynecology and related specialties, including hormone therapy, contraception, treatment for infertility, and medical alternatives to surgical procedures for sterilization and pregnancy termination.

Dr. Hager's views of reproductive health care are far outside the mainstream and a setback for reproductive technology. Dr. Hager is a practicing OB/GYN who describes himself as "pro-life" and refuses to prescribe contraceptives to unmarried women. Hager is the author of "As Jesus Cared for Women: Restoring Women Then and Now"; The book blends biblical accounts of Christ healing women with case studies from Hager's practice. In the book Dr. Hager wrote with his wife, entitled "Stress and the Woman's Body," he suggests that women who suffer from premenstrual syndrome should seek help from reading the bible and praying. As an editor and contributing author of "The Reproduction Revolution: A Christian Appraisal of Sexuality, Reproductive Technologies and the Family", Dr. Hager appears to have endorsed the medically inaccurate assertion that the common birth control pill is an abortifacient.

Hager's mission is religiously motivated. He has an ardent interest in revoking approval for mifepristone (formerly known as RU-486) as a safe and early form of medical abortion. Hager recently assisted the Christian Medical Association in a "citizen's petition" which calls upon the FDA to revoke its approval of mifepristone in the name of women's health. *

More on this can be found at: http://www.duke.edu/~aak4/

This is but one appointee. The Bush regime is appointing reactionaries, stacking judgeships and enacting laws that are turning the clock back on women and minorities alike. On April Fool's Day, 2004, Bush signed a mandate proclaiming "the personhood of the fetus." This is but one of the steps on the way of reversing Roe vs Wade.

Many women know this, however. A majority of minorities know their rights have eroded under Bush. It is my belief that they voted against Bush in 2000 and 2004. Yet another **huge** group of voters that should have made a difference in the outcome of the last election. Who then voted for Bush?

Health Care

"I expect the Bush Administration will go down in history as the greatest disaster for public health and the environment in the history of the United States."
- Sen. Jim Jeffords, the ranking minority member on the Environment and Public Works Committee.

Much information has been compiled concerning this ever important area. I will cite Judd Legum, who wrote "100 [UNSPUN and referenced] Facts and 1 Opinion: The Non-Arguable Case Against the Bush Administration" (The Nation), who has done an excellent job of collecting facts. The numbers listed below tell you what tidbits await you with his entire list of 100 facts. Read on and pull out your hankies (they're affordable).

59. The Bush Administration authorized twenty companies that have been charged with fraud at the federal or state level to offer Medicare prescription drug cards to seniors.
Source: American Progress
60. The Bush Administration created a prescription drug card for Medicare that locks seniors into one card for up to a year but allows the corporations offering the cards to change their prices once a week.
Source: Washington Post
61. The Bush Administration blocked efforts to allow Medicare to negotiate cheaper prescription drug prices for seniors. Source: American Progress
62. At the behest of the french fry industry, the Bush Administration USDA changed their definition of fresh vegetables to include frozen french fries.
Source: commondreams.org
63. In a case before the Supreme Court, the Bush Administrations sided with HMOs--arguing that patients

shouldn't be allowed to sue HMOs when they are improperly denied treatment. With the Administration's help, the HMOs won. Source: ABC News64. The Bush Administration went to court to block lawsuits by patients who were injured by defective prescription drugs and medical devices.
Source: Washington Post

65. President Bush signed a Medicare law that allows companies that reduce healthcare benefits for retirees to receive substantial subsidies from the government.
Source: Bloomberg News

66. Since President Bush took office, more than 5 million people have lost their health insurance.
Source: CNN.com

67. The Bush Administration blocked a proposal to ban the use of arsenic-treated lumber in playground equipment, even though it conceded it posed a danger to children. Source: Miami Herald

68. One day after President Bush bragged about his efforts to help seniors afford healthcare, the Administration announced the largest dollar increase of Medicare premiums in history. Source: iht.com

69. The Bush Administration--at the behest of the tobacco industry--tried to water down a global treaty that aimed to help curb smoking. Source: tobaccofreekids.org

The Environment

"It is amazing how brazen the administration is in its disdain for the public."
Sierra Club conservation director Bruce Hamilton, May 2003

"The industry drilled more natural-gas wells from 2000 to 2002 than in any three-year period in the last half-century."
Time, 21 July 2003

Robert F. Kennedy, Jr., the country's most prominent environmental attorney, wrote **Crimes Against Nature: How George W. Bush and His Corporate Pals Are Plundering the**

Country and Hijacking Our Democracy.
He charges that this administration has taken corporate cronyism to such unprece-dented heights that it now threatens our health, our national security, and democracy as we know it. "In a headlong pursuit of private profit and personal power," Kennedy writes, "George Bush and his administration have eviscerated the laws that have protected our nation's air, water, public lands, and wildlife for the past thirty years, enriching the president's political contributors while lowering the quality of life for the rest of us." Mr. Kennedy wrote a very brave letter declaring that the 2004 election was stolen, by the way. It was ignored by most media.

The Clean Air Act was passed in 1970; the Clean Water Act in 1972. Note that these environmental Acts were passed during the Republican Nixon administration. The Bush regime is rewriting these regulations so that companies can continue to pollute our air and water without impunity. Bush refused to renew the tax on toxic-waste polluters, which is the main source of income for the cleanup of abandoned superfund sites. Funding for clean water programs have been slashed. Plans are to remove protection from 60% of the nation's wetlands. What is he thinking? In true short-term fashion, he is leaving environmental decisions to the marketplace and to individual states. When will we learn? *The market doesn't care about the environment.* Period. "It"is interested in profits. In this economic downturn, states are cutting all kinds of "non-essential" programs (as if water and air were non-essential!).

> I cannot believe that the majority of Republicans are against clean air and water, and that they would rather sell off our natural resources at the expense of parks and national forests. Your party has been hijacked!   SP

After declaring states rights, by the way, the Bush regime overruled the state of California's attempts to regulate greenhouse -gas emissions from SUVs, not to mention, on another matter, overruling dozens of state and community referendums on medical marijuana. States rights... unless your superiors in

Washington, DC, disagree!? You can't have it both ways, Dubya. Or are we back to that control thing?

Like his stance on the environmental Kyoto Treaty, Bush will ignore past agreements and just have us "adapt" to worsening conditions. Here's the Bush plan: Those who live next to a polluted area, just use your extra stock dividends, pack your Hummer, and move away!

The Clear Skies program is basically a policy of unequal environmental protection, according to Carl Pope, director of the Sierra Club. And what about that wonderfully named "Clear Skies" proposal? Trading pollution credits? So one cleaner industry in one state can sell its quota units to a dirty polluter elsewhere? How absurd. How about this for a simple solution: We congratulate the clean company, and encourage the polluting company to clean up its act for the good of all.

John Graham, Bush's boy in the Office of Information and Regulatory Affairs at the Office of Management and Budget, evidently made it common practice to slash environmental rules and to allow businesses to do as they will. The Environmental Protection Agency (EPA) is under attack:

> - logging is a way to prevent forest fires.
> - snowmobiles are good at Yellowstone. Grizzly bears don't need protection there, however.
> - chemical plants, pulp mills, auto factories and steel mills are exempt from stringent air-pollution controls. What else is there?
> - wilderness areas are now open to oil and gas exploration. Bush's friends are salivating over the Arctic National Wildlife Refuge, which relatively speaking doesn't have that much oil to begin with; evidently its total capacity would be used up in six months at current American fuel levels. The coal-methane lobbies are also seeing eye to eye with Mr. Bush.
> - trapping dolphins while netting tuna is now OK. The ludicrous *self-regulating* policy can allow fishermen to

use the "dolphin safe" labels. To their credit, the 3 largest tuna companies Chicken of the Sea, Starkist and Bumble Bee have pledged to adhere to the older, stricter dolphin-safe rules.

- Molly Ivins, the witty writer of "Bushwhacked," informs us that there will be lower standards of meat inspection in the United States. *Production* is the catchword in some factories, and the employees better have a Very Good reason to stop an assembly line.

- Bush's dirty plan for clean hydrogen research begins by taking money away from wind, geothermal, bioenergy and renewable energy research and projects. And, since the huge oil and automobile industries are deeply involved, the production of hydrogen for fuel cells is coming from, guess what?, burning oil and coal! This plan will negate the whole intent of clean energy! Hello?!

- Bush is seeking exemptions to the international ban on methyl bromide, an ozone depleting pesticide. The list goes on.

By the way, George Dubya Bush's nickname for environmentalists: "Green-green-lima-beans." This is right out of junior high.

>>~o~<<

From a joint statement by Defenders of Wildlife, Friends of the Earth, Natural Resources Defense Council, National Parks Conservation Association, The Ocean Conservancy, and The Wilderness Society in early 2003, printed in Washington, DC's, Pathway Magazine, titled "There He Goes Again: Bush Budget Bashes the Environment" we have the following points:

From day one the Bush administration has assaulted the environment on two fronts: starving federal agencies of resources, and redirecting them towards weakening environ-mental protections.

Bush has reduced budgets, laid people off, and plans on eliminating many enforcement personnel (who monitor clean and healthy standards) by repositioning them to less active roles. This adds up to lower standards and more pollution.

"Polluters make the mess, taxpayers foot the cleanup bill." Businesses are paying for 70% of the cleanup. Guess who pays the rest? The oil industry is exempted from liabilities at various sites, "ensuring that it will never be held responsible for its toxic pollution even though it no longer contributes to the Superfund tax." Guess who's pro-oil?

Bush's Clear Skies Initiative would actually weaken present standards, allowing for more pollution. As for carbon dioxide, a main contributor to global warming, there are no new controls.

Bush promised to "fully fund the LWCF," or the Land and Water Conservation Fund. This was an out and out lie, for his budget proposal actually cut it by 50%.

At least $10 million is allocated to develop oil and gas production on Bureau of Land Management lands. In a cynical parlor trick, the administration is suggesting, furthermore, that some of the revenues from Alaska's Arctic National Wildlife Refuge be earmarked for alternative energy research.

"Bush administration claims of large increases for wildlife protection are accounting gimmicks." Need we say more?

The 2004 budget proposal will "cut core programs that fund solar, wind and geothermal research and development, as well as programs that reduce commercial and residential energy use."

"Fossil Fuel Energy Research and Development: Clean Coal is an Oxymoron." The proposed 2004 budget contains $320 million for coal research!

There is a preposterous tax credit of $75,000 for small business owners who use large, gas guzzling SUVs (more than 6000 lb.) for business purposes! Good for Hummers!

Nuclear power continues to fascinate George, for he proposes yet more money for the industry, even though we are creating radioactive waste for generations unborn. Overlooking facts again, the 2004 budget for the Yucca Mountain Nuclear Waste Repository will be $591 million. Two problems: there are 33 earthquake faults there, and the drinking water for nearby residents come from this area.

Last but not least, the National Ocean Service, working to preserve America's coastal resources, is slated to be cut by $100 million, or 20% of its budget. Coastal waters? Big deal.

> In short, the Bush regime is clearly anti-conservation and anti-environment, even though its spin doctors lie about it. The numbers are in, and this beautiful land of ours is in big trouble. For the sake of plants, forests, wildlife, our water and even our air, people of common sense should indict the traitors now.
Aren't we getting tired of the Bush and Gun show?
Let's clear the air.

Where is this Leading?

Hiding behind the flag and declaring national security at the drop of a shoe - or boot, this secretive government is essentially a bunch of control freaks. Regulations and codes are being drawn up daily – for our own good. Our civil rights are deteriorating rapidly. William D. Hartung, who has done some great investigative work, has stated, "We have witnessed immigrants and U.S. citizens being held incommunicado on unspecified charges, awaiting trial before secret tribunals."

There was a lot of howling the end of 2005 and into 2006 when it was discovered that there was a well established spying program on US citizens. As far as I can tell, these outrages erupt and seem to be an important issue for about 3 or 4 months. Then taking little notice on the back pages. This pattern has been working to the benefit of George and the gang. Of course, who prints things on the back pages? The media. Who owns the media? Oh, yes, we've been through that already. You know, ...

... and *you know what to do.*
>>~o~<<

The following, some say, are merely aberrant and extreme examples of neo-cons taking things too far. My sense is that they represent their basic philosophical core as well as things to come. Scary things. Fascist things. For instance, many were outraged when a blatant example of civil rights abuse gained national attention. ... and this involved a lawyer who knew his rights, but was jailed anyway. The crime:
"Lawyer Arrested for Wearing a 'Peace' T-Shirt" March 4, 2003:

NEW YORK (Reuters) - A lawyer was arrested late Monday and charged with trespassing at a public mall in the state of New York after refusing to take off a T-shirt advocating peace that he had just purchased at the mall.

According to the criminal complaint filed on Monday, Stephen Downs was wearing a T-shirt bearing the words "Give Peace A Chance" that he had just purchased from a vendor inside the Crossgates Mall in Guilderland, New York, near Albany.

And how about this: DeNeen L. Brown, Washington Post foreign service writer, informed the reading public in October 2003 of a Canadian citizen who was deported to Syria by US officials in New York, where he was jailed for a year and tortured. Maher Arar, 33, was born in Syria and emigrated to Canada as a teenager. Passing through NY after a family vacation, the US officials declared him connected to al Qaeda and deported him to Jordan. From there he was sent to a prison in Syria. The Canadian government pressured Syria to return him. Canadians have begun an investigation and have asked some embarrassing questions. Why wasn't he deported to Canada? He was a Canadian citizen, after all. Why Jordan? If he was a terrorist, why did the US allow him to leave at all? The Bush White House would rather not discuss it.

YUSUF ISLAM (CAT STEVENS) DENIED U.S. ENTRY (9/22/2004):
http://groups.yahoo.com/group/nhnenews/message/7914
CAT STEVENS CALLS U.S. DEPORTATION 'RIDICULOUS' (9/23/2004):
http://groups.yahoo.com/group/nhnenews/message/7922

Cat Stevens, who converted to Islam in 1977, was detained for 33 hours - without family contact or access to lawyers or civil rights - and deported back to Britain. Had he used his famous stage name, he probably wouldn't have been hassled. This is called "profiling" based solely on a Muslim name. Here is what this entertainer, who has devoted his time and money to charity work worldwide, had to say:

"I am a man of peace, and I denounce all forms of terrorism and injustice; it is simply outrageous for anyone to suggest otherwise. The fact that I have sympathy for ordinary people in the world who are suffering from occupation, tyranny, poverty or war is human and has nothing to do with politics or terrorism."

Sounds suspicious to me. We should keep such people out of this country, dammit! Smash his records and CDs! No more un-Christian music! He was probably on his way to conspire with the Dixie Chicks!

Un-American Activities

What do inept and embarrassed government neo-cons do when individual reporters make them look bad? When stories about misjudgment, ignorance and misplaced priorities in the Bush government began to be published in the New York Times and elsewhere – making Bush and crew look bad on national security connected to the suspicious handling (and cover-up) of the 9/11 attacks – instead of learning from their mistakes and improving the performance of their duties, they pressured the reporters to find out "who leaked." Yes, punish the whistle-blowers, tighten the web of secrecy, and control the media ... and ignore the First Amendment. Here is another eye opening piece to look at in your spare time: Larry Neumeister of the Associated Press, September 28, 2004, told us about this dangerous and illegal tactic in his article,
N.Y. TIMES SUES ASHCROFT IN LEAK PROBE.
http://apnews.myway.com/article/20040928/D85CV3100.html

The International Herald Tribune, Oct 5, 2006, informed Europeans about the CIA spying on their bank accounts:

Dan Bilefsky reported from Brussels that there was a general outrage with the European Central Bank and SWIFT (Society for Worldwide Interbank Financial Telecommunications) for handing over confidential financial information to the Bush administration. The bank knew of this CIA spying program as early as June 2002, but the official news broke in the NY Times in late summer 2006. "Under European law, companies are forbidden from transferring confidential personal data to another country unless that country offers adequate protections. The European Union does not consider the United States to be a country that offers sufficient legal protection of individual data." Francis Vanbever, Swift's CFO, said that failure to comply with U.S. subpoenas for information could have resulted in fines and a possible prison sentence.

> Here we go again: comply with European law, or pay fines and go to jail. Force and threats prevailed again and a rather large, international company quietly acquiesced to Bush might (and fright). SP

If you are not for us, you are against us. You are un-American if you question the US Government, I mean, the Bush policy. We are going way beyond unpatriotic with this "reasoning"; If you do not toe the line, perhaps you are "one of them." Here is a piece that opens new territory on social protest and swift action against unpopular notions:

October 14 2004 - MEDFORD, OR
"President Bush taught three Oregon schoolteachers a new lesson in irony – or tragedy – Thursday night when his campaign removed them from a Bush speech and threatened them with arrest for wearing t-shirts that said "Protect Our Civil Liberties," the Democratic Party of Oregon reported.
The women were ticketed to the event, admitted into the event, and were then approached by event officials before the president's speech. They were asked to leave and to turn over their tickets...."

Yes, one has to watch those subversive teachers. As reported by CNN.com and others, in late February, 2004, Bush's Education Secretary Rod Paige "shocked the nation when he compared America's teachers to terrorists. In a closed-door meeting with the nation's governors, Secretary Paige referred to the National Education Association, which represents 3 million teachers, as a 'terrorist' organization." Why wasn't he immediately fired? Could this be the core paranoia of the inner circle? At any rate, Bush took care of "his own" and the Rod Paige story slipped into the back pages... again. Just like Trent Lott, and Tom DeLay, and Bill O'Reilly, and Dick Cheney, and Henry Kissinger, and ....

Although the number of outrageous incidents are many, here are three telling items released by the Associated Press just before the 2004 election (If more Americans had been informed of these outrages, perhaps they wouldn't have voted for Herr Bush. Or did they vote for him?):

- When Vice President Dick Cheney visited Eugene, Oregon on Sept. 17, 2004, a 54-year old woman named Perry Patterson was charged with criminal trespass for blurting the word "No" when Cheney said that George W. Bush has made the world safer.
- One day before, Sue Niederer, 55, the mother of a slain American soldier in Iraq was cuffed and arrested for criminal trespass when she interrupted a Laura Bush speech in New Jersey. Both women had tickets to the events.

- Graphic Designer Fired After Heckling Bush
MARTINSBURG, W.Va. (Aug. 21) - A man who heckled President Bush at a political rally was fired from his job at an advertising and design company. The graphic designer said he was told he'd embarrassed and offended a client who provided tickets to the event.
Hiller was escorted from Hedgesville High School on Tuesday after shouting comments about the Iraq war and the failure to find weapons of mass destruction there. The crowd had easily drowned out Hiller with its chant: "Four more years."

>>~o~<<

Another Homeland Security scandal... A Texas Brew
In 2003, republicans in Texas used an arm of the Homeland Security Department for their own use – hunting down elected

Democrat lawmakers: Texas House Speaker Tom Craddick illegally used the Air and Marine Interdiction and Coordination Center, in Riverside, California, in his search for Democratic legislators who left en-masse as a protest against right wing Texas republicans. This arm of Homeland Security traced a particular plane belonging to someone rather suspicious – an elected Democrat. Once these desperadoes were tracked down, Craddick sent officers of the Texas Department of Public Safety to escort them back to Austin, which they refused to do. He then sought federal assistance to arrest the lawmakers. The republican aim, among other things, was to redistrict Texas so that there will be fewer Democrats in the US Congress. By this writing, I'm afraid they succeeded. This means more power and authority to carry on this national takeover. Republicans are aiming towards a one party system. Sound familiar? This example in Texas (of course) lets us all know what is coming next. Doesn't all of this sound like a bad TV show, or a "B" horror movie? Is our Cold War nightmare now coming true--*after* the fall of the Soviet Union? The theatrics continued; On the internet was found the following from a piece called

AWOL DEMOCRATS HOLE UP IN OKLAHOMA MOTEL:

> The legislative walkout erupted from months of growing tension that the Democrats described as the "tyranny of the majority," resulting from the Republican takeover of the House for the first time since Reconstruction.
> The walkout was triggered by a congressional redistricting plan being promoted by U.S. House Majority Leader Tom DeLay, R-Sugar Land. The plan would give Republicans an opportunity to win four to seven seats now held by Democrats and erase the Democrats' 17-15 congressional delegation majority.
> But Democrats said the blame falls on Craddick and the Republican-dominated House, which has run over the Democrats time and again on issues such as state spending and putting caps on lawsuit damage awards. Republicans mostly refused to debate the Democrats on the budget, voting down one Democratic amendment after another.

The unfolding scandal that was swept under the rug – termed "damage control" by politicians and a "cover-up" by citizens – was reported by Glenn W. Smith in *Common Dreams* (May 14, 2003):

Republican leaders in Texas and Washington are furious. They have called the Democrats, holed up in a Holiday Inn in Ardmore, "cowards" and "terrorists."

State troopers have followed the Democrats wives, parents and children.

Troopers even staked out a hospital where one lawmaker's premature twins are being cared for. Staffers have been harassed. All this has happened after the location of the Democrats was known.

Now, in a chilling revelation, we discover the Homeland Security Department was apparently used to try and track the Democrats' whereabouts.

The warnings of civil libertarians appear to have been justified. Even if it turns out that some half-crazed Republican staffer or independent investigator called the Air and Marine Interdiction and Coordination Center, it raises disturbing questions about the operations of Homeland Security and the lengths Republicans will go to enforce their will.

Please note how easily Gestapo types throw around the word terrorist to hush criticism. Such labeling, like Pinko, Commie or Communist sympathizer, are old maneuvers to intimidate and squelch dissent. And how about state troopers tagging or following the families of elected officials. How safe do *you* now feel? When does this end?

! A note to troopers and police: When do you say "No, I won't do that?!" "I will not spy on nor harass my fellow Americans just because my *superior* told me to!" "I will not shut down and drive back peaceful protesters who are actually citizens expressing their rights of free speech!" Who are the criminals here?! Even the poster girl for Iraqi torture pics at Abu Ghraib stated that she was merely following orders. Evidently remorseless about her involvement in the international scandal, she refused to take responsibility. (She got jail time, as we know, but no top official did.) Remember that "following orders" was no defense at Nuremberg. The British chief prosecutor at those trials, Hartley Shawcross, had this to say: "There comes a point when a man must refuse to answer to his leader if he is also to answer to his conscience." - SP

Homeland Official Arrested on Child Porn Charges
by Michelle Spitzer, AP - MIAMI (April 5, 2006)

The deputy press secretary for the U.S. Department of Homeland Security was charged with using a computer to seduce a child after authorities said he struck up sexual conversations with an undercover detective posing as a 14-year-old girl.
Brian J. Doyle, 55, is the fourth-ranking official in the department's public affairs office. ...
Doyle found the teenager's profile online and began having sexually explicit conversations with her on the Internet on March 14, the sheriff's office said in a statement.
He sent the girl pornographic movie clips, as well as non-sexual photos of himself, officials said. One of the photos, released by the sheriff's office, shows Doyle in what appears to be DHS headquarters. He is wearing a Homeland Security pin on his lapel and a lanyard that says "TSA."
The Transportation Security Administration is part of the Homeland Security Department.
During online conversations, Doyle revealed his name, who he worked for and offered his office and government-issued cell phone numbers, the sheriff's office said.

-- feel safer now?

Big Brother and the Holding Tank

Project Censored is a media research group out of Sonoma State University. Its mission is to educate people about the role of independent journalism in a democratic society and to tell *The News That Didn't Make the News* and why. The Project gathers stories from many sources and contributors and publishes annual lists and studies called the "Top 25 Censored Stories of the Year." The link below will take you to this important group. Although I am not including the list here, please note that the great majority of newsworthy items censored are directly connected to Bush and conservative, corporate control and greed, both nationally and internationally. PROJECT CENSORED http://www.projectcensored.org/about/index.html

Take a look at this – and note that the person in question was a former member of Congress, by William Fisher (Inter Press Service / CommonDreams), dated November 30, 2004: ACTIVISTS CRAWL THROUGH WEB TO UNTANGLE U.S. SECRECY http://www.ipsnews.net/interna.asp?idnews=26472

NEW YORK - To combat the Bush administration's penchant for secrecy, U.S. citizens have been forced to unearth new sources for information they once read in their daily newspapers. ...
"The Bush administration has taken secrecy to a new level. They have greatly increased the numbers and types of classified documents," says Steven Aftergood, who conducts one of the most widely used "open government" programs – the Federation of American Scientists (FAS) Project on Government Secrecy http://www.fas.org/sgp – which publishes 'Secrecy News', which recently disclosed: "Americans can now be obligated to comply with legally-binding regulations that are unknown to them, and that indeed they are forbidden to know."

As an example, the website reports the effort of a former conservative member of Congress to board a commercial airplane. "She was pulled aside by airline personnel for additional screening, including a pat-down search for

330

weapons or unauthorized materials. She requested a copy of the regulation authorizing such pat-downs, and was told that she couldn't see it."

Why? "Because we don't have to," said an official of the Transportation Safety Administration (TSA). "That is called 'sensitive security information'. She's not allowed to see it, nor is anyone else," he added, according to 'Secrecy News'. "She refused to go through additional screening (without seeing the regulation), and was not allowed to fly."

US SENATOR KENNEDY COMPLAINS OF FALLING ON ANTI-TERROR NO-FLY LIST, AFP, August 19, 2004 http://news.yahoo.com/news?tmpl=story&cid=1541&u=/afp/2004 0819/en_afp/us_kennedy_air_security_040819230633

WASHINGTON - He is among the most recognizable politicians in the United States, but liberal lawmaker Ted Kennedy said that even he has fallen victim to the tightened air security of the terror-conscious, post-9/11 era.
At a hearing of the Senate Judiciary Committee Thursday, the Massachusetts Democratic senator described having endured weeks of inconvenience after his name ended up on a watch list barring persons deemed to pose a threat to civil aviation or national security from air travel.
Kennedy said that on several occasions last March, he was nearly denied permission to board a US Airways shuttle from Washington to Boston because his name landed on a no-fly list in error.

In each instance, he said, an airline supervisor was called and he was eventually allowed to board the flight.

But the misunderstanding persisted for weeks – even after US Homeland Security Secretary Tom Ridge personally intervened.

"It happened even after he called to apologize," Kennedy said at the hearing, "because my name was on the list at the airports and with the airlines."
"He (Ridge) couldn't get my name off the list for a period of weeks."
Kennedy directed his remarks to Homeland Security Undersecretary Asa Hutchinson at the hearing, suggesting that if a well-known US senator can have such difficulties in clearing up such misunderstandings, the average traveler must have a much harder time.

A spokeswoman for the Transportation Security Administration, Yolanda Clark, confirmed Thursday that the senator had on at least two occasions been subjected to additional pre-flight screening, but added "he was not on the no-fly list."
However, she said "his name was similar to an alias of someone who was on the list," leading to the confusion that complicated Kennedy's travel.

> Come on, his name was similar ...! What was she going to say, "Yes, we've been watching those Kennedys!" or "Mr. Bush doesn't feel that Senator Kennedy is loyal enough ... or American enough...?!" People, if Ted Kennedy can get stuck on the no-fly list, why do you think You would be exempt?! When You are mistaken for a security risk, are you going to call Tom Ridge, or flash your congressional ID?! This is part of the intimidation show, and it is quite effective at making people behave, obey, and just follow orders.

* By the way, notice how this piece is reported? I am thankful that it was reported at all, but to use the phrase "leading to the confusion that complicated Kennedy's travel" slants the picture somewhat. *Confusion* and *complicated one's travel* are polite euphemisms. And the security official? "... the senator had on at least two occasions been subjected to additional pre-flight screening..." Again, sugar-coated "professional-speak." Such wording is partly why the vast majority of Americans are not alarmed (the phraseology is hypnotic and dulling – no cause for

alarm); no, these stories, when we perceive what is really being said and what is really happening in this country, is this: we are looking at a breakdown in our civil rights and mass hypnosis aimed at social conformity to reactionary ideals. We are steadily moving towards a police state in which we are being monitored, searched, and numbered. Remember, I'm not referring to this one (famous) incident alone, but to a collected list of grievances and "confusion" nationwide. I am citing but a few of the thousands of examples.

~ ~ ~

Lee Douglas, a reporter for Reuters / Washington Post, wrote a chilling vision of this new, safer republican America that looks more like George Orwell's Big Brother in action. Below he describes how an "OREGON LAW WOULD JAIL WAR PROTESTERS AS TERRORISTS":

PORTLAND, Oregon (April 2, 2003) - An Oregon anti-terrorism bill would jail street-blocking protesters for at least 25 years in a thinly veiled effort to discourage anti-war demonstrations, critics say.
The bill has met strong opposition but lawmakers still expect a debate on the definition of terrorism and the value of free speech before a vote by the state senate judiciary committee, whose Chairman, Republican Senator John Minnis, wrote the proposed legislation. Dubbed Senate Bill 742, it identifies a terrorist as a person who "plans or participates in an act that is intended, by at least one of its participants, to disrupt" business, transportation, schools, government, or free assembly."

>   Can you believe that? Blocking the road while marching across it is an act of terrorism that could put you behind bars for 25 years? THAT will discourage dissent. And then the state senate has the gall to debate the value of free speech? And this is from the supposedly progressive West coast! Let's look at the East coast now.

333

While the TVs reported speeches and flag waving inside of the Republican National convention, New Yorkers themselves saw something completely different. Received during the RNC 2004 in NYC; this by lawyer David Jacobus:

Friends,

Please take a minute to read my experience of the past few days. While the TV makes things appear as if everything is ok here, in truth it is not. Coming home from work and turning on the TV reveals a frightening difference between what is outside my door and what is reported.

For those of you that don't know, I currently live in Times Square which is blocks away from the RNC and where many of the delegates are staying. Our skies have gunships, our waters have gunboats, our streets have machine gun, shotgun, and tear gas wielding uniformed officers lining the street. Plainclothes officers make arrests without showing IDs or announcing who they are. Blimps with military photography equipment monitor from above and trucks with cameras line the streets. Police cars, motorcycles, trucks, and tinted window escorts drive up and down the streets with their sirens on all day for no apparent reason. FBI agents are questioning people on the streets and making arrestees fill out personal questionnaires in jail which include questions such as your opinion on interracial marriage. Searches of everyday Americans are being conducted on the streets without probable cause.

Currently between 1,000 and 2,000 people arrested the past few days are being held in an abandoned pier (Pier 57) which has razor wire covered fenced out cells and no seating. Detainees are forced to stand or lie on the oil covered cement floor while they await processing. These people are merely awaiting Desk Appearance Tickets which are literally a ticket which give you a court date and don't require lengthy incarceration. Some reports indicate there are detainees who haven't even been officially arrested or read rights. It's hard to tell though because currently people are being held for up to 36 hours without access to lawyers, who are turned away at the detention camp.

I'm sure many of you think, as the Republicans do (according to the rhetoric of the past few days), that this is all part of the necessary and tireless resolve in the face of terrorists or the "anarchists" that the media has spent so much time discussing. Currently, anyone who opposes the current administration as well as those who happen to be near them on the streets are being considered suspect and treated as such. I have been approached only a block from my apartment with the question, "Are you an anarchist?" while wearing merely my law firm attire (shirt and tie). I am also scared to death because I was confronted with an attempt to entrap me in conspiring to commit a capital felony down the block from my apartment. These are not lies, they are happening to others too.

> How much time did the media give to such reports and eye-witness accounts during the Convention - or during any public collection of people who differ with the policies of the present government? In effect, there is a republican contingent that is so controlling and ultra-conservative that it borders on fascism. It is centrally positioned in the executive office but it is to be found, for sure, within the Republican Party. The right wing Christian Coalition showed others how this could be done in the 1980s. Newt Gingrich led yet another phase in the 1990s. He and his republican muscle men were so heavy handed and Machiavellian that they had to retreat from public view. Some dubbed their elitist and heartless program the *Contract* **on** *America*. Guess what? *They're ba-ack!*

In fact, their troops are alive and well in California. The Recall initiative of Governor Gray Davis is another example of a republican preemptive strike: They aren't even waiting for a due election to govern, but righteously ousting the inferior Democrats mid-stream. Hardly anyone is taking notice that the main force

behind the recall movement was a wealthy republican who wanted to be governor himself (no, it wasn't Arnold). Conflict of interest? And the chief complaint? A deficit of $45 billion – caused by a national recession, the Iraqi War, rising oil prices, and Enron's huge theft during the energy crisis that it partly created! These facts ignore the embarrassing reality that G. W. Bush has pushed the whole country into a deficit more than Ten Times that amount! Where was the Recall Initiative there? Is anyone going to call the bluff?
The hypocrisy?

Hmmm. Why not a similar initiative to recall G. W. Bush? Of course, this would be legitimizing his election; and to this author, such a recall would be better than he and his cohorts deserve.

> To recap, we have a president who was selected under questionable circumstances, who has used the power of his office and his right-wing network in the media and think tank worlds to advance the partisan and financial interests of his cronies. He has also undermined our basic freedoms in the name of fighting terrorism. It would be a vast exaggeration to say that our democracy is in as sorry a shape as the pale reflection of a representative republic that Rumsfeld and company are building in Iraq. But it is fair to say that during George W. Bush's term, our democratic freedoms have been diminished, while the power of wealthy individuals and corporations has been enhanced. That's why we need to be at *least* as concerned with the future of democracy in *America* as we are with the future of democracy in Iraq.
> - William D. Hartung

Technology & the Takeover

It is clear what must be done – and soon. This regime will use any means necessary to get its way. Think a moment about the 2004 election. Why should a group who manufactured the results of 2000 worry about the fair results of 2004? or 2006? or

2008? – especially since they absolutely believe they have the right to rule America? And who do you suppose fabricate the new electronic voting machines that were used? Diebold and other right-wing controlled companies. And no paper trail! Perfect!

I have cited the following article already, but it is well written and documented. If you are interested in the important details of electronic voting today, please take some time to review this investigation – it is revealing.
HOW E-VOTING THREATENS DEMOCRACY
  by Kim Zetter - Wired (March 29, 2004)
http://www.wired.com/news/evote/0,2645,62790,00.html
>>~o~<<
Those e-voting machines were protected from analysis in the 2002 Georgia election by wily conservative lawyers. They hid behind the clever "we cannot reveal the *trade secret* software" that was running the non-paper-trail voting machines (can you say cover-up?). Many analysts of that election were surprised that the popular Democrat, Max Cleland, who was doing well in the exit polls, lost the election. This upset helped establish Republican control of the Senate in 2002. It was another trial run for 2004; the exit polls told the same story as in 2004. John Kerry and the Democrats were ahead -- but they lost. The right wing neo-cons, with their God given sense of entitlement, have taken the country.

Furthermore: LOST RECORD OF VOTE IN '02 FLORIDA RACE RAISES '04 CONCERN by Abby Goodnough, New York Times, July 28, 2004
http://www.nytimes.com/2004/07/28/politics/campaign/28vote.final.html
    And check out THE VOTERGATE RESOURCE CENTER:
http://miamedia.com/votergate.html

Video on voting fraud:
http://www.youtube.com/watch?v=DaEECHjWptU

David Mathison, of Be The Media, has posted the film link for *Hacking Democracy* on his website. The whole film is available by going to: **http://www.bethemedia.org/**

Michael Moore, urging liberals and Democrats to get out there and campaign just before the fall 2006 election, reminded his readers not to assume anything:

"Yup. Just like it was when we won the popular vote in 2000 and when we were ahead in the exit polls all day long in 2004. You know the deal -- the other side takes no prisoners. And just when it seems like things are going our way, the Republicans suddenly, mysteriously win the election."

Post mid-term Elections, 2006 and beyond

> The pebbles that have started slipping, seemingly unnoticed, down the mountainside – like the 'sudden' realization that maybe invading Iraq wasn't such a great idea after all – are merely the precursor to the inevitable avalanche of desperate Republicans who will, over the course of the next few months, denounce the actions of the very president whose praises they could not sing loud enough over the past six disastrous years.
> We will not forget the times we were called "Godless" as you condoned torture, "unpatriotic" as you allowed this president to ignore the Constitution without consequence, "bereft of moral values" as you protected the corrupt among you, or "defeatists" as we embraced reality rather than the propaganda you spewed in an attempt to garner support for what you knew, or ought to have known, was a lost cause in Iraq.
> - Nancy Greggs, WE WILL NOT FORGET, 10 Dec 2006

>>~o~<<

Before we start celebrating the Democratic victory in the 2006 election - an obvious sign that this stolen election thing is paranoia, think about how many more Dems could have won:

REPORT EXPOSES 'EXCESSIVE' E-VOTING MACHINE FAILURES IN 2006 ELECTIONS
By Christian Avard, Raw Story, January 4, 2006

http://www.votetrustusa.org/pdfs/E-VotingIn2006Mid-Term.pdf

RAW STORY has now obtained a report that documents persistent and widespread voting machine malfunctions across the country on Election Day.
VoteTrustUSA, VotersUnite.org, and Voter Action have released a joint report titled "E-Voting Failures in the 2006 Mid-Term Elections: A sampling of problems across the nation"

My conclusion?

The 2006 election was a give-away. (Too many people observing the machines.) The cut-throat neo-cons may be wishing to retire Bush, who has gone too far for even them (in his speeches and behavior anyway). Some are obviously distancing themselves, shining up their image, hoping the American public will forget what the republicans have done all of these years. Time for a new show – with the same methods and ugly results. I expect re-doubled efforts by the neo-cons to fix the next elections in 2008 -- unless they are stopped in their tracks. Now.   - SP

Meanwhile, notice some of the strange reactions by certain countries over the Republican defeat in the fall 2006 mid-term elections - a resounding rejection of Bush and his policies. Especially note the irony in the fact that American conservatives are appreciated by communist Chinese. It is a strange world, and stranger bedfellows.

Election Sweep Big News Across the Globe, by PAUL HAVEN, AP:

MADRID, Spain (Nov. 8, 2006) - The electoral rebuke for President Bush and the resignation of his defense secretary, both deeply unpopular away from American shores over the Iraq war, was celebrated throughout Europe, the Middle East and Asia.
...
There was also some concern that Democrats, who have a reputation for being more protective of U.S. jobs going

overseas, will make it harder to achieve a global free trade accord. And in China, some feared the resurgence of the Democrats would increase tension over human rights and trade and labor issues. China's surging economy has a massive trade surplus with the United States.

"The Democratic Party ... will protect the interests of small and medium American enterprises and labor and that could produce an impact on China-U.S. trade relations," Zhang Guoqing of the state-run Chinese Academy of Social Sciences said in a report on Sina.com, one of China's most popular Internet portals.
The prospect of a sudden change in American foreign policy could also be troubling to U.S. allies such as Britain, Japan and Australia, which have thrown their support behind the U.S.-led invasion of Iraq.

> Listen up, Dems! This could be a vote producer in your next elections! The fact that the communist Chinese government would rather have the Republicans in charge because the Democratic Party "will protect the interests of small and medium American enterprises and labor." You can't ask for a better campaign endorsement!

How *did* George Bush respond to the fall 2006 voting reversal (greatly influenced by the unpopular Iraqi War, in which only 25% of Americans approve - Dec 06) that created a Democratic Congress? He finally admitted a mistake. Before we start the band, however, the mistakes he admitted to in early 2007 were 1) not sending more troops to Iraq and 2) not giving our military forces there more free rein.
He stayed the course of course.

Bush was in the thick of a Smoke & Mirror show as the new year – and the new Democratic Congress – began in early 2007: He immediately put a lot of military options on the collective plates of the new Congress by pushing for a military increase of 21,500 more troops - and the extra money that that folly would cost! (Do note the escalation, or surge, of troops, the talk of an

340

Iran invasion, etc., either overwhelms or obscures the main issue of being in Iraq in the first place - smoke-screen!) Just in case they would see past this ploy, he did a hat trick of misdirection; besides pushing for more troops for Iraq - an *I dare you to stop me cause I am the President!* maneuver - Bush sent US planes to bombs Somalia, claiming to be retaliating for embassy bombings in the 1990s. Umm, isn't that a tad late, and actually already done by President Clinton years ago? More Smoke.
And killing.
And deception.

Clear the air and look back at Iraq: Bush's "blueprint" would boost the number of U.S. troops in Iraq - now at 132,000 - to 153,500 - and at an *extra* cost of $5.6 billion. Just so the rest of us don't get side-tracked, or side-swiped, this Iraqi War as of early 2007 has cost the lives of more than 3,000 U.S. troops (more than were killed on 9-11) as well as more than $400 billion. Bush is a pit bull – his jaws are locked.

The bottom line on this ploy is that Bush is defying the new Democratic Congress. "I am the decider!" It now begs the questions: Is he out of control by wanting to maintain absolute control? and Is this an indicator of how he will continue to show the world he is *the (unrepentant) Boss*?

~ ~ ~

Putin accuses U.S. of sparking arms race
By Slobodan Lekic, Associated Press Writer, 10 Feb 2007
http://news.yahoo.com/s/ap/20070211/ap_on_re_eu/security_conf erence;_ylt=Ai9tiExHyiiH7Fb3qECLABCs0NUE

MUNICH, Germany - Russian President Vladimir Putin on Saturday blamed U.S. policy for inciting other countries to seek nuclear weapons to defend themselves from an "almost uncontained use of military force" — a stinging attack that underscored growing tensions between Washington and Moscow.
"Unilateral, illegitimate actions have not solved a single problem, they have become a hotbed of further conflicts," Putin said at a security forum attracting senior officials from around the world.

"One state, the United States, has overstepped its national borders in every way."

The Bush administration said it was "surprised and disappointed" by Putin's remarks. "His accusations are wrong," said Gordon Johndroe, Bush's national security spokesman. ...

But Putin said it was "the almost uncontained hyper use of force in international relations" that was forcing countries opposed to Washington to seek to build up nuclear arsenals.

"It is a world of one master, one sovereign ... it has nothing to do with democracy," he said. "This is nourishing the wish of countries to get nuclear weapons."

Time for Bush to Go! by Robert Parry, Consortium News, 08 December 2006

George W. Bush had a point when he disparaged the Baker-Hamilton commission's plan for gradual troop withdrawals from Iraq by saying "this business about graceful exit just simply has no realism to it whatsoever." It's now obvious that there can be no exit from Iraq - graceful or otherwise - as long as Bush remains President.

Despite wishful thinking about Bush "making a 180" and taking to heart the bipartisan Iraq Study Group's 79 recommendations, the President is making it abundantly clear that he has no intention to reverse course, negotiate with his Muslim adversaries or pull American combat troops out of Iraq.

Bush continues to present the Iraq War and the broader conflict in the Middle East as an existential battle between good and evil, a scrap between black hats and white hats, not a political struggle that can be resolved through respectful negotiations and mutual concessions.

~ ~ Robert Parry broke many of the Iran-Contra stories in the 1980s for the Associated Press and Newsweek. His latest book: **Secrecy & Privilege: Rise of the Bush Dynasty from Watergate to Iraq**

"I think Bush and Cheney have to go for a number of reasons. One of them is that, frankly, if there is...another 9/11, while they are in power, then I think you will not distinguish this country very much from the police state in Germany in the summer of 1933...We have to get them out...."

- Daniel Ellsberg, 4 January 2007, National Press Club/ World Can't Wait, Washington, DC

Did the Republicans learn anything from the mid-term elections of 2006? Apparently not. The Economist told us that ... "Senator TRENT LOTT, who was forced to resign from the Republican leadership in December 2002 after he made racially insensitive remarks at a birthday party, returned to the Senate's centre of power by winning election as the minority whip in the next session. Mr Lott will be second-in-command to Senator Mitch McConnell, who replaced Bill Frist as minority leader in the Senate."

> This is another classic conservative move, perhaps instructed by the legacy of *Tricky* Dick Nixon: the public has a short memory, so just come on back and take charge again. It doesn't matter what you, I mean, a fellow republican, has done or stood for in the past; A conservative brother will always get another chance. This is an example and a warning, my friends. In ten years time George Bush will be regarded as the grand old statesman, the one to call on for advice - and pay him for it. It is an old and ignominious story.
I would rather take Garrison's advice:

Early Retirement, by Garrison Keillor, Nov. 1, 2006

"The Current Occupant, who is two years and three months away from retirement, was quoted last week as saying, 'They can say what they want about me, but at least I know who I am, and I know who my friends are.' A pathetic admission of defeat for one who has owned all three branches of government for the past six years -- did he seek power so that he could attain self-knowledge? If so, the price is too high. The beloved country

343

endures a government that merges blithering corruption with murderous incompetence.

Congress, which once spent an entire year investigating a married man's attempt to cover up an illicit act of oral sex, has shown no curiosity whatsoever about a war that the administration elected to wage that has killed and maimed hundreds of thousands and led our own people to commit war crimes and squandered hundreds of billions of dollars and degenerated into civil war. The contrast is deafening. Republicans haven't tolerated much dissent in their ranks, the voice of conscience has not been welcome, and now the herd finds itself on the wrong side of the river. It's discouraging seeing so many people go so wrong all at once. It makes you question the idea that each of us has unlimited potential for good."

>>~o~<<

Impeachment by the People

by Howard Zinn, AlterNet; February 3, 2007
http://www.alternet.org/rights/47467/

Courage is in short supply in Washington, D.C. The realities of the Iraq War cry out for the overthrow of a government that is criminally responsible for death, mutilation, torture, humiliation, chaos.

But all we hear in the nation's capital, which is the source of those catastrophes, is a whimper from the Democratic Party, muttering and nattering about "unity" and "bipartisanship," in a situation that calls for bold action to immediately reverse the present course.

These are the Democrats who were brought to power in November by an electorate fed up with the war, furious at the Bush Administration, and counting on the new majority in Congress to represent the voters.

But if sanity is to be restored in our national policies, it can only come about by a great popular upheaval, pushing both Republicans and Democrats into compliance with the national will....

>>~o~<<

Vermont Senate Calls for Bush Impeachment
Lawmakers Also Call for Impeachment of Cheney,
by ROSS SNEYD - AP

http://news.aol.com/topnews/articles/_a/vermont-senate-calls-for-bush/20070420104609990001?ncid=NWS00010000000001

MONTPELIER, Vt. (April 20, 2007) - Vermont senators voted Friday to call for the impeachment of President George W. Bush and Vice President Dick Cheney, saying their actions in Iraq and the U.S. "raise serious questions of constitutionality, statutory legality, and abuse of the public trust."

The resolution was the latest, symbolic, effort in the state to impeach Bush. In March, 40 towns in the state ... voted in favor of similar, non-binding resolutions at their annual meetings. State lawmakers in Wisconsin and Washington have also pushed for similar resolutions.

~ ~ ~

After the 2006 mid-term elections, there was talk about ...
A Time For Accounting, by Joseph L. Galloway;
TomPaine.com, 10 November 2006

Where did our money go? Billions of dollars of taxpayer money disappeared down various rat holes in Iraq, forked over to contractors without even so much as a handwritten receipt. Who got the money? What did they do for it? This is a fertile field that can be drilled for years, with a steady stream of indictments, trials and prison sentences.
What about those no-bid Defense Department contracts that were parceled out to the Halliburtons and KBRs and Blackwaters in Iraq and Afghanistan, and other more costly weapons and equipment contracts that went to big defense industry conglomerates accustomed to writing very generous checks to the Republicans?
Why did an administration that was hell-bent on going to war, with the inevitable and terrible human casualties among our troops, consistently underfund the Veterans

Administration, which is charged with caring for our wounded and disabled?

...

Who at the top bears responsibility for the torture and mistreatment of prisoners and detainees at Abu Ghraib prison and the Guantanamo detention camp? A score of Pentagon investigations got to the bottom of the chain of command but declared that the top, in Rumsfeld's office and the White House, was innocent.

... Simply put, the jig is up. President George W. Bush, Vice President Dick Cheney and Rumsfeld have come to the end of their free ride. No longer can they act without thought or ignore the boundaries of the Constitution, the law and common sense.

Did they really think they could get away with all of this without ever being called to answer to history and the American people?

They all deserve what's about to descend on their heads. They deserve every subpoena. They deserve every indictment. Most of all, they deserve a reserved place atop the ash heap of history.

-- Joseph L. Galloway is former senior military correspondent for Knight Ridder newspapers, columnist for McClatchy Newspapers, and co-author of the national best-seller We Were Soldiers Once ... and Young.

Rep. Dennis Kucinich, D-Ohio, logically asserts that if the newly elected Democratic Congress votes for new Iraqi War appropriations (this looking like a staggering extra $160 billion proposed for spring 2007), they essentially would be voting for Bush's War, and enough money to keep the troops in Iraq another two years at least. We will see how brave and independent the Dems are. So far they have not been the bravest in the band. He is running for president; notice that the media tries to ignore him. The official mirrors will be pointing the public elsewhere.

"They" don't want you to pay too much attention to this elected representative. They don't like what he says, and so they will divert your collective attention. And this in the U.S.A..

But it is time, way past time, that the newly elected Democratic Congress, and all of us striving for justice in the world, to
Be Brave. Be Fearless!

You are up against a fierce opponent. The neo-cons will knock you down at the first opportunity. It is their nature. They are righteous and arrogant. This thing of the unpopular Bush is probably seen as a time to re-group and strategize. They are looking for your weaknesses and ready to publicize your flaws. They are down right now. They are just catching their breath... waiting, unrepentant.

It is your turn. *Our* turn. Be quick and be strong. We just need the conviction to oust them.

- SP

~ ~ ~

In the months ahead, we'll hear a lot about what's really been going on these past six years. And I predict that we'll learn about abuses of power that would have made Richard Nixon green with envy.

- Department of Injustice by Paul Krugman, The New York Times, 09 March 2007

Lee Iacocca's 9 C's of Leadership
Excerpt from his book, **Where Have All the Leaders Gone?**
(2007)

Am I the only guy in this country who's fed up with
what's happening? Where the hell is our outrage? We
should be screaming bloody murder. We've got a gang of
clueless bozos steering our ship of state right over a cliff,
we've got corporate gangsters stealing us blind, and we
can't even clean up after a hurricane much less build a
hybrid car. But instead of getting mad, everyone sits
around and nods their heads when the politicians say,
"Stay the course."

Stay the course? You've got to be kidding. This is
America, not the damned Titanic. I'll give you a sound
bite: Throw the bums out!

You might think I'm getting senile, that I've gone off my
rocker, and maybe I have. But someone has to speak up. I
hardly recognize this country anymore. The President of
the United States is given a free pass to ignore the
Constitution, tap our phones, and lead us to war on a pack
of lies. Congress responds to record deficits by passing a
huge tax cut for the wealthy (thanks, but I don't need it).
The most famous business leaders are not the innovators
but the guys in handcuffs. While we're fiddling in Iraq, the
Middle East is burning and nobody seems to know what to
do. And the press is waving pom-poms instead of asking
hard questions. That's not the promise of America my
parents and yours traveled across the ocean for. I've had
enough. How about you?

I'll go a step further. You can't call yourself a patriot if
you're not outraged. This is a fight I'm ready and willing
to have.

My friends tell me to calm down. They say, "Lee, you're
eighty-two years old. Leave the rage to the young people."
I'd love to -- as soon as I can pry them away from their

iPods for five seconds and get them to pay attention. I'm going to speak up because it's my patriotic duty. ...

WHO ARE THESE GUYS, ANYWAY?

... Some of us are sick and tired of people who call free speech treason. Where I come from that's a dictatorship, not a democracy.

What happened to the strong and resolute party of Lincoln? What happened to the courageous, populist party of FDR and Truman? There was a time in this country when the voices of great leaders lifted us up and made us want to do better. Where have all the leaders gone?

A leader has to show CURIOSITY. He has to listen to people outside of the "Yes, sir" crowd in his inner circle. He has to read voraciously, because the world is a big, complicated place. George W. Bush brags about never reading a newspaper. "I just scan the headlines," he says. Am I hearing this right? He's the President of the United States and he never reads a newspaper? ... As long as he gets his daily hour in the gym, with Fox News piped through the sound system, he's ready to go.

... The inability to listen is a form of arrogance. It means either you think you already know it all, or you just don't care. Before the 2006 election, George Bush made a big point of saying he didn't listen to the polls. Yeah, that's what they all say when the polls stink. But maybe he should have listened, because 70 percent of the people were saying he was on the wrong track. It took a "thumping" on election day to wake him up, but even then you got the feeling he wasn't listening so much as he was calculating how to do a better job of convincing everyone he was right.
... George Bush prides himself on never changing, even as the world around him is spinning out of control. God forbid someone should accuse him of flip-flopping.

349

There's a disturbingly messianic fervor to his certainty. ... Leadership is all about managing change -- whether you're leading a company or leading a country. Things change, and you get creative. You adapt. Maybe Bush was absent the day they covered that at Harvard Business School.

A leader has to COMMUNICATE. I'm not talking about running off at the mouth or spouting sound bites. I'm talking about facing reality and telling the truth. Nobody in the current administration seems to know how to talk straight anymore. Instead, they spend most of their time trying to convince us that things are not really as bad as they seem. I don't know if it's denial or dishonesty, but it can start to drive you crazy after a while. ...

A leader has to be a person of CHARACTER. That means knowing the difference between right and wrong and having the guts to do the right thing. ... Bush has shown a willingness to take bold action on the world stage because he has the power, but he shows little regard for the grievous consequences. He has sent our troops (not to mention hundreds of thousands of innocent Iraqi citizens) to their deaths -- for what? To build our oil reserves? To avenge his daddy because Saddam Hussein once tried to have him killed? To show his daddy he's tougher? The motivations behind the war in Iraq are questionable, and the execution of the war has been a disaster. A man of character does not ask a single soldier to die for a failed policy.

A leader must have COURAGE. I'm talking about balls. (That even goes for female leaders.) Swagger isn't courage. Tough talk isn't courage. George Bush comes from a blue-blooded Connecticut family, but he likes to talk like a cowboy. You know, My gun is bigger than your gun. Courage in the twenty-first century doesn't mean posturing and bravado. Courage is a commitment to sit down at the negotiating table and talk.

If you're a politician, courage means taking a position

350

even when you know it will cost you votes. Bush can't even make a public appearance unless the audience has been handpicked and sanitized. He did a series of so-called town hall meetings last year, in auditoriums packed with his most devoted fans. The questions were all softballs.

... Bush has set the all-time record for number of vacation days taken by a U.S. President -- four hundred and counting. He'd rather clear brush on his ranch than immerse himself in the business of governing. He even told an interviewer that the high point of his presidency so far was catching a seven-and-a-half-pound perch in his hand-stocked lake.

It's no better on Capitol Hill. Congress was in session only ninety-seven days in 2006. That's eleven days less than the record set in 1948, when President Harry Truman coined the term do-nothing Congress. Most people would expect to be fired if they worked so little and had nothing to show for it. But Congress managed to find the time to vote itself a raise. Now, that's not leadership.

... Maybe George Bush is a great guy to hang out with at a barbecue or a ball game. But put him at a global summit where the future of our planet is at stake, and he doesn't look very presidential. Those frat-boy pranks and the kidding around he enjoys so much don't go over that well with world leaders. Just ask German Chancellor Angela Merkel, who received an unwelcome shoulder massage from our President at a G-8 Summit. When he came up behind her and started squeezing, I thought she was going to go right through the roof.

A leader has to be COMPETENT. That seems obvious, doesn't it? You've got to know what you're doing. More important than that, you've got to surround yourself with people who know what they're doing. Bush brags about being our first MBA President. Does that make him

351

competent? Well, let's see. Thanks to our first MBA President, we've got the largest deficit in history, Social Security is on life support, and we've run up a half-a-trillion-dollar price tag (so far) in Iraq. And that's just for starters. A leader has to be a problem solver, and the biggest problems we face as a nation seem to be on the back burner.

You can't be a leader if you don't have COMMON SENSE. ... George Bush doesn't have common sense. He just has a lot of sound bites. You know – Mr. they'll-welcome-us-as-liberators -no-child-left-behind-heck-of-a-job -Brownie-mission-accomplished Bush.
... I think our current President should visit the real world once in a while.

Leaders are made, not born. Leadership is forged in times of crisis. It's easy to sit there with your feet up on the desk and talk theory. Or send someone else's kids off to war when you've never seen a battlefield yourself. It's another thing to lead when your world comes tumbling down.
On September 11, 2001, we needed a strong leader more than any other time in our history. We needed a steady hand to guide us out of the ashes. Where was George Bush? He was reading a story about a pet goat to kids in Florida when he heard about the attacks. He kept sitting there for twenty minutes with a baffled look on his face. It's all on tape. You can see it for yourself. Then, instead of taking the quickest route back to Washington and immediately going on the air to reassure the panicked people of this country, he decided it wasn't safe to return to the White House. He basically went into hiding for the day -- and he told Vice President Dick Cheney to stay put in his bunker. We were all frozen in front of our TVs, scared out of our wits, waiting for our leaders to tell us that we were going to be okay, and there was nobody home. It took Bush a couple of days to get his bearings and devise the right photo op at Ground Zero.
That was George Bush's moment of truth, and he was

352

paralyzed. And what did he do when he'd regained his composure? He led us down the road to Iraq -- a road his own father had considered disastrous when he was President. But Bush didn't listen to Daddy. He listened to a higher father. He prides himself on being faith based, not reality based. If that doesn't scare the crap out of you, I don't know what will.

A HELL OF A MESS

So here's where we stand. We're immersed in a bloody war with no plan for winning and no plan for leaving. We're running the biggest deficit in the history of the country. ... Our schools are in trouble. ...
But when you look around, you've got to ask: "Where have all the leaders gone?" Where are the curious, creative communicators? Where are the people of character, courage, conviction, competence, and common sense? I may be a sucker for alliteration, but I think you get the point.

Name me a leader who has a better idea for homeland security than making us take off our shoes in airports and throw away our shampoo? We've spent billions of dollars building a huge new bureaucracy, and all we know how to do is react to things that have already happened.

Name me one leader who emerged from the crisis of Hurricane Katrina. Congress has yet to spend a single day evaluating the response to the hurricane, or demanding accountability for the decisions that were made in the crucial hours after the storm. Everyone's hunkering down, fingers crossed, hoping it doesn't happen again. Now, that's just crazy. Storms happen. Deal with it. Make a plan. Figure out what you're going to do the next time.
...
I have news for the gang in Congress. We didn't elect you to sit on your asses and do nothing and remain silent while our democracy is being hijacked and our greatness is

being replaced with mediocrity. What is everybody so afraid of? That some bobblehead on Fox News will call them a name? Give me a break. Why don't you guys show some spine for a change?

HAD ENOUGH?

Hey, I'm not trying to be the voice of gloom and doom here. I'm trying to light a fire. ... If I've learned one thing, it's this: You don't get anywhere by standing on the sidelines waiting for somebody else to take action. Whether it's building a better car or building a better future for our children, we all have a role to play. That's the challenge I'm raising in this book. It's a call to action for people who, like me, believe in America. It's not too late, but it's getting pretty close. So let's shake off the horseshit and go to work. Let's tell 'em all we've had enough.

~ ~ ~

It is clear where this narrowly focused band of selfish power lords stand on many issues: this group of republicans, neo-cons, and opportunists have denied or ignored the United Nations, international law, the Geneva Convention, the sovereignty of other nations, environmental protection, and civil rights. They promote a self-serving strategy while tolerating or promoting the destruction of the oceans and its creatures, air and forests, global warming, land mine use, and the development and production of weapons of all sorts– all for profit. They are ruthless in their pursuit of public power and will do anything to get it and keep it. They use intimidation, propaganda, surveillance, fear and force to keep people like you and I in line.

SP

>>~o~<<

The Neo-Con Players

    We have our own "terrorists" to deal with and
we need our entire focus returned to them so that
we can one day live in a country where the people
once again pick the president, a country where the
wealthy learn that they have to pay for their
actions. A free country, a safe country, a peaceful
country that genuinely shares its riches with the
less fortunate around the world, a country that
believes in everyone getting a fair shake, and
where fear is seen as the only thing we truly need
to fear.
- Michael Moore, *Dude, Where's My Country?*

~ ~ ~

We will not forget the Bankruptcy Bill that lined the
pockets of the credit card companies and financial
institutions at the expense of hard-working middle-class
citizens, nor the policies that funneled billions into the
accounts of the pharmaceutical industry while our most
vulnerable citizens sickened and died because they could
not afford life-saving medication.

We will not forget the cronyism that elevated the
incompetent to positions that required decision-making in
situations that literally meant the difference between life
and death.
We will not forget the homeless you have ignored, the
jobless you have created, the numbers of uninsured you
have contributed to.

We will not forget the victims of Katrina, those who fell
below the poverty level during your tenure in office, nor
the corruption that led to the investigation, indictment and
imprisonment of your own party members whose greed
literally knew no bounds.

We will not forget that as you debated non-issues like
flag-burning, everything our flag symbolizes –

355

democracy, freedom, working together for the common good of the country – was being dragged through the mud. We will not forget that you were all too willing to turn a blind eye to things like signing statements and executive actions contrary to law, while rubber-stamping every whim of the petulant, immature idiot you placed in the White House under questionable, if not outright fraudulent, circumstances.

We will not forget that as that president broke the laws of the land, spied on American citizens, lied the country into war and then displayed an ineptitude in conducting that war and governing the nation literally unsurpassed in the annals of our history, you not only gave your unwavering support, but had the audacity to question the loyalty of those who demanded a return to the very freedoms this democracy was founded upon.

- Nancy Greggs, WE WILL NOT FORGET, 10 Dec 2006
http://journals.democraticunderground.com/NanceGreggs/133

"Men who have no respect for human life or for freedom or justice have taken over this beautiful country of ours. It will be up to the American people to take it back."
- Howard Zinn

The indictable players in this seditious crime are as follows (with many more hiding in the shadows, laundering money, negotiating contracts, rigging elections, altering legislation, and setting divisive policies). In fact, it will be very illuminating to find out who are the prime contributors to Bush's election 2004 war machine, with over $200 million contributed. They aren't giving money because they like him. We are talking PAYBACK.

The Neo-Cons

George "Dubya" Bush
Dick Cheney
Carl Rove
Donald Rumsfeld
Paul Wolfowitz
John Ashcroft
Antonin Scalia
Clarence Thomas
William Rehnquist - too late
Anthony Kennedy
Sandra Day O'Conner
Jeb Bush
Katherine Harris
Condoleezza Rice
James A. Baker III
Colin Powell; retirement after aiding in the coup and Iraq - how comfortable
Ward Connerly
Vin Weber; Choice Point's DC lobbyist
Clayton Roberts; FL Div of Elections
Richard "profit on 9-11" Perle - Defense Policy Board (DPB), consultant, and principle behind investment firm Trireme
Tom DeLay – disgraced House majority leader ... in the thick of things in Florida and Texas; by 2006 confronted with federal investigation and changing the rules for his benefit; stepped back but still there
Ari Fleischer - just because you retired ...
Scott McClellen - who took Ari's job of disinformation (obviously a burn-out job. Conscience?) Nah
Richard Armitage - Deputy secretary of state
Dan Bartlett - communications director, spin meister
Edward Pozuolli, R., FL
Bill Scherer - lead counsel in FL
Elliot Abrams - National Security Council
Bill Frist - Senate majority leader
John Graham; OMB (Office of Management & Budget)
Lewis Libby - Cheney's chief of staff; got caught leaking the Plame case; implicating others like Rove and his boss!

John Snow; Treasury Secretary
Jack Abramoff, right wing lobbyist, presently under investigation, and perhaps talking
Gale Norton - Interior Secretary
Karen Hughes - Bush spokesperson
Spencer Abraham - Sec. of Energy (in 2000 he voted to abolish this department!)
Rod Paige - Sec of Education
Grover Norquist - anti-government lobbyist and Bush advisor on tax cuts for the rich
Emmett "Bucky" Mitchell - lawyer for Katherine Harris
Don Evans - Sec. of Commerce
Tommy Thompson - Sec. of Health & Human Services
Andrew H. Card, Jr. - Whitehouse Chief of Staff
Ann Veneman - Sec. of Agriculture, not wanting to scare Americans by labeling genetically altered foods
Mitch Daniels, Jr. - Director, OMB
James Sensenbrenner (R-WI), congressman and overlord
Douglas Feith - Undersecretary of Defense, CSP (Center for Security Policy), JINSA (Jewish Institute for National Security Affairs)
Ralph Reed - GOP strategist, Enron consultant and former head of the Christian Coalition
Dennis Hastert - speaker of the US House
James Roche - Sec. of the Air Force
Dov Zakheim - Pentagon Comptroller
Ted Forstmann - Empower America, neo-con
R. James Woolsey - former CIA Director, DPB member
Newt Gingrich - will he never go away?
John Poindexter - various posts, lots of damage
John Minnis - Senator "Menace"
Dr. W. David Hager - cited in this work, FDA
Frank Gaffney - Center for Security Policy
John Bolton - assistant Secretary of State for Arms Control, rabid NRA advocate; U.N. reprehensible
David Steinmann - JINSA, CSP
Michael Ledeen - JINSA, CSP, Pentagon adviser and warhawk
Jay Garner - retired general
Bill Luti - Deputy Assistant Secretary of Defense

Thomas White - Sec. of Army
Harvey Pitt - chairman of the SEC
Robert Joseph - National Security Council
Stephen Cambone - Rumsfeld advisor
Phil Gramm - U.S. Senator, Texas, and ...
Wendy Gramm - Commodity Futures Trading Commission
chairwoman; another rip-off husband and wife team
Stephen Hadley - Deputy National Security Advisor – Condi
Rice's right-hand man
Marc Racicot - chairman of the Republican National Committee
George Tenet - CIA Director; took the fall, but helped the insiders
and the plan
Pat Wood - Federal Energy Regulatory Commission
Kenneth Adelman - Pentagon Advisory Board, Defense Policy
Board ... so, Iraq would be a cakewalk, huh?
Andrew Card - chief of staff, ex-GM lobbyist, packager of the
Iraq War sale
Ed Gillespie - RNC Chairman and former Enron lobbyist
David Jeremiah - retired Navy Admiral, DPB and paid consultant
for Boeing = conflict!
Ronald Fogelman - retired Air Force general, DPB and paid
consultant for Boeing = conflict!
Joe Allbaugh - New Bridge Strategies, a consulting firm cashing
in on Iraq = conflict!
Porter Goss - presently Bush's director of the CIA ; as Rep. Co-
-chairman of the joint House- Senate intelligence panel
investigating 9/11, he suppressed information about the Saudis
for Bush ... and this is our man objectively collecting data for our
national security? No, this is a post given for loyalty to the
president, not the people.

Trent Lott - how clever of the Republicans to handle this bigot
themselves, keeping his public stance lauding segregation an
internal affair, while sidestepping the democratic process of recall
or impeachment. And, oh yes, very close ties to the weapons
industries. After the 2006 mid-term elections the republicans
brought him front and center again.

All members of the Project for the New American Century

359

(PNAC)

Committee on the Present Danger (CPD) - against the Soviet threat. Is it still around?

Center for Security Policy (CSP) - masterminded by Frank Gaffney

Empower America - neo-con group; Ted Forstmann

The Heritage Foundation

National Institute for Public Policy (NIPP) - Dr. Keith Payne

American Enterprise Institute (AEI)

Jewish Institute for National Security Affairs (JINSA); advocating regime changes throughout the Middle East, brought about and paid for by USA

The Federalist Society for Law and Public Policy Studies; turning back the legal system

Trireme - consulting firm headed by Richard Perle

Vinson & Elkins law firm

Key members of the neo-con Media, such as in ...

>
> Fox TV
>
> Clear Channel
>
> Conrad Black and his cohorts

Corporations involved to date in the 2000 & 2004 Elections are, coincidentally, conservative businesses that favor Bush and crew. If it is found that they manipulated and altered the vote in any US election, should their executives and board members not go to jail for treason?

- DIEBOLD ELECTION SYSTEMS
- ELECTION SYSTEMS & SOFTWARE
- HART INTERCIVIC
- SEQUOIA

Questionable, but implicated:

Ted Olson - Solicitor General

Richard Pombo; R., CA

Rich Santorum, R. Pa, GOP Conference Chairman, equating gay rights to incest and bestiality

John Sununu
Frank Keating
Asa Hutcheson - Deputy Undersecretary
Edward Badolato - Vice President for Homeland Security, The
Shaw Group
John Ellis - Bush cousin, FOX employee
Roger Ailes - FOX News chief
Michael Powell - FCC Chair (giving away our airwaves to the
right people)
Jeane Kirkpatrick - various posts, lots of damage
Gordon England - Sec. of Navy
Rudy De Leon - lobbyist
Tom Hicks - Clear Channel vice chairman
Bennett Zier - Regional Executive Vice President, Clear Channel
Fred Smith - President/CEO, Federal Express
Paul O'Neill - ex Sec. of Treasury (does your exposé exempt you
from your greedy past?)

The Carlyle Group
Lockheed Martin - military and war is good for business
Boeing - military and war is good for business
Northrop Grumman - military and war is good for business

* Propagandists such as Sean Hannity, Brit Hume, Bill O'Reilly,
Michael Savage, William Safire, Rush Limbaugh, Chris
Matthews, Ann Coulter, Laura Ingraham and other loud-mouthed
liars. What has Jim Bohanon - National Late-night Broadcaster -
been saying? We can assume that the TV, radio and news
organizations that promote these neo-cons approve of their views.
That includes people like Rupert Murdoch, Fox media merchant
and propagandist, and William Kristol, neo-con editor of the
Weekly Standard.
There are more ...

One can find more scoundrels on Right Web, an
investigative online information source that is dedicated to
naming the names and pointing out the right wing conservatives
(and their organizations) who are pushing this country into more
militarism and dangerous reactionary politics. http://rightweb.irc-

online.org/
* Have moved on:
Kenneth L. Lay - presidential advisor, ex-Enron executive; arrested in July 2004, convicted in 2006, then took off on a vacation to Colorado, and died of a heart attack

William Rehnquist - too late for this chief justice to pay his dues. If we do nothing many in this theft will retire, get their pay-offs and pensions, then die ... escaping justice and probably believing to the end that they did the right thing for God and their country. They did the *Right* thing all right.

As of late 2006 some of the hypocritical and dangerous ones have left, thank God, but they are in the side lines, and may want to run for some office again. Let us hope we collectively wake up. But let's cherish their departure (and remember their names) here: "Vaya Con Dios, My Darlings - Wonkette" http://www.wonkette.com/politics/bloodbath/vaya-con-dios-my-darlings-213488.php

~ ~ ~

Loud and threatening voices will come to defend these people; they will have various motives:

"Though I would carefully avoid giving unnecessary offense, yet I am inclined to believe, that all those who espouse the doctrine of reconciliation, may be included within the following descriptions. Interested men, who are not to be trusted; weak men who cannot see; prejudiced men who will not see..."
- Thomas Paine

The True Patriots

Meanwhile, the good citizens of the United States are responding to the tenets and clear arguments from many voices within our own borders, including Chalmers Johnson, Howard Zinn, Dennis Kucinich, Molly Ivins, Noam Chomsky, Greg Palast, Ramsey Clark, Thom Hartmann, Michael Moore, Caroline Kennedy, and thousands of others. These are brave and patriotic souls who care enough to stand up to tyranny and to let their voices be heard. Do not be afraid to stand up too, especially you who feel you have more to lose:

> Rich men are notoriously timid. It is the have-nots and the men who are on the make who encourage social disturbances. The Tories were not blind to [John] Hancock's importance; they would have paid a high price for him... He, the owner of the greatest business in New England, stepped forth boldly as the champion of the revolutionary cause, well aware that if it came to hanging, he, above all others, would be the one the Tories would most delight in hanging.
> - Kenneth Umbreit, *Founding Fathers*, 1941

~ ~ ~

"... we must prepare to take on a Republican machine that has already corrupted the electoral process in the past three elections, and knows how to "pull a Ukraine" in any state at any time with single a phone call to Jim Baker or Tom DeLay. In a preemptory move, Republicans are now calling for an end to exit polls in the USA because, as RNC Chairman and former Enron lobbyist Ed Gillespie noted on November 4th, 'In 2000 the exit data was wrong on Election Day, in 2002 the exit returns were wrong on Election Day, and in 2004, the exit data were wrong on Election Day – all three times, by the way, in a way that skewed against Republicans and had a dispiriting effect on Republican voters across the country.'"

- Thom Hartmann, HOW TO TAKE BACK A STOLEN ELECTION (Common Dreams, Nov 29, 2004)

Bill Moyers has been a voice of reason and common sense for decades. Please take to heart his inspiring "This is Your Story - The Progressive Story of America. Pass It On." - Text of speech to the Take Back America conference; sponsored by the Campaign for America's Future, June 4, 2003, Washington, DC:

What I can't explain is the rage of the counter-revolutionaries to dismantle every last brick of the social contract. At this advanced age I simply have to accept the fact that the tension between haves and have-nots is built into human psychology and society itself – it's ever with us. However, I'm just as puzzled as to why, with right wing wrecking crews blasting away at social benefits once considered invulnerable, Democrats are fearful of being branded "class warriors" in a war the other side started and is determined to win. I don't get why conceding your opponent's premises and fighting on his turf isn't the sure-fire prescription for irrelevance and ultimately obsolescence. But I confess as well that I don't know how to resolve the social issues that have driven wedges into your ranks. And I don't know how to reconfigure democratic politics to fit into an age of soundbites and polling dominated by a media oligarchy whose corporate journalists are neutered and whose right-wing publicists have no shame.

...

What will it take to get back in the fight? Understanding the real interests and deep opinions of the American people is the first thing. And what are those? That a Social Security card is not a private portfolio statement but a membership ticket in a society where we all contribute to a common treasury so that none need face the indignities of poverty in old age without that help. That tax evasion is not a form of conserving investment capital but a brazen abandonment of responsibility to the country. That income inequality is not a sign of freedom-of-opportunity at work, because if it persists and grows, then unless you believe that some people are naturally born to ride and some to wear saddles, it's a sign that opportunity is less than equal.

364

That self-interest is a great motivator for production and progress, but is amoral unless contained within the framework of community. That the rich have the right to buy more cars than anyone else, more homes, vacations, gadgets and gizmos, but they do not have the right to buy more democracy than anyone else. That public services, when privatized, serve only those who can afford them and weaken the sense that we all rise and fall together as "one nation, indivisible." That concentration in the production of goods may sometimes be useful and efficient, but monopoly over the dissemination of ideas is evil. That prosperity requires good wages and benefits for workers. And that our nation can no more survive as half democracy and half oligarchy than it could survive "half slave and half free" – and that keeping it from becoming all oligarchy is steady work – our work.

...

What's right and good doesn't come naturally. You have to stand up and fight for it – as if the cause depends on you, because it does. Allow yourself that conceit - to believe that the flame of democracy will never go out as long as there's one candle in your hand.

So go for it. Never mind the odds.

The Bottom Line, Restated

The 2000 election in the state of Florida was fixed by Jeb Bush and Katherine Harris and their co-conspirators – before the voting began. In the ensuing controversy, a biased supreme court then selected the president of the United States. There was a bloodless coup in December 2000. This takeover was planned, in part, by members of the Project for the New American Century, who also planned the Iraqi invasion for position, power and oil. They and the people in power since the takeover committed treason at home and war abroad. They are traitors and war criminals.

The richest and most powerful nation in the world has been hijacked by a small group of arch-conservatives with happy visions of 1955. They feel entitled to rule us all, and wish to drag America back to those good days of J. Edgar Hoover, atomic supremacy, Joe McCarthy and apple pie. How much compassionate conservatism can we take?

We are fighting for no less than our country, our ideals, and our freedom.

I shall wrap this up with an open letter of fact and action.

Dear Citizen, Friend and Neighbor

This is a desperate time. Neo-cons have taken our country, the USA. They have been lying, manipulating and controlling at home, and arrogant, aggressive and militant abroad. Their deluded sense of righteousness, inability to admit mistakes, their militancy and greed are almost too much.

There was such hope and idealism for this 3rd millennium. The world is now threatened by a surprise enemy: the nation that has stood for justice, progress, innovation, and democracy has become an aggressive and dangerous rogue nation. The most powerful country on earth has been hijacked by some profiteers and mercenaries, while its citizens have been conned into believing that all is well and legitimate in this land.

March 2003 witnessed this clear threat to world peace – the Bush regime, after failing to achieve UN acceptance for its invasion of Iraq, ignored international law and preemptively attacked that nation. Saddam and his repressive government will not be missed, but it is well known by now that the world was not in danger from this petty tyrant. There is now a bigger and more violent tyrant to worry about, controlling a government that is not afraid to use force anywhere in the world – and has the power to do so. This rogue nation scoffs at world opinion, believing it is closer to God and truth. It does not have to answer to lesser nations, to the Geneva Convention, nor to the people of the United States itself.

The international threat is real. Bush spokesmen like Dick Cheney and Condoleezza Rice have threatened the governments of Iran, Syria, North Korea and Cuba, and have implemented punishments ("policies and sanctions" are the official terms) to countries like France and Germany for disagreeing with the Iraqi invasion. The whole NATO alliance is in jeopardy. The precedence for pre-emptive war has been set. The world is less secure because of it.

Am I being too critical or over-reacting? A poll of nations and non-profit organizations including Amnesty International and the Red Cross have listed the USA as one of the biggest threats to world peace. We have a clear pattern of endemic deception, belligerence and cover-up. The invasion and occupation of Iraq? As usual, George W. Bush is not taking responsibility for the deceit used in selling the threat; he passed the blame of "flawed intelligence" (which conned many into joining the illegal invasion) on to a lone and well paid (by our own government) Iraqi informant, and to fall guy and former director of the CIA George Tenet, and to unspecified British sources. Evidently following this arrogant precedent, and with official memos condoning torture, our men and women in uniform, protecting our nation (?), are the focus of ugly revelations of physical, mental and sexual abuse of Iraqi prisoners at Abu Ghraib and other prisons, plus the even more shocking crimes of revenge killings and even massacres. And this by the *liberating* forces of George W. Bush's America.

As this circus of falsehood continues, Bush is soiling the good name of the United States while losing this War on Terror through ignorant short-sightedness, incompetency and overt aggression. This arrogant Texas cowboy is inspiring Middle Eastern militants daily. Osama bin Laden predicted that imperialist America would soon occupy an Arab land – and Bush answered his prayers. Our soldiers–who shouldn't be there in the first place–are in more danger today than when the "war was won" in the spring of 2003. There is well over three thousand US dead, tens of thousands wounded on "our" side, and untold hundreds of thousands of innocent Iraqis buried in this selfish oil and power grab.

The preemptive war and occupation of Iraq is not the main accusation here; it is just an egregious example of the Bush regime's tactics as usual. This regime will push, sue, manipulate, deceive, coerce, threaten and then initiate a strike to get what it wants, which is exactly how they came to rule in the first place.

Here's the news that no "mainstream" person dares admit: Bush should *not* be calling the shots here at home nor abroad. Before "we" take our liberating forces out into the world, toppling dictators who gained their power in coups, we need to clean up our own mess here at home.

A crime was committed against the American people at the election polls. I am not referring to the 2004 election; no, while investigators and statisticians are reviewing that mess, we have a bona fide and **verifiable** stolen election several years before that. Millions of people stood by in disbelief as opportunistic lawyers and judges intervened in the US election of 2000. We were shocked when the US Supreme Court, overstepping its own bounds, overruled the Florida Supreme Court. And then, with a flimsy excuse but with the authority of the highest court in the land, the "supreme" court *selected* the next president of the United States for us. It was a **coup d'etat**, bloodless and arrogant. The debacle of the stolen election of 2000 was more than some clever political strategy. As been stated elsewhere:

Traitors have taken the government of the USA in a coup.

And Yes. We are talking treason.

It is not too late to overturn this injustice. Some pundits and conservatives would tell us "This is old news. The decision has been made years ago. Let's move on." Let me say that there is no statute of limitations on political theft, sedition, and now, war crimes. Now that this dangerous band of usurpers are in power – and they are connected with the manufacturers of the voting machines (Hello??!), do you believe there will be any fair elections in our future?
Why bother? We have stepped over the line into a new era for our Republic.

It happened to Rome, why not here? Why, because this is "America" and stuff like that doesn't happen here? Look around, read the "other" news, talk to political activists, check the internet and the world press. My friends, right now we have a dynasty (George the Second?) and a ruling class that have no intentions of relinquishing power on their own.

The 2000 US election was a coup and the 2004 election was rigged – assuming that Bush and Cheney were eligible to run *as felons of the 2000 coup.*

Their friends and supporters are looking at 2008....

There comes a time when citizens of a free republic must stand up to a self-serving and dangerous regime and demand their removal. For the sake of our children, our families, and our very ideals, we the people of the United States of America must throw out those who have betrayed our trust and choose again to live as free citizens of a just and fair land. It is crucial that we wrest the power away from these neo-con extremists and put them where they belong – in jail.

Think about it. We could swing back to that idealism warranted of a new millennium in a bold move. We could put the whole lot of neo-cons behind bars (including the Supreme Court Justices that aided the coup), repeal and dismiss all of their draconian laws (including the dangerous Patriot Act) since 2001, cripple their whole hypocritical party for decades, overturn disastrous policies promoting militancy, global warming and environmental pollution, reassert our *progressive* place in the international community, and demonstrate to the world that justice and democracy *can* come from the shores of America.

For the sake of our trampled democracy, our polluted land, our miserable economy, our threatened civil rights, and for the sake of world peace, these dangerous fanatics must be stopped. It is the responsibility of people of good conscience and common sense to stand united and prepared in the face of such obvious falsehood, deception and crimes.

We are fighting for liberty and democracy,
     here and now.

It is time.
Stephen Paine

http://www.culturefix.org/common_sense_revisited_treason/evidence

Contact your representatives in Congress and "suggest" that they make a brave stand and take back the stolen executive branch - http://www.congress.org/congressorg/directory/congdir.tt Careful whom you contact, though; some of them will have you watched.

It is not too late.

First, a reminder of the founding principles, rights and choices in this country, the United States of America, this experiment in government:

When, in the course of human Events, it becomes necessary for one People to dissolve the political bands which have connected them with another, and to assume among the Powers of the Earth the separate and equal Station to which the Laws of Nature and of Nature's God entitle them, a decent Respect to the Opinions of Mankind requires that they should declare the causes which impel them to the Separation.

We hold these Truths to be self-evident, that all Men are created Equal, that they are endowed by their Creator with certain unalienable Rights, that among these are life, Liberty, and the Pursuit of Happiness – That to secure these Rights, Governments are instituted among men, deriving their just Powers from the Consent of the Governed; that whenever any Form of Government becomes destructive of these Ends, it is the Right of the People to alter or to abolish it, and to institute new Government, laying its Foundations on such Principles, and organizing its powers in such Form, as to them shall seem most likely to effect their Safety and Happiness. Prudence, indeed, will dictate that Governments long established should not be changed for light and transient Causes; and accordingly all Experience hath shewn, that mankind are more disposed to suffer, while Evils are sufferable, than to right themselves by abolishing the Forms to which they are accustomed. But when a long train of Abuses and usurpations, pursuing invariably the same Object, evinces a Design to reduce them under absolute Despotism, it is their Right, it is their Duty, to throw off such Government, and to provide new Guards for their future Security. ...

Declaration of Independence, July 4th, 1776

Call to Action

When a country is taken over by a treacherous power elite, pushing aside the candidate who won the popular vote, is this not sedition? When the mechanism of voting is undermined in a supposedly democratic country, is this not traitorous? When an aggressive group of pirates intimidate the opposition, usurp the legal institutions, and storm the executive office, is this not treason?

Our Legal Grounds

The US Constitution - and the Amendments - are bases in which those who wish to have legal certainty in this indictment can then rest in peace ... and have some legal ground to sign the warrants.

Here it is, folks: The Constitution, Article. II., Section. 4. *The President, Vice President and all civil Officers of the United States, shall be removed from Office on Impeachment for, and Conviction of, Treason, Bribery, or other high Crimes and Misdemeanors.*

My fellow Americans, they can be successfully tried for **all** of these crimes – as stated in the Constitution! Treason, bribery (what do you call it? Business deals?), high crimes **and** misdemeanors!

George W. Bush has sworn before the American people, and the whole world, twice (two inaugurations), the following, as directed by Article. II., Section.1., Clause 8: *Before he enter on the Execution of his Office, he shall take the following Oath or Affirmation: – "I do solemnly swear (or affirm) that I will faithfully execute the Office of President of the United States, and will to the best of my Ability, preserve, protect and defend the Constitution of the United States."*

Thus, he has perjured himself, far greater than President Clinton, for he has not defended the Constitution of the United

States. On the contrary, he has abused it and crippled it – and us, the citizens of this country.

Furthermore, just to let us know that the forefathers anticipated some strange happenings, they gave us Article II., Section.1: *The Congress may by Law provide for the Case of Removal, Death, Resignation or Inability, both of the President and Vice President, declaring what Officer shall then act as President, and such Officer shall act accordingly, until the Disability be removed, or a President shall be elected.*

It turns out that we can fire "Supreme Court" justices a lot easier than urban legends describe. Article. III., Section.1. gives us the following: *The judicial Power of the United States, shall be vested in one supreme Court, and in such inferior Courts as the Congress may from time to time ordain and establish. The Judges, both of the supreme and inferior Courts, shall hold their Offices **during good Behaviour**, and shall, at stated Times, receive for their Services, a Compensation, which shall not be diminished during their Continuance in Office.*

My goodness, *"during good Behaviour"* is rather broad! However, their behaviour has been very bad. Very bad indeed.

When can we arrest those guilty? From the Bill of Rights, Article [V.] *No person shall be held to answer for a capital, or otherwise infamous crime, unless on a presentment or indictment of a Grand Jury, **except in cases** arising in the land or naval forces, or in the Militia, when in actual service in time of War or **public danger***

The public is in danger. Now.

The powers of Congress are clear according to the Constitution. Their duty in this particular instance is found in Article I, Section. 8., Clause 15: *To provide for calling forth the Militia to execute the Laws of the Union, suppress Insurrections and repel Invasions.*

374

As this book – and thousands of other exposés – prove, we have an insurrection (in business suits) on our hands. An official meaning of insurrection is "a conflict in which one faction tries to wrest control from another." The coup of 2000 was indeed a "wresting" of control. Can an invasion come from within? This is the implication of a cabal, a small but forceful group determined to take over a government no matter what means. This is treason.

The cautious may wonder if we can arrest members of Congress. In Article I, Section. 6. Clause 1, we find this: *The Senators and Representatives ... shall in all Cases, except Treason, Felony and Breach of the Peace, be privileged from Arrest during their Attendance at the Session of their respective Houses.*

Thus, as they have indeed committed these very crimes, then we can proceed with the arrests. This will create, undoubtedly, a great division in this land; one we haven't seen since the Civil War. The similarities to this time are revealing. Not unlike the Civil War, when members of a single family were on opposite sides of the conflict, we have some members of Congress guilty of abetting and aiding the enemies of the State, and we call upon other members of Congress to do their duty to carry out that which must be done. These patriots have the power to make the laws to fit the crime (If the crime lies outside of the present law, which I don't think is the case.) However, the following Article may make some of these legislators breathe easier. Article. I.., Section. 8., Clause 18: *To make all Laws which shall be necessary and proper for carrying into Execution the foregoing Powers, and all other Powers vested by this Constitution in the Government of the United States, or in any Department or Officer thereof.*

Once we have weeded the Congress of the aiders and abettors, then the Constitution comes to our aid again: Article. III., Section. 3., Clause 2: *The Congress shall have Power to declare the Punishment of Treason.*

Shall we look at treason itself? The Constitution tells us in Article. III., Section. 3., Clause 1: *Treason against the United States, shall consist only in levying War against them, or in adhering to their Enemies, giving them Aid and Comfort. No Person shall be convicted of Treason unless on the Testimony of two Witnesses to the same overt Act, or on Confession in open Court.*

This begs the questions: Who are the enemies of the States? - those individuals, groups and corporations that weaken, deprive, deceive, pollute, demean, and abuse these United States – and send its sons and daughters off to be killed for personal greed? As you see, this description in the Constitution is rather broad. Good. I think we've got a case. We can easily find two witnesses; in fact, with much of the 2000 election fiasco beamed out to the American public, there were millions of witnesses.

> Adhering to their Enemies, giving them Aid and Comfort? My friends, the enemies of the States are the extremist neo-conservatives, who have formed bonds of profit with countless enemies of our Republic – putting our country into danger internationally, while corrupting the Constitution they were supposedly defending, plus their undermining of the Bill of Rights and other freedoms. The list of crimes are mentioned throughout this indictment.

The facts are before you. The path of action is clear for those with common sense. Before there is any more damage done, let us stop the insanity and injustice.

Let us weed the garden.

I propose "Operation American Freedom."

Ω Arrest Bush and Crew, the four surviving supreme court justices, and their accomplices.

These manipulators, liars, opportunists and despots are guilty of treason, theft and war crimes and must be t removed from positions of power and jailed for the good of all. Arrest warrants should be written now. With this bold move, we would cripple their whole hypocritical party for decades. Don't argue and threaten these people, nor give them time to retaliate. Beware of conciliation and stalled negotiations and counter legal bluff. Remember, you are dealing with people who subvert the legal system to their ends, and who are not afraid of violence and preemptive strikes to those who oppose them.

Ω Pay Us All Back

Officials, lawyers, contractors and businessmen have been stealing from the American people for decades. How far back should we go? To the millions stolen from the tax coffers and spent on the outrageous seven year Clinton investigation (and how much was the infamous Mr. Starr and his intrusive staff paid?) that only uncovered a private matter but blew into a humiliating and ugly impeachment? [This was a politically motivated witch trial that told all concerned that the Republicans would use anything to take you down. Message? Do not defy us or get in our way. Result? Weak-kneed reactions to the 2000 Coup and their other trespasses.] If we merely go back to 2000, they owe us for the corporate rip-offs (and the "lost" retirement funds), the special appropriations, the kick-backs, and the hugely expensive military defense institution and the wars which seem to justify them in an unending circuit of fear, war and death.

Americans are worried about the expenses of health care, retirement, education, social security, community services, and the environment. In a land as prosperous and resourceful as ours, there has been no reason for these worries. No, one reason: The money was diverted, siphoned off into private hands. They stole billions and have to pay us back.

* All of those billions, however, will not bring back the young men and women who obeyed the call to fight a foreign "enemy" that happened to occupy an oil rich land. These crimes cannot be paid back in money. The con men who manufactured these bogus wars have to stand before an international court for war crimes.

Ω Rescind all of their Rules, Appointments and Regulations

With a bold stroke, we could swing towards a progressive future (not some mythical past), repeal and dismiss all of their draconian laws (including the dangerous Patriot Act) since 2001, and overturn disastrous policies promoting fear and paranoia, militancy, global warming and environmental pollution. You know what to do.

Ω Get Out of Iraq ... and many other Countries

We could continue the aggressive policies that made us the number one power in the world, with installations or troops in over a hundred countries and a military budget greater than the rest of the world combined. Let us however use our common sense and see the truth: It is a tremendous waste of energy and resources. We are not secure and we are not admired. The United States has been following a paranoid policy of international intervention, coercion and nation building for too long. This reactionary policy has not made any of us safer – it has only created animosity, fear and hatred ... and more weapons. Merely withdrawing from Iraq and all of the other countries will not be enough, however. As I stated earlier, it is imperative, for reasons of national security, that the Bush regime be removed from office and put behind bars. By ridding ourselves of the coup, we are declaring, simultaneously, a statement to the world that Americans ultimately strive for justice and can achieve it at home and abroad. Those who say this is idealistic and foolhardy will merely prolong the irrational and destructive policy of the neo-conservative world view. They would pull us back into more fear and weapons. These theorists and apologists will stare you in the eye and declare their pragmatic reasoning, or bluff you with fabrications and threats. Don't listen to them. They are liars, manipulators or deluded. They are emotional hot-heads and chicken-hawks or self-serving businessmen and lawyers who are looking out for number one. We must break free of them. If we fail in this noble stance, we will continue to be vulnerable to them and to the terrorists they help create.

Let us reassert our *progressive* place in the international community and demonstrate to the world that justice and democracy *can* come from the shores of America. We should be expanding Kennedy's Peace Corps internationally and our own AmeriCorps nationally. We could make the United Nations relevant again. We could be part of an international community of cooperative nations.

Ω   **Abolish the Electoral College, Reform the Court**

Reflect upon the facts given. I hope I have convincingly stated my case. Not only do we need to jail the traitors, but to ensure that such an outrage cannot happen again, we need to overhaul the US Supreme Court system and abolish the Electoral College.

If we were living in a democracy, the close election in Florida would not have been an issue. Al Gore won the popular vote by more than half a million votes (which totally eclipsed the small number of voters in Florida). Some say we shouldn't tamper with the Constitution and just leave the voting system and the Electoral College alone. This is a ludicrous argument, for it overlooks many important changes to that document, including civil rights amendments and even the Bill of Rights. The very people who tell us the Electoral College is sacred are the ones who want a Constitutional amendment concerning pro-choice and alternative lifestyles. Some argue that the electoral college offers the small states more clout during elections. Two sobering thoughts:

1) Smaller states with uncertain election results in 2000, 2004 and almost any other election are regularly **ignored** because the larger states (Florida in 2000, Ohio in 2004) have more electoral votes. For instance, in 2000 New Mexico was won by 366 votes – remember the news media there for that close race?

2) There is already a powerful institution which represent small states – it is called the Senate, which is in session every year, not a quick voting experience one day every two years.

Ω Amends for Blowback

Our international business and military policies came back to bite us in the blowback experience of 9/11 as well as numerous other "retaliations" around the world. Let us not play favoritism with belligerent countries, nor follow hypocritical policies, nor back right wingers (anywhere), and definitely let us not pander to businesses following the bottom line *at any cost*. Let us weed from our agencies, military, and government those who create enmity due to selfishness, lies and deceit.

We need to redirect our security agencies and re-write their intentions of purpose. We need to mix information gathering with international good will projects and progressive educational programs. The Cold War is over. Are we living in the past? No, let us live honestly now, with a progressive eye on the future; for a conscientious life now, and a positive life for future generations.

We are living in the third millennium – let's act like it.

Stop pretending that we are a democracy – we are a republic (look it up). However, we are a participatory republic. Contact your progressive Congressmen, judges, marshals, and officials and demand that we follow a higher course. Perhaps we could be an admired and even be a beloved country!

Ω Change Course

It will be a great and longer work to change the course of this country; however, it must begin by improving the educational system to enable Americans to discern and refute lies attractively packaged. Let us teach common sense, practical living, ethical behavior and philosophical reflection. Let us mix schools and learning into business and the workplace. Perhaps the responsibility of teaching children the ways of trade and the market would invite more ethical behavior from our executives, businesspeople, and military personnel.

Our whole social and political system is unnecessarily complex – right now we need experts and lawyers and intermediaries to let us know what we can do and what is permissible and when to act in our communities. Fewer police, more teachers. Fewer laws, more ethics. Fewer rules, more common sense. Let's keep things simple:

"I draw my idea of the form of government from a principle in nature, which no art can overturn, viz., that the more simple any thing is, the less liable it is to be disordered, and the easier repaired when disordered."
Thomas Paine, 1776

Be smart, be quick, be thorough. And don't delay.

Stephen Paine

>>~o~<<

"The only thing necessary for the triumph of evil is for good men to do nothing."

- Edmund Burke

Please share this with your friends and family, especially with those who have the power and courage to arrest the fanatics. We need a concerted presence to meet this menace.

Please urge those who can do something about this to act, and soon.

A determined group of visionary activists and leaders with integrity can make the difference.

Each time a man stands up for an ideal, or acts to improve the life of others, or strikes out against injustice, he sends a tiny ripple of hope, and those ripples, crossing each other from a million different centers of energy, build a current which can sweep down the mightiest walls of oppression and resistance.

Robert F. Kennedy

~ ~ ~

Destiny is not a matter of chance,
it is a matter of choice;
it is not a thing to be waited for,
it is a thing to be achieved.

William Jennings Bryan

Books & Documentaries

The word is out! There are many voices:

The Best Democracy Money Can Buy by Greg Palast
Overruling Democracy: The Supreme Court vs. The American People by Jamin B. Raskin
How Much Are You Making On the War, Daddy? By William D. Hartung
The Re-Count Primer by Timothy Downs and Chris Sautter
Down and Dirty: the Plot to Steal the Presidency by Jake Tapper
Jews for Buchanan by John Nichols
The Greatest Sedition is Silence by William Rivers Pitt
War On Iraq by William Rivers Pitt (with Scott Ritter)
Blowback by Chalmers Johnson
Dude, Where's My Country? and *Stupid White Men* by Michael Moore
Pigs at the Trough by Arianna Huffington
The Great Unraveling: Losing Our Way in the New Century by Paul Krugman
The Lies of George W. Bush: Mastering the Politics of Deception by David Corn
Had Enough? A handbook for Fighting Back by James Carville
Fear's Empire: War, Terrorism, and Democracy by Benjamin R. Barber
Bushwhacked: Life in George W. Bush's America by Molly Ivins and Lou Dubose
Thieves in High Places: They've Stolen Our Country and It's Time to Take It Back by Jim Hightower
Perpetual War for Perpetual Peace: How We Got To Be So Hated by Gore Vidal
American Dynasty: Aristocracy, Fortune, and the Politics of Deceit in the House of Bush by Kevin Phillips (a Republican!)
The Book on Bush: How George W. (Mis)leads America by Eric Alterman and Mark Green
The Price of Loyalty: George W. Bush, the White House, and the Education of Paul O'Neill by Ron Suskind (an insider shares tales of treachery, arrogance and foolishness)

Crimes Against Nature: How George W. Bush and His Corporate Pals Are Plundering the Country and Hijacking Our Democracy by Robert F. Kennedy, Jr.

Fraud: the Strategy Behind the Bush Lies and Why the Media Didn't Tell You by Paul Waldman

Lies and the Lying Liars Who Tell Them: a fair and balanced look at the right by Al Franken

Big Lies: the Right-Wing Propaganda Machine and How It Distorts the Truth by Joe Conason

Weapons of Mass Deception by Sheldon Ramton & John Stauber

The Five Biggest Lies Bush Told Us about Iraq by Christopher Scheer, Robert Scheer & Lakshmi Chaudhry

The President of Good & Evil: the Ethics of George W. Bush by Peter Singer

It's The Crude, Dude: War, Big Oil, And The Fight For The Planet, by Linda McQuaig

Corporate Predators: The Hunt for Mega-Profits and the Attack on Democracy by Russell Mokhiber and Robert Weissman

Four books by Thom Hartmann: *"The Last Hours of Ancient Sunlight," "Unequal Protection: The Rise of Corporate Dominance and the Theft of Human Rights," "We The People: A Call To Take Back America,"* and *"What Would Jefferson Do? A Return To Democracy"*

State of Denial and *Plan of Attack* by Bob Woodward

The Corporation: The Pathological Pursuit of Profit and Power by Joel Bakan, a professor of law at British Columbia Law School (Free Press, 2004) It is now a documentary/ movie

Secrecy & Privilege: Rise of the Bush Dynasty from Watergate to Iraq by Robert Parry

The U.S. versus George Bush by Elizabeth de la Vega

The Raw Deal: How the Bush Republicans Plan to Destroy Social Security and the Legacy of the New Deal by Joe Conason

The Bush Agenda: Invading the World, One Economy at a Time by Antonia Juhasz

documentaries

"Unprecedented: the 2000 Presidential Election" - documentary by Robert Greenwald, Joan Sekler, Richard Ray Perez and others.
Order this video at www.unprecedented.org
Or (800) 847-9835
- There is now another video of the same quality and professionalism produced by Robert Greenwald entitled "Uncovered, The Truth About the War in Iraq."
www.moveon.org has more information.

Iraq for Sale: As Not Seen on TV
"Iraq for Sale," the latest documentary from Robert Greenwald, tells a depressingly familiar tale of corporate corruption and war-profiteering in Iraq. Focusing on companies like Halliburton, CACI International and Blackwater Security Consulting, it recites a litany of rapacity and exploitation that ought to have American citizens swarming Congress.

"Fahrenheit 911" by Michael Moore and friends

"The Corporation: The Pathological Pursuit of Profit and Power" by Joel Bakan and friends

"Unconstitutional: The War on Our Civil Liberties" written, produced and directed by Nonny de la Peña, executive producer Robert Greenwald ("Outfoxed" and "Uncovered"); on the Patriot Act and what it means for us.

"The Power of Nightmares" a three-hour documentary written and produced by Adam Curtis about the paranoid notions that Cheney and Rumsfeld have had all of their lives.

Videos and Online sources:

There are also numerous videos of broadcasts to stay informed. Here is but one example; stay awake:

"Keith Olbermann | We Fight for Liberty by Having More Liberty, Not Less"

or http://www.truthout.org/docs_2006/120106S.shtml

Pink sings "Dear Mr. President" on Jerry Kimmel Live 4/10/07 http://www.youtube.com/watch?v=45IZWvPdA-A

Humor in these sad times; it is the comedians and satirists who are telling the truth in society.: http://folksongsofthefarrightwing.cf.huffingtonpost.com/

Will Ferrell playing George Bush - on Global Warming: http://www.transbuddha.com/mediaHolder.php?id=1147

Can Bush screwing the country be funny? www.glumbert.com/media/roleplay

~ ~ ~

Websites and Articles concerning Iraqi War Vets and Soldiers of Conscience

ACTIVE DUTY SOLDIERS CALL FOR END TO IRAQI OCCUPATION (12/18/2006): http://groups.yahoo.com/group/nhnenews/message/12292

PERSPECTIVE: THE ANTI-WAR ESSAYS OF CAMILO MEJI (3/22/2006): http://groups.yahoo.com/group/nhnenews/message/11029

ARMY REACHING BREAKING POINT (1/26/2006): http://groups.yahoo.com/group/nhnenews/message/10739

U.S. ARMY RAISES MAXIMUM AGE FOR ENLISTMENT (1/22/2006):
http://groups.yahoo.com/group/nhnenews/message/10710

ANY SOLDIER WILL DO (11/13/2005):
http://groups.yahoo.com/group/nhnenews/message/10335

WAR VETERANS PASS ON TRAUMA TO FUTURE GENERATIONS (8/16/2005):
http://groups.yahoo.com/group/nhnenews/message/9750

PERSPECTIVE: IRAQ WAR: TALKING WOUNDED (8/10/2005):
http://groups.yahoo.com/group/nhnenews/message/9711

PERSPECTIVE: IRAQ WAR: 'WHAT HAVE WE DONE?' (8/10/2005):
http://groups.yahoo.com/group/nhnenews/message/9710

IRAQ VETERANS TURN WAR CRITICS (1/27/2005):
http://groups.yahoo.com/group/nhnenews/message/8760

PERSPECTIVE: THE COURT-MARTIAL OF STAFF SGT. CAMILO MEJIA (5/21/2004):
http://groups.yahoo.com/group/nhnenews/message/7236

Smoke & MiRRORS

THE TRUTH iS OUT

Smoke & Mirrors

Appendix: Essays Wise and True

- Received on the internet during the election crisis of 2000.
Authorship unknown.

A history professor from Uppsala Universitet in Sweden read an article in which a Zimbabwe politician was quoted as saying that children should study this event closely for it shows that election fraud is not only a phenomenon of the developing world.

1. Imagine that we read of an election occurring anywhere in the third world in which the self-declared winner was the son of the former prime minister and that former prime minister was himself the former head of that nation's secret police (CIA).

2. Imagine that the self-declared winner lost the popular vote but won based on some old colonial holdover (electoral college) from the nation's pre-democracy past.

3. Imagine that the self-declared winner's victory turned on disputed votes cast in a province governed by his brother.

4. Imagine that the poorly drafted ballots of one district, a district heavily favoring the self-declared winner's opponent, led thousands of voters to vote for the wrong candidate.

5. Imagine that the members of that nation's most despised caste, fearing for their lives/livelihoods, turned out in record numbers to vote in near-universal opposition to the self-declared winner's candidacy.

6. Imagine that hundreds of members of that most-despised caste were intercepted on their way to the polls by state police operating under the authority of the self-declared winner's brother.

7. Imagine that six million people voted in the disputed province, that the self-declared winner's 'lead' was only 527 votes, fewer, certainly, than the vote counting machines' margin of error, and that the person responsible for ensuring the integrity of the vote was a member of the self-declared winner's inner circle.

8. Imagine that the self-declared winner and his political party opposed a more careful by-hand inspection and re-counting of the ballots in the disputed province or in its most hotly disputed district.

9. Imagine that the self-declared winner, himself a governor of a major province, had the worst human rights record of any province in his nation and actually led the nation in executions.

10. Imagine that a major campaign promise of the self-declared winner was to appoint like-minded human rights violators to lifetime positions on the high court of that nation.

None of us would deem such an election to be representative of anything other than the self-declared winner's will-to-power. All of us, I imagine, would wearily turn the page thinking that it was another sad tale of pitiful pre-or anti-democracy peoples in some strange elsewhere.

THE IDENTIFYING CHARACTERISTICS OF FASCISM
By Dr. Lawrence Britt, political scientist
Free Inquiry Magazine, a journal of humanist thought
Spring 2003
   http://www.secularhumanism.org/library/fi/index_23.htm

Dr. Britt's article is published online (above link). His points are distilled here. He studied the fascist regimes of Hitler (Germany), Mussolini (Italy), Franco (Spain), Suharto (Indonesia), and Pinochet (Chile) and found these regimes all had 14 things in common, and he calls these the identifying characteristics of fascism.

The 14 characteristics are:

1. Powerful and Continuing Nationalism – Fascist regimes tend to make constant use of patriotic mottos, slogans, symbols, songs, and other paraphernalia. Flags are seen everywhere, as are flag symbols on clothing and in public displays.

2. Disdain for the Recognition of Human Rights – Because of fear of enemies and the need for security, the people in fascist regimes are persuaded that human rights can be ignored in certain cases because of "need". The people tend to 'look the other way' or even approve of torture, summary executions, assassinations, long incarcerations of prisoners, etc.

3. Identification of Enemies/Scapegoats as a Unifying Cause – The people are rallied into a unifying patriotic frenzy over the need to eliminate a perceived common threat or foe: racial, ethnic or religious minorities; liberals; communists; socialists, terrorists, etc.

4. Supremacy of the Military – Even when there are widespread domestic problems, the military is given a disproportionate amount of government funding, and the domestic agenda is neglected. Soldiers and military service are glamorized.

5. Rampant Sexism – The governments of fascist nations tend to be almost exclusively male-dominated. Under fascist regimes, traditional gender roles are made more rigid. Opposition to abortion is high, as is homophobia and anti-gay legislation and national policy.

6. Controlled Mass Media – Sometimes the media is directly controlled by the government, but in other cases, the media is indirectly controlled by government regulation, or through sympathetic media spokespeople and executives. Censorship, especially in wartime, is very common.

7. Obsession with National Security – Fear is used as a motivational tool by the government over the masses.

8. Religion and Government are Intertwined – Governments in fascist nations tend to use the most common religion in the nation as a tool to manipulate public opinion. Religious rhetoric and terminology is common from government leaders, even when the major tenets of the religion are diametrically opposed to the government's policies or actions.

9. Corporate Power is Protected – The industrial and business aristocracy of a fascist nation often are the ones who put the government leaders into power, creating a mutually beneficial business/government relationship and power elite.

10. Labor Power is Suppressed – Because the organizing power of labor is the only real threat to a fascist government, labor unions are either eliminated entirely or are severely suppressed.

11. Disdain for Intellectuals and the Arts – Fascist nations tend to promote and tolerate open hostility to higher education, and academia. It is not uncommon for professors and other academics to be censored or even arrested. Free expression in the arts is openly attacked, and governments often refuse to fund the arts.

12. Obsession with Crime and Punishment – Under fascist regimes, the police are given almost limitless power to enforce laws. The people are often willing to overlook police abuses, and even forego civil liberties, in the name of patriotism. There is often a national police force with virtually unlimited power in fascist nations.

13. Rampant Cronyism and Corruption – Fascist regimes almost always are governed by groups of friends and associates who appoint each other to government positions, and who use governmental power and authority to protect their friends from accountability. It is not uncommon in fascist regimes for national resources and even treasures to be appropriated or even outright stolen by government leaders.

14. Fraudulent Elections – Sometimes elections in fascist nations are a complete sham. Other times elections are manipulated by smear campaigns against (or even the assassination of) opposition candidates, the use of legislation to control voting numbers or political district boundaries, and the manipulation of the media. Fascist nations also typically use their judiciaries to manipulate or control elections.

http://www.ratical.org/ratville/CAH/fasci14chars.html

The Self-Impeaching President
by Steve Bhaerman, January 15, 2007
http://www.wakeuplaughing.com/news.html

And so the next step in moving the upwising forward is taking on two inconvenient and uncomfortable truths. The first is -- expressed tersely -- that we are not in Iraq to keep the peace, we are there to keep the pieces. The Democrats have made a strategic, if not moral, blunder in failing to contextualize our misadventure in Iraq as a necessary and predictable move of a nation that has forsaken its founding as a republic to become an empire. The real issue -- and this is one the mainstream media has avoided as much as it has the questionable answers around 9/11 -- is that we have to choose as a people whether or not we are willing to pay the economic and moral price of empire.

The American people up to this point have been able to have it both ways. They've been able to take cover behind the various lies the Bush regime (and their enablers in Congress on both sides of the aisle) have perpetrated about why we invaded Iraq. They can now jump on the get-out-of-Iraq bandwagon for the wrong reason -- we aren't winning, and the Iraqi people are incapable of governing themselves. The real truth -- vividly exposed in Iraq but just as true during the Clinton years where corporate globalization continued to devour local autonomy throughout the world -- is that our economy as it exists today has become frighteningly dependent on death and destruction.

If you haven't done so already, go rent the DVD Why We Fight. [http://www.sonyclassics.com/whywefight/]and invite a bunch of friends over to watch it with you. There you will see vividly the elephant (and its jackass fellow travelers) in the living room. Our entire house of cards economy is based on beating plowshares into swords, all for the benefit of a few. It's completely consistent and congruent that Vice President Cheney invited only the leaders of the oil industry into his conference to discuss energy policy nearly six years ago, and the ostensible conversation was how to divvy up the oil fields [http://www.judicialwatch.org/iraqi-oil-maps.shtml] of Iraq.
For a more updated take on how the oil industry has already achieved its objectives, please see this article by Chris Floyd. - http://www.truthout.org/docs_2006/printer_010807A.shtml
...

The President's call for an anti-insurgent surgency in Iraq is not just a way for the President to "save face." He is trying to save his ass. Because when we pull away the cover of "preemptive self-defense" and see the Iraq war for what it is -- a long-planned invasion [http://pnac.info/index.php/2003/4-years-before-911-plan-was-set/] of a sovereign nation -- then the war becomes a war crime. Add to that the deception to get us involved, torture and lack of due process for "suspects," use of 9/11 and the war as a pretext to remove civil liberties, and the use of secrecy to cover up other criminal acts, and all of a sudden we're looking at a crime scene.

Meanwhile back in the States, there has been a growing and inexplicable state of malaise, cynicism, low-level fear and high-level mistrust. While some of this undoubtedly dates to the Kennedy assassination and the likely cover-up of what really happened, underneath it all Americans know they are being lied to. According to a Zogby poll [http://zogby.com/news/ReadNews.dbm?ID=1116] last May, trust in government and media has hit "Iraq bottom." Only 11% trust the media, and just under 25% trust the President -- and this was before the voter fraud story broke, and before the President's intransigence reached its current level of dysfunctionality. In this current awakening and "upwising" we see people finally beginning to connect their own inner malaise with the evidence that we may actually have more to fear from our own government than from those terrorists they've been getting us worked up about.

In the either/or, black-and-white world the media likes to present (the more divided we the people are, the more conquerable), we are not expected to be able to think and chew gum at the same time. If we are suspicious of our own leaders, we must be supporting the terrorists or certainly not taking the threat seriously enough. If Americans learn nothing else during this Age of Nefarious, we must understand that the "enemies" of real freedom on both sides, from Islamofascists to Neocon con artists, are more alike than they are different. Each has an "us or them" world view that justifies their immoral and illegal actions. Each has a stake in demonizing the other side. Each uses selfish-righteous religious dogma to mobilize their masses. Each insists you're either with them or against them, with no middle ground. Each uses fear, force, and fabrication as their primary weapons.

The greatest threat to either of these obsolete and dangerous thought systems is for people who have been thrust into one camp or another to wake up, wise up, and recognize that all humans have a common interest that transcends fighting one another. That old doomsday clock is still ticking, only this time in addition to the nuclear bomb, we face a population bomb and the environmental bomb of global warming. Interestingly, what we've come to call the "biological imperative" includes not just survival of the individual but survival of the species as well. And we now stand at a dangerous time where the former is at odds with the latter.

So ... back to the issues at hand, the upwising and prospects for regime change in America. We can expect that the President will use every weapon in his arsenal to bring recalcitrant Republicans back into the fold. He may very well be able to enact his escalation plan without any oversight whatsoever. Nevertheless, this too will be an opportunity for greater awakening and understanding on the part of the American people. ...

A Quest for Integrity
by Congressman Dennis J Kucinich, Dec 7 2006

Dear Friends,

I am on a quest for integrity in Washington this week. The Democratic leadership plan to continue the war in Iraq by supporting yet another

appropriations bill that is likely to go to the floor early next year granting an estimated $160 BILLION, the largest appropriation so far for the Iraq war. You can read my comments in an interview with Truthdig yesterday.
http://www.truthdig.com/interview/item/20061206_dennis_kucinichs_showdown/

There is $70 billion already in the pipeline that can be used to bring the troops home.

There is only one way to end the war in Iraq – by cutting off funds. In October this year, $70 billion was appropriated for FY 2007; the $160 billion supplement will take the budget for the war in 2007 to $230 billion. 2006 saw $117 billion spent on the war, 2007 will be almost double. This will expand war, increase the violence, send more troops to the region, and push our nation into even further indebtedness.

Already over 18% of our tax dollars goes to service the interest on our national debt and 28% to the annual military budget (not including wars in Afghanistan and Iraq), whilst only 2% goes on housing and 0.3% on job training. (See tax chart
http://nationalpriorities.org/auxiliary/interactivetaxchart/taxchart.html)

Last week I published a series of articles on the web which analyze the responsibilities of congress, the Campbell v Clinton case, of which I was part, which rules that appropriating funds is implied consent for the war (i.e., voting for appropriations = voting in favor of the war), looks at the voting record in the House and Senate, and puts forth a plan for US withdrawal and UN handover. Click here to read the articles. - or ...
http://www.huffingtonpost.com/rep-dennis-kucinich/
Yesterday the Iraq Study Group issued their Iraq report, which I read in full last night and spoke about on the floor of the house today.
http://kucinich.us/

The report cites how 500,000 barrels of oil are being stolen per day in Iraq. That is $11.3 billion worth per year. This is interesting, since the Ministry of Oil was the first place our troops were sent after the invasion of Iraq and we now have 140,000 troops there.
How can we expect the end of the Iraq war and national reconciliation in Iraq, while we advocate that Iraq's oil wealth be handled by private oil companies?

It is ironic that this report comes at the exact time the Interior Department's Inspector General says that oil companies are cheating the

US out of billions of dollars, while the Administration looks the other way.

Is it possible that Secretary Baker has a conflict of interest, which should have precluded him from co-chairing a study group whose final report promotes privatization of Iraq oil assets, given his ties to the oil industry? Is it possible that our troops are dying for the profits of private oil companies?

What kind of logic is it that says we need to appropriate $230 billion in a single financial year? The largest appropriation for the war in Iraq? The money is there to bring the troops home now.

A defective logic has invaded Capitol Hill. Democrats won the election because the American people want to end the war in Iraq, yet members feel they can say they oppose the war in Iraq while at the same time support an appropriation of $160 billion. They say the appropriation is to "support the troops," yet will result in keeping them in Iraq for another two years.
We must work together to transform this destructive thinking.
I need your help.
Please contact your member of congress
http://www.congress.org/congressorg/directory/congdir.tt and the Democratic leadership, urging them to vote NO on the appropriations bill. An appropriation of $160 billion is enough to keep us in Iraq for another two years. In Government Oversight Committee hearings, I have personally questioned military officials, who state clearly that this war cannot be won militarily.

Would you buy a used war from this administration?
There is $70 billion already in the pipeline that can be used to bring the troops home and implement a real plan for stability in the region.

Sincerely,
Dennis J Kucinich

    Mr. Kucinich is again running for President in 2008. The Media, as before, ignores him. This would be enough to pay attention to him, based on who they endorsed in the past. As I tried to tell Congressman Kucinich in the last presidential election, if he were to get Oprah Winfrey as his running mate he would win the election. (I hope she's not a republican!) Think about it.
His website: http://kucinich.us/

Letter to the Editor of *Time* Magazine

Written Feb 13 2004; *Time* chose to ignore it.

Dear Time Magazine

Congratulations on your choice of "Persons of the Year - 2003." U.S. Soldiers.

They are now - and have been for years - sexually assaulting one another. Our female soldiers are the targets of lustful advances, social pressures, and old boy cover-ups. Things haven't changed since the San Diego Tailgate - or was that WhiteTail? - fiasco and the Colorado Academy's scandal.

On the international front, these same soldiers are pushing around, bullying, and "containing" Iraqi citizens daily, creating increased animosity against all Americans. We can't blame the average soldier, of course. He is only following orders. And yes, one cannot discount the honest majority because of some really scary and brutal members of the military. Moreover, in this nationalistic climate, it would be unpatriotic to criticize those "defending our country."

Which leads me to your clever, politically motivated choice of the soldier as person of the year in the first place. Perhaps you did not want to be obvious and forth-coming by backing up Bush's War on Iraq directly and naming him, or Colin Powell, or Cheney, or Rumsfeld, as heros. Perhaps you didn't want to lose your more liberal or democratic subscribers. But since the only major event involving US troops in 2003 was the War on Iraq, then you indirectly applauded Bush's involvement in a self-serving grab for land and oil.

And how much stock do you own in Halliburton? And which conservative stock holders are pulling your strings and inking your presses?

When you came to your annual "vote" by December 2003, it was obvious to all but the most dense that there were no weapons of mass destruction, no immanent danger, and thus, no reason to send our troops to that foreign land to be shot and killed.

Our soldiers are pawns and dupes in a big game of acquisition. They don't have much say-so in the matter. To disobey is to face court-marshal. If they were ordered to attack France or Mexico - or wherever - they would do it. Now that the new foreign policy looks a lot like a Texas posse, with guns a-blazing, I, for one do not feel that secure in this neo-con America.

Is this what you voted for?

There are many good people in the military. The system itself is to blame. It is a hierarchical chain of command; a "do or die" mentality. It is a cult of the alpha-male masculine, so women (and protesters) beware. If it is aggressive, dysfunctional, and violent at the bottom, then it reflects the same at the top.

Stephen Russell
a veteran

~ ~ ~

Lincoln (Weeps)

Bill Moyers, October 03, 2006

Bill Moyers is a veteran television journalist for PBS and the president of the Schumann Center for Media and Democracy. "Capitol Crimes," the first episode of Bill Moyers' latest series of documentary specials, airs Wednesday on PBS. (Check local listings.) Audio of commentary: http://www.pbs.org/moyers/moyersonamerica/lincolnweeps.mp3

Back in 1954, when I was a summer employee on Capitol Hill, I made my first visit to the Lincoln Memorial. I have returned many times since, most recently while I was in Washington filming for a documentary about how Tom DeLay, Jack Abramoff, Ralph Reed and Grover Norquist, among others, turned the conservative revolution into a racket—the biggest political scandal since Watergate.

If democracy can be said to have temples, the Lincoln Memorial is our most sacred. You stand there silently contemplating the words that gave voice to Lincoln's fierce determination to save the union—his resolve that "government of, by, and for the people shall not perish from the earth." On this latest visit, I was overcome by a sense of melancholy. Lincoln looks out now on a city where those words are daily mocked. This is no longer his city. And those people from all walks of life making their way up the steps to pay their respect to the martyred president—it's not their city, either. Or their government. This is an occupied city, a company town, and government is a subservient subsidiary of richly endowed patrons.

Once upon a time the House of Representatives was known as "the people's house." No more. It belongs to K Street now. That's the address of the lobbyists who swarm all over Capitol Hill. There are 65 lobbyists for every member of Congress. They spend $200 million per month wining, dining and seducing federal officials.
Per month!

Of course they're just doing their job. It's impossible to commit bribery, legal or otherwise, unless someone's on the take, and with campaign costs soaring, our politicians always have their hands out. One representative confessed that members of Congress are the only people in the world expected to take large amounts of money from strangers and then act as if it has no effect on their behavior. This explains why Democrats are having a hard time exploiting the culture of corruption embodied in the scandalous behavior of DeLay and Abramoff. Democrats are themselves up to their necks in the sludge. Just the other day one of the most powerful Democrats in the House bragged to reporters about tapping "uncharted donor fields in the financial industry"— reminding them, not so subtlety, of the possibility that after November the majority leader just might be a Democrat.

When it comes to selling influence, both parties have defined deviancy up, and Tony Soprano himself couldn't get away with some of the things that pass for business as usual in Washington. We have now learned that Jack Abramoff had almost 500 contacts with the Bush White House over the three years before his fall, and that Karl Rove and other presidential staff were treated to his favors and often intervened on his behalf. So brazen a pirate would have been forced to walk the plank long ago if Washington had not thrown its moral compass overboard.

Alas, despite all these disclosures, nothing is happening to clean up the place. Just as the Republicans in charge of the House kept secret those dirty emails sent to young pages by Rep. Mark Foley—a cover-up aimed at getting them past the election and holding his seat for the party —they are now trying to sweep the DeLay-Abramoff-Reed-and-Norquist scandals under the rug until after Nov. 7, hoping the public at large doesn't notice that the House is being run by Tom DeLay's team, minus DeLay. All the talk about reform is placebo.

The only way to counter the power of organized money is with organized and outraged people. Believe me, what members of Congress fear most is a grassroots movement that demands clean elections and an end to the buying and selling of influence—or else! If we leave it to the powers that be to clean up the mess that greed and chicanery have given us, we will wake up one day with a real Frankenstein of a system—a monster worse than the one created by Abramoff, DeLay and their cronies. By then it will be too late to save Lincoln's hope for "government of, by, and for the people."

~ ~ ~

News and Views from other Lands

On the other side of the world, the Israelis are contemplating arresting their President. A mirror for us?

It will be instructive to find out if the following scandal, now playing out in Israel, is a political mirror of what we could do in the US -- A sitting President has been accused of some serious crimes, and the police have pressed charges. In January 2007 President Katsav was accused of sexual harassment, electronic eavesdropping and granting pardons in exchange for cash. The Israeli police have charged him (Ah, if only our police, or FBI, or CIA, or members of Congress or the Pentagon were to be this brave about bringing charges against Bush, Cheney and the crew...). The President's resignation is being called for, and a trial is supposed to ensue soon. His crimes are different than Bush's - they do not involve killing as far as I know.
One of the headlines: **Israeli President May Face Rape Charge** By RAVI NESSMAN - AP

> JERUSALEM (Jan. 23, 2007) - Israel's attorney general said Tuesday he intends to indict President Moshe Katsav on charges of rape and abuse of power, a stunning accusation against the country's ceremonial head of state.
> ... If indicted, Katsav would be Israel's first sitting president to be charged with a crime.
>
> The decision by Attorney-General Meni Mazuz came just days after authorities launched a criminal investigation into Prime Minister Ehud Olmert's involvement in the sale of a government-controlled bank in 2005. Several other high-level politicians have also been implicated in other scandals.

From another source we discover that ...
"Moshe Katsav is a staunch defender of Israel's controversial 'separation barrier' in the West Bank, parts of which were denounced as illegal in a non-binding ruling from the UN International Court of Justice and slammed by the Palestinians as a land grab."
http://www.news.com.au/dailytelegraph/story/0,22049,20588288-5006003,00.html

> - notice the euphemisms used by propagandists in other lands? Do they all go to the same school? A *separation barrier* sounds so much more benign than The Berlin Wall or the Iron Curtain.

And writing of *coming from the same neo-con school*, this President also came out swinging when his crimes were about to be revealed: "... ironically, it all started off with the president himself going to the attorney general and complaining that he's being blackmailed. This very soon turned around into an array of women - up to 10 women - who all came out of the closet, so to say, and began to file complaints, in retrospect, against the president."
http://www.npr.org/programs/morning/transcripts/2006/oct/061016.goldman.html

So, this scandal from another land could instruct us here on how to proceed against our own mess; or it might be quietly swept under the Israeli rug, political strings being pulled in the background. We will see if justice shines anywhere.

~ ~ ~

And then we look to another land, South Africa, and a very revealing letter from a journalist who experienced Apartheid and now sees something ugly here in the USA:

Allister Sparks used to come to the U.S. for inspiration, but he won't any more
COMMENTARY | January 16, 2007
A personal note from one '62-'63 Nieman Fellow to another, and in it a harsh repudiation of American newspapers and TV
By Saul Friedman, saulfriedman@comcast.net

Allister Sparks, of South Africa, is my closest and dearest friend although we are thousands of miles apart. We have been friends since we were Niemans together in 1962-63. And each in our own countries, we have done journalism the old fashioned way, he reporting on the evils of apartheid, I covering the struggles for civil rights in the south.
...
But recently, I heard from a friend that Allister, a winner of the Louis Lyons award, among others, no longer wished to visit the United States because of its behavior since Sept. 11, 2001. I asked him why and suggested I convey his thoughts to others, just as I wrote once for an American audience a long time ago about apartheid in South Africa. Allister still writes a syndicated column and works as a consultant for a South African bank. Here's what he replied:

> "What I said was that I had no wish to visit the U.S.... I shall probably have to in the course of my work for the bank -- although I may well be denied entry because of all the stamps

of Arab countries in my passport -- especially Syria. A friend of mine, the head of political analysis at our important Human Sciences Research Council, was turned back from Kennedy Airport the other day for that reason. Or it may have been because he has a slightly dark skin and a Muslim name, Adam Habib.

But I must confess that I have felt paralyzed, too, by your challenge to me to write for a U.S. audience about your country, or at least to write to you so that you can communicate those thoughts in the stuff you are writing for the Nieman alumni. This is hard to explain. I guess it's a bit like the break-up of a love affair. For so long the U.S. has been a kind of lodestar for me in my more idealistic beliefs, beginning with my Nieman experience and the idealism of the Kennedy years, the civil rights campaign and all that followed.

Whenever I felt down, struggling to maintain a sense of optimism in all the gloom of life in the midst of a twisted ideology and personal defeats, I would travel to the U.S. to have my batteries recharged.

But now that pattern of my life has been reversed. My own country has emerged, albeit still with many faults, as a beacon of racial reconciliation and co-existence that gives me at least some sense of personal fulfillment in my evening years, while my old moral lodestar, the U.S., has slipped into an abyss of moral degeneracy, of political lies and casuistry, of torture and cruelty and of a contempt for human rights and human decency that violates your own supposedly sacred Constitution. For me emotionally, it is as though the United States has become the old South Africa – and although you challenge me to write about this in the U.S., as you yourself once did in South Africa, I find that, frankly, after all I have been through, I do not now, at the age of nearly 74, want to revisit the old South Africa. To fight that fight once in a lifetime is surely enough.

I must stress that it is not only the behavior of the Bush Administration that repels me, but the craven obsequiousness of the U.S. media, both television and newspapers. As you know I was in the U.S. at the time of 9/11 and so I am aware of and sensitive to the shock of that terrible event, but I have been appalled from the very beginning at the meek and uncritical

402

way television and even the great newspapers have reported and commented on the decision to go to war in Iraq – the triumphalist coverage of the "shock and awe" bombardment of Baghdad with no thought for the thousands of Iraqis being incinerated in it.

On my several visits to the U.S. in the course of this war I have been disgusted by all the cheerleading for your "brave boys in Iraq," the flagwaving and the craven desire to be seen as patriotic that wiped out the journalistic duty to ask the tough questions about why the war was being fought, who told the lies, or even to portray the carnage that was taking place inside Iraq. I was appalled to see newspapers and journalists I had admired, old friends and colleagues, fall into the conformist trap of jingoistic patriotism. Even the op-ed page of my own old newspaper, The Washington Post, was fully in step with Bush, Rumsfeld and the other neocons.

I felt betrayed. I had faced all those pressures for patriotic coverage when my own country went to war against those it called "terrorists" in what is now Namibia and in South Africa itself, and when I defied those huge pressures I was applauded and given awards (including the Nieman Foundation's Louis M. Lyons award) by the American journalistic establishment.

I came to despise the very concept of patriotism, which so often through the ages has been used to command support for evil. Now I had to watch while that journalistic establishment that had applauded me itself succumbed to the patriotic pressures. To such an extent that it was left to a few magazines, notably The New Yorker, to expose the crimes against humanity that were being committed.

Only now, as the tide of fortune is turning and it is clear that America is losing the war, is the press reportage and commentary turning against the war – in an opportunistic way that I find almost equally contemptible. If it looks like you're winning, the war is wonderful; when you start losing, it was all a wretched mistake.

And even now, the essence of the new opposition to the war is that too many American troops are being killed. More than 3,000. Never mind the 150,000 Iraqis that have been slaughtered, or the fact that their country has been destroyed, perhaps for generations to come. The cry is to get out. Bring the brave boys home. Forget the shattered lives and the shattered country left behind. Turn now to carrying the "war on terrorism" to Somalia – and maybe Iran, and who knows where else.

Nor is the Iraq War the only thing that has disillusioned me about the country I once so admired. I was in the Middle East at the time of the Palestinian elections and was shocked by the refusal of the U.S. to accept the clear victory of Hamas, even though the election was declared "free and fair" by Jimmy Carter's observers, among others. Wasn't the final justification for the Iraqi war that it was being waged to bring democracy to the Middle East?

After talking to Palestinians in Qatar, including both the Managing Director and Editor-in-Chief of Al Jazeera, who have become friends, I began to suspect that my own impressions of Hamas may have been distorted by stereotyped reporting in much the same way that my impressions of the ANC had been in South Africa – even though I had thought myself immune to Apartheid regime propaganda. Even liberal South Africans shunned the ANC as a "terrorist organization. So when I ceased to be Editor of the Rand Daily Mail and other papers and became a foreign correspondent for the Washington Post, et al, I decided to visit the ANC in exile and check out those preconceived impressions. As I think you know, it was an eye-opening experience for me to discover how sophisticated and pragmatic they were. It was an experience that changed my entire outlook on what should happen in my own country.

Recalling that, I decided to do the same with Hamas. So last September, on my own account and for my own personal interest, I flew to Damascus and spent two days at Hamas headquarters talking to their exiled leaders. Again it was an eye-opening experience to hear their side of the story and discover the degree to which they, too, are sophisticated, pragmatic people who I believe are the only ones capable of negotiating a peace agreement that could stick – since, like the ANC, they are the only ones whose control extends to the people with the guns.

I came away with five hours of tape recorded conversation with these key leaders whom the authorities of both Israel and the US refuse to speak to – because they are "terrorists." [Why haven't other] Western journalists done this. Why? Why haven't these men and women who have preached to me over so many years about the importance of balanced reporting and getting "the other side of the story" done what I, with no funding or backing of any big organization, did?

...

Just as you did in the old days, I draw a sharp distinction between a country and the many fine individuals in it. I admire your idealism and your resilience, and the determination with which you keep the voice of sanity alive in a country – and within a profession – that has lost its way. But the task is too big for me.

I don't want to look back into that abyss from which I have only just emerged."

Saul Friedman, a 1963 Nieman fellow, is a former White House correspondent for Newsday and Knight Ridder newspapers.

~ ~ ~

Martin Luther King said in 1967,

"My government is the world's leading purveyor of violence."

He was killed, as we all know.

When will it end?

>>~o~<<

Backing up this book, and indictment, are hundreds of pages of information, research, and evidence.
They are found on the web at ...
http://www.culturefix.org/common_sense_revisited_treason/evidence

Smoke & MiRRORS

concise

The ultimate measure of a man
    is not where he stands
        in moments of comfort and convenience,
but where he stands
    at times of challenge and controversy.

- Martin Luther King, Jr.

Fair Use Notice

This report may contain copyrighted material the use of which has not specifically been authorized by the copyright owner. Making such material available is an effort to advance the understanding of environmental, political, human rights, economic, democratic, scientific, religious, spiritual, and social justice issues, etc. This constitutes a 'fair use' of any such copyrighted material as provided for in section 107 of the US Copyright Law. In accordance with Title 17 U.S.C. Section 107, this material is distributed without profit to those who have expressed a prior interest in receiving the included information for nonprofit educational and research purposes.
Furthermore, the material has been collected to guarantee the future rights of all citizens, regardless of intellectual property rights. When the nation, and the world, is in jeopardy, the defense of copyright must be weighed against the disintegration of the commonwealth.
ps: Ask Alejandro Jodorowsky the movie director about copyrights and intellectual property.

~ ~ ~

Links are provided as a convenience to the reader and allows for verification of authenticity. However, as originating pages are often updated by their originating host sites, the versions cited may not match the versions found on the Original links. Internet archives, however, will have the exact quotes and citations published herein.

~ ~ ~

Smoke & MiRRORS